PRAI

THE GIRLS OF GOOD FORTUNE

"A captivating blend of intrigue and heart, celebrating the resilience of a woman determined to reclaim her life... Richly layered, this novel reminds us that even in the darkest places, light and love find a way to endure."

—Jean Kwok, *New York Times* bestselling author of *Searching for Sylvie Lee* and *The Leftover Woman*

"McMorris is a master in the art of storytelling, weaving a heart-pounding adventure of freedom and survival... With vivid characters and a history long buried now unearthed, *The Girls of Good Fortune* brings legend to life. A must-read you don't want to miss."

—Patti Callahan Henry, *New York Times* bestselling author of *The Secret Book of Flora Lea*

"In this page-turning, propulsive read, McMorris shines a light on a forgotten corner of America... A gripping tale of family, identity, and redemption that I simply couldn't put down. One of McMorris's best yet."

—Fiona Davis, *New York Times* bestselling author of *The Stolen Queen*

"Novels like this are why I read historical fiction... A thoughtfully crafted, intimate, and deeply felt tale... McMorris once again kept me up all hours reading to learn how her heroine would find justice...and love."

—Janie Chang, *Globe & Mail* bestselling author of *The Phoenix Crown*

PRAISE FOR *THE WAYS WE HIDE*

An Instant International Bestseller

"Readers interested in historical fiction, Houdini's illusions, Depression-era United States, wartime London, and the Nazi Resistance in Holland will be quickly captured."

—*Booklist*, Starred Review

"Framed by on-the-record tragedies and Britain's famed use of special skills in its MI9 efforts, *The Ways We Hide* makes for compelling reading, both as a historical novel and a sad rumination on the lifelong scars of childhood trauma."

—Historical Novel Society

"Epic in scope and breathless in pace...this book will educate, inspire, and awaken you. It also just might convince you of the magic behind the illusions."

—*Book Reporter*

"Just like her heroine, Kristina McMorris works magic in this twisting tale of James Bond's Q meets World War II. I love this book!"

—Kate Quinn, *New York Times* bestselling author of *The Rose Code* and *The Briar Club*

"A riveting tale of intrigue and illusion, danger, and historical mystery but, at its heart, the story of one woman's struggle to escape her own past."

—Lisa Wingate, #1 *New York Times* bestselling author of *Before We Were Yours*

PRAISE FOR *SOLD ON A MONDAY*

A *New York Times* Bestseller
A *USA Today* Bestseller
A *Wall Street Journal* Bestseller
A National Indiebound Bestseller

"A tender love story enriches a complex plot, giving readers a story with grit, substance, and rich historical detail."

—*Publishers Weekly*

"Poignant and compulsively readable... Based upon a haunting historical photograph, this story will linger long after the pages have all been turned."

—Stephanie Dray, *New York Times* bestselling author of *America's First Daughter* and *Becoming Madame Secretary*

"A masterpiece that poignantly echoes universal themes of loss and redemption...both heartfelt and heartbreaking."

—Pam Jenoff, *New York Times* bestselling author of *The Orphan's Tale*

"The story has grit, a complex plot, and historical detail depicting the tragedies of families who are poor and ill. A good read."

—*The Daily News*

"[A] finely told, emotionally satisfying gem of a novel."

—*Historical Novels Review*

ALSO BY KRISTINA McMORRIS

The Ways We Hide
When We Had Wings
Sold on a Monday
The Edge of Lost
The Pieces We Keep
Bridge of Scarlet Leaves
Letters from Home

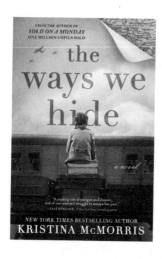

THE
GIRLS OF
GOOD
FORTUNE

A Novel

KRISTINA McMORRIS

sourcebooks
landmark

Published by Sourcebooks Landmark, an imprint of Sourcebooks
P.O. Box 4410, Naperville, Illinois 60567-4410
(630) 961-3900
sourcebooks.com

Library of Congress Cataloging-in-Publication Data

Names: McMorris, Kristina, author.
Title: The girls of good fortune : a novel / Kristina McMorris.
Description: Naperville, Illinois : Sourcebooks Landmark, 2025.
Identifiers: LCCN 2024047223 (print) | LCCN 2024047224
(ebook) | (trade paperback) | (hardcover) | (epub)
Subjects: LCGFT: Novels.
Classification: LCC PS3613.C585453 G57 2025 (print) | LCC PS3613.C585453
(ebook) | DDC 813/.6--dc23/eng/20241004
LC record available at https://lccn.loc.gov/2024047223
LC ebook record available at https://lccn.loc.gov/2024047224

Printed and bound in the United States of America.
LSC 10 9 8 7 6 5 4 3 2 1

To my beloved mom and Grandma Jean,
the original storytellers in my life

PREFACE

While this story is a work of fiction, it is rooted in historical realities, including the use of language and terminology reflective of the era as well as, most notably, depictions of the atrocities that occurred in Rock Springs and Snake River Canyon (known fittingly today as Hells Canyon). More details about these shocking, lesser-known incidents, along with the author's personal experiences and inspirations as the proud daughter of an Asian immigrant, can be found in the Author's Note.

The sky can change unexpectedly.
Overnight, people's fortunes can rise or fall.

—Chinese proverb

PROLOGUE

Pingshu. It's what the Chinese call the "art of storytelling." No less so, I suppose, than the brushstroke characters on scrolls tracing back to centuries-old dynasties and ancestors, both the tales themselves and the way they're told are considered a means of sharing culture and history as well as identity.

I've thought of that word a lot lately—*identity*—as I continue to define who I am at even this late stage of life. Only with time and experience, above all as a mother and now a grandmother, have I come to fully comprehend how much I've been shaped by not just those on the branches of my family tree but also their stories.

Perhaps from the latter even more.

One in particular hovers at the forefront of my mind as I ready for my drive to the cemetery. Not for a service on this occasion—a regular event at my age—but for a delivery. A message to bring closure to a story, or at least peace at some level, even if a hundred years overdue. How greatly so many lives back then would have been altered with the knowledge revealed on the page in my hands.

The staunch historians I've encountered, much like scientists, often give little or no credence to accounts lacking evidence or documentation. They grumble over so-called lore spread by animated guides of "mysterious" underground or city walking tours—or their least favorite, surely, the ghost tours. Today, I'm reminded yet again that reality typically lies somewhere in between and that the most extraordinary events—especially involving love and betrayals, tragedies and triumphs, sacrifices and regret—too frequently never make it into the textbooks.

My family's history is a prime example.

In that vein, perception is a funny thing. With our continually growing lineage of strong, successful, brightly natured women—many born in the years of the most coveted sign, the dragon—friends began calling us the "girls of good fortune." And while in many ways, it applies, it hasn't always—not for everyone.

Not if you know the whole story.

1888

—

JULY

CHAPTER ONE

Dirt. The damp, earthy scent of it was the first thing she registered. Distinct and familiar, it reached through the thick haze of
Celia's mind, like smelling salts luring her to consciousness. She
was lying face down. The ground was cool and hard against her
cheek. A chill penetrated her dress and sent a shiver through her
veins. Had she nodded off in the barn again?

She worked to open her eyes with the effort of muscling a
stubborn window. Even with her lids raised partway, the blackness remained. No sunshine nor moonlight slanting between
planks. At the sense of blindness, her pulse quickened.

She struggled to lift her head, suddenly throbbing and heavy as
a boulder. One of her hands lay pinned beneath her. She pulled
it free and, despite the numbness, flattened both palms on the
packed soil to press herself upward. While slogging through every
inch, she noted the air was tinged not with the odors of livestock
and hay but with those of a back alley, a mix of stale liquor and
men's sweat. Urine.

Her vision strained for purchase. Through the dimness,
she made out a ceiling. Dark and uneven. Same as the walls
surrounding her fully.

Her heart pounded against the shrinking confines of her chest.

A faint flickering, amber-hued, nipped at her periphery. She traced the glow to a gap below what seemed to be a lone weathered door. A potential exit—from wherever this was.

On hands and knees, she edged her way over. As if her body had instantly aged by decades, each movement was a chore.

Finally there, she ran her fingers up and over the rough, grooved wood in search of a handle. A futile hunt. Her breaths turned quick and shallow.

Was it an illusion, or was the room closing in?

Desperate for air, she lowered her mouth to the space beneath the door. The smell beyond was no better, so pungent she could taste it. But with the wavering light suggestive of a lantern, she remained in place and looked for signs of movement.

"Help..." Her voice eked out weak and gravelly. She repeated herself louder, sending the word into a ricochet within her skull. Upon a third try, her throat, dry as dust, plunged her into a coughing fit. She clutched the collar of her dress while calming her lungs.

Only it wasn't a dress covering her body...

By feel, she discerned a vest. And a shirt, somewhat loose on her slender frame. The garments reeked of tobacco. Baffled, she patted downward, over the baggy trousers that swallowed her legs to the bulky boots on her feet.

Droplets of sweat slipped from her temple, and a tickle arose on her cheek. Reflexes drew her hand to the spot, where she felt something foreign. *A spider?*

Panic surged. She swatted at the creature, only to find it unmoving, inanimate. It was a layer of short bristles, beard-like, that ran from one cheek to the other. She followed the trail upward. Atop her head sat a short wig and brimmed hat, providing confirmation.

She was dressed as a man. Disguised.

Whatever for?

Confusion riddled her thoughts. Wading through them, energy draining, she slumped against a wall. It was cold and rough, made of stone. A familiarity seeped in and a revelation emerged, overcoming her with the force and terror of a riptide:

She was trapped underground.

Imprisoned in the tunnels.

1885

—

JUNE

CHAPTER TWO

The girl was missing.

Again.

"Blast it." Celia voiced this strictly under her breath, fighting the impulse to say worse. A respectable lady, she'd been taught—to an exhaustive point—refrained from spouting even euphemisms in public.

Not that her station in society would award her such a title. She merely hoped her mother wasn't peering down from the heavens with those kind yet scrutinizing eyes, the same shade of hazel Celia had inherited, as sailors and lumberjacks now ogled her in passing. She could feel their weighted gazes roving the high collar of her dress to the tips of her heeled boots as if she wore nothing at all.

Granted, even in broad daylight on a Saturday, no "respectable lady" would be seen in Portland's North End, through which she had no choice now but to traipse.

All because of Abigail.

That maddening child.

Celia tightened her grip on the ribboned handle of the hatbox swaying at her side, aware that every step, every bump against her leg, could damage the contents she'd been tasked with fetching: a delicate, feathered and brimmed accessory special ordered for the mayor's wife, Mrs. Bettencourt. A frilly overindulgence, in Celia's view. Sent all the way from New York City, it was easily worth two weeks of her wages.

She could only imagine the amount she'd be penalized for losing track of the couple's sole daughter...

No meandering off, Celia had stressed to Abigail upon reaching the hat boutique back at the city's center. It was the singular condition for allowing the girl to linger outside to dote on a collie leashed to a hitching post—pets, after all, were out of the question in the Bettencourts' home. When Celia reemerged, the dog remained, yet Abigail had vanished.

"Eh, pretty lady!" On a bench next to a barbershop, a grizzled man flashed a yellow-tooth grin. "C'mon over and make yourself cozy." He patted his thigh, a liquor jug resting crookedly on his other knee.

Celia's desire to shoot him a glare was overtaken by a dark thought, specifically what men of his sort might do to a girl like Abigail, enticed by her golden ringlets and porcelain skin, despite her meager age of thirteen.

Perspiration, from more than the summer heat, trickled down Celia's back.

Hastening her mission, she angled to cross the cobblestone street and waited anxiously for a horse-drawn streetcar to roll past. The instant the path cleared, she charged onward to reach the Silver Dollar. The saloon was but one among the plethora that dotted every block in the area, though given its Vaudevillian shows meant to keep patrons indulging, it was the very spot she'd found Abigail during their last errand together, from which the girl had impulsively strayed. Same as today.

"Take a walk and stay out!" On the unseen man's orders, a compact fellow was shoved through the swinging half doors of a tavern. He landed on all fours a few strides ahead, halting Celia. His traditional black braid, a queue, slipped from his hat and dangled over his shoulder. "You heard me, you dumb coolie," the aproned barkeep added while stepping outside. "Crawl back to Chinatown and stick to your own kind!" He reinforced this by jerking his thumb in the corresponding direction.

The Chinese man attempted to gather himself as several Oriental bystanders looked away; they faced enough troubles of their own without borrowing that of others.

Celia leaned down to help. Just in time, logic stopped her short, and the urge to keep her identity shrouded led her around the stranger to resume her route.

Surely he had committed a wrongdoing to warrant such treatment.

She told herself this, adamant, wishing to believe it.

In truth, with the dwindling of the gold rush and the completion of the transcontinental railroad, Chinese men who'd been so eagerly recruited for backbreaking labor in America were now deemed threats to white men's jobs, resented for their willingness to endure longer hours and lower pay. Thus their relocating in search of work, particularly to port cities such as this, where the population was escalating at exponential rates—ironically, due to the very tracks they had laid—only further stoked racism that seemed to grow with every passing day.

As Celia rounded a corner, a low, drawn-out whistle caused her to wince. The call, thankfully, was directed not at her but at a woman behind a second-story window of the Dewdrop Inn. In the house of ill repute, she was smoking while observing the bustling street, her long, fiery locks draping her silky robe. With painted lips and rouge coloring skin as fair as Celia's, even appearing the same age of eighteen, she looked markedly unabashed of her obvious profession.

Especially given her beauty, why ever would she stoop to such a low?

Celia's gut churned with pity, dashed with repulsion. She averted her eyes just as a man stumbled out the entrance. He was reapplying his suspenders, an evident customer of either the redhead or another so-called lady of the night. It was far more accurate than calling them "seamstresses," a laughable title used to evade laws that, presumptively through payoffs, went blatantly unenforced.

The jaunty tune of a piano emanated from the opened entry of the Silver Dollar, reminding Celia of her task. She followed the notes to the threshold. Brushing from her eyes umber strands let loose from her low bun, she scanned the room for Abigail. In the bog of tobacco smoke scented with ale, there was no shortage of drinkers, even this early in the day.

"Bring out da...l-ladies!" Parked at a table, a man with the hunch and leathery skin of a gold panner bellowed toward the stage, which mercifully lacked suggestive female dancers. Rather, a fellow in a top hat and tails was performing a modern shuffling number, accompanied by an elderly pianist who plinked away on the keys. It was just the type of amusement to attract Abigail.

Except this time, she was nowhere to be seen.

Celia hustled to the bar, where the bearded barkeep she recalled from her last visit stood busy filling pints.

"Sir, pardon me," she said, summoning his gaze. "But have you seen the little girl I tracked down here before? Blond curls, about this high—" Celia was raising her hand when he cut in.

"Yeah, yeah. I 'member." An encouraging reply, until: "Ain't seen her." With that, he continued his work.

Celia tensed. She scrambled to deduce where else the child might have gone.

Already they had swung by the bakery, a place that felt like home and was always Celia's first stop—even on days like this, when not assigned to buy pastries, just pausing to look. Abigail had been antsy from the start despite the heavenly scent of baking dough and the trays of mouth-watering tarts. She had tagged along on the day's errands only to acquire new hair ribbons—

That was it. She must have ambled off to obtain them on her own.

"Simple as that," Celia decided. Though as she exited and faced another brothel, rumors returned to her: tales of abducted women in Portland sold into prostitution; how before being secretly shipped off, they were held in cells amid an alleged grid of tunnels connecting basements in the waterfront area. Said to be built by Chinese laborers several decades ago, the passages for transporting goods had gained a reputation for nefarious usage.

Celia attempted to block all this out, yet powered by fear, her clip approached frenzy as she wove in and out of shops known to sell ribbons. Between each elimination, she dodged wagons and carriages and knots of strangers, all while seeking glimpses of Abigail's pink dress with a soft-yellow sash—or were the colors reversed?

A passing sailor pulled Celia's worries toward the river.

Within walking distance, the Willamette hosted ever-lively docks full of crewmen and ships, scavenging birds, and moving cargo. Abigail's swimming skills were decent but, like Celia's, had been accrued in the serenity of lakes, not in fast-moving currents. Even for relief from the heat, Abigail knew better than to dip a toe in—didn't she?

A hefty woman bumped Celia's arm. The hatbox slipped free and landed hard on the ground.

"Watch it," the woman growled, smelling of whiskey, and continued on.

Not bothering to be contrary, Celia swiftly recovered the box, any potential damage to its contents a secondary priority. All that mattered was finding Abigail.

Although averse to relying on others—and Timothy Vale, the family's driver, of all people was one she had no desire to owe—she couldn't very well scour the whole area alone. She just hoped he was back from repairing equipment for the Bettencourts' horses before it was too late.

She was hurrying his way when a vision struck, one of Abigail at the open-air carriage, waiting to head home. The logical possibility raised Celia's hopes until, from fifty paces, the transport came into view. Entirely vacant.

A wave of panic rolled through Celia. The air turned impossibly heavy.

At the adjacent corner, a pair of police officers were exiting a boardinghouse. Both were likely on the grift, as most lawmen were known to be in this city. Nonetheless, she prayed they'd be willing—

"Miss Celia?"

The voice, lofty and familiar, spun her around. She found Abigail's big, crystal-blue eyes not ten feet away.

"Thank goodness. There you are!" Celia rushed to close the distance. "Mercy, you gave me such a fright."

The girl's brow twitched as if from surprise, and her expression softened. The extent of Celia's concern seemed to blunt the razor-sharp edge Abigail had directed increasingly at Celia over the past year.

"Where on earth have you been?"

Hesitant, Abigail shifted her gaze away. "I...went to fetch ribbons. When I returned to the hat shop, you were gone."

There was a small coin pouch in her grip but nothing more. No paper-bound package. No evidence of a purchase.

"Oh? And where are those ribbons?"

Abigail lifted a shoulder. "Couldn't find the color I wanted." From the angle of her face, the sun highlighted a mark near her mouth—a pink smear.

Ice cream.

Celia's relief dissipated. The child's obvious lie, let alone her defiance of a clear order—two, in fact—flooded Celia with frustration. She jabbed her finger in the air. "Young lady, your mother made it abundantly plain you were not to indulge in sweets."

Abigail's eyes widened and shot down to her dress, a search for the betraying tell. She touched her face, found the sticky dab, and began wiping it away.

"If you think I'm going to keep your misbehavior to myself this time, including from your father, you are very much mistaken."

The threat dangled for mere seconds before Celia dreaded the idea of following through. Already she realized that her gruffness derived, more than anything, from worry, from care.

At the start of Celia's employment with the family three years prior, Abigail had found in her a new playmate, just as the interests of Abigail's older brother turned toward schooling and away from indulging his baby sister with rounds of hide-and-seek. While Celia dusted and laundered, Abigail's muffled giggles or her polished shoes peeking from below the drapes had served as reliable giveaways.

Now, in contrast, Abigail responded with a gaze bearing no amusement nor endearment. "Go right ahead," she replied. "I'll only deny it." Her tone was flat, strikingly icy in its nonchalance. "Then we'll see which one of us they figure for the liar."

Celia had failed to maintain her guard, still off-kilter, and the implication pierced like a knife.

"Besides," Abigail said, "you're awfully fond of keeping secrets. Wouldn't you say?" She added this as a twist of the blade. A reminder: among the few who knew of Celia's heritage, Abigail was in fact the one who'd discovered and revealed it to her family.

Or...was she implying knowledge of something more?

Abigail sauntered away and boarded the carriage in preparation for the ride home, a journey of quiet tension that would plague Celia with questions of what else the girl might have learned.

CHAPTER THREE

The Bettencourts' neighborhood, a residential area of northwest Portland known as the Alphabet District, usually evoked a sense of safety and comfort. Even its single-lettered street names bore predictable order. Currently, however, Celia's concerns since leaving downtown shunned any of those offerings.

Timothy slowed the carriage before the mayor's Victorian house. Compared to several others in the vicinity that boasted Queen Anne turrets and wraparound porches, the family's powder-blue three-story residence was equally charming, if somewhat dainty.

As the horse came to a stop, Celia considered presenting Abigail with a truce, but in a whirl, the girl hopped off and bounded toward the front door, her gait practically a skip. It was the demeanor of a child confident no punishment would be forthcoming; she was banking on Celia's discretion.

Gratingly, she wagered right.

Even so, Celia had another pressing issue at hand, quite literally. Maintaining a protective hold on the hatbox, she rose from her seat just as Timothy hustled around to the carriage step. In his standard gray suit, which hung slightly loose on his lanky frame, he extended a palm and his usual slanted smile.

"Help ya down, Miss Hart?" A subtle southern accent tinged his voice. Framed by dark-brown hair sharply parted, his eyes shone earnest as ever.

She gauged her ability to maneuver carefully with the box on her own, then acquiesced with reluctance. Once planted on the dirt road, she withdrew her hand from his lingering grip.

"Thank you, Mr. Vale," she said politely and proceeded to the service entrance at the back of the house.

Timothy was a nice-enough fellow with a boyish face, not at all unpleasant. But her thoughts of him ended there, for more than one reason.

—

The curtains were normally kept drawn during the day to ward off heat. Celia opened them just a smidge, inviting a shard of light to cut through the room designated as hers. On the third floor among the servants' quarters—and just large enough for a bed, small bureau, and a basic desk with chair—the space afforded her the privacy needed in moments like this.

Braced for any damaged contents, she cracked open the hatbox; Mrs. Bettencourt would be expecting the special order, and her eagle eyes missed very little. Closely, Celia reviewed the feathers and other embellishments. Each remained whole and in place. She blew out a sigh, which she immediately retracted as an arm from behind lassoed her waist and a hand sealed her mouth.

A vision of Timothy, having misread her intentions, crashed into her mind. At the feel of lips against her ear, instinct trounced her shock. She swung her elbow backward into him, hard as could be, causing him to grunt and loosen his grasp. Breaking away, she lurched for her bureau, nabbed the first metal object within reach, and spun around, prepared to strike.

"Stop," he rasped. He held his middle with one hand, the other splayed to reinforce his order. "It's *me*." He looked up, revealing features not belonging to Timothy. Rather, his slate-blue eyes and sandy-blond hair, styled with tonic yet somehow always tousled, confirmed his identity.

"Stephen…"

"Doggone it, Celia. You got me right in the ribs."

Relief swept through her, though not free of irritation. Her heart continued to pound. "Well, what did you expect? You scared the living daylights out of me." Granted, she might have immediately figured it was him if not for her already frayed nerves.

He let out a breath, gradually rising to his full five inches above her. His cotton shirt hung casually on his broad frame, his suspenders askew and sleeves rolled to the elbows. Even without the dirt smudges on his forearms, she could easily guess where he'd been: at a family friend's local farm, checking on the livestock's latest wounds and ailments. It was voluntary work his mother groused over yet Celia admired, for it illustrated his passion for aiding even animals with medical care he so yearned to apply to people.

"What do you say you put that weapon down?" he said, then his lips curved upward. "Unless you're planning to brush me to death."

She glimpsed the item she was clutching: a measly hairbrush. While this indeed compounded her feeling of being foolish, it didn't tamp her desire to give his skull a good whacking. After all, they'd long agreed that either of their rooms was too risky for a rendezvous.

She glanced at the door, verifying it was shut, and dropped her volume to a minimum. "What are you doing here anyway?"

"I saw the carriage return and simply had to see you."

"But I thought we were to meet later, after the party."

"We are," he said, approaching her. "I just couldn't wait...for this." He leaned down, and his lips joined hers in a kiss that was soft and gentle, further muddling her thoughts. As he drew his head away, she attempted to retain her indignance.

"I...still don't forgive you."

"In that case"—a smirk emanated from his husky tone—"let me try again."

His second effort was more passionate, with one of his hands on her back, his other at the nape of her neck. The heat rippling down her spine was no less powerful than that from their first romantic encounter, back in November. That was when their friendship, deepened through nights in the den warmed by firelight and quiet laughter over chess and cribbage—both of them falsely claiming insomnia—had finally culminated in a breath-stealing kiss.

"Better?" he whispered.

"You're infuriating," she managed, entirely noncommittal.

"I'll interpret that as a yes."

She couldn't help but mirror his smile as he caressed her cheek with his thumb, the motion nearly hypnotic.

"How was your outing with Abby?"

Celia took a moment to reflect on the debacle and groaned. "It's best if you don't ask."

He chuckled. "She's young. Give her a little time and she'll outgrow this rebellious phase of hers."

At the memory of Abigail's words, Celia stilled his hand on her cheek. "Do you think she knows? About us?"

He cocked his head. "Did she say something?"

Abigail's remarks, while pointed, admittedly had been vague. "Not specifically." As Stephen pondered this, Celia's gaze fell to the box on her bed, and she remembered with a start. "Gracious. I need to deliver the hat to your mother before she comes looking for it."

"Say no more." He kissed her again, this one a sweet peck. "Meet me at our usual spot?"

She nodded before being struck by how soon they'd be ceasing to visit their *usual spot*. In three short days, he would set off for England to attend King's College, where his father's friend was a visiting professor who touted courses in groundbreaking medical procedures. Until Stephen's return—initially for Christmas, if travel somehow proved feasible—there would be no contact between him and Celia, as a letter exchange could raise suspicions.

Come to think of it, this impending reality had likely drawn him here, violating their established rule. She had largely succeeded in suppressing thoughts of their separation. Now pushing through, they tightened her chest.

"Ah, I almost forgot," he said. From his trouser pocket, he produced an envelope.

The sender, of course, was evident at a glance. Her father's writing skills were far better in his native Chinese characters; hence, his childlike penning of the address in English typically made her smile. This time was no exception. And yet in accepting the post, she recalled what had recently become his standard message about his path for her life, and her lips leveled.

"All right then," Stephen said. "I'll see you soon." As he turned for the door, she spoke without planning.

"Wait."

He angled back, and her harbored worries gathered in her throat: *After being away, experiencing the world, will you feel the same? About me and us? Will you—will we—still want to marry after virtually four years apart?*

"Celia..." His forehead creased with concern. "What is it, love?"

She opened her mouth, but fear of his answers dissolved the queries before they could reach her tongue. "Make sure...the coast is clear."

He half laughed. "I think I know as much."

Indeed, he did.

After a cautious peek into the hall, he slipped out undetected. A small triumph.

The achievement, though, gave her little reprieve. For already his absence held hints of a void, a yearning in the face of a future daunted by the unknown—and by a decision to be made.

She looked back at the envelope, and old memories churned.

Throughout childhood, Celia often lamented her father's lengthy absences due to his job with Union Pacific's railroad division. Whereas her mother's sufficient care had prioritized instilling in Celia a proper disposition, her father, while dutiful, exuded bountiful warmth. So much so, after her mother's death from consumption five years ago, he became Celia's whole world. She'd even accompanied him then as he laid tracks, until he ruled the nomadic lifestyle ill-suited for a young daughter and sent her to Portland to work for a Cantonese couple. Despite her knack for cooking and passion for baking—skills also ingrained by her mother—her limited knowledge of Oriental cuisine had meant employment as a house girl. When the couple moved back to China, she'd accepted the best job she could find that offered room and board, as a servant with the Bettencourts.

Now her father had been transferred to the company's coal mines in Wyoming Territory. In what he viewed as a stroke of good fortune for them both, he'd finally achieved his goal of settling in one place, a town appropriate for her as well—even the name Sweetwater County conveyed quaint charm—and expected her to join him.

Her excuse of staying in Portland to save funds, much of which she regularly sent his way, would hold up for only so long. Which begged the question: Did she have reason enough to defy him?

CHAPTER FOUR

Amid the din of conversations in the drawing room, Celia slowly registered Mrs. Bettencourt's voice, her tone a command.

"*Well?* Tut-tut, off you go."

At Celia's bewildered pause, Mrs. Bettencourt drew her head back, magnifying features made more severe by her updo. From her pronounced jaw to her flaxen hair, she closely resembled Stephen, but in appearance only. In contrast to his easygoing nature, Georgia Bettencourt was a product of her wealthy East Coast breeding, her poise as cool and statuesque as the silhouette on the brooch adorning the high collar of her dress.

"Another circling of the room," she stressed and nodded toward the silver tray in Celia's hands, where small crystalline stemmed glasses held assorted cordials.

"Oh—yes," Celia said, remembering her assigned routine. How long had she been standing in place, staring off absently? "My apologies, ma'am."

Mrs. Bettencourt waggled her hand with a trace of impatience, naturally unaware of the subject consuming Celia's thoughts: her father's shocking news.

Not that Celia would divulge such matters to the woman;

Mrs. Bettencourt kept her personal life to herself and expected the same of her staff. Moreover, the topic of letters from Celia's father had already proven a near detriment a year prior when Abigail playfully hid under Celia's bed and found a stowed collection of posts from Chung Jun, revealing him as Celia's father. To secure a job, Celia had quickly learned to present her surname not as *Chung* but *Hart*, her mother's maiden name. Even her prideful father hadn't objected to the pragmatic charade.

Although Abigail had distanced herself since the discovery, over either Celia's falsity or bloodline, Abigail's parents—the mayor, more explicitly—had allowed Celia to stay in their employ. Obviously, it was under an agreement of mutual discretion over her status as a Chinese "half-breed." The reasons for this, even now, remained painfully clear at the current gathering of all-white dinner guests.

Steeling herself, Celia embarked on another round of the room. In formalwear, the eight uppity attendees were clustered in various discussions, some standing, others parked on the matching settees before the unlit fireplace. Several men traded their empty glasses for fresh ones, including Stephen; his and Celia's facade through courteous exchanges came second nature at this point. Most of the wives declined, claiming they would refrain until seated for the meal.

Taking up the slack, Gordon Humphrey, a lumber baron with a mustache as thick as his middle, accepted a third imbibement while proclaiming to the mayor, "A ten-year ban on the Chinese is unmistakably insufficient." Two neighboring gentlemen murmured their concurrence. "Frankly, should a village be threatened by dragons, a shrewd slayer doesn't aim to hold them at bay but temporarily. For given the chance, the beasts will inevitably return in greater force and burn all to ashes."

The *beasts*, he called them.

A deep twisting wrought Celia's chest, as much from the word as the context. The Chinese Exclusion Act, prohibiting Chinese laborers from immigrating to America, would remain in effect for seven more years, yet already chatter centered on a permanent ban.

One such laborer, the erosion of him, flickered through Celia's mind. She saw her father's sloping shoulders and raw, blistered hands, the scarring of his forearms, the encroaching wrinkles at his eyes.

"Thank you, Celia," the mayor inserted. The gentle nudge was to detour her from the unnerving exchange. As usual, Edwin Bettencourt's paradox of towering height and soft, round features lent him a rare commanding yet approachable demeanor. No doubt the trait contributed to the steady success of his wholesale-grocery firm and now his political feats.

Celia mustered an agreeable nod. "My pleasure, sir."

Just as she turned, he offered her a subtle smile. It was a recurring message of kindness: not to pay any mind to the hateful talk of blustering guests—members of the Knights of Labor among them. The group openly opposed Chinese immigrants, but its support had been crucial to Mr. Bettencourt's mayoral win and likewise would be for any similar future aspirations he might have.

Aware of the compromises required, Celia returned to her post along a cream fabric-lined wall. There, she stood essentially invisible—to all but Stephen, whose furtive glances emitted warmth that would normally expand her enthusiasm over their imminent encounter.

Tonight, though, her father's latest note repelled that joy with an update far more distressing than she had foreseen.

Beloved daughter,

 Work here very busy still. Long hour. But good news! We not need wait to save money for home in Rock Springs. New matchmaker in Chinatown. He found good husband for you here. Fine family. Nice home. I soon share more.

Your father,

Chung Jun

Matchmaker. Husband. Soon.

Together the words bore down, adding the pressure of a ticking clock. Like a countdown to an explosion.

CHAPTER FIVE

In the shadows of a dusky sky, Celia stepped into the hay-scented barn where Stephen often tended to the animals—or, as he had coined it, their "usual spot." His awaiting presence provided much-needed calm but, hampered by her circumstances, only a meager dose.

As she slid the door closed, the shifting of horse hooves sounded from a far stall. Stephen welcomed her with an embrace, this time free of startle. His eyes gleamed from the lantern aglow on the floor. Already, he had laid out a woolen blanket, their standard upon which they'd sit and talk and cozy up together, sometimes dozing off until one awakened and roused the other to ensure they returned home before morning.

After a tender kiss, he said, "I've wanted to do that all night."

She pushed up a smile.

If only she could as easily push away the ponderings that had burdened the half-mile walk here. "Stephen…I have something to tell you."

"That you love me desperately and will miss me every minute we're apart?"

Skilled at adding levity to dim situations and despite his claim being weighted and true, he would expect a laugh. At her silence, he retracted slightly to listen.

"My father," she continued, "in his letter—" A sudden lump formed in her throat, an obstacle to prevent solidifying the quandary as real.

"Love, what is it? Is your father all right?"

The misconception bolstered her will to finish. "He's found me a match."

A crinkle split Stephen's brow, a show of puzzlement before clarity ironed the pleat away. He was aware of the cultural tradition. "Then you'll tell him no, that you refuse." When she paused—as it wasn't as simple as that—Stephen's hands dropped from her waist, and his speech slowed. "You don't...*want* to accept, do you?"

"No," she insisted and touched his arm. "Of course not. I just don't see what other choice I have."

He released a small exhale and shook his head. "Darling, that choice is standing right in front of you."

Did she really need to voice the obvious?

"In this moment, yes. But you're leaving. For four years."

"And I've assured you, I'll return every chance I get."

His statement carried such confidence, she didn't doubt his intent. Yet with his rigorous class load and the school's location, how often would that be?

Before she could say as much, he added, "The instant I have my diploma in hand, I'll be sailing back to propose to you properly, down on one knee and with a gold band to slide onto this lovely hand of yours." He raised her ring finger to his lips tenderly, as if her skin were milky smooth, not roughened from years of cooking, scrubbing, and, harshest of all, laundering through winters.

Ironically, the very idealism she found so magnetic in Stephen also fed her worries.

Did he fully comprehend the expansive hatred in their city, much less in the house they shared? Not to say tonight's dinner guests were her greatest concern. True, her father, of anyone, would understand love as the impetus for marriage regardless of race; after all, in China, he had wedded her mother, the daughter of a widowed American missionary who'd long resided, then passed away there—some village in a southern province Celia could never pronounce. Apparently, Celia's father was among the few converts from a respected and educated family, which thereafter scorned his sense of judgment. Escaping their scrutiny as well as the tribulations of the second Opium War, the couple had left all their connections behind and moved to America, a place advertised as idyllic—*Gam Saan,* many called it: the "Golden Mountain"—only to face a fresh set of hardships.

Given all Celia's father had endured, could she really strip herself from the remainder of his life? No doubt this would happen once she married Stephen, for the sake of her husband's best interests—and, admittedly, her own.

Also, what of Stephen's parents? Despite his father's sympathetic gestures, Stephen felt it best to shroud any marital plans until the completion of his schooling. Then he and Celia could move to Washington Territory—where, unlike in Oregon, their marriage would be legal—and he could stand financially on his own. The potential of his being cut off from his family, in every aspect, went without saying.

All due to Celia.

A dreaded notion.

She opted to put it simply. "You can't tell me you believe your parents will ever approve."

"Celia, we've been over this. They know about your heritage, and they clearly care for you enough to keep you in their home."

"As a maid," she stressed. "That doesn't mean they'll feel the same about my becoming your wife. Or their daughter. Not just because of my station but as a half-breed—"

"Stop. You're being foolish."

While perhaps warranted—and really, didn't she want him to counter her points?—his exasperation was irking. Besides, she wasn't the one being naive.

She broke away and retreated to the other side of the blanket. With her back to him, she summoned the courage to broach a topic they'd surely both considered but never addressed.

"What of our children?"

A quiet beat passed, unsurprisingly, before he replied. "Lord willing, we'll have beautiful, healthy babies. A whole litter if I have my say." His overly casual tone made clear he was evading the issue.

"But what if our children look…" Her question trailed off, and Stephen, now behind her, gingerly grasped her waist and rotated her around.

"They'll look like you. And me. A perfect blend of both."

"Or," she said, amounting to a rasp, "like any one of the Chinese on the streets being shunned and beaten."

She didn't have to explain the biological, if rare, possibility of features skipping a generation or more. Just months ago, at a Bettencourt dinner party, gossip made the rounds about a dove-white woman in Portland's high society who'd learned she was a quadroon only after giving birth to a baby the color of cinnamon. Despite her banker husband uncovering documents that traced his wife's lineage to a Southern plantation, he publicly declared the baby illegitimate by way of a man with unknown ancestry. Because in the eyes of many, the adulterous scenario was better than the truth: that his wife and child were part Negro. Undesirables. Like the Chinese.

"No matter the circumstances," Stephen asserted, "I'll protect our family."

Forever?

The rhetorical challenge would do no good. Celia sighed and turned her head away. She stared unseeing but for dust motes floating in the lantern light.

"Darling, look at me." The directive, though firm, held gentle sincerity.

Reluctant, she met his eyes.

"There is nothing we can't conquer together. Nothing. And the same will be said of our children. They'll be fine because they'll be loved fiercely and raised to be strong. Their skin could be purple...or orange. Green, for that matter."

The images lured Celia's lips into a partial smile.

But Stephen remained fervent. So much so, she couldn't help but want to believe him.

Then again, she wasn't the rest of the world. While not to be disagreeable, she felt compelled to remind him: "Tonight, you heard Mr. Humphrey speak of the ban, of efforts to make it permanent."

A muscle shifted in Stephen's cheek, further highlighting his jawline. "Do you know the willpower it took for me not to slug that bastard—pardon my language—square in the face?"

Hearing the sentiment aloud did serve as a comfort, if not a solution.

"In that case," she said, "you can imagine how greatly the laws will worsen by the time you're home for good."

"I can," he conceded. "But by then, I'll have the credibility as well as the personal resources to help strike them down. And I assure you, if any of them pose the slightest threat to you, I'll fight them tooth and nail."

She was tempted to tease, as she sometimes did, that he ought to instead become a lawyer despite his aversion to the related paperwork and bureaucracy.

"Do you love me?" he asked, and she blinked, though purely from the redirect.

"Of course I do."

"Then you need to have faith in me. In us."

Alone with him in this barn, a universe of their own making, with his hands resting on her hips, she felt protected, cherished. Finding it all too easy to agree, she nodded before remembering where their conversation began.

"And how am I to answer my father?"

"You'll tell him…" Stephen contemplated briefly. "You'll tell him to read my letter."

"Your letter?"

"The one I'm going to be writing while I sail to England, laying out our plan. And," he said, "asking for his permission to take you as my wife."

The very idea, a tangible show of Stephen's devotion, spurred in her a fluttering sensation that she swiftly tempered. "What if he says no?"

"Not a chance. I have a flair for being persuasive. I already succeeded in winning you over, didn't I?" His eyes crinkled at the edges from a smile that proved infectious, an ability that had made winning her over secretly easy. Then he brushed aside a stray lock of hair from her forehead. "We'll wait to marry, only because you deserve the grandest of weddings and a full-fledged doctor for a husband who can provide for you properly. However, in… the meantime…" He looked over her shoulder and oddly stepped away, surveying the ground as if seeking a dropped object.

"Is everything all right? Did you lose something?"

He raised a pointer finger, a signal to wait. After picking up an item too small for her to identify, he wrestled with it a bit, then returned and gazed into her eyes. "Celia Therese Chung." Lowering onto one knee, he displayed a strand of cotton string tied into a loop. "Promise you'll marry me, and with this temporary band, we'll hereby be engaged—at least known by us, the only ones who truly matter."

It was all so absurd—comical, even. Still, the ring could just as well have been crafted from gold and lined with diamonds, and it would have altered nothing for Celia. In that moment, of singular importance was the love she felt between them, so strong it verged on electric.

With eyes welling, she answered, "I promise."

His smile widened as he slid the loop onto her finger. Then he stood and embraced her, sealing their pact with a kiss that sent her heart racing in the most wondrous of ways.

Though increasingly and on numerous occasions, they had been physically intimate to a proper limit, that night on the blanket, amid the soft flickering of the lantern, with each whisper and caress and adoring entanglement, any boundaries melted away as they united as would a husband and wife.

It was a bond Celia clung to throughout the proceeding days. For it helped barricade her emotions—first as she watched Stephen leave on the depot-bound carriage, then in the interminable weeks that followed, particularly when his letter arrived for his family.

To exclude Celia had been sensible on his part. Expected. Knowing this, however, didn't lessen the sting nor the hollow ache from his absence, both of which she'd do well to grow accustomed to. Until his return, there would be no assuring posts for Celia. For her, there would be only longing and trusting and waiting in silence.

CHAPTER SIX

On any given day, the head housekeeper possessed a glower so constant it might well have been carved in stone. But on the afternoon of this specific Wednesday, as Celia was pressing the linen napkins amid the interim calm of the kitchen, Miss Waterstone interrupted with a unique look, her eyes unreadable.

"Come with me."

The addition of two words—her standard for acquiring assistance being a mere *Come*—was also curious. Even so, Celia complied by adjusting her grasp on the cloth-wrapped handle of the iron, still hot from the stove, and stood it upright. Then, wiping her hands on her apron, she trailed Miss Waterstone through the adjacent corridor. The woman's hair barely jostled with each step. Ever short and tidy, it was naturally graying from her age of fifty-three—or, as she claimed, from the five staff members under her charge, all requiring perpetual scrutiny.

As she led Celia through the dining room, the clacking of their bootheels and rustling of their uniform dresses remained the only sounds between them. In the foyer, they passed an array of painted ancestral portraits, familial photographs, and decorative vases that would later need dusting. Still imparting no hints, Miss

Waterstone maintained her deliberate strides, reminiscent of the teacher from Celia's one-room schoolhouse.

Back then too, Celia had reined in her instinct to question directives and certainly to protest or challenge. Attention was something to be avoided. The fellow children in her small town in Washington Territory, being aware of her father's origin, had immediately labeled her "different." As such, she'd learned to focus on academics and keep to herself. The latter still a penchant of hers, to drift into another world, she relied on books. That and the meditative rhythm of kneading dough.

She felt the same desire now to escape as Miss Waterstone halted at the drawing room. Again, the woman's eyes shone with an unsettling flicker. But just as soon, it was gone, as was she.

"Come in." The mayor motioned with a wave, tight as his tone. "Close the door behind you." In his regular three-piece charcoal suit, he stood beside the settee where his wife sat poised, suggesting a formal purpose for Celia to have been escorted to a room she well knew how to find.

Back stiffening, she did as commanded and stepped onto the Persian rug to appear before the couple. Beyond the trio of windows on the far wall, a scattering of clouds largely cloaked the sun, cooling a mid-September day that was suddenly anything but comfortable.

"Good afternoon, sir. Ma'am." Celia proffered a smile, which elicited no reciprocation.

On the claw-footed table in front of Mrs. Bettencourt was a porcelain teacup filled with a brew that smelled of jasmine. But no sign of steam. As if it had been there a while, cooling, ignored.

Celia's mind raced, seeking the issue. She could think of only one possibility…

In what seemed a wordless prod, Mrs. Bettencourt shot a

glance at her husband, who exhibited a manner Celia recognized; it was his precursor to a speech he found unpleasant yet necessary to deliver.

"Celia," he said, "we have summoned you for a most unfortunate cause. Some startling news has…come to our attention."

They knew. About her engagement to Stephen. But how? After the passing of nearly three months, how had they learned of it?

Celia's mouth went dry as Mrs. Bettencourt spoke to her husband. "Edwin, go on and show her. Let her read for herself." A mystifying reference.

With a slight nod, the mayor pivoted to cross the room, and the likeliest source occurred to Celia:

A letter from her father.

She had delayed responding to his post, allowing ample time for Stephen's to reach him first. Now it seemed her father had conveyed his objections in writing, not to her but directly to the people who'd ensure the marital plans were stopped.

Celia girded herself, instinctively clasping the promissory loop on her finger—discreet and unconventional but no less binding.

If only Stephen were here, they could make their stance known together.

The mayor rustled what sounded like paper on the fireplace mantel, over which was mounted the saber from his service as a Union soldier. Like most veterans, he shared little about his time in the Civil War—aside from his duty protecting mail routes, entailing dealings with various Indian tribes. His occasional remarks about their unjust treatment—an expression of sympathy rarely afforded the outcasts of white society—was never more notable than now.

He circled back, but not with stationery. Rather, he passed

along a newspaper folded in half, his face somber. "Read there, toward the bottom."

Equally daunted and perplexed, Celia scanned the front page and, below the middle crease, stopped at a headline.

ROCK SPRINGS RIOT LEADS TO TRAGEDY

"Rock Springs," she said, processing. "Why, that's where my father is…" She stole a glance at the Bettencourts before it dawned on her that she'd already shared her father's location and that of course this was their reason for presenting the paper.

Her attention dropped back to the article. She strained to concentrate, warding off panic.

On the second of September, it said, in Pit 6 of a Union Pacific coal mine in Sweetwater County, a fight broke out between a group of white and Chinese miners over working a desirable area, a common contention point for men paid by the ton. Later that day, approximately 150 white miners—mostly Cornish, Irish, Swedish, and Welsh—descended on Chinatown.

Celia's hands trembled as she read on with increasing speed.

By that evening, seventy-nine company coal houses had been burned to the ground. Damages had yet to be fully assessed but so far were estimated to total an astronomical $150,000. Twenty-two arrests were made, a state legislator among them. Although the mob's actions were being widely rebuked, the burden of responsibility, according to the article, lay with the Union Pacific Coal Department. Specifically, it said, the management's "calamitous decision" to bring in Chinese strikebreakers a decade prior had resulted in Chinese miners now outnumbering the whites by more than double, and all at lower wages. This stoking of animosity was not only foreseeable but preventable, the report claimed, and had given the white workers just cause for resentment—

This stopped Celia cold.

Just cause? For burning down homes? For terrifying Chinese people simply trying to get by?

Anger and helplessness swirled within her. She envisioned her father, faced by a vengeful mob amid the smoke and flames of a town set ablaze.

"I need to go there," she decided aloud and rapidly considered how fast she could pack and how soon a train would leave for Rock Springs.

"Dear," Mrs. Bettencourt said, reminding Celia of the couple's presence, "that won't be necessary." A definitive statement, a ruling made.

Celia withheld a scoff, as taking leave from her job would require permission. "I won't be gone long. I give you my word."

Mrs. Bettencourt released a breath, yet her expression didn't waver. "Quite frankly, it would be safer if you stay."

The observation wasn't unfounded. Still, the incident happened almost a week ago. Things had to have settled some.

"He's my father. I just need to make sure he's all right."

"Celia—*no.*"

The retort was jarring. Indeed, Celia was being obstinate, though for good reason. She straightened, readying to press her case, when the mayor piped in. "Your father has passed."

Celia halted with lips parted, silenced by the word.

Passed. The lone syllable echoed in her ears, reverberating through the tunnels of her memories. From a doctor in her childhood home, pronouncing her mother gone. At Celia's age of thirteen, the reality of her mother's death had still come as a shock, yet there had been warnings. Months of illness. But now? With her father? No.

No, there was no sense in it—only a logical explanation.

"You're mistaken." She strove to be insistent. "The article said nothing of the like. You've simply assumed the worst."

The mayor, without taking the newspaper from her, flipped to another page. He gently pointed. "There's more."

Gripped by heightened dread, Celia risked lowering her eyes to the paper. She forced herself to continue through the article.

Far more than homes were decimated in the rampage, it said. Lives were taken. Twenty-eight confirmed dead, listed by name. All Chinese.

Vaguely, Celia felt a hand on her elbow, supporting her, just as her knees buckled at her recognition of a victim.

Chung Jun

CHAPTER SEVEN

Only upon reflection did Celia decipher the look in Miss Waterstone's eyes, the anomalous flicker...

It was pity.

Since Celia's allotted period of mourning would entail reprieve from her duties, Miss Waterstone had been informed that Celia's father died—even before Celia was told—though minus the circumstances. This was according to Mrs. Bettencourt, offered as an assurance to Celia.

All to say her bloodline remained a secret among few.

Concerns over its discovery, however, weren't the cause of Celia's reclusion in the immediate days that followed. Certainly, she held doubts that justice would be served. But more than that, even more than grief—besides, how could a person truly grieve without a proper funeral?—it was guilt that weighed on her, heavy as lead: shame for not answering her father's letter; for not being the obedient daughter he deserved; for her selfishness, in thought and intention if nothing else.

Curled up in bed, with morning light seeping through the curtained window, she opened her mother's oval locket. Typically, she kept the inherited keepsake tucked away in her bureau. The wedding portrait inside was the sole photo of her parents that she owned. Grainy in warm-brown tones, the bride stood elegantly in a dress with a high laced collar, long hair swept up and adorned with a peony, her hand resting on the crook of her groom's suited arm. He too looked distinguished, with ebony hair slicked back and thin mustache neatly trimmed. They gazed forward—without smiles, of course—but they leaned toward each other just enough to reveal their affection.

And now both were gone.

Was Celia considered an orphan now, even as a grown woman? Either way, she felt altogether alone.

A knock rattled her door, a cursory alert before it creaked opened.

Instinctively, she pulled the locket to the chest of her nightgown and beneath her coverlet.

Miss Waterstone entered and placed a tray of bread and soup on the nightstand, same as she had periodically for the past two days. "Eat," she said, not unkindly. It was her usual instruction despite Celia's utter lack of appetite. But then she added, "Next, you shall sponge yourself clean and dress. You are going downtown."

Celia blinked, slow to comprehend. "Downtown?"

"Indeed. Mrs. Talbert has a list of items requiring purchase. The fresh air should do you good."

Although loath to venture from the cocoon of her room, particularly for a reason as trivial as an errand for the cook, Celia reminded herself of her station.

She was a servant, not a guest.

———

Through the jostling carriage ride, Timothy made casual conversation over his shoulder, all while Celia clutched the empty cloth sack on her lap. With each bump over a rock or divot, the salty bone broth she'd compliantly ingested now surged up her throat. It took considerable strength to keep the soup where it belonged.

Downtown at last, they pulled to a stop on Morrison Street. This time, she didn't hesitate in accepting Timothy's help to climb off.

"Thank you," she managed, though she was far more grateful for the unmoving ground beneath her boots.

He flashed his slanted smile. "I'll be waiting right around here for whenever you want to head back."

She nodded genially. Then, gathering her shopping list and bearings, she took a breath and proceeded with her mission— which, she suspected, had been assigned strictly for her well-being. The house's stolid cook was a paragon of efficiency; her systematic planning of daily meals and food deliveries left scant room for error. Any offers of assistance Celia had made before, to help with even dinner rolls, were spurned as an encroachment on the woman's territory.

But Miss Waterstone was likely right; if nothing else, the fresh air could do Celia good.

Unfortunately, entering Miss Tracy's Tea Shop negated any refreshing gains. There, an onslaught of herbs scented the air to an unusually repugnant level. As such, the clerk's every movement and calculation seemed to move at glacier speed. The instant Celia finished buying tea for Mrs. Bettencourt, she returned to the street and exhaled with relief.

Then she recalled her next stop: the Spice House, to acquire cardamom for supper and cloves for a breakfast loaf. Thoughts of the latter at least reminded her why she most loved to bake:

whether for bread or pies or any number of sweets, the process was formulaic. Measured. The outcome predictable.

Pressing on with the errand, she crossed several streets, weaving around wagons and horses and passersby, to reach the store just off Burnside. She slowed only at the sight of a handwritten sign displayed in a window.

Owners from Japan
All welcome

Likely seeming inviting and innocuous to most, the message struck her with an underlying meaning:

Owners not Chinese
Safe to shop here

Even for the lowest rungs of society, there was a hierarchy.

Celia stomped out the notion, useless as it was and of no help to her sullen state. Best to focus on matters within her control: her own meager obligations. She was gearing up to step into the spice shop when she glimpsed, off to the right, a distant figure. In a ribbon-secured coolie hat and a quilted tunic, a fellow glanced over. The man was Chinese and…her father.

A breath snagged in her chest.

Not a moment later, he turned and disappeared into the bustling center of Chinatown.

But no—it couldn't have been him. Or could it?

From inquiries into the riot, the mayor had relayed that there would be no funerals for the victims, saying he believed they'd already been buried in a shared, likely unmarked grave. Now Celia wondered: In the chaos, could some identities have been mistaken? White authorities overseeing the aftermath could certainly have misheard a Chinese name. Many were difficult for even Celia to pronounce.

Of course, if her father was alive and in town, he would have come to the house. But what if he'd only just arrived?

Her legs didn't wait for a conclusion to the hypotheticals; already, she was striding in the man's wake. She paused at the street corner to scan the crowd. The man's face, still too far for her to identify with confidence, blinked between people's heads.

She needed to get closer.

In a rush, she threaded through the sea of bodies, bumping several while trailing the conical bamboo hat as it floated down the road. She made her way past outdoor vendors of poultry and seafood. Scents of anise and cloves and garlic wafted past as she wove around peddlers toting baskets of vegetables until she again lost track of him.

Panic shot through her.

"Chung Jun!" Her voice turned several faces, though not the man's she sought. She rotated in place, straining her eyes, searching.

Beyond a decorative red lantern hanging over a storefront, the hat reappeared, along with the same man's profile. He'd stopped moving, near enough for a clearer view.

It was him. Somehow. Her father.

Heart racing, she dashed toward the side of the street where he was speaking to a rickshaw driver. Celia reached out and earnestly touched her father's arm. He spun toward her, revealing a face that...she didn't know.

A stranger's.

Her insides plummeted.

Both fellows stared back with a quizzical look.

"I…I'm sorry," she murmured. "I thought…" She ebbed away, nearly stumbling, and turned to retreat into an alley where she forced herself to breathe deeply.

Good heavens, was she going mad?

She strove to purge her emotions, her nonsensical thoughts, her stunning disappointment. Soon, with an inhale, came a familiar smell. One distinctly reminiscent of childhood days spent with her father.

She worried she was imagining this too before she traced the source.

Roughly twenty feet away, white, puffy bao were being steamed by a Chinese woman wearing a headscarf knotted at her forehead. While using chopsticks to plate the filled buns, the lady chatted intently with an older woman, their near-identical features suggestive of siblings.

Celia suddenly recalled making bao with her father. During his visits home, they would stuff the buns with custard or a sweet red-bean paste. Finally, they would eat them while giggling over the flour that would inevitably cover her nose, drawing a laugh from even her mother.

Celia must have been six when she told her father she no longer cared for the foreign food. A lie. She merely wanted the treats real American girls ate, like peppermint sticks and licorice. She wanted to bake molasses cookies and lemon snaps.

Now she so wished her parents were here, her father especially, to share with her a whole plateful of that soft, delicious bao…

And yet as the two women conversed, it wasn't nostalgia that ultimately reeled Celia over; her train of thought was diverted by two words in their discussion, the only ones she recognized from a language that, like all its related dialects, she otherwise couldn't understand.

"…Rock Springs…"

Until this instant, it hadn't occurred to her, though it should have, that news of the tragedy would be a common and passionate topic among Chinese people even in Oregon. The older woman was gesticulating in animated movements while the cook was shaking her head with a scowl.

We need to be patient, the mayor had told Celia regarding the impending investigation. Given the scale of the crimes, with not just the twenty-eight Chinese murdered but also fifteen more injured, she had to believe those responsible would be punished—especially now that President Cleveland had intervened to an extent, having sent army soldiers to safely escort the Chinese who'd fled the area to return to Rock Springs, either to work or simply to retrieve any salvageable belongings.

Patience would come easier, of course, if Celia at least knew more about how her father had died—hard as it might be to hear. Perhaps these two women similarly had ties to others affected or had even just gathered more details.

"Pardon me, ladies."

They noticed Celia's presence only then, and the older one took her leave, slipping through the back entry of a restaurant.

"You want to buy?" The cook indicated the bao with her chopsticks. "How many?"

"Oh. No…but thank you."

The woman frowned and swatted away flies from a finished stack.

"Ma'am, about Rock Springs, the riot there. Do you happen to know details beyond what's in the papers?"

The woman narrowed her eyes. Maybe she didn't understand, her English potentially limited. Her round face pinched in confusion—or suspicion.

Celia explained, "I knew someone there. Someone who was killed." Reality, from saying this aloud, sprang moisture to her eyes.

The woman must have noticed, because she appeared to soften, if only a fraction.

"Do you know how that happened?" Celia pressed. "How people were hurt?" As she fought to withhold her tears, the woman continued to stare.

The moment stretched with an awkward silence.

What more was there to say? A tear slid down Celia's cheek, let loose by yet another setback. Left with no other choice, she angled to leave.

"Chinese were hiding. In houses."

When Celia turned back, the woman glanced about as if to confirm no one was in the vicinity. Then she resumed in a low tone, "White group came with many weapons. Knives, guns. They make fires and start shooting."

The images crowded Celia's mind. Horrendous as they were, they closely resembled the scene she'd envisioned until the woman added, "Some bodies, they leave on ground. Others, thrown in flames. Some, cut to pieces."

Celia became aware she had gasped only from the story abruptly stopping. The visions in her head, of the terrors her father must have endured, charged on regardless and pummeled her gut.

The woman lowered her eyes before stoically returning to her work, her report finished.

Somewhere in the shock of Celia's thoughts came an understanding. Not of the mob's ghastly crimes by any means but of the evident lack of funerals. Because for at least some who were killed, there was no body to bury.

CHAPTER EIGHT

"Done already?" Timothy asked, leaning against a carriage wheel.

Celia followed his surprised eyes, aimed at the shopping sack dangling from her grip. Even if she were toting more than a single tin of tea, she would have forgotten the bag was there. Just as she had forgotten the other tasks on her list.

"I don't feel well." The truth.

He hurried to stand upright, concerned. "Well, don't you fret. I'll get you on home." He guided her onto the carriage, then hustled up to the driver's seat.

A smack of the reins, and they were off with a jerky shake.

Celia yearned to divulge what she had learned, to Stephen above all. How the headline had been wrong, that it wasn't a riot—it was a massacre.

In light of his absence, she imagined relaying the details to his father until realizing the mayor surely already knew and had amended the gruesome parts to spare her. Now they played in her head on a merciless loop, fueling her burden of guilt.

The rest of the ride passed in a queasy, draining blur that lessened only slightly when she returned to the haven of her bed.

She remained there for the next few days, mornings blending with nights, longing for dreamless sleep.

Even Abigail peeked in on occasion, curious. Or perhaps she still cared.

Late one morning, a doctor with spectacles and a white wreath of hair was called to the house. He asked Celia a seemingly endless list of questions, about her cycles of sleep and eating and all else. So despondent was her state that even her concerns over modesty fell away as he thoroughly examined her body.

Once done, he refastened the buckle on his medical bag and summoned Mrs. Bettencourt, who proceeded to observe with arms folded. "By all indications," he declared, "I would say the girl is not ill."

Mrs. Bettencourt looked rightly bewildered. "Well then, what on earth is wrong with her?"

She's grief-stricken, Celia expected to hear.

Instead, his reply, cold and sharp as a sword, pierced what remained of Celia's guard and sliced straight through her.

"She is with child."

CHAPTER NINE

When beckoned to the drawing room two days later, Celia didn't need to be instructed to shut the door behind her. This time, she was fully aware of the dreaded subject awaiting.

"Have a seat." The mayor, again standing behind his wife's position on the settee, gestured to a cushioned chair set adjacent to them both.

Ever since the doctor's announcement, Celia had been bracing for this discussion. Her mind had spun incessantly with how best to explain. Although still grappling with her father's death and related nightmares, she had to admit that not needing to inform him of her news was at least a small consolation. For while she couldn't be prouder of bearing Stephen's child, in society's eyes—and likely her father's—a pregnant woman out of wedlock deserved a heap of shame.

Celia perched on the assigned chair, heart thumping. From the ominous gray sky, afternoon rain dotted the windows.

Mrs. Bettencourt's gaze gave away nothing.

Subtly, Celia clutched the string loop on her finger while recalling the sentences she'd mentally rehearsed, praying the couple would support Stephen's plan. Just earlier than anticipated. Including an imminent wedding, upon which he'd now naturally insist.

"We're pleased you are well enough to join us," the mayor said.

Celia hesitated. "Thank you, sir. The doctor's tonic has done wonders."

"I am very glad to hear it."

His greeting was surprisingly affable. Why?

Was it possible he already suspected the father's identity? Had he caught one of their many traded glances?

Or had Stephen merely decided to divulge the truth in his letter home?

Whichever the case, perhaps news of the pregnancy—now three months along, affirmed by the doctor's estimate—had swayed the couple to accept the engagement, even if reluctantly.

The mayor cleared his throat. "Celia, I shall put this as delicately as I am able, as pertains to your *condition*."

His utterance of the descriptor was no less fitting for a terminal illness—a contagious one at that. Yet Celia offered only a nod, hoping that in the end she would have to say very little.

"You shall pardon my bluntness," he continued, "but…if this is…well, the result of a man's forcing himself upon you, you should feel free to confide as much."

Despite the notion being fair, compassionate even, Celia balked. Thoughts of Stephen and his gentleness in every way compelled her to defend his honor. "Gracious, no. That is not at all what occurred."

The mayor's expression dropped, and Mrs. Bettencourt raised a knowing brow at him. A smug look of being proved right.

Celia couldn't hold back. "Stephen and I are engaged."

The couple's eyes snapped toward her and went equally wide.

Celia scrambled to regather the speech she'd prepared. "Once he set off for King's College, he was going to write to my father to request his permission. Whether or not it reached him... before..." She needed to be strong, assured. She straightened in her seat. "Stephen and I had planned to tell you of our engagement together. I can assure you that we'd intended to marry only after he earned his degree."

This much at least, the practicality of their initial thinking, would hopefully lessen the blow of their secrecy.

"Just one minute." Mrs. Bettencourt tilted her head, squinting, as if Celia's words were floating in the air, scribed on invisible parchment for review. "Are you saying the baby is Stephen's?"

Celia forced a hard swallow. "I am."

"And therefore," Mrs. Bettencourt went on ponderously, "our grandchild?"

Celia's hand touched her stomach reflexively as she watched the woman comprehending the connection. "Yes."

"And hence, I presume, *our* responsibility."

Celia was about to respond when she absorbed the barbed implication. "No. Of course not. That is not what I'm saying."

Mrs. Bettencourt exaggerated a sigh. "Oh, well, isn't that a grand relief."

"Georgia," the mayor interjected. "Let the girl finish."

"Finish what precisely?" She rose to her feet and faced him. "More despicable falsehoods? I daresay I most certainly will not!"

The outburst was so uncharacteristic that Celia chimed in but feebly. "Ma'am, I-I'm telling the truth."

"Oh? The same as you did of your lineage? Even of your name, for heaven's sake." Celia was struggling to counter the indisputable when Mrs. Bettencourt muttered, "This whole matter is an abomination."

Intended or not, the term matched that of a recent sermon

in which the local kind-faced preacher warned against the "unnatural mixing of bloodlines." *Abominations*, he had called the consequential products. The memory again panged Celia as Mrs. Bettencourt redirected her ire toward her husband.

"You were the one who insisted she could be trusted regardless. And this is the gratitude she shows us—by attempting to sully our son's good name! And all while he's not in the country to defend himself. How very convenient."

Flustered, desperate, Celia wished for even a scrap of evidence, then recalled the token on her finger. She sprang to her feet. "This." She held up her hand. "Just days before leaving, Stephen made this ring for me. On the night he proposed in the barn."

The sound from Mrs. Bettencourt's mouth seemed like a gasp. But when the corners of her lips curled up, it became clear she was scoffing. "Naturally. Where else would it have taken place?" If not for the disgust in her eyes, she almost looked amused.

But it wasn't only at Celia's expense; it was also that of her and Stephen's child, who was in fact real, no matter what anyone else claimed or desired to be true.

Celia held her belly, this time deliberately, protectively, and appealed to the mayor. "Sir, you must believe me. What reasons would I have for fabricating such a tale?"

Mrs. Bettencourt answered for him. "What reasons indeed! Status. And finances, no doubt. Perhaps she thinks threatening to spread such filthy gossip would be worth a pretty penny. Meanwhile, I can only presume the actual man responsible has chosen to shirk his obligations."

Tears pricked Celia's eyes from a collision of horror and sadness and rage. "That's absurd!"

"What's *absurd* is thinking we would believe this nonsense. As a matter of fact"—Mrs. Bettencourt paused, clearly hit by a thought—"for the two of you to marry wouldn't even be possible. This alone puts a rather large gap in your story, wouldn't you say?" Her tone conveyed pride over the point, which Celia was quick to counter.

"Actually, no. It doesn't." In truth, just across the border, in Washington Territory, her parents' own nuptials had been in jeopardy at one time, but only briefly before the interracial-marital laws there had been repealed. "Because we plan to marry in Seattle."

Oddly, the woman smirked. "Ahh, yes. An answer for everything."

Celia barely kept herself from shouting. "Just ask Stephen, then. Ask for yourself."

The woman's smugness vanished at that. She held a glare, heated as the sun. "I will do no such thing. Our son needn't lower himself to dignify such accusations. Particularly from a lying half-breed servant who couldn't manage to keep—"

"*Enough.*" The mayor raised his hand. He was halting a brawl, which, in an instant, had become one sided, having rendered Celia speechless.

"But, Edwin—"

"We have all heard plenty for today," he replied firmly.

Mrs. Bettencourt, remembering herself, tightened her lips and said no more.

Then the mayor angled back to Celia, his voice thick. "Return to your room, and remain there until I decide what is best."

Best. For whom?

The answer was obvious. Yet with no other place to go nor any way to contact Stephen herself, Celia could only abide by the mayor's order—and wait.

CHAPTER TEN

For the next several days, Celia remained sequestered in her room, trapped above all by her circumstances.

Having sent much of her wages to her father—funds forever lost, like so much else—she had little means to get by on her own. Even if she found other work, how long before her physical state became evident and any proper employer would put her out on the street?

Such dilemmas tumbled in her mind as she sat in bed through yet another endless morning, her only breaks from the monotony being trips to the servants' privy. Attempting to read a book she could scarcely focus on, she allowed her gaze to drift to her fraying ring.

She prayed nightly Stephen would return early for a visit. Then his parents could sooner acknowledge the full truth—as could even Miss Waterstone. The sole person to breach the confines of Celia's quarters, the woman came strictly for meal deliveries. With all other staff members steering clear, the single knock on the door now raised no mystery of the person paying a call.

Carting a breakfast tray of milk and porridge, Miss Waterstone entered without a greeting and avoided all eye contact. This manner had become her norm, making clear her awareness of the pregnancy, though presumably little more.

She set the tray on the desk.

"Thank you," Celia said, knowing better than to anticipate a response.

Rather than turn to walk out, however, Miss Waterstone remained to speak. "The mayor has instructed me to inform you that he has graciously secured for you a new arrangement."

The word *graciously* poked at Celia, but she continued to listen.

"At an establishment downtown, room and board shall be provided. This will be in exchange for your duties there as a housekeeper."

Celia had considered the possibility of being relocated. At least it wasn't to a convent or any such place rumored to be stringent and bleak.

"When am I expected to leave?"

"Eleven o'clock."

Celia blinked. "This morning?"

"An earlier hour if you are ready. Here is the address." From her apron pocket, Miss Waterstone handed over a slip of paper bearing the mayor's penmanship.

97 Halsey Street

"Do you require assistance with your packing?"

It was all happening so fast.

Celia scanned her meager belongings in a space that, over the course of three years, she had come to consider her home. Swiftly she was reminded that it had never been that at all.

She replied with a shake of her head.

"Then I shall return shortly to gauge your progress." Miss Waterstone turned and headed for the door.

"How long is the arrangement to last?"

The woman slowed to a stop. After a weighty pause, she answered over her shoulder, gaze to the side: "The retainment of your services will naturally be at the discretion of your new employer—who, I am told, is aware of your condition. As related to this house," she finished with scarcely a glance, "the arrangement is permanent."

———

The house staff was all busy working, a small blessing. Alone at the servants' entrance, bundled in bonnet and coat, Celia gripped her canvas valise and proceeded outside. Dampness from the morning rain clung to the air.

The Bettencourts' carriage sat along the street, readied with a horse, prepared to dispose of her.

Timothy met her partway and relieved her of her bag. He even guided her onto the carriage though all the while remained silent with gaze averted.

She took her seat, determined not to look at the house. At this point, she possessed no reason for sentimentality nor the desire to give any judgmental onlookers the satisfaction of a pitiable glance.

By the time Timothy climbed onto the driver's seat, she sensed someone watching. She managed to keep her attention forward until her periphery caught on a familiar figure up in a window.

On the second floor, Abigail peered from between her bedroom curtains, the very ones she'd often hidden behind as Celia called her name and pretended the girl was nowhere to be found. Celia, nudged by the memory, found herself raising a gloved hand in a small wave. In turn, Abigail's palm lifted halfway and rested on the glass, a seeming attempt to reach out.

Mrs. Bettencourt arrived at the window then. At her sighting of Celia, she moved her daughter aside, and just as the carriage jerked into motion, she yanked the curtains closed.

—

At long last, Timothy halted the horse. There had been no conversations en route, yet Celia couldn't say she minded the quiet.

Though absent any enthusiasm, he came around to help her down. She hesitated, only because their present location, while downtown, was several blocks from the prescribed street.

"The address I was given," she said, "I believe is on Halsey."

He responded in a murmur, "I was told this here would do."

Being rather early in the pregnancy, she was fully capable of tackling the distance, even lugging her travel bag. All the same, the Bettencourts' order to deposit her short of her destination seemed a final slap.

"I see."

He said nothing more, simply guided her down and handed off her bag. With a glance suggestive of disappointment, he said, "Take care." Bypassing his usual smile, he reboarded the carriage and left.

Celia inhaled a steadying breath. Borrowing Stephen's optimism, she assured herself that all would be righted in due time.

With address slip in hand, she ventured down the teeming street ahead. Once on Halsey, she sought numbers on the buildings. She shouldn't have been surprised that they led her to the North End, but still her apprehension rose.

73...79...

Saloons peppered every few buildings. One such "establish-ment" could very well be her new home. She cringed at the vision of mopping up liquor and urine and vomit from the floors, swatting away drunken men's wandering hands.

85...93...

At the sight of 97, shock plowed through her and rooted her in place.

She understood then why Timothy wasn't permitted to deliver her to her destination: The arrangement the mayor had made was with a business to which no respectable family desired to be linked. Not a saloon but worse.

It was the Dewdrop Inn.

A brothel.

CHAPTER ELEVEN

A flush of heat shot up Celia's neck from the leers of passing men. As one whistled, another gleefully remarked about the arrival of a "new girl."

Granted, what else were they to think of her, standing alone with a travel bag before a brothel?

Desperate for an alternative, she scanned the area. A variety of boardinghouses and hotels lay within view, yet practical reasoning saved her a useless trek. Her savings would cover no more than a shabby rented room, undoubtedly infested with fleas and lice. She had not only her own safety to consider but also that of her child.

She dragged her attention back to the Dewdrop Inn. It was but a temporary solution. She just wished she had a way to contact Stephen. If only she'd peeked at the return address on his post to his family before they tossed her out like a pile of rubbish...

Oh, stop.

She gave her head a quick shake, ridding the notion along with self-pity. Neither would do her an ounce of good.

Suppressing enough pride to act, she plodded to the front

door. She was reaching for the handle when two men stumbled out together. They were grinning like Cheshire cats, the clear source of their joy appalling.

Before her nerve could escape her, Celia continued inside, where floral perfumes and the stench of tobacco assailed the air.

"This ain't that kinda inn," a blond proclaimed from just off the entry. The lone person in the parlor, she was reclined on a chaise lounge by the unlit fireplace while buffing her fingernails. Her scanty robe shifted, exposing her drawers and, even more shocking, her bare bosoms.

Celia dropped her gaze to the scuffed wooden floor, and her cheeks flamed. Deciphering the remark based on her luggage, she replied, "No—yes, I understand. I'm here to work." She rushed to clarify, "As a housekeeper, that is." Did that sound disparaging? "Not that there's anything wrong with…what you do…or rather your line of work…"

"Golly. I'm tickled to death you approve." Sarcasm coated the blond's tone. Or was that amusement?

Celia thought to apologize. Due to her fluster, it seemed safer to detour. "I was told, upon my arrival, to ask for—" The contact escaping her, she went to reference the note in her grip and discovered it gone. Oh mercy, she must have dropped it.

"Marie is the name," a lilting voice supplied, the correct name of the overseer turning Celia around. On the stairs that ran along an entry wall, the woman descended with fiery locks draping the shoulders of her silky robe, which at least was properly closed and tied.

Celia had seen her before in a window, holding a lit cigarette, same as now. "You're Marie?"

"Don't I bloody wish." A laugh lined her brogue. "It'd be grand giving the orders round here for a change." At the base of the staircase, she pulled a drag from her cigarette. "I'm Lettie. And you are..."

"Celia. Celia Hart."

"Well, Celia Hart"—Lettie exhaled a gray stream from the side of her mouth—"I hope you're not like the last housekeeper. No one took to her much. Ended up kickin' the bucket." A punctuating smirk implied a sinister end. "She's upstairs. First door on the left."

Aghast, Celia looked upward, then back. "The housekeeper— her body's still here?"

"I was talking about the madam. You want to see her about the job, don't you?"

Celia swallowed, relieved, and nodded.

"Off you go then." Lettie tipped her head toward the stairs before sauntering into the parlor. A haze of smoke drifted in her wake.

Celia collected herself, then proceeded up the steps. At the described door, she knocked.

Nothing.

She knocked harder, growing anxious.

"Madam Marie, I'm Celia Hart," she called out. "I was told you were in need of—"

The door opened partway, revealing a compact woman in a navy housedress. She looked to be in her forties, with short, black hair that stylishly framed intelligent eyes. And she was Chinese.

"What's this you say?" Her tone carried a rasp.

Celia reset her thoughts. "I've come to be your housekeeper." Although yearning to add *for an extremely short while*, she tacked on a polite "Should you find that agreeable."

"Show me both hand."

Celia stared for a second. But then, recognizing the reason—a test for toughness—she set down her bag and extended her palms, which Marie quickly examined. Surely she did the same when hiring ladies of the night, though in a gauge for softness. She then eyed Celia from head to toe.

The possibility of being rejected for a job at a brothel was shamefully dumbfounding.

Celia had the urge to counter whatever had been relayed about her character and morals, her baby's father no doubt conveyed as being unknown. Instead, given the woman's cool bearing, she volunteered, "I can also cook. And bake—at which I'm particularly skilled."

Culinary duties would even be preferable.

But Marie flitted her hand at the suggestion as if swatting away a flea. Past her shoulder, a ribbon of earthy-scented smoke plumed from a small black cabinet. Its splayed doors presented a framed photograph of grainy figures, various trinkets, and rice mounded in a blue Oriental bowl. A shrine.

As a child, Celia had once discovered a similar exhibit tucked away in her family's home—an especially intriguing find, given that both parents were Christians—mere seconds before her mother intervened. *Your father's private belongings are not to be disturbed*, she'd said, then shut and removed the cabinet, which was never seen again.

Finally, Marie grunted her verdict and wagged a finger. "You work hard or no food, no bed."

"Yes, of course." Celia's reply came far too earnest to her own ears.

"You clean everything *very* good. I check close." The woman tapped the outer corner of her eye for emphasis.

"Yes, ma'am. I understand."

A sudden notion of the soiled sheets to be washed caused Celia a queasiness she did her best to ignore. Then Marie flicked her fingers again, making clear Celia was now the flea.

"Begin," Marie said and went to close the door.

Celia rushed to procure the most basic of details. "In which room shall I stay? And where might I find cleaning supplies?"

Whether or not Marie heard, the door fully shut.

Once again, Celia was left to fend for herself.

———

Fortunately, with a bit of investigating, Celia located all she needed to get by. This included her bedroom, which was the size of a linen closet and musty as an old rag. As commanded, she went straight to work. She swept and mopped the dirt-tracked floors, pausing to scrub stubborn marks until her neck and back ached, making sure to be thorough.

At six o'clock, on the cusp of the busy hours, Marie ordered her to stop. Celia was to resume at dawn—but quietly, so as not to disturb the "girls."

Alone in the kitchen, Celia ate the last of the stew left by the cook, a middle-aged Polish woman who spoke minimal English and made clear she was there solely to work. The other ladies had already eaten in preparation for their evening activities.

Given the widely known nature of the inn, a thought came to Celia: Could the Bettencourts have sent her here with an underlying purpose? If unsavory presumptions were made, would her claims of Stephen as the father be more easily discredited?

"A moot point," she answered herself decisively. Stephen would be the first to declare the child as his own—as soon as he knew.

After washing her bowl, Celia headed for the privacy of her

room. The walk there resembled how she imagined it would be to tread backstage as actors prepared for a show. Costumes were donned, from ribboned garters to boas and corsets, set off with dramatic makeup and feathered updos. Stoicism was replaced by smiles and giggles. A few accents emerged where previously none had been. The cast was ready to perform.

Too soon, a cacophony of gut-churning sounds affirmed as much.

While Celia lay in bed with a pillow held tight to her ears, only partially muffling a clash of moans and squeaky bed frames, she prayed that every hardship endured through this period of her life would soon be a distant memory.

1888

—

JULY

CHAPTER TWELVE

In the dimness of the underground, an unseen man bellowed, "Lemme out! You hear me? Lemme out, damn you!"

A rattling followed, a door being shaken. Not Celia's. Despite her dizzy haze, being seated against her own door, she knew this much. Still, the noises were loud enough to suggest they were from a neighboring cell.

Then came more rattling, more shouts. They further swelled the ache in her brain before the man quieted.

At least she wasn't entirely alone.

She was about to call to him to share her presence but thought better of it. The effort would only further deplete her energy. Besides, what good would it do?

And so she kept silent, seeking scraps of memories, clues to what had led her here and why on God's green earth she was dressed as a man.

She recalled running. Through the darkness. In the tunnels.

There had been a whistle. High pitched, from a distance and—

The thought broke off, interrupted by a shaking against her spine. She twisted around. Someone was pounding on her cell door.

"Stand back!" The muffled command came in a man's nasal tone.

The bottom center of the door shifted, and more light shone through. A square, no more than a foot wide, was opening away from the cell.

"Stand back, I say! Or you get no food!"

Celia struggled to obey by moving on all fours.

The door within the door swung fully open. In the rectangular shaft of light, a hand shoved a metal plate inside. Then the small door shut, followed by a sliding noise, a lock returned to its place.

"Stand back!" he repeated, farther away. Another lock scraped open; then came a low creak. A food slot being lifted.

Celia expected the sound of his resecuring the lock. Instead, the man burst into a scream. "Help! He's got my arm!"

"*Shut your trap.*" The prisoner's voice had gained menacing gruffness. "Unlock my door, or I'll rip your damn arm off."

From an intensified shriek, Celia visualized the guard's forearm on the ground, enduring the weight of a booted foot.

"All right, all right!" the guard yielded through his panting. "I'll do it. I'm tryin'. I'm trying...to reach..."

Celia pictured him on his side, much like a fish out of water, flopping and writhing while stretching upward for the bolt. From somewhere in her mind, a notion arose: If the ploy worked, could she too be saved?

"*Hurry up,*" rasped the inmate, eerily deep, "or I'll crush your arm, I swear it."

"Wait—I've almost got it! There... Yeah, I got it..."

A louder scraping indicated an unlocking of the door, and a hinge-like creak swiftly mixed with scuffling noises. Clearly the prisoner had pushed open the cell door, shoving the guard along with it.

Celia needed to speak up, to beg the inmate for release before he was gone. "Help…" The call triggered a cough that smothered her voice. Bypassing a second attempt, she scurried toward the door to pound an alert. Just as she got there, a clash of voices erupted, including that from a third man. Layering the shouting were sounds of hitting and punching and kicking.

Celia cowered instinctively into a ball. Her quickened breaths only slightly muted the raging fight.

Then, at last, it stopped.

"What'd I tell you to do?" the new voice chided. "You shove the plate in fast. And that's after you peek inside, ya dunce."

A pause followed. Then a nasally reply: "So what we do with him?"

"Just put him back in there. They'll take him even if he's dead."

Soon came dragging sounds. By the time the neighboring cell door slammed shut, Celia was trembling with such force she wondered if her bones would shatter—not just from the vision of a murdered man in the next cell but also from the loss of her one, perhaps only, chance at escape.

1885

—

OCTOBER

CHAPTER THIRTEEN

"We needing opium."

Celia ceased her sweeping of the hall, befuddled as to how Marie's words pertained to her until the woman passed over a small red pouch. Coins within it clinked. Made of silk with intricate gold stitching, the bag was cinched with a pair of black strings.

"Instruction inside." Eyes watery, Marie rubbed her temple as if fending off a headache. Past her robe sleeves, gooseflesh covered her quivering arms.

Since Celia's arrival a week prior, she had yet to see Marie in such a state, though the cause was clear: withdrawal. During the short time Celia traveled with her father, she'd witnessed the ailment in several railway workers who, in the evenings, often indulged in the vice.

But her familiarity with the reaction didn't mean she had any desire to venture into an establishment that sold the substance. What was more, given the exorbitant taxes on opium—100 percent, according to the papers—sellers were known to often distribute smuggled supplies.

"Maybe it would be best," Celia suggested, "if one of the other girls ran the errand, to ensure you receive exactly what you need."

"They sleeping. Need rest for work tonight." Marie *tsked* as if Celia should know this—which, of course, she did. It was only ten in the morning. "You think you are more important?" She waited for a reply with crossed arms.

"No. Certainly not." Celia leaned the broom against a wall and unfastened her apron, preparing to trade it for her coat.

Though she had provided the right answer, in all truth, it felt like a lie.

———

Projected through a large white cone—a megaphone, people called it—a man's rant in Chinese dominated Chinatown, drawing a crowd like a carnival barker.

Celia stayed close to the storefronts and away from the stream of people while striding anxiously toward the penned address. Standing on stacked crates, the speaker waved a flyer with a passion reflective of his tone.

Celia comprehended nothing, of course. For a time as a young child, she'd begged her father to teach her words in his dialect, as they seemed an amusing code that others couldn't crack. Yet he'd refused. He had been insistent she sound "American"—until years later, when finally he yearned to teach her. By then, she'd lost all interest and, more than that, became averse herself to being viewed as different.

Per Marie's directions, at the Xi Ping bookstore, Celia turned into an alley. A dead end awaited her fifty-some feet ahead. Nerves humming, she tried to ignore the sense of being boxed in. At the unmarked door on the right, she glanced about with caution, confirming she was alone.

She rapped with her knuckles. During the wait, something

coiled around her ankle. She jumped back with a gasp before spotting the cat she'd inadvertently pushed aside. No doubt a stray, with gray fur matted and an outline of ribs showing, the animal startled and its tail shot upright.

Celia caught her breath. She reached down to pat the feline in an act of amends, but the creature reared back. It hissed with fangs bared just as a man's voice sounded.

"What do you want?"

A peep-through in the door had swung open. Dark Asian eyes. Perfect English.

Celia rushed to recall her instructions. "Madam Marie at the Dewdrop Inn—she requires a new supply."

He scanned Celia with the type of scrutiny she always sought to avoid.

Latching on to a diversion, from her coat pocket, she held up Marie's bag. Whether from recognition of the pouch or just the promise of its contents, he clapped the window shut and opened the door.

"Get in."

Celia slid past him, and he closed the door behind them. Then he secured the bolt, enclosing them on a landing lit dimly by the lantern in his grip.

"Follow me."

So surprising was his youth given the nature of the sale— he couldn't have been older than fifteen—Celia stalled as he embarked down the stairs.

He suddenly peered back. "You coming?"

"Yes. Sorry."

Utilizing the handrail made of weathered planks, she descended cautiously, whereas the boy's fast feet suggested a path frequently used. The smell of opium vapor, sweet and cloying, intensified near the base. Once there, the kid set his lantern on a small square table and held out his palm. A demand for money.

Was this how it should be done? She'd presumed the trade would be simultaneous.

"You want the stuff or don't you?"

An error on her part could cost her another home. Desperately hoping she was doing this properly, she poured all the coins into his hand. By the fluttering light, he calculated the change with a near-instant glance.

"Wait here."

He turned and slipped through a split in a dark, raggedy curtain, releasing a more potent waft. A two-inch gap invited a peek. Thick with smoke and aglow with oil lamps used to heat opium, more than the room's aura resembled an inferno. A mix of men and women were sprawled on cushioned cots that filled the space like a maze, their minds spiraling through mental trails from slow, deep inhales off their pipes.

From behind Celia came a peculiar sound.

She listened closer. The soft cry of a baby. Had a child been set aside so its mother could get high in the parlor?

Seconds later, the cries grew insistent, indicative of hunger. With the doorman yet to return, an urge to check on the babe tugged at Celia.

Beneath the shadowed staircase, a brick wall hosted a squatty doorway. Following the wails, she peeked through the opening. A set of parallel walls made of stone stretched narrowly into the dimness.

A tunnel.

It appeared the rumors were actually true, about a labyrinth of passageways underlying Chinatown. Whether they were several floors deep and featured hideaways for sordid dealings, this much was irrefutable: it would be an inconspicuous place to abandon a child.

Prodded by thoughts of the one growing within herself, Celia couldn't resist ducking through the entrance. Dirt scented the air, stale and dank. A shiver ran up her spine.

She returned the silk pouch to her pocket and headed to the right, toward the hoarsening cries. Their volume escalated, guiding her to a rectangular board, about four feet high and propped against a wall. Envisioning a lone newborn behind it, she slid the board partly aside and gawked.

There indeed was a baby, but not alone.

In a room illuminated by kerosene lanterns, a Chinese woman stood rocking the swaddled child, who wailed away. The lady stared at Celia, and she wasn't the only one.

Spread about the room were at least a dozen other Chinese people in a wide range of ages, the majority looking her way. Among them were several children circled in a game of marbles and a man standing while smoking a pipe. Its spiced sweetness mingled with the smell of sweat and a tinge of urine—from a chamber pot, presumably. Some elderly folks were cross-legged on grass sleeping mats, small piles of bedding beside them. Off to the side, two women were squatting by a basket into which they were snapping peas. A pot over a small burner belched steam in waves.

"Pardon my intrusion," Celia said, embarrassed though also confused by the scene in such a place. "I heard the crying..."

A few exchanged worried looks. Then one of the older men flicked a hand, muttering words clearly meant to shoo her out. A younger fellow grabbed hold of the board and slid it closed, returning her to the darkness.

Incredibly, the family—perhaps a combination of more than

one—had made the sunless world of the underground their home.

"Hey, miss!"

Celia's pulse sprinted as she spun toward the voice. It was the boy who was to fetch the opium. He was craning his neck from the entry under the stairs.

Reminded of why she'd come, she hurried back and returned to the spot where he had left her.

"What were you doing in there?"

"Nothing. Sorry..." She diverted, "Do you have it for me? The madam's supply?"

He surveyed her face but briefly. Then he handed over a small tin fastened with twine.

"Thank you." She had no inkling if it contained a fair amount—or, really, if it held anything at all—its weight being too light to judge, yet she simply followed him up the steps. The instant she exited, he shut and locked the door.

A couple of strangers were wandering into the alley. Celia stored the tin in her pocket and averted her eyes while heading for the main street, eager to return to the inn.

On the makeshift stage, the speaker was still ranting, only now he was joined by two men distributing flyers. One of those papers lay on the ground just ahead of Celia. Without pausing her steps, she scooped it up. Beneath dusty shoeprints were row after row of Chinese characters.

A burst of shouts arose from the crowd. Several fists were raised and shaking in support, the anger ramping up. Even more concerning was the sight of a few young men in black with menacing looks and long braids wrapped atop their heads. Based on warnings from Celia's father, they had all the signs of being "highbinders," dubbed so for their fight-ready hair. Alleged to carry small hatchets, they were known as hired killers for the sworn brotherhoods called *tongs*.

The latter—most having fallen steeply from their origins as benevolent associations—dealt chiefly in gambling halls and prostitution, both voluntary and forced. While territorial wars among the various gangs were common knowledge, Celia imagined the members had even less affection for white lawmen, like those currently posted on the fringes of the rally.

Gripping their batons, the officers were shifting their gazes between the gathering and each other. The setting resembled a volcanic island on the verge of eruption, with a similar threat of casualties.

And here was Celia, carting around potentially illegal opium.

Sweat formed on her scalp as she shoved the flyer into her pocket and treaded around the crowd. Nearing a policeman, she detoured as subtly as possible and wove around passersby.

A whistle rang out. A cop's warning.

She didn't stop to investigate, just hastened her strides as a throng of people bumped past her. They were dashing from the assembly, chaos breaking out. In seconds, she was pulled into a run.

As with so many of her nightmares, in which she failed to reach her father through the tangle of an angry mob, she kept pace with the fleeing strangers. She halted only upon reentering the inn, where she released a deep breath.

When she pulled out the tin, relieved it hadn't fallen out, the crumpled flyer came with it. On the backside was what appeared to be an English translation of the Chinese text.

She flattened the creased page across her hip, then read.

Triggered by the riot in Rock Springs, it claimed, a flood of anti-Chinese violence and mass expulsions was spreading rapidly through the American West, particularly in Washington Territory. In the city of Tacoma, a mob of six hundred forced the residents of Chinatown to clear out. The so-called peaceful expulsion had been touted as such a success by white authorities that the "Tacoma Method" was being employed in city after city.

Celia winced at her own ignorance. Consumed lately by her personal tribulations, she had little knowledge of what was occurring beyond her current walls. And now she realized: the families in the tunnel were likely seeking safety from just such dangers.

The treatment was utterly unfair, to be sure—as the flyers made clear. And yet she couldn't help but question the sensibility of a public protest. If anything, wouldn't that add to justifications for pushing the Chinese out?

Reading on, she discovered an update not only related to the Rock Springs massacre but specifically about it. She gripped the page tighter, gearing up for what she now feared was the greatest impetus of the gathering—and outrage—in Chinatown.

Despite the murders being committed in broad daylight and in plain view of hundreds, it reported, not a single white witness agreed to testify, a right to which Chinese people were legally barred. Hence, the grand jury ultimately refused to indict.

Shock encircled Celia's throat, strong as a choke hold, as the ramifications fully set in.

Every murderer, including her father's, would walk free.

CHAPTER FOURTEEN

Fortune rests in misfortune.

It was an old proverb Celia's father had passed along, an ancient belief of balance: that good and bad luck were intertwined, with one inevitably, in some form, following the other. Considering her current situation, Celia yearned to believe a positive turn was coming—beginning with reaching Stephen.

More than ever, she needed to share what was happening—about the baby and brothel, of course, but now her father's injustice. She was desperate to hear that all would be fine, that there was no reason to give up, and most of all, that something significant could be done.

But how to contact him?

Despite its high chance of failure, a potential solution propelled her back to a place she dreaded with every inch of her being: the Bettencourts' home.

Approaching the servants' entrance, shaded from the autumn sun, she properly adjusted her hat. Sweat lined the inner brim from her lengthy walk. She'd kept a brisk pace, as she couldn't afford to dally. Being Sunday, her day was free of work, but the Bettencourts would soon be back from church.

Once at the door, she steeled herself. Any staff member might well answer with dismay over her return, even disgust over her "condition."

Chin raised, she knocked.

The person she'd planned to call upon opened the door, to Celia's relative relief.

"Good afternoon, Miss Waterstone."

Although the woman's expression gave away nothing, she flitted a glance at the midsection of Celia's coat, where the closure stretched a bit.

A cordial prelude seemed wise. "I'm very glad to see you, ma'am. Are you well?"

Miss Waterstone was quick to intone, "Did you leave a personal belonging?"

There would be no idle chatter.

Celia followed the cue, though in a cautious undertone. "No, ma'am. Rather, I've come to you for a favor."

The edges of the woman's eyes tightened with slight curiosity. More likely over the sheer audacity of the request.

"Quite...a large one, I'm afraid." Celia was aware she was stalling, as the favor would require an ethical violation. Though it involved a mere tidbit of information, for Miss Waterstone to divulge any of the family's private details could put her livelihood and professional reputation at risk.

Still, Celia had to try.

"Praying you somehow have enough mercy in your heart for me, I'm asking—pleading, actually—for your help in locating a postal address I direly need."

The woman blinked—twice. This wasn't what she'd been expecting.

"You see, it's essential I make contact as soon as possible."

Miss Waterstone cocked her head a little. "Whose address precisely are you seeking?" Her query lacked a knowing tone. For any chance at her assistance, Celia would have to answer.

"Stephen Bettencourt's."

After a second, Miss Waterstone shot another glance toward Celia's stomach, this time openly. Comprehension played out in her eyes, and the conclusion spurred a look of at least mild distaste. She knew none of the context, surely leaving her to think poorly of Stephen as well.

"Ma'am, if I may explain—"

Miss Waterstone raised a palm. "This is no business of mine."

"But if you'll only hear me out—"

"Good day." She went to shut the door, but Celia reflexively reached out, blocking it from closing. Miss Waterstone gasped lightly, taken aback.

Celia needed to finish before the woman called for reinforcement.

"I love him, Miss Waterstone, and he loves me. We plan to marry. I realize you might find the notion ludicrous, my being in such a position, but I swear it's God's honest truth." Throat thickening with emotion, she swallowed as Miss Waterstone's eyes softened a fraction, hinting to a notable resonance.

Celia had always presumed the head housekeeper, never married and rigidly devoted to her occupation, would be unable to relate to such feelings. But what if, on the contrary, her lifestyle and demeanor actually resulted from a loved one being out of reach?

Seizing upon the possibility, Celia forged on. "Ma'am, if ever in your life you've cared for anyone so much that your heart physically ached when you were apart, at times making it difficult to breathe, then I beg of you. Please. Please, help me." Her voice broke as she dared confess for the first time, including to herself: "I simply can't do this on my own."

Through tear-misted eyes, she awaited Miss Waterstone's reply. But there was none. After a moment of contemplation, the woman merely resumed her effort to shut the door.

Celia's chest went taut, halting her breaths, until the door stopped just short of closure. Beyond the gap, Miss Waterstone appeared to be confirming the absence of anyone within earshot, revealed when she turned back and replied in a clipped yet hushed voice.

"The mayor has decided it best for his son to devote the entirety of his efforts to his academics. He will, therefore, not return until completing his courses."

Celia scrambled to delineate the news. "Are you saying...he won't be back until summer?"

Miss Waterstone exhaled, impatient, if understandably so. "No, I am not."

The answer brought a dash of relief before she clarified.

"I am informing you that he will not be provided the means to travel home until having earned his medical degree."

"His...degree?"

"I'm sorry, but I can be of no further help." With that, Miss Waterstone closed the door fully.

Celia stood there, unable to move as the implications, sharp as talons, took hold. Vaguely, she felt hot tears stream down her face, released at the idea that she would have no contact with Stephen—for more than three years.

CHAPTER FIFTEEN

Focus on the tasks before you, and your time apart will pass all the faster.

The advice, supplied in her mother's ever-practical tone, was meant to be the singular salve whenever Celia, as a young girl, had grown sullen over her father's long stints away. *Missing him is to be expected, Celia. I indeed feel the same. But moping about will not return him a minute sooner.*

Now, several days since the shock about Stephen, Celia was relying again on her mother's words, as well as on hope that Miss Waterstone's news was merely mistaken, to help keep her anxiety to a simmer. Stephen would indubitably insist she stay healthy for the baby's well-being and for her own.

As it was, her father's death made giving in to devastation tempting enough.

Thus, it didn't help when, in her distracted state, she knocked over a bottle of Marie's favorite perfume while dusting the woman's vanity, causing a small portion to spill out.

"So clumsy!" Marie spat. "If old housekeeper not move away, I bring her back *now*." Then she waved Celia into the hall and shut the door.

On its own, the scolding wasn't what set Celia's mood to a

boil; it was the added revelation of her predecessor's true fate. Comprehending Lettie's deception over the matter—done apparently just to frighten Celia, toying with the nervous newcomer on her first day—she charged straight to the gal's room.

There, on her four-poster bed, Lettie sat in a robe, sketching on rough-edged paper by the waning light from her window. Her bedroom decor always made clear she was a lucrative attraction at the brothel, from her finely lacquered armoire and tufted lounge chair to the collection of patrons' gifts on her vanity—flowers, jewelry, a mother-of-pearl brush set. All the more reason for Celia's resentment.

"Why did you lie to me?"

Lettie's eyes raised in puzzlement. "Lie? What about?"

"The last housekeeper. You told me she'd died."

Lettie's expression smoothed into one of nonchalance. She flipped shut her leather folder, storing her drawings. "What I *said* was that we weren't fond of her, and so she kicked the bucket—which she did."

According to Marie's remark, that was altogether false. Celia went to state as much when Lettie added, "The day she left, the cantankerous cow deliberately knocked over a bucket of filthy suds all down the stairs. Marie threw a ruddy fit. 'Twas quite the event."

Celia strove to retain her frustration. But as a vision of the scene took shape, paired with the double meaning of Lettie's words—despite the misunderstanding surely being intentional—her smile couldn't help but slip out.

Lettie grinned in turn. The exchange no sooner ended, however, at the quick succession of two claps.

"Get ready!" Marie called out from the hallway. "All lady, work hard tonight!" *All* only applied to Marie if one counted friendly mingling.

Granted, as the girls' overseer, she did have other responsibilities—namely turning a regular profit, which the "big boss" collected through henchmen. The brothel was said to be too sullying for the man, though clearly not its funds.

Lettie stood and tucked her folder under the bed. Just then, Marie appeared at the door focused on Celia, surely to resume her reprimand.

"Tomorrow, midwife come for tea," Marie said. "Before leaving, she will check on you."

Grateful for the surprise offering, Celia replied, "Thank you. That would be kind of her."

When Marie treaded away, Lettie muttered something about the midwife. Her disdainful tone wasn't missed on Celia, raising her concerns as Lettie headed for the door.

"Lettie, wait."

She turned back.

"Do you know something about her?"

"Who?" Lettie said after a beat, not quite meeting Celia's eyes.

"The midwife." Celia strained to withhold her impatience, not in the mood to play games again.

Lettie shook her head and shrugged. "Nothing of importance. Now, if you'll excuse me, I need to ready myself for work." She strode out and toward the commode.

This time, it was immediately clear:

Lettie was lying.

CHAPTER SIXTEEN

One monotonous day after another, autumn crept into the gloom of winter. A small bright spot came from Mrs. Downey—to Celia's cautious relief. With each of the midwife's occasional check-ins, the pregnancy now five months along, Celia's wariness of the woman decreased. And thankfully so, given the many risks of childbirth. Her stoutness exuded capability and fortitude, while her soft-spoken assurances rang with sincerity.

Evidently, Celia had just misgauged Lettie's reaction to Marie's first mention of the midwife, or perhaps Celia and Lettie simply differed in their impressions of others. In any case, at least for now, Celia would trust her personal intuition.

The same applied to her latest strategy to reach Stephen.

Still lacking his specific address, she figured: What could it hurt to send him periodic letters in care of King's College? If even one found its way to him, the efforts would prove more than worthwhile.

As for distracting herself from waiting and worrying, she relied on literature, an old standby. Seated in bed on yet another Sunday evening, she now opened a book borrowed from a shelf in the parlor and propped it on her expanded middle. The half-melted candle on the nightstand cast ghostly shadows across the pages.

She'd read *The History of Tom Thumb* as a young girl. Three times, in fact, having found a particular connection to a character viewed and treated differently by others. Presently, with just two weeks until Christmas, she hoped to find comfort in the pages, to help fend off an onslaught of loneliness.

True, last year her father's work had left him unable to visit for the holidays. But that separation currently paled in comparison, knowing that he, like her mother, was gone forever. Stephen previously had been there to help fill the void; now Celia prayed nightly he would do the same again—in person. Soon she would learn if that prayer was to be answered, for on Christmas Eve, she would call on the Bettencourts with hopes that he'd managed to finagle a visit home, regardless of the distance and mayor's wishes. Even if not, what was the worst his parents could do? Order her away a second time?

"Celia…may I?"

She looked to the doorway, where Lettie stood in her cotton nightgown, plain and modest like Celia's; this was, after all, Lettie's weekly night off. Not waiting for permission, she entered the room, hair worn loose and arm draped with gray woolen dresses.

"Thought these might be of use to you," Lettie said, "what with your belly stretching inches by the day." She deposited the garments at the foot of the bed and smirked. "It'll only be a matter of time before your usual clothes split right down the middle."

Although Celia had continued to stay mostly to herself, the two had formed a habit of trading pleasantries in passing, so the generous offer, while unforeseen, wasn't a shock.

Celia reached out and touched the waistline of the top dress, noting its liberal width. Without warning, for more cause than the coming holidays, a surge of sadness broke through her defenses.

"Thank you," she said quickly and dropped her gaze to the book. Her hair swept forward over her cheeks, helping cloak the emotion surely surfacing.

"Ah, for heaven's sake." Lettie sighed. "You're growing a baby inside. Would you rather be shrinkin'?"

"No—of course not." Then Celia added brusquely, an invite to exit: "Thank you for coming by."

After a moment, she found relief in the creak of a floorboard, a sign of Lettie's departure, only to realize from a glance that she'd in fact stepped closer.

"What in the name of God is troubling you?" Lettie pressed.

Wishing to be left alone, Celia scrounged up half a smile. "I'm just tired. Otherwise, perfectly fine."

Lettie groaned and planted both fists on her hips. "Are you really going to make me drag it out of you? 'Cause mark my words, I can and I will."

Celia was tempted to blurt out that her personal business was her own, that they were housemates, not friends. But she refrained. Much like a stray cat accustomed to relying on itself for survival, she seemed to have hardened to tokens of kindness— which clearly this was.

"I appreciate the dresses, truly I do."

"But..."

"But I suppose...I hadn't figured on requiring such things. Not while still living here."

Lettie regarded the garments, and a glimmer of compassion entered her eyes. Then she gave Celia's shoulder a squeeze. "You'll be all right. One way or another."

Celia took this in. About to nod, she gasped from a sensation that rippled through her gut. She wrapped her arms over the area, and her mind spun. She'd grown increasingly careful during her cleaning duties while still fulfilling them. Had she somehow pushed herself too hard?

"It's the baby," she said, her voice tight.

"Easy now, girl. If need be, I'll run and fetch the midwife straightaway."

The baby wasn't due until April. Celia didn't have to be told what could happen if she went into labor this early, already aware of how commonly pregnancies ended in complications, even fatalities, for both mother and child.

"First off," Lettie said, "tell me what's it feelin' like."

Celia aimed to focus through her worry. "There's a strong tingling. In my stomach. No, wait—it's fading now."

"Tingling? Like…a fluttering, would you say?"

"Yes. *Precisely.*"

"A bit like bubbles, rising inside?"

"Yes. Yes, that's it. Why? Is that a bad sign? Should we call for a doctor?"

"We could if you like. But only if you want the man to tell you what I already know. That it's just the babe movin' about." Lettie laughed, though softly and not in a mocking way.

"Honest?"

"I'd swear to it."

"How can you know for sure?"

"Trust me. I *know.*"

There was such certainty in the reply that Celia released an exhale just as a thought appeared to settle over Lettie, dimming her demeanor.

Celia glanced at the dresses, each meant for a woman with

child. She recalled Lettie's muttering about the midwife that suggested familiarity and realized: "You're a mother."

Lettie opened her mouth, yet her voice seemed to catch in her throat. After a pause, she nodded pensively. "I was," she said. "But not like you think."

Celia's mind hadn't yet delved into the potential circumstances. Though indeed, given Lettie's occupation, there was a natural conclusion many would make.

"If you're willing to share," Celia offered, "I'm here to listen, about anything. Lettie, you can trust me too."

Lettie contemplated for a long moment. Then with reluctance, she lowered onto the side of the bed. Gazing off at an indistinct spot, she explained, bordering on a murmur. "It seemed a fine idea at the time, sailing over as a mail-order bride, what with the famine back home. It was three years ago when I stepped off the train in Portland. The groom was right there to greet me. Not as dashing as his photograph, but handsome enough." She lifted a shoulder before continuing.

"Told me there was no need for a ceremony, that we were already married. I figured it was done differently in America. How was I to bloody know?" Her voice hardened as she spoke through gritted teeth. "Turned out the dirty bastard had met another woman the week prior. Changed his mind about wedding me, he did. But apparently he still fancied what he saw, because he chose not to tell me. Not till after he'd had his way with..."

As her words trailed off, the implication gripped Celia with disgust at the unthinkable ruse.

Lettie briskly shook her head as if to expunge the memory and resumed in a fortified tone. "Being an Irish woman, finding work was challenge enough. By the time I discovered I had a wee one on the way, my options were even more miserable. Marie saw me on a street corner, begging for food. She offered me a bed and three square meals with an agreement that once the baby was born, I'd work off the debt. Marie held up her side of the bargain, and I honored mine."

Absorbing the unexpected—about Marie included—Celia thought aloud: "So that's why you're here."

Lettie faced her then, but with a defensive air. "Where else was I to go? How was I to eat? And now with reputation sullied…"

"I understand," Celia assured her. "Truly I do."

In various ways, they were both just doing what was needed to survive.

Celia reached over and touched her hand. Not only did Lettie allow it, but her posture eased.

How harshly Celia had judged her, along with the others. "And your baby?" she asked gently. "Was it…healthy?"

"Indeed. But far more than that, she was"—Lettie sought out the word, and a warm smile curved her lips—"perfect."

A girl. Lettie had a daughter.

The sex of Celia's child was a consideration she'd consciously avoided. She told herself Stephen would want them to ponder it together. But really, she feared that giving the baby a name before its birth displayed an arrogance guaranteed to tempt fate.

She dared to ask: "Where is your daughter now?"

The answer came quick and fervent. "A right fine home," Lettie said. "Mrs. Downey promised. Swore on the Holy Bible, she did, for I demanded it. And Marie vowed the same."

The idea of a mother giving up her newborn sent an ache through Celia. But as Lettie had said, what were her options?

Celia tendered a smile of support. "That was good of them both."

"Oh, don't be fooled. They won't say as much, but you can't

tell me they didn't receive a sum for their troubles. Even more reason, though, to have kept their word. A wedded couple with a fine home is far more likely to pay—and to pay well."

The view was starkly logical, cushion for a heartrending act. It also made Celia wonder: Was her own pregnancy, the potential profit from it, a factor in Marie's willingness to employ her? And for the midwife's early attention?

She wadded up the pointless thoughts, as her baby would remain her own. "Well, I'm sure you made the right decision."

Lettie took a breath, then smiled wistfully. After a few seconds, she straightened in her seat and patted Celia's hand. "Morning will be here in a blink. We best get some sleep." She rose to her feet, and Celia found herself not wanting Lettie to go.

"Wait—please." When Lettie turned, Celia scraped for a response. "Do you have any special plans? Tomorrow, I mean."

"Special plans?" Lettie echoed and added in a hoity-toity fashion, "Well, now, I'd have to check my schedule. Why do you ask?"

Celia remembered then: Marie had prepared and packed dumplings earlier today, as she did periodically, always delivering them the next morning to friends, with whom she'd spend several hours. This meant Celia would be able to sneak out for a bit and without shirking her duties, so long as she started them earlier. "How about a stroll in the park once you're up?"

"Hmm..." Lettie folded her arms and tapped her chin in debate, perhaps still teasing. "I've got a better idea. 'Tis the holidays, a grand time to visit the boutiques in town. How would you fancy that?"

Boutiques? Apparently, Lettie had earned her way out of Marie's debt to suggest such a venture. As Celia's present finances were not as comfortable, she replied candidly, "I'm afraid I can't afford to purchase any dresses. Even so, what you've given me here is plenty."

"Who said anything about purchasing? I said only that we'd be visitin'."

"I'm...confused."

"Ah, sweet girlie." Lettie grinned. "You won't be for long."

CHAPTER SEVENTEEN

A light breeze skimmed the pleasant December morning, though Celia found it difficult to savor. The cloak and day dress Lettie had persuaded her to wear—lavish as it was, with an abundance of burgundy silk, lace trim, and dainty buttons—lent her the feel of an impostor. The addition of a blond wig replete with updo and ringlets only exacerbated the issue.

Lettie, in her similar outfit of a cloak and sunflower yellow dress, carried herself with a remarkably natural countenance. It helped, perhaps, that her hat bore a veil that half shielded her face and of course that she'd worn the garments many a time before. Same for the burgundy getup. An older patron regularly paid her to wear his late wife's clothing along with the wig to resemble the woman's locks, then to curl up with him in bed. Nothing more. Then there were other men who simply wanted to talk, some confiding in Lettie as if in a priest or in a sweetheart they wished they had. A few even feigned proper courting, without fear of rejection.

In sum, not all the brothel's customers sought the sort of companionship Celia had presumed.

Setting the thoughts aside, she accompanied Lettie from one downtown boutique to the next, where they inquired over the latest styles and fabrics. Lettie skillfully hid her brogue; she was accustomed to playing a role—as was Celia, really. At any rate, Celia's confidence rose with every stop, and by the time they entered a new hat shop, she took pride in leading the charge. Ironically, the more uppity her manner, the better the treatment.

"I shall have to ponder this," she said to the bespectacled salesclerk, who displayed in his hands an emerald-colored brimmed hat for her consideration. "My cousin in San Francisco has one nearly identical. I wouldn't want to be *unoriginal*." She said the word as if it soured her tongue.

"Madam, if I may be so bold, I insist you could never be that."

"So I have heard." She conjured a smug look.

"Perhaps you might try it on and admire it in the mirror."

"Mmm. Possibly." As she couldn't risk detection of her wig, she diverted by patting one of her ringlets. "Though I would hate to disturb my hairstyling for naught." She angled toward the back of Lettie, who stood at the counter that featured a feathery pinned adornment. "What say you, Miss Johnston?"

Lettie didn't answer, missing her cue to hem and haw before she was to recommend they move along to the next shop.

"Miss Johnston?"

Still no response, which wasn't entirely peculiar, since the surname was false. To prevent suspicion from the clerk, Celia strode over primly and touched her friend's shoulder.

Lettie startled as if yanked from a trance. "Yes—sorry?"

"I was curious if I should bother trying on the hat over there."

Lettie glanced toward the clerk and adhered a smile that appeared to take effort, her face gone slightly pale. "Why, certainly."

At the incorrect reply, Celia lowered her volume. "Are you all right?"

Lettie supplied a nod just as a youthful giggle broke out.

Nearby, a girl of roughly four was modeling a bonnet for a woman clearly her mother, their similar faces equally aglow. It was a charming interaction that Lettie had been watching. One that, sadly, she and her daughter would never have.

Celia wondered how much to say, but the clerk was waiting. She projected amply enough for him to overhear. "You know, dearest, all this holiday shopping is quite taxing. I daresay a breath of fresh air is in order." She turned to the man. "Sir, I am afraid we shall have to return another day."

He hid his disappointment rather well. "Absolutely, madam. I look forward to welcoming both of you again very soon."

She twisted back toward Lettie, only to find her friend halfway to the door. Celia followed her outside, where Lettie paused to inhale the late-morning air. Her pallor was returning when a dog's happy bark drew Celia's gaze across the street. In a pink coat, the girl kneeling to pet the mutt wore a ribbon atop blond hair that Celia knew at a glance.

Abigail...

Celia's lungs pulled a sharp breath. For a moment, she just stared; then her senses grabbed hold, shaking her into action. The child was alone. Approachable. Now was Celia's chance.

She hustled to cross the street, barely dodging a stagecoach in passing. Lettie's voice called to her from behind, but Celia couldn't stop. Abigail could vanish in an instant.

Upon halting before the girl, Celia was about to speak when Abigail looked up with a smile that fell only partially. Her brow crinkled, not with dismay but curiosity. She took Celia for a stranger—and no wonder, what with the clothing, the hair.

"Abigail, it's me."

Recognition rolled over her face. The brightening of her eyes sent through Celia a surprising rush of warmth. Yet as Abigail

rose to her feet, her levity slipped away, no doubt from the recollection of Celia's ousting.

Celia skipped to an essential. "Is your brother coming home?
In time for Christmas?"

Abigail hesitated. Then she shook her head no, and Celia's
chest tightened.

But no matter. If Stephen knew of the reason for urgency,
surely he would find the resources for a prompt return.

"Could you write to him, then, on my behalf?"

Abigail remained reluctant before answering. "I'm sorry,
but...I can't."

Can't or won't? Celia squelched the retort and opted for a plea.
"A mere sentence or two. That's all I'm asking."

The crinkle on the girl's brow reappeared, now from an internal struggle. "Mama says I'm not to utter a word about you ever
again, especially to Stephen."

Celia leaned down, leveling their gazes. "Abigail, I understand
what you've been told. Regardless, this is far too important. You
simply must."

Abigail was weighing the assertion when a woman's voice cut in.

"The only thing the girl *must* do is obey me." Mrs. Bettencourt
approached from the side. Clad in a coat and scarf and holding a
wrapped parcel under her arm, she skewered Celia with her eyes.
"Parading about under a guise, I see. How very typical."

The jab was cheap but stung nonetheless. Celia was tempted
to explain the harmless fun of her attire, but why?

Mrs. Bettencourt waved her daughter toward her. "Abigail, let
us be off. *Now.*" Then, to Celia: "You'll keep clear of my family
or be put out on the street."

As they angled to depart, it was a gamble, to be sure, but Celia
reached for the woman's elbow. "Wait."

Mrs. Bettencourt retracted, dramatically, as if the mere touch might infect her with an illness.

Celia allowed space between them but pressed on. "Ma'am, I implore you to listen. For the baby's sake, if nothing else."

At the reference, Mrs. Bettencourt's attention dipped to Celia's middle. Despite the cloak and bunched fabric of her dress preventing confirmation of a widened belly, the woman's demeanor marginally eased. Maybe she was recalling when she herself was with child. Just as well she could be envisioning the baby to come—a boy, perhaps, who would inherit his father's looks, his manner, the legacy of a name: Stephen Nicholas Bettencourt Jr.

Whichever the cause, she was contemplating, seeming to waver.

Anticipation tensed Celia's every limb.

"Ah! Georgia!"

The high-pitched voice stole Mrs. Bettencourt's focus. With practiced precision, she applied a smile for the socialite emerging from a shop. "Juliana Nicole, how lovely to see you."

"Isn't it though?" The lady chortled at her own wit. As the wife of an oil tycoon, Juliana Nicole Stone wore a smart tailored coat and matching gloves. Same for her daughter, approximately Abigail's age, who trailed with a bored glower. "Shall we find a spot to take hot cider, or are you still occupied with shopping?" She gestured toward Mrs. Bettencourt's package. "I wouldn't want to sidetrack you."

Celia looked intently at Mrs. Bettencourt, praying she would decline.

"Cider," she replied, "would be splendid."

Celia's heart dropped, heavier than a concrete block. While Mrs. Bettencourt ushered Abigail to join them, Mrs. Stone abruptly noticed Celia's presence.

"Dear me." She put a hand to the base of her neck and looked at Mrs. Bettencourt. "Did I interrupt you, Georgia?"

Mrs. Bettencourt afforded Celia but a glance and leaned toward her friend's ear. "You arrived just in the nick of time. She is no one of consequence." The ice in her tone, even more than the choice of words, sent a chill through Celia.

While the ladies scuttled off with their daughters, Celia's sense of humiliation hardened to anger. She could halt them all in a single swipe of truth by calling out to Mrs. Stone and sharing the family's predicament. Whether or not believed, the gossip in their circles would subject Georgia Bettencourt to a similar lash of embarrassment.

Celia was about to speak out when a glimpse of Lettie, observing nearby, gave her pause. The lingering emotion in her eyes served as evidence: that the greatest sacrifices for loved ones were often made in silence.

Celia turned back to the departing group. Despite a driving urge—perhaps even out of hope for amends one day—she couldn't justify the untold damage her public declaration could cause.

Not to the family.

Above all, not to Stephen.

CHAPTER EIGHTEEN

The joy of their excursion gone entirely, Celia returned to the inn with Lettie, who barely needed to probe to decipher the situation. And yet from the fresh dose of reality, Celia cared only about a barrage of daunting notions.

Would Stephen know nothing of his child before the delivery, and just how long after would that be? Was a brothel to be the baby's first home?

The prospects stalked Celia as the days trudged on, whispering during her daily chores and growing in volume through her idle hours, like now.

What else could she do but use distractions to stave off panic?

With supper finished and patrons soon to amass, she fetched from the parlor a book to reread out of the house's limited supply. *Alice's Adventures in Wonderland.* A fitting story of tumbling down a vexing path and yearning for escape.

She was crossing the foyer when the front door swung open and a man stepped inside. When he removed his cap, the sight of his features stopped her cold.

"Mr. Vale..."

Timothy's eyes widened a smidge before he issued a nod.

"Good evenin'." He tightened his lips and fidgeted with his hat, suggesting shame over the reason for his visit.

Apparently, he hadn't been informed where she'd been exiled after all.

"Miss Hart," he said, "I've come here to... See, the thing is, I came because—"

"It's all right," she interjected to save him further embarrassment. A true irony in that. "You don't have to explain."

"But I'd like to." He met her eyes then, causing Celia's to lower.

"Honestly, Mr. Vale, your dealings here are none of my concern." Eager for the solitude of her room, book held at her side, she resumed her path toward the stairs.

"They could be though."

At the base of the staircase, she twisted back, befuddled.

A grizzled customer passed between them, and Timothy edged closer. "Is there somewhere more private we could go?"

Celia stared at him. "I beg your pardon?"

"Oh, no. I didn't mean—" He gripped his cap tighter, his neck reddening. "Just to converse. If you're willing."

From the sincerity in his tone—and, admittedly, Celia's curiosity—she found herself giving in with a nod. Aware the parlor was occupied, she guided him to the kitchen and discovered the space vacant.

She gestured toward the table. "Would you care to sit?"

"Standing'll be just fine."

The notion that he wouldn't be staying long delivered a dose of relief.

"Look here, Miss Hart. What I was tryin' to say is I didn't come for the inn's usual companionship."

Again, she couldn't help but drop her gaze. The degradation of her surroundings was inescapable.

"The point is I know you're in quite a pickle."

An understatement if ever there was one. She clutched the book to her middle, as if that alone could deflect from the evidence of her indiscretion.

"And, well, I'd like to help out." He let the statement dangle, luring her focus back to his face. "I've given it a whole lotta thought, and it just seems right."

Could he have learned of her conversation with Abigail? Or months ago, perhaps he'd overheard Celia's appeal to Miss Waterstone. A postal address was still all she needed.

Her hopes swelled, even as she tried her darndest to constrain them. "Oh? How so?"

"My brother lives in Colorado," he said. "He doesn't know of your situation, so we could tell him anything at all, and he'd believe it."

A burst of distant giggles further hindered Celia's grasp of Timothy's offer. "Your brother is going to help me?"

"Us, really."

"I'm afraid I don't understand."

Timothy advanced to just a few feet away, unsettling her slightly. "He's found me work up there on a ranch. Long days, but the pay is decent, and room and board would be included for us both—for all of us, rather." His now-obvious intent material- ized as he took one of her hands. "Celia, be my wife."

Her pulse raced, an instant gallop.

"I promise I'll take good care of ya—the baby too," he said. "And, of course, we could have some little ones of our own." His eyes glimmered as if envisioning the prospect, and his lips slanted warmly.

She'd long known he cared for her, though not to what extent. In this moment, his display of affection, highlighted by his willingness to act as the father to her child—remarkably, that by another man—stalled her instinct to decline.

He was proposing more than marriage; he was proposing a new life. A fresh start.

She peered down at his fingers clasping hers. Upon her other hand, which still gripped the book, the string looked aged and thinned from wear. It was, in fact, only a string...

Marrying Timothy would solve everything. Her reputation would be salvaged as a wife and mother while sparing her baby shame. They could enjoy the contentment of a respectable life. And who was to say her fondness for Timothy couldn't grow with time?

She was striving to imagine them together on the ranch when flashes returned of a barn. From them came Stephen's candlelit face and the memory of a promise, ceasing thoughts of all other possibilities. Despite her reality of floating untethered, she couldn't go back on her word. She couldn't betray Stephen nor her heart.

Holding on to the faintest shred of hope, she provided her answer. "It's all so generous of you, Mr. Vale. Unfortunately, I just can't accept."

He stared for a bit before withdrawing his hand. All kindness left his expression.

"I'm sorry," she added, wishing he understood, wanting to say more. But he pulled on his cap with a tug as sharp as his gaze, his humiliation palpable.

"You're a fool, Celia. And you'll live to regret this."

She didn't respond. She simply watched him leave, fearing deep inside he would well be proved right.

CHAPTER NINETEEN

"I need more towels." Mrs. Downey spoke the words evenly, yet a note of urgency tinged her tone. Across the dark ceiling, the lamplight swayed as the portly midwife, wearing an apron and cap, remained stationed at the foot of Celia's bed.

"Is something wrong?" Celia asked through her exhaustion. Lying with knees bent and nightgown drenched in sweat, she was resting from the latest labor pains that had torn through her core.

"I'll go and get 'em," Lettie volunteered. She went to release Celia's hand, but Celia refused to let go.

"*Please*, don't leave."

"You're grand," Lettie said. "All is running like clockwork."

It was April. The baby was coming as scheduled, though the hours since Celia was first instructed to push were stretching into eternity.

Lettie smiled softly. "Be back in a jiffy."

Celia yielded, less from the assurance than fatigue. As Lettie hustled away, Celia looked to Marie for comfort. But Marie remained unreadable in a corner of the room, where she stood while periodically checking in. And so Celia clenched her hands, pressing her nails into her palms to detract from their emptiness.

If she allowed herself to dwell on whose grip was missing or on Stephen's absence altogether, she'd break down into a blubbering heap, wasting what little strength she had left.

Again, she asked Mrs. Downey, "Is everything all right?"

"Yes, dear, it is." Her reply was tight as she dropped a used towel into a bucket. Piled upon others, the cloth peeked from the top. Soaked with blood. A startling sight. Then she murmured something too quiet to hear.

Celia was about to request that Mrs. Downey repeat herself when a snippet reached Celia's ears, and with a rush of panic, it dawned on her...

The midwife was praying.

CHAPTER TWENTY

Night had given way to morning—as best as Celia could figure. Without a window for reference, she'd lost all sense of time. Her world had narrowed to seemingly endless rounds of labor pains. Moisture brimmed her eyes from exertion and desperation, but still she dammed her tears from falling.

"One more now," Mrs. Downey commanded. "Just one more push."

At her side, Lettie chimed in, "Keep it up now. You're gettin' there."

Celia longed to stop, even fearing herself incapable of pressing on, but somehow she bore down, and at last came a watery release, and from it, her baby.

She collapsed back onto her pillow before noting a sudden, discomfiting quiet.

Tension pervaded the room as Marie joined Mrs. Downey and Lettie in a huddle around the child, blocking Celia's view.

Chinese, Celia realized with dread. Her newborn's features were surely Chinese, causing confusion for all.

Then came a smack, the sound of skin being slapped, followed by a wail. The three women breathed a collective sigh. The delay of the baby's crying had been their sole concern, made clear when Mrs. Downey bundled the child in a blanket and revealed the girl's hair, a golden shade of honey, her other features no less fair.

A daughter.

"Please—let me hold her." Celia edged herself upright and extended her arms.

Marie ordered Lettie out of the room as Mrs. Downey slowly brought over the baby, now soothed and calm. Once near Celia's outstretched hands, the midwife appeared to hesitate.

A shiver of worry ran down Celia's spine.

But then Mrs. Downey surrendered the infant, and Celia cradled the baby to her chest. A tide of emotion, an overwhelming sensation she could identify only as love, enveloped her.

Celia stared in awe at the child's wide and shimmery eyes—blue gray like her father's—her dainty nose, her rounded chin. How could anything be so…perfect?

Mrs. Downey's voice floated into Celia's consciousness. "A true blessing," she said with an admiring tone, "despite a most unfortunate situation."

It took Celia a moment to recall her predicament.

"Yes," she answered simply.

"After all, this is scarcely the sort of place to raise a child."

As if on cue, a thumping sounded from the floor above—a headboard striking a wall.

Celia held her daughter closer, as though this alone could protect the purity of her tiny, shelled ears.

"Thankfully," Mrs. Downey added, "you do have options."

Once again with the options.

As winter had rolled into spring, the midwife sprinkled hints of a decision Celia would need to make, mentioning several well-to-do couples in want of a child. Always, Celia had replied while moderating any feelings of offense: *They all have my sympathies, ma'am, yet my baby's father will soon be returning.* Mrs. Downey's skeptical looks hadn't gone unnoticed, nor had the growing doubt in Celia's own pronouncement.

Now the child was here, but Stephen was not.

"Celia, you must consider this." Mrs. Downey suddenly took a more direct approach. "It would be an entirely selfless act. You could give your daughter a respectable life in a loving, God-fearing home." She gave the baby's crown a gentle stroke. "I know just the couple who would treat this beautiful girl as their own, fulfilling her every need. And when of age, with a generous dowry, she'd be practically guaranteed to become the wife of a splendid, upstanding man."

The proposition was so civilized. Pragmatic. And yet to Celia, the very suggestion of giving away her child…

Well, it was ludicrous.

Wasn't it?

Marie touched her shoulder. "You love baby?"

Celia's gaze swung to Marie's. "Of course I do." So much so, she could never fully describe it. The extent of the feeling was irrational, really, for a creature she'd only just met.

Marie gave a nod. "Then do what best for her."

Celia recalled Lettie's remarks, about the financial gain for Marie and Mrs. Downey from such arrangements. Still, that didn't lessen the truth in their words.

Celia looked back at her daughter, innocent and helpless, relying on her mother to decide correctly. Finally, Celia's well of tears broke through. They spilled down her face and onto the baby's blanket.

She squeezed her eyes closed, and when she reopened them and gazed upon her child's face, right or wrong, whether or not destined for regret, she made her choice.

1888

—

JULY

CHAPTER
TWENTY-ONE

Braced against the cell wall, with deep breaths, Celia gradually reduced her shaking, though not the burning of her throat. So parched had she become, it hurt to swallow.

By light from under the door, an object glinted in the cell. A tin cup. It sat on the served plate, which held something square. She inched herself over and grabbed hold of the drink. Liquid sloshed over her fingers as she raised the cup to her lips. She managed to resist just enough to test a sip.

Indeed, it was water, if lukewarm and tasting of dirt. She chugged it down all the same. Drips ran from the corners of her mouth and dampened her bearded chin.

She traded the empty cup for the square, a piece of hardtack. It was terribly dry and bland, yet her stomach growled from hunger. Only then did she register the hollow depth in her gut. She gobbled up the flavorless food, wishing she'd saved some water to guide it down.

When was her last meal? How long had she been here? Had it been days?

Had anyone noticed she was missing?

The last thought summoned an image, an indistinct face from

her memory. On the brink of definition, the lines and shapes blended and blurred. A wave of drowsiness was washing them away.

She glanced back at the cup. Her water...must have been drugged.

Her eyelids turned impossibly heavy.

As she battled to stay awake, on the shores of her mind, a sketch of the face floated back. Its features, still hazy, were just clear enough to discern. Recognition triggered a panic that flooded Celia's veins, but for only a moment. The clutches of sleep returned with a vengeance, dragging her under, even as she reached futilely for the receding image of the child she'd left behind.

1886

—

JULY

CHAPTER
TWENTY-TWO

Only a week remained. One week before Celia would be out on the street unless she found a solution. There would be no extension, and asking again could jeopardize what little time she had left.

As it was, though grudgingly, Marie had allowed her to maintain their work arrangement—*a very kind thing*, Marie repeatedly stressed—but for the length of just three months and with strict conditions: Celia's housekeeping efforts could not suffer, nor could the brothel's profits. The latter required her ensuring ample quiet through the girls' late-morning sleeping hours as well as in the evenings to not irritate patrons.

In short, the baby—named Pearl, after Celia's mother—needed to be virtually silent and invisible, an agreement made the night of her birth.

Despite being pressured for many a valid reason, Celia had refused to give up her child. She'd thought of Lettie's melancholy over the relinquishment of her own daughter, and she couldn't imagine ever forgiving herself, let alone facing Stephen, if she did the same. Not when there was still hope of uniting as a family. Obviously, Marie was as dismayed as Mrs. Downey, but not enough to immediately send Celia and her baby packing.

Of course, nothing had prepared Celia for the extreme challenge of keeping a newborn soothed nearly round the clock.

With most nights spent nursing and swaying and bouncing Pearl at even her smallest fuss, Celia would work through the day with the child bound to her in a sling. At least the night-mares involving Celia's father lessened, one benefit of being too exhausted to dream. If only the unsavory elements of evenings at the inn could also fade. The noises to which she'd become so accustomed that she had barely noticed them anymore, suddenly, in the company of her child, blared in her ears, amplifying fears of being an unfit mother. Especially next to Lettie, who, as the oldest of her five siblings in Ireland, shined maternally—current occupation aside.

Prior to her nightly work hours and in other free times, Lettie would sneak in visits with Pearl, allowing Celia breaks to eat, regroup, and nap in order to wakefully last the nights.

How was Celia going to fare in a new residence without such help? Presuming she could even find and afford a new home. Her funds were increasingly limited...

And yet here she was, preparing to spend even more on a gamble.

Sweltering from the July heat, she bounced a fussing Pearl while waiting in line at the post office, ten minutes till closing. Perspiration dampened Celia's dress as she shifted between feet, anxious to send another letter to King's College with hopes that this would be the one, at last, to reach Stephen.

Pearl burst into full cries over Celia's shoulder, as if sensing the growing direness of their situation.

"*Sh-sh.*" Celia rocked her and patted her back with stronger effort. "It's all right. Everything's all right."

A fib. Everything was far from that.

The gentleman ahead of them in the queue, ordering a wired

message from the postmistress, snapped to look their way. Celia avoided his glare of annoyance by diverting her attention to the window.

Beyond the glass stood a few of the many local hotels and saloons that had considered her request of a room-and-board exchange. In each case, the disclosure of her baby had earned her firm declines. Without a recommendation from the Bettencourts, resuming her work as a private housekeeper was also out of the question.

A bead of sweat slipped from her temple as Pearl's cries escalated.

"Hush now," Celia urged—pleaded, really. "I promise we'll be home soon."

Behind them, a toddler in finely threaded clothes sucked his thumb in enviable silence. He held the hand of a middle-aged woman—a nanny, based on her uniform—who stared intently at Celia, no doubt observing her ineptitude.

Since residing at the inn, Celia had further toughened to strangers' sneers and presumptive looks. But in this moment, sleep deprived and with fraying patience, she couldn't stop tears from springing to her eyes.

She angled forward to mask them. Then something brushed her shoulder, and reflexes turned her around. The nanny's hand lingered in the air. She'd had the audacity to tug away the collar of Pearl's threadbare cotton dress, acquired from Mrs. Downey, and was scanning the child's face.

"I beg your pardon?" Celia said as Pearl continued to bawl.

In truth, it wasn't the first time Celia had wondered if her daughter's features appeared unique. Not overtly, but with a subtle "other" quality that couldn't be pinpointed. Admittedly, her nose did resemble that of Celia's father. But weren't all babies' noses rounded at this age? And yes, there was a slightly darker tint to her skin, though from jaundice—a minor and common enough case that would fade, according to Mrs. Downey.

Without answering, incredibly the nanny reached out and touched Pearl's cheek—worse yet, with her wrist, as if not to sully her fingers.

Taken aback, Celia pulled her daughter to her chest.

"The child is quite ill." Authority lined the woman's tone.

Pearl's cries had turned hoarse, and her nose was runny. But this was often the case when she became upset.

"When last did she eat?" the nanny pressed.

Placed on the spot and with each day blending into the next, Celia couldn't say precisely. Indeed, Pearl had been struggling at the breast. As her mother, though, Celia would have sensed something greatly off. Wouldn't she?

What did a stranger know anyway?

"It's just a touch of a summer cold, I am sure."

"I daresay it's more than that." The response was sharp, resembling a challenge. "Feel her."

Celia resisted at first. She complied only to prove the woman wrong. "Naturally, she's warm. She's been crying, and given the weather—"

That was as far as Celia got before fully registering the heat emanating from Pearl. Skin blotchy and scarlet-hued, she wasn't just hot, she was burning up.

"Get her home. Cool her down, quick as can be."

The woman deserved to be thanked, even acknowledged for being right. More crucially, Celia should have asked for advice on how to best reduce the fever. But all this occurred to her later. In that instant, with Pearl snug in her arms, instincts launched her out the door, vaguely cautioning her not to trip and fall as she verged on sprinting to the inn, praying she wasn't too late.

CHAPTER
TWENTY-THREE

The path of several city blocks stretched into miles. Pearl continued to wail as Celia murmured assurances that she herself yearned to believe.

Finally back at the Dewdrop, she flew up the stairs to reach the first person who came to mind.

"Lettie!" She pounded on her friend's door an instant before barging in, interrupting a half-dressed man about to untie Lettie's corset, laces in hand.

"Hey!" he exclaimed. "Whaddya think you're—"

Celia ignored him. "Pearl is sick."

Her tone must have held sufficient gravity, because Lettie merely glanced at Pearl before shooing her customer out, pausing only to shove his clothes and boots into his arms.

"I need to cool her," Celia told Lettie, "fast." It was the nanny's one instruction, common sense as it was.

"A cold sponge bath ought to help. Strip her down. I'll dash to the icehouse cross the road." Lettie had barely thrown on a robe when she tore out of the room, the layers of her skirt rustling. The footfalls of her shoes traveled rapidly down the hall and stairs.

With trembling hands, Celia laid Pearl on the bed and

removed her little sweat-dampened dress. The redness of her face matched that of her entire naked body.

"You'll be fine, sweetheart." Celia strove for a calm voice. "Mama's here."

Pearl's cries persisted nevertheless. The sight of tears escaping her tightly closed eyes renewed the welling of Celia's.

Had there been earlier signs of the child's worsening health? Ones that Stephen would have caught? From the medical textbooks he used to pore over and now from a year of formal courses, surely even from experience with the ailing animals he'd cured, he would know what to do.

But he wouldn't be coming. Not in time.

Lord in heaven, would he lose his child before even knowing she'd existed?

Celia stomped out the thoughts—useless, the lot of them. Solutions were all that mattered.

She gave the room a quick scan. On the bureau sat a pitcher and washbasin. She raced over and poured water into the bowl. Anxious, waiting for the ice, she dipped and lightly wrung out a rag before hurrying back and applying it to Pearl's skin, yet the water was as warm as the air strangling the room.

They needed a fan, paper or silk—anything would do. Not seeing one, Celia recalled Lettie's drawing folder and retrieved it from under the bed. Back and forth, she waved the leather folder to forge a breeze over Pearl. The shock of air interrupted her wails, a welcome pause that lasted only a moment. Celia continued fanning regardless and lowered herself to sit on the mattress. Willing Lettie to return, she threw a hundred glances toward the open window. Every second passed as if slogging through mud. What was taking so long?

A figure arrived at the door, delivering a pinch of relief until Celia realized it wasn't Lettie.

"Why baby not quiet?" Marie demanded. "Where Lettie now? Why she make customer go?"

The truth would neglect to appease the woman, but Celia was beyond caring. Not about anything save her daughter's survival.

"I need ice for Pearl's fever. Lettie went to fetch some."

Marie took this in. She treaded to the bed and touched Pearl's temple. Then she gave the baby a once-over, her expression neutral.

Celia braced for a dismissal of any concerns. She verged on responding without a shred of restraint, but the bed started to shake. Pearl's arms and legs were stiffened and twitching. Her eyes were open yet rolled back in her skull.

A deluge of fear and confusion burst through Celia.

She scooped up her daughter, whose temperature now rivaled that of an iron fresh off the stove. "Pearl," Celia said, voice cracking. "Pearl, stay with me."

A quick succession of footsteps preceded Lettie's charge into the room. Her red curls disheveled from running, she held a package wrapped haphazardly in brown paper. "I've got it!"

Pearl went limp. Her eyelids fell closed.

Celia shook her gently but failed to rouse her. "*No, no, no.* Not you too." She couldn't die. She simply couldn't.

Celia's tears broke free just as Marie rested a hand on Pearl's chest. The act seemed one of mourning, turning Celia's panic to terror.

"She alive," Marie said, though tightly. "Still breathing." Then she regarded Lettie, who'd stalled by the door. "Put ice in bowl."

Lettie nodded, and within seconds, all three women were kneeling on the floor around the prepared basin and Pearl, having been moved to the cushion of a shawl. Celia used the cooling water to remoisten the rag and ran it over the length of Pearl's body.

The child didn't so much as shudder.

Celia repeated the routine several times, prayers looping in her head. The clinking of ice against the bowl's edge and the noises of city life from the window were the sole sounds in the room. Those and the mumbled conversations downstairs from the inn's ladies greeting customers.

Pearl remained stubbornly red—or was that now from the chilled water? Although she'd cooled a little, her fever refused to yield, which Marie also clearly found, based on her silence upon regauging Pearl by feel.

Lettie piped in, "I'll go and fetch Mrs. Downey."

Marie held Lettie's elbow, stopping her from rising. "No. She cannot help."

Celia thought to ask why and how to know for sure, but Marie's tone was so decisive, and the inquiries would waste time that Pearl couldn't afford to spare. "A doctor then," Celia urged. "We should get a doctor."

Marie shook her head. "Doctor take money, though also cannot help."

"But—he has to!"

"How? No tonic for fever. Not for babies. He tell you to wait for morning, see if baby will live."

Celia wanted to rail against the defeatist notion. And yet her recollection of similar accounts indicated Marie wasn't wrong. From gossip in the Bettencourts' home, whispered tales of even wealthy families losing their children to a score of illnesses, often with unbreakable fevers, affirmed there was little to be done.

Marie rose without another word and strode from the room, evidently leaving Pearl to God's will or the Fates or perhaps just the cruelty of happenstance.

Lettie's eyes sullenly misted.

Celia clutched the dripping rag, desperate and fearful, and recalled the blood-soaked cloths from her labor. Her hope and strength had waned that day, yet she hadn't given up. And she wouldn't now.

"We have to keep trying!" She plunged the rag into the basin, sending cold water sloshing, and resumed her efforts with fervor. Achieving no better result, however, she fought to suppress her panic. She wanted to scream.

Just then, Marie returned and closed the door behind her. She again knelt at Celia's side but now with a lidded palm-size bowl, ceramic and Oriental in nature. "You trust me?"

The question was so unexpected, so broad, Celia faltered in answering. Was Marie suggesting opium as a cure? Was it wrong to rule out anything at this point?

"We try. Yes?" Marie lifted the lid to reveal not drugs but, just as startling, a pile of needles. Unlike the sewing type, each was particularly short and slender.

Celia had heard vaguely of a Chinese practice involving such instruments, a means to treat various ailments, even phobias. But it had all seemed as contrived and nonsensical as the countless superstitions brought from the Far East. Like being cursed with bad luck when struck by a broom, especially in the head. Or from dropping chopsticks or sporting mustaches or using the number four, since the sound of it in Chinese resembled death.

Marie picked up a needle. "Turn baby over."

"Celia, no." Lettie's furrowed brow matched the warning in her face.

Marie huffed, impatient. "It not hurt."

In all candor, Celia trusted neither Marie nor what she was proposing. But having lost both her mother and father, unable to prevent either of their deaths, unable to so much as try, for even the slightest chance of now saving her daughter, she couldn't second-guess the singular alternative before them.

Onto her drenched lap, she laid Pearl tummy-side down. Lettie watched slack-jawed while Marie ran a hand over Pearl's back as if mapping out a strategy. Or was she unsure what to do? Presumably, she had done this before.

Celia was about to confirm as much, but Marie poked the tip of a needle into the back of Pearl's shoulder, breaking through the skin.

Celia gasped, though it didn't stop Marie from retrieving another needle.

"That's enough," Celia told her.

Marie *tsked*. "Need many more to end fever."

The idea of adding even a second one, let alone a slew of them, was wholly unnerving. Celia hastened to decide. Only from the fact that Pearl didn't react was she able to nod, a signal to continue.

Methodically, Marie laid a trail of needles across Pearl's shoulders and down either side of her spine. When the supply ended, she set down her ceramic bowl.

No one spoke. They only stared at the protruding needles, a frightening design that seemed straight from a book of witchcraft. With nothing to do but wait once more, Celia hoped to high heaven that she hadn't wagered wrong.

CHAPTER
TWENTY-FOUR

Moonlight through a dusty window slanted hauntingly across
the room.

Groggy, Celia pressed herself to sit upright on the hardwood
floor—Lettie's—having fallen asleep. Small puddles shimmered
beside the half-filled washbasin draped with a rag. She touched
the crumpled shawl beside her, the indent from Pearl's body still
damp. She scanned her surroundings.

No sign of her daughter. No sign of...anyone.

Pearl's fever had broken. Celia recalled this with relief. Marie
had removed the needles but warned that the baby's temperature
could spike again. By the time Marie had left to check on the
inn's patrons, having sent Lettie off to fulfill her nightly duties
in another room, Pearl looked peaceful enough to ease Celia's
tension—to the point of her dozing off.

But where was Pearl now?

Between rounds of customers, Lettie must have retrieved her to
allow Celia a bit of rest. Warily, she came to her feet and entered
the hall, where she recognized a petite blond from behind. At her
elbow was a man she was guiding toward the stairs.

"Harriet, where's Lettie?"

Harriet glanced back over her shoulder, then nodded toward a door halfway down the corridor. "Cynthia's old room, I think."

Cynthia had become smitten with a longtime customer and recently run off to elope, an act Marie ruled as "ungrateful" and had since groused about regularly.

Celia was nearly at Judith's door when a man stumbled out with a lofty smile. If Lettie indeed was inside, Pearl would not be.

The moment the man cleared the threshold, Celia peered into the room. Standing by the foot of the bed, Lettie was fastening her silky robe, and Celia's concerns doubled. "Have you seen her? Have you seen Pearl?"

Lettie shook her head. "Back with you, last I'd seen."

Celia hadn't an inkling how long she'd been asleep. "When?"

"A few hours, I'd say."

That long?

Celia bristled. "Well, she's not there. When I awoke, she was gone."

Lettie squinted, perplexed. "Have you asked Marie? Perhaps she's taken her to...that is, maybe she..." The rest dropped away. Either Lettie was stumped for an explanation or, far worse, upon imagining reasons, she was hesitant to voice them.

Celia suddenly envisioned Marie in Lettie's room, finding Pearl not hot but cold at Celia's side. Ice cold and absent of breath.

Although if true, surely she would have woken Celia.

The scenario, discarded, gave way to one nearly as dark: of Marie judging Celia an unfit mother who'd even missed signs of a life-threatening illness. With the child now in the clear, she and Mrs. Downey could have felt justified in selling Pearl off, particularly to a suitable, God-fearing couple.

The thought caused Celia an intake of breath, drawing her hand to her mouth.

"What?" Lettie said. "What is it?"

Celia didn't bother to answer. She scrambled toward Marie's room, ready to pound on the door. As it was open a quarter, she charged inside. By a lantern's dim light, there was no sight of Pearl—on the bed nor elsewhere—just Marie planted before the window, her back to Celia.

Terror rebounded, gripping Celia once more. "Where is she? What did you do with her?"

The moment that followed, as Marie pivoted around, was interminable. It seemed the earth itself had ceased to spin.

And yet there was a murmuring, the words Chinese, the cadence like a lullaby. Marie was singing. Celia noticed the object in Marie's arms just as the tune broke off. It was Pearl, alert in what appeared to be a freshly pinned diaper, her presence so welcome Celia's knees almost gave out.

"Fever gone." Marie declared this with finality, even as she continued to gently sway.

Celia approached to check for herself. At the cool feel of Pearl's forehead, the sight of her lovely paleness, Celia's impulse to weep was quelled only by the shame of her suspicions.

"How did you know?" she asked Marie. "About using needles on a baby?"

"Grandfather teach me. So I do this, many time."

Pearl was gazing at Marie now, soothed. The way the woman held her conveyed a comfort derived from experience—beyond her disquieting yet effective needle treatments.

"As...a mother?" Celia hazarded to ask.

Marie's attention stayed on Pearl as she shook her head. "At orphanage, in China."

Celia stared, surprised by the rare divulgence. "You're an orphan?"

"No." Marie winced. "Only work there." The response might have been insulting if not for her care of Pearl. Evidence of a softer heart than Marie normally let on. Then she added, "That is how I come here, to America. As nanny. But I grow tired... of saying goodbye."

A heaviness in her words suggested at least some of the partings, perhaps at the orphanage, were grim in nature.

As though sensing the observation, she held out Pearl. "Here. Take baby."

Celia accepted gladly, savoring the feel of her child safe in her arms. When Pearl looked up at her with a loving sense of recognition, all else for Celia drifted away, specifically every memory of motherhood she'd viewed as a hardship. They scattered into the distance like leaves in a breeze.

"Go now." Marie flitted her hand. "I needed for work."

Before abiding, Celia thought first to say, "Thank you, Marie. For everything."

Marie absorbed this. She didn't reply but yielded a partial nod.

Celia was midturn when Marie said, "Our cook much too busy. You also do baking now."

Celia stared, puzzled by the expansion of her duties despite her job ending soon.

Marie clucked with slight annoyance. "Fine. I pay. But not big amount." Then she pointed emphatically. "I want good bread in fall." The remark, delivered as a condition, lightly cloaked a vital message: Celia and Pearl's stay had been extended through at least the season ahead.

Celia battled back a smile, as making a hoopla of the offer just might jeopardize it. "Of course."

Never would she have imagined calling a brothel her home. Even so, she was grateful.

CHAPTER
TWENTY-FIVE

The newspapers described it as the Haymarket Affair. A mild term for it, to be certain.

Although the tragedy occurred four months past, amid the May Day protests and in the faraway city of Chicago, effects of the clash between police and labor activists in Haymarket Square—culminating in eleven deaths from a bomb explosion and subsequent gunfire—were still reaching as far as Portland. Fortunately, on this particular Sunday, one of the results was of the positive sort.

Lively as a carnival, the rally was meant to boost a movement to establish an official holiday supporting workers—Labor Day, they were calling it—making Oregon the first state to pass such a law. Throughout the park blocks that ran parallel to the river were bunting and flags aplenty, vendors hawking goods, and a trio of fellows performing a peppy folk song with a banjo, harmonica, and washboard. In the afternoon shade of trees, umbrellaed by leaves on the cusp of autumn's hues, families were picnicking on blankets as if commemorating the Fourth of July.

"Would you look at all this fuss," Lettie said, walking beside Celia on a footpath.

Celia glanced about while pushing Pearl in a baby carriage, partially distracted by its wheels. Squeaking aside, the canopied wicker buggy—compliments of a woman in Marie's mah-jongg group—made Celia feel rather fancy. Pearl was just as appreciative, made plain by her cooing while staring up at the scattered white puffs in the cerulean sky, her grip on a rattle impressively tight. At five months of age, she grew more aware and capable with each passing day.

Lettie huffed. "Makes no sense to me at all."

"What is that, precisely?" Celia dared ask.

Lettie gestured toward a line of banners, of which the most prominent read *Labor Built This Republic and Labor Shall Rule It.* "If they get their way and make it a true holiday, they'll be celebratin' workers by telling them not to work."

Celia considered this and laughed a little. "I suppose you have a point."

"Besides, what would the holiday mean to me anyhow? Can you imagine Marie allowing us girls to laze about on a regular bloody work day?"

Lettie wasn't wrong. Nor, in this regard, would the girls be alone. That the movement also excluded Chinese laborers went painfully unspoken. The surrounding sea of fair-skinned faces reinforced as much.

Granted, Chinese locals appeared to be venturing beyond their homes and shops with increasing rarity. It seemed a shrewd precaution, given the rise in reported murders of Chinese immigrants in the American West, not to mention the perpetual expulsions—more than 150 incidents, according to talk in Chinatown, a place Celia visited only when needed. And not with Pearl.

Never with Pearl.

Lettie halted with a gasp, impelling Celia to do the same.

"What is it?" Celia pressed, and Lettie pointed.

"Over *there*."

Celia rushed to trace the issue through the crowd. In the distance, a standard mix of ships and boats floated past on the Willamette. "What are you seeing?"

"Why, there's sticky apples!"

Relief struck, though Celia then groaned. "Don't frighten me like that. I thought it was something important."

"'Tis indeed. They're my favorite." Lettie wrinkled her nose. "Then again, I really shouldn't. Because of your fine pastries, I've already had to loosen my corset."

The compliment, echoing those from the other ladies since Celia had taken over the inn's baking two months ago, effectively eliminated her agitation. "Nonsense. Your figure is lovely as ever." And that was the truth.

"Well..." Lettie shrugged. "I suppose there's no harm in a peek." She grinned and scuttled right off. As usual, even as she strode through the crowd that no doubt held some of her former and current patrons, her posture didn't falter. Only on occasion during her weekly strolls with Celia did her eyes flicker with recognition of men in passing. Those with their wives or proper dates were a tad less subtle, averting their gazes or guiding their companions on a divergent path.

While the nature of Lettie's work was still unsettling to Celia, she couldn't help but admire the way her friend carried herself. Assured. Without apology.

Pearl's cheery babbling nudged out the thought. Her two bottom front teeth had recently broken through the gums, making her—and therefore Celia—far happier, though the drooling hadn't relented. Celia reached down to wipe the saliva and stopped at a fresh sound.

Had she heard it correctly? She bridled her zeal so as not to startle the child. "Was that a laugh, angel?"

Pearl gurgled, then blew tiny spit bubbles.

Celia leaned down to better listen through the event's bustling. "Can you laugh again? Can you do that for Mama?" Adding encouragement, she tickled her daughter's tummy.

Pearl wriggled in her dress, eyes twinkling, and let loose a giggle.

"That's it! That's my girl!"

When her small cupid lips curled up, an apparent show of pride, Celia had to consciously keep from dwelling on the absence of the person she most wished were here. Not for the first time, she drew strength from the memory of her father's time away, his efforts similarly dedicated to serving as a family provider. Though she still longed for Stephen's return, she'd learned from her parents that distance alone wouldn't weaken a true relationship—nor, in the end, would it lessen the bond between a father and daughter.

Thus, in the interim, she looked around for Lettie, eager to showcase Pearl's new skill.

A crowd's applause broke out from the direction of the stage, set along an edge of the park. At the podium stood a man whose presence froze Celia in place.

The mayor. Edwin Bettencourt.

He waved at the audience and worked his way toward the steps, appearing to have just completed a speech. From Celia's recollection of their last exchange, instinct demanded she hightail it out of the vicinity.

How had she not foreseen this? Aware of his impending reelection, she should have bypassed the event out of caution. Now, with her guard presently down, his beaming smile revived memories of the compassion and kindness he'd often shown her—before his wife's harsh stance and Celia's banishment from their home. Well before the birth of Pearl, the couple's precious grandchild.

A vision flashed at Celia. She imagined the mayor spotting the baby and all else fading away. He'd send word to his son and insist Celia and Pearl move into the house, where even his wife, despite initial hesitation, would welcome them back.

The scenario was obviously far reaching. Celia wasn't naive enough to believe otherwise. Still, logic suggested that given the passage of time and with no sign of Mrs. Bettencourt—always averse to attending these to-dos—the mayor might well be receptive.

Moreover, even the slimmest chance to reconnect with Stephen, for Pearl's sake above all, was worth an attempt.

Nerves humming, Celia pushed the baby carriage toward the area to the right of the stage, where suited men were shaking hands with the mayor. No more than ten feet away, she waited. She was arranging her appeal when his gaze stalled on hers.

A smile of recognition stretched his lips. Then his eyes lowered toward the buggy, its canopy preventing a clear view of Pearl, and his expression became unreadable.

Celia's pulse raced with anticipation.

Beside him, a gentleman followed the mayor's eyeline and peered curiously. A regular dinner guest at the Bettencourt home, Mr. Humphrey then rotated back and slapped a friendly hand on the mayor's shoulder.

Whether or not the man recognized Celia, as servants tended to be invisible, she most definitely remembered him. His tone alone when referring to "Chinamen" turned the common term derogatory. In endless rants standard for the Knights of Labor, he'd likened Chinese immigrants to locusts and cancers, even menacing dragons in need of slaughter.

And now, just as vile, greeting the mayor was another distinctive figure: Sylvester Pennoyer. Deceivingly dapper with his neat white mustache and beard, he'd chaired an assembly a year prior to set a thirty-day deadline for a statewide ouster of all those *tainted*—his choice of word—by Chinese blood.

So consumed had Celia been with personal challenges, namely pregnancy, that she'd learned of this only after a security force in Portland, the majority volunteers, pushed back—citing not a moral factor necessarily but the legalities of a treaty with China. Although Pennoyer's crusade had failed, leading some to even call Portland a refuge for the targeted immigrants, his campaign cry of "Keep the Mongolians Out" was still effectively aiding his ambitions as he charged toward the governorship.

Pay their words no mind, the mayor would say to Celia when such men visited the house. And she'd agreed amenably. But in this instant, considering all the hatred and violence they continued to perpetuate, the thought of him accepting their blood-drenched support churned her stomach.

Right then, Mayor Bettencourt shifted away to consort with more members of the Knights of Labor—the very organization that, at least indirectly, had caused the death of Celia's father. Of this, the mayor was disturbingly aware.

A child's rattle jangled. Pearl was chewing intently on its handle, all trace of her glee depleted. The same as Celia's.

"Time to go," she informed her daughter and, without pause, reversed their path. They would find Lettie on their way to the inn, where tomorrow, as usual, Celia would await the mailman's delivery. And if no reply came from Stephen, she would simply send another post.

"Your father's going to be home soon," she assured Pearl and tacked on: "I promise."

Not intended as cursory, the two words carried a certainty felt deep within—a surety that proved to be fleeting.

Ultimately, it would stand in glaring contrast with the seemingly countless months that followed. For as the current year flowed into the next, each season dissolving into another and another, Celia often reflected on that day and suspected the vow was one she never should have made.

CHAPTER
TWENTY-SIX

"Please, come quick."

Over the laughter and chatter drifting distantly from the parlor, Harriet's summoning reached through Celia's doorway, if at a hushed volume; it was a thoughtful effort to prevent rousing Pearl. Despite the comfort of the toddler snuggled beside Celia in bed, with her little exhales a lulling rhythm and her body warm and soft as a biscuit fresh from the oven, Celia hadn't yet dozed off.

"You'll need the mop," Harriet muttered with a look of disgust. Then she disappeared into the hall, leaving a shaft of light from the door open a crack.

Celia sighed, the situation clear. At this late of an hour, no doubt an overindulging customer had produced a mess requiring cleanup—of one type of bodily fluid or another.

Though reluctant, she eased out of the covers and pulled a robe over her nightgown. Now in early March, the floor wasn't nearly as cold as it had been through winter, but due to the filth of her task, she threw on her slippers. To keep Pearl resting and cozy, Celia cocooned her with the coverlet. The child's outlined form emphasized just how fast she was growing.

It was hard to believe she'd be turning two in a few short

months. On her birthday last year, she'd relished fistfuls of a multilayered silver cake, which Celia had proudly baked using sweet milk and extract of peaches. The unconventional party—a first birthday celebrated with ladies of the night wasn't exactly common—had marked the occasion with gaiety. *One in a lifetime of milestones.* Celia had assured herself this as the child's sole parent in attendance, ever awed by Pearl's constant expansion of skills. The transition from crawling to walking, though with the charming wobbles of a baby giraffe, had occurred practically overnight. Same went for the evolution of her speech, from indecipherable babbling to a slew of distinguishable words. *Mama*, admittedly, continued to be a tingling source of pride.

Strange, the way some days stretched into eternity while the months, at least upon reflection, passed in a blink.

With solemn awareness, Celia touched a kiss to Pearl's crown of silky curls. The crinkle above her nose, matching her father's look of concentration, indicated she was deep in a dream. Her new penchant for long stretches of sleep left her generally undisturbed by the sounds of the inn's activities—for the time being. Long before she could comprehend such things, she'd be settled in a far better place. A true home.

It was a notion Celia clung to, yet again, before treading out of the room to fetch supplies for her sordid chore.

———

In the shadows behind the inn, Celia had just emptied the dirty pail of water, thankfully having mopped up only urine on this occasion, when something moved in her periphery. Slumped on the rain-dampened ground against an oak barrel was a lean fellow. Relatively young for the premises, not much older than eighteen, he had a clean-cut face with youthful, if heavy-lidded, eyes. And clutched upon his shoulder was a revolver.

Celia startled at the realization, almost dropping the bucket.

"Whatcha doin' back here?" A slur barely softened his gruffness. He lowered the weapon to his side, bumping a tipped bottle. "Go on 'n' git!"

Celia's feet stalled as she registered where the gun had been aimed—straight at his temple.

Good heavens, he'd been gearing up to launch a bullet at himself.

"You simple-minded? I told ya to go!" He jerked his chin toward the brothel, further disheveling his dark hair.

This man's travails had nothing to do with Celia. Besides, she'd witnessed enough customers made mean by liquor—moonshine, in particular—to know that in his condition, anyone near him could wind up shot, intentionally or not.

Gripping her pail, she turned for the back door. As she reached for the knob, the man released a lengthy exhale threaded with a quiver. Far from rage, it conveyed a feeling she knew well: desperation—evidently on the most extreme of levels. No doubt magnified by drinking.

Celia battled her compulsion to flee. She couldn't deny that, when in need, she'd benefited from the aid of others. Moreover, if this stranger was on the verge of committing the ultimate sin, would she be any less innocent if she walked away?

While keeping a cautious distance, she swiveled to face him. "Sir..." she began gently, as *young man* might provoke him. "Whatever your predicament, I guarantee it won't seem nearly as burdensome come morning, once the alcohol has worn off and—"

"Booze got nothin' to do with it!"

She scoured for another approach. "Is there a friend nearby? One who could lend a hand?"

He scoffed and shook his head. "A pal done brought me here tonight. Swore it would cheer my mood." After a pause, the fellow's gaze dropped to the six-shooter still in his hand, now resting on his leg. "I tried...with a lady here. She was plenty pretty and all... It wasn't 'cause of her...I...I just couldn't..."

A flush of embarrassment heated Celia's cheeks. She detoured with a casual shrug. "Perhaps a good night's sleep would do you well."

"Ain't you listenin'?" His gaze cut to hers, causing her to retract a step. "I can't sleep. Can barely eat. I lie there for hours each night as the pictures in my brain go round and round, the sounds too. Can't shut the damn things off." He squeezed his eyes closed and pressed his free hand to the side of his head. "After all that's happened, ain't nothing gonna make it right...not ever again."

His raw vulnerability, a rare display among men, tugged like twine in Celia's chest. Despite the inference of guilt—really, at his age, how terrible an infraction could it be?—she attempted a personable tack. "What did you say your name was?"

Muffled conversations from the inn filled the space between them until he mumbled, "Frank."

Gingerly, she set down her pail. Though wary of his finger hovering over the trigger, she dared to kneel on the cool ground to meet his level. "Well, Frank, whatever it is you've done, I can't imagine you deserve to lose your life over it."

At last, slowly, he opened his eyes but directed them straight ahead—unseeing, if contemplative. She sensed he'd inched back from the edge of a cliff, yet one wrong word or move on her part could send him into a leap.

She was weighing her next action when he spoke, as if musing to himself, "That apply to murder?"

Stunned, she merely waited. The topic could be far less grim than it sounded. She dearly hoped that was the case as he continued in a near whisper.

"Spent days chewing on it, out in the schoolyard...me and Robert and Omar. We'd first heard it from JT, another member of our gang, about a group of 'em mining flour gold. He said they'd been camped in a cove along the Snake for more than half the year. That long in one spot, it must've been a major strike of dust and nuggets, we reckoned."

Failing to track all the names he'd rattled off, Celia trained her attention on the main points of his story.

"We plotted it out, feeling like real-life Robin Hoods. Way we saw it, they was plundering riches they got no business takin', and all to send to family on the other side of the world. 'What about the good citizens from right here?' we said. 'What about *our* families?'"

The potential origin of the gold miners, those supporting relatives from so great a distance, needled Celia with dread as he went on.

"Rest of the gang jumped right on board. Not long after, the bunch of us rode off to a hideout just a few miles from the cove. While we was settling into the cabin, one of the fellas headed over to steal a glimpse. Sure enough, he said, there they was on the gravel bar. Ten in number, panning in Dead Line Creek, deep down in the canyon."

The name of the creek held familiarity. Why? Where had Celia heard it?

Unimportant, she decided and refocused.

"Come mornin', we loaded up and set off according to plan. Being only a kid, Robert was to mind the horses. Carl and Hiram split ways as lookouts: one downstream, one up. Then to surround the camp, I followed Blue—the leader of us—far below while JT and Omar stayed above on the hillside. I was holding my rifle to my chest. My heart was pounding so hard, it being my first time. I considered turning back—hand to God, I did—but then shots rang out. And the screams. They were echoing off the cliffs, terror filled and bloodcurdlin'. Over even the gang's whoops and hollers while picking 'em off one by one. That bowl-shaped cove was an outright trap. Nowhere to hide, no way out."

Horrified by the imagined scene, Celia could feel the cliffs closing in. The agonizing screams and the blasts of rifles clashed distantly in her ears as he asserted, "I had no choice. What with Blue right there, eyeing me. I was too scared to do nothing else. We'd made a pact, see. Unless I wanted the lead poured in me too…"

Celia prayed his tale had come to an end as his chin trembled and teeth clenched, appearing to bar his next words until they pushed through.

"Then JT pulled out an axe."

She gasped, a half breath. At that point, a viselike grip was constricting her lungs.

"The blood, it was splattered and spilling out everywhere. By then, none of it felt real. Like being in a nightmare. All those bodies lying about like torn-up rag dolls, with heads and backs sliced, limbs chopped. Blue ordered us to strip and dump 'em in the river. Till that day, I reckon I saw them people as different as can be. Somehow not…human…" He shook his head marginally, then pressed on in a rasp, "Turned out one was still alive. He was crawlin' toward a skiff, trying to get away. Since we was out of bullets, I figured we could let that one go. But a couple of the fellas grabbed some rocks. They didn't quit swinging 'em till that last Chinaman was gone."

The cruelty, the gruesomeness, was too much to fully

comprehend. This was beyond a slaughter; it was an act of pure evil, of searing hatred. Simply because they were Chinese.

A sob caught deep in Celia's chest, emitting a sound that caused Frank to flinch. As if reminded of her presence, he dragged his gaze up to meet hers. Emotion welled in his bloodshot eyes.

"So tell me again," he said after a moment of quiet. "Why is it I deserve to live?"

Despite the blatancy of his shame, her compassion for him had been decisively smothered. What was she to say? Reassure him with a lie? Tell him regret alone made him worthy of forgiveness?

From the gap in his shirt collar, a necklace peeked out—a small wooden cross. The level of irony was repulsive.

He was awaiting a response.

The words he truly deserved were clamoring in her mind when, once more, she glimpsed the revolver in his hand. Through her muddled thoughts, she realized…

She knew far more than she should.

"Vaughan!"

Her heart jumped. She swung toward a corner of the inn, where the interjecting man stood. Moonlight shone on his lightly bearded face, pockmarked scars visible on his upper cheeks.

"There ya are, damn you." He spat tobacco juice at the ground. "Up and at 'em. You've had plenty of time to cozy up with this one here."

He presumed she was one of Marie's gals. A logical conclusion, what with her dressed in nightclothes, kneeling in the shadows with Frank.

"C'mon now. We got more horses to break in bright 'n' early."

Frank mumbled something that resembled agreement. Loosely grasping his gun, he endeavored to climb to his feet without falling.

Only after he'd staggered off with his friend did Celia allow her emotions to surface, and for more reasons than she could discern, she remained on the ground and wept.

1888

—

JULY

CHAPTER
TWENTY-SEVEN

With concerted effort, Celia forced her eyes to open. They were heavily sealed, feeling almost swollen. The room returned in dim, blurry streaks.

It seemed only minutes had passed since she'd last drifted off.

On her side, she still lay on the hard ground, and yet a textured fabric, reminiscent of a feed bag, rested beneath her cheek. She reached out to probe further.

The floor had changed. It felt of wood. Weathered planks. They were damp. Same as the air. She struggled to comprehend, to assemble the pieces.

Creak...creak...

Creak...creak...

The gentle rhythm kept time like a metronome, reminding her of a lovely Chinese song her father used to hum.

Creak...creak...

She perceived a swaying motion.

The world was rocking her, like a chair lulling a babe. She was being soothed as if by her mother, encouraged to sink back into the cottony grayness of sleep. It was drawing her in with the comfort of her mother's flour-dusted hands.

Then through the fog came a series of sounds. Distant and muffled, they were the calls of birds, a type Celia knew but couldn't place.

And still there was creaking. Crates being moved at the docks. Or were they the sounds of the docks themselves? She easily envisioned them, off the waterfront in Portland, enduring the whims of the river.

She strained to make sense of the clues. Gradually, like driftwood on the currents, they floated together and formed a revelation.

Though free of a cell, she was now on a ship.

1888

—

MARCH

CHAPTER
TWENTY-EIGHT

The nightmares that had eventually faded didn't just return; they worsened.

No longer was Celia struggling to reach her father through a violent uprising. Upon noting the bat in her grip, she realized she was a member of the attacking mob. She'd awaken from the shock, quaking and covered in sweat, sometimes rousing Pearl.

It seemed her conscience viewed her as an accomplice to murder—not to those in Wyoming Territory but in Oregon. Over the three long days and even longer nights since her run-in with Frank Vaughan, she couldn't ignore the impetus to do something, anything, with the information she'd been given.

But what?

The slaying of ten Chinese gold miners, she since recalled, had been reported in *The Oregonian* sometime late last year. That was the reason Dead Line Creek, tucked away in the northeastern corner of the state where it emptied into the Snake River, had seemed familiar. The murders were discovered only when bodies began washing ashore, far from their encampment and badly decomposed from several weeks in the water.

In truth, Celia had never finished the article. The status of the crimes as "unsolved yet under investigation" had stopped her short. She could easily speculate the meager amount of resources being spared for a maddening outcome. To save herself from sinking back into darkness, she'd determined to purge the account from memory.

Of course, that was before Frank and his admission invaded her life.

She wished for the hundredth time that Stephen were here for guidance. Although she could wait for his return, by then Frank's urges to confess could evaporate like raindrops in the summer heat, leaving little or no trace. Contrarily, an escalation of his guilt could lead to another suicide attempt, perhaps even achieved.

Ideally, he'd instead come forward, preventing at least the most heinous of the killers from roaming free and the victims' families from continuing to suffer without justice.

But to sway him would require assurance—specifically from a person who could credibly vouch that a judge would grant him leniency. Based on the mayor's discussions Celia had overheard regarding various cases, such a trade seemed standard for incriminating, reliable testimony.

In fact, perhaps the mayor would be willing—

No, not him. Even if he hadn't already shown his aversion to Celia's presence, her bruised yet enduring pride wouldn't permit her to stoop so low as to request his help.

She could think of just one type of authority potentially open to her approach, the sort with both the obligation and capacity to act.

—

From across the room, the clacking of a typewriter by a young cop—among the handful of officers present in the downtown police building—reverberated off the walls. A drunkard's snore filled the intermittent pauses from a cell in the corner.

At the largest desk, having just listened to Celia's relating of events, Officer Glenn reclined in his chair, legs crossed in navy trousers. He continued to puff on his pipe and, just as he had throughout her summary, maintained a neutral look—disturbingly so. But then murder was common in his line of work, requiring a degree of callousness.

Still ruminating, he expelled smoke through the thick brush of a black mustache that harbored his lips.

Celia staved off a cough. In the worn wooden seat before him, she subtly waved the haze away from Pearl, who was fidgeting on Celia's lap while holding a yellow yarn doll by its skirt.

"Mama, hungwy," she whined.

"I know, angel," Celia whispered. "We'll be home soon." She'd hastily departed the inn after speeding through her chores and neglected to bring a snack. Now, with the supper hour approaching, Pearl's teetering mood only added to Celia's apprehension in wait of the officer's response.

Finally, he said, "And this schoolboy, Frank Vaughan, he shared this story of his at the Dewdrop after enjoying its services?"

The last bit wasn't quite right. But graciously, for herself included, she'd skip mention of Frank's intimate mishap—which, incidentally, she'd since investigated and traced to Louise at the brothel, who knew nothing of him beyond his name. "Yes, that's correct."

"To just you. A *stranger* with whom he had no acquaintance."

Celia tensed at the flippant phrasing. She hoped the lawman was merely being discerning. "Given the monstrous nature of the crimes, he evidently needed an ear."

The officer started to reply just as Pearl lurched toward him. Celia barely prevented her, though not the doll, from plummeting to the floor.

"*Staah*," Pearl said, reaching for the seven-point star on the man's vest. Its silver reflected the early-evening light from the window. Not banking on him being the paternal type, Celia shifted Pearl away and retrieved the yarn doll, a tenuous distraction.

Officer Glenn waited, expectant. What had he asked?

"I...apologize. Could you please repeat that?"

His cheek twitched. "I *said*: And you believe he'd been drinking before he confessed about murdering all those Chinamen?"

The summation was jarringly succinct after all she'd relayed and especially blunt in Pearl's company. Celia had to remind herself that much of the conversation would mercifully pass her daughter by.

About to nod, Celia felt the need to clarify, still somewhat conscious of her words: "Indeed, he seemed somewhat inebriated, though I didn't get the impression that he...did away with many of the miners on his own—if any of them, come to think of it. He conveyed only that he did participate."

"After egged on by a pal's glare," the officer supplied. The terminology held more levity than Celia would have preferred; thankfully, his tone did not.

"That's correct. As I explained, apparently he was also fearful for his life should he back out."

"Because of a pact."

"Yes."

Pearl began squirming, accompanied by mumbling. Celia bounced her lightly as the officer drew from his pipe and exhaled.

"So they stripped down the bodies, and...why was that exactly?"

To be honest, Celia hadn't given it thought. Any guess in this instant would be just that. "I am afraid I didn't ask."

"Seems odd, doesn't it? Taking the time to remove the clothing of victims already chopped up when they're just going to dump the parts in the water. Forgive me for being indelicate."

With Pearl distracted, Celia shook her head that he was fine, as there was nothing delicate about the topic—though she couldn't disagree with his point. Then again, liquor had been a factor. "I'd venture to say he may have simply misstated the order of events or other details."

"Yes. Yes, I imagine so." Officer Glenn took another puff from his pipe. "He didn't indicate any evidence to back all this up, I suppose? Anything not already published in the paper?"

"Well…no. It doesn't mean some can't be found."

"And you feel confident this young fella wasn't just spinning a tale, trying to impress you?"

The outlandish suggestion took her off guard. How would such a tale impress any woman? "I have every reason to believe he was being truthful."

The officer nodded, appearing to accept the answer. Yet between the tidy stacks of documents on his desk, a pencil continued to rest on a blank sheet of paper, unused since Celia's arrival.

"Pardon me for asking. But shouldn't you be writing any of this down?"

"Oh, not necessary, Miss—Hart, did you say? Got everything right here." He tapped his temple, just as well highlighting his receding hairline. "In fact, I believe I've collected all the information we need. Naturally, I'll let you know if we require anything more." With that, he stood from his chair and towered over Celia. "I'm much obliged to you for coming in." His mustache lifted at the corners from what she feared was a veiled smirk.

On the verge of making a fuss, Pearl too was ready for their departure.

And yet, concerned the claim was being dismissed, Celia remained seated. While the officer might not have more questions for her, she had one for him—delivered politely. "Could you first tell me, sir, how you plan to proceed?"

His mustache lowered. Then he released a condescending sigh that affirmed her suspicion, setting her nerves further on edge. "Ma'am, what is it you would like me to do precisely?"

How about your job?

She clamped her jaw shut to contain the retort. Perhaps on the grift, he might be one to operate in the gray area of the law, looking the other way with business violations—but this was different. This was murder on a massive and brutal scale, demanding amends. The type too often unmet.

She therefore answered as though his question was genuine. "I suspect Mr. Vaughan could be persuaded to testify. He might require but a nudge."

"A nudge."

"Reassurance that his own punishment would be minimal in exchange for speaking out."

"You mean for turning on his pals."

The choice of words conveyed a tattletale, at best; at worst, it made informing on his companions seem a greater offense.

"For reporting the *killers*," she corrected.

The officer huffed under his breath, not missing the gouge.

Celia needed an ally, not an enemy. She smoothed her tone while centering on what mattered. "Furthermore, who's to say Mr. Vaughan won't convince others to confess as well? He cannot possibly be the only one among them to know it was wrong. His school friends at least. Sir, you must agree this merits considering."

After a moment of silence, save a series of small grunts from Pearl, Officer Glenn proffered a nod. "How about this…"

Celia couldn't help but perk up.

"I do my job the way I see fit, and you grab a broom and worry about yours." Although his voice remained level, his pointed words, reinforced by his gesture to the door, made clear that no good would come of her staying.

CHAPTER TWENTY-NINE

From the police building, Celia did return to the inn, but rather than work, she vented her aggravation to the one friend there she wholly trusted. As Celia paced, Lettie listened from the bed while feeding Pearl a bowl of porridge. The child was rubbing her eyes between bites when Lettie interjected.

"Celia..." She hesitated, a rarity that paused Celia's feet. "'Twas a tragedy in that canyon, to be certain, but..."

Celia had to consciously control her impatience. "But?"

Lettie finished a bit tentatively, "You just seem to be taking the whole thing awful personal."

Celia's jaw slackened.

Did the massacre of Chinese immigrants mean nothing to Lettie? Had she not taken in the grisly details?

"And you think I shouldn't?" Celia took the liberty of providing the most obvious reason: "Because they weren't white, I presume."

Now Lettie was the one who went still, exasperated. "Jesus, Mary, and Saint Joseph. That isn't what I'm saying at all."

Pearl whimpered, an unrelated reaction—or was it from the spike in tension? Regardless, a protective wave surged through

Celia. She swooped Pearl up and, holding her close, guided her head to rest sleepily on her shoulder.

"All I was saying," Lettie clarified with an air of defense, "was that you can't read a single newspaper nowadays without learning of one murder or another."

Celia digested the point, a sad truth, easing her indignation and clearing a path to view the hurt in her friend's eyes, just as Lettie pressed on.

"Do you really believe I'd think that way about those poor miners?"

Celia regretted the assumption immediately. Almost as much as her accusation.

"Of course not." Her tone lacked the full conviction the assurance deserved. As Lettie set aside the bowl, Celia added with resolve, "Sincerely."

Lettie averted her gaze nonetheless.

To fill the fissure between them, Celia would need to share the true source of her frustration—granted, to a cautionary limit for her child's sake.

Relaxing her hold on Pearl, whose breaths were turning heavy, Celia sat beside Lettie on the bed. "A miner who was killed," she began with measured words, "was very dear to me."

Lettie looked back at her, astounded. "Among those in the cove?"

"No—no, a different massacre. In Rock Springs." The fact that she had to clarify which one, let alone her personal connection to it, stirred up her buried emotions. She did her best to keep them in check as she explained simply, "It was by a mob of white miners and townsfolk."

Lettie appeared puzzled but only briefly; the incident, after all, had made national news.

"Not a solitary person paid for those crimes," Celia reminded her.

Sympathy seeped into Lettie's face, followed closely by under-standing. The parallels of the tragedies went without saying.

Then she twisted to face Celia, who braced herself; questions over the person she had lost would be natural.

"I understand," Lettie said. "Still, I reckon you've done all you can do, going to the police and all."

Relieved by the lack of prying, Celia nodded before her thoughts swung back to Frank, and she realized Lettie was wrong. A distinct option remained at Celia's disposal.

Though not free of risk, she had to try.

CHAPTER THIRTY

In addition to calling Frank by his surname, the man who retrieved him outside the inn had inadvertently left a second clue. His mention of breaking in "more horses" implied it was standard in their jobs, a deduction that led Celia to inquire at several local saddle shops in search of a connection. To her dismay, however, even a description of the man's pockmarked face failed to produce the pair's whereabouts. Only upon leaving the third shop did an adjacent sign pull her focus:

HAL'S FEEDSTORE

The common supplier of ranchers in the area might well know of him, she figured.

It was a notion that, after describing him to a balding clerk, luckily proved true.

"Nice-enough boy," he said, for which Celia fought a cringe. The man wiped his hands on an apron too snug for his belly. "Been helping out for a stint, o'er yonder at Collins Ranch."

Celia's thrill from the discovery was soon tempered by a

thought. The success of her sleuthing meant she no longer had a choice: she had to charge forward.

—

Two days later, under the canopy of a pewter sky, Celia caught a wagon ride with a chatty elderly driver headed in a similar direction. She nodded periodically, masking her inability to absorb his words. Her mind was too busy readying for the confrontation ahead.

She had delayed the trek until Sunday afternoon, when Pearl could nap under Lettie's care. This enabled Celia to pay Frank a visit on her own—a necessity, as an expanded audience would surely seal his lips. Unless she'd misgauged, he alone didn't strike her as a personally dangerous threat, particularly since her intervention appeared to have saved his life.

Celia disembarked at a literal crossroads. The air, dusty in the wagon's wake, deterred her from lingering and propelled her the last quarter mile to reach Collins Ranch. Its white crisscrossed gate, chipped and peeling from the weather, greeted her unlocked.

She nudged it open. The creak of the hinges sent a shiver up her back.

With a bolstering breath, she proceeded up the dirt drive.

A scattering of horses grazed on the surrounding fields. Some fifty yards away awaited a lengthy barn and, beyond that, a quaint farmhouse.

In bed at night, she'd explored the likeliest scenarios. If informed that Frank was absent, for instance, she would request his location—for a personal matter involving family, she'd say. The excuse was authentic at its core—for her certainly—and one she could also use to obtain privacy should she find him in the company of others.

Unfortunately, these mental preparations did nothing to prevent her nerves from jittering. As she rounded the first structure, they sharply escalated at the sight of a lean fellow. On a walnut-brown horse, he was approaching at a leisurely pace from a fenced-in riding area. His wide-brimmed hat shadowed the upper half of his face while sunrays highlighted his clean-shaven jaw. Chaps covered his legs.

He tugged the reins to slow before her, then tipped his hat. "What can I do for ya, ma'am?" His familiar tone and youthful features confirmed him as Frank Vaughan, prickling the tiny hairs on the nape of her neck. Or perhaps it was from the way he was peering down at her from such a height, which, paired with the horse's display of broad muscles, made her feel markedly small.

She delved in regardless. "Good day, Mr. Vaughan. I trust you remember our recent exchange."

Intrigued, he gave her face a swift review yet shook his head. "Afraid I can't say I do…"

Had he really been that intoxicated?

She studied his face in turn, though for hints of dishonesty, of which she found none. "It was at the Dewdrop Inn," she said. At the quirking of his brow, she immediately wished to clarify. "Outside of it, rather. We had spoken of"—she lowered her voice to a cautious volume—"a most distressing occurrence."

He scratched under the brim of his hat, just above his temple. As he strained to think, revulsion climbed within her. That his mind could so easily eradicate their discussion despite its subject pushed her to add, "Specifically at Dead Line Creek."

Recognition—of the referenced incident at minimum— flickered in his eyes. His mood darkened. He glanced around, as if to verify the area was clear, before muttering, "I downed a whole lotta drink. Must've been rambling nonsense." Then he clucked his tongue, cueing the horse to resume its path at a clip that gave her no chance to respond.

But the conversation was far from over.

She promptly followed him into the barn, where she stood just inside as he dismounted.

"Not to be contrary," she said, despite that being precisely the case, "but I do believe the account you shared to be true." Though by softened means, she was calling his denial a lie, an accusation that hit its mark, based on the set of his jaw.

His attention veered from her as he removed the horse's saddle. "Got chores here to see to. Appreciate you going on your way."

What was essentially a grim order magnified a daunting fact: that she was alone with a man who'd helped commit cold-blooded murder. Neither his relative youth nor his regrets over his part—presuming he still had any—did anything to lessen the dread pooling in her stomach.

He led the horse into a nearby stall. The spurs on his boots rattled with each step.

Celia could walk out unscathed, or she could force an exchange that risked morphing into a detriment.

It was a decision made easy by a sudden vision of her father. Fueled by the relevance of his death, she marched forward, ramrod straight, and into Frank's view.

"I presume," she said, "that you're still troubled by the memories and nightmares you spoke of."

He froze. Although he neglected to meet her eyes, she continued.

"I understand being haunted by such things. The difference is that *you* can do something to better yours. Perhaps even stop them."

Silence stretched the air, expanding like yeasted dough, but she let the statement be, in hopes of reeling him in.

At last, without sparing a glance, he replied, "Oh? And how would you propose that exactly?" His tone suggested a challenge. Belying it, however, a hint of sincerity invited an answer.

"You could deliver justice for their deaths."

This provoked a low laugh. "Justice, huh?"

"Yes. *Justice*."

He shook his head in a patronizing manner.

Her frustration flared. She controlled it just enough to reason, "While you can't bring back the men who were killed, you could give solace to their families, their loved ones."

He conveyed no mockery this time, but neither did he respond. He simply resumed his task by removing the horse's bit, acting as though she'd taken her leave.

She was reminded then of how their first encounter began, how she'd defied his demand that she depart—to his personal benefit.

"Clearly it *must* matter to you. Enough for you to have considered taking...extreme measures." A rather mild description. "Do you honestly believe guilt of such magnitude will vanish on its own?"

He went still again. But then he clutched the reins—a seeming display of control—while removing the bridle and transferred it to a hook on the wall.

She raked her mind, desperate for words to sway him, yet stopped short of spouting a threat. Even a moderately natured animal could turn vicious when cornered. Moreover, when it came to the shootings, under duress or not, Frank was no innocent.

And so she latched on to her sole remaining point.

"What about your school friend—Robert, was it?"

Having just returned to the horse, Frank paused. He looked at her. "What of him?"

She had at least regained his attention.

"Why, you could convince him to come forward. The two of you together."

His eyes narrowed, incredulous. "And land us behind bars?"

"No—not necessarily." She hastened to add, "You said he's the youngest of the gang so was only put in charge of the horses. What's more, if you felt pressured by the others, surely he did too. I can't fathom a judge not being sympathetic. Especially if you both dared to bravely speak up."

Frank's gaze continued to hold, though relaxed slightly. He was pondering, a tenuous thread of consideration. As she suspected it would quickly fray, she called to mind his pendant, a wooden cross. His devotion to faith could well be flimsy—his transgressions being indicative—but she had nothing else.

"Mr. Vaughan, if for no other cause, what of your soul? And Robert's? This could be his one chance at salvation."

He stared at her, stoic, yet she sensed him further wavering.

Then his face snapped toward the stall's open window, pulled by a sound. In the fields beyond the farmhouse, a group of horses was being led by a couple of men riding among them.

Frank shifted back to Celia with an expression that tightened with his voice. "Like I said, time you get a move on."

She didn't argue.

CHAPTER
THIRTY-ONE

The subsequent days passed as if awaiting a break in a relent-less ceiling of winter clouds. Celia couldn't help but hope for progress. Perhaps, though improbable, a visit from Officer Glenn to request more details for an investigation ultimately deemed worthwhile. Or better yet to inform her that Frank, with or without persuasion, had officially submitted a confession, even corroborated by the young schoolboy.

But there was no visit. No word. And the earth kept right on spinning as the guilty went unpunished.

Already she'd ruled out returning to the ranch. Frank's final tone struck her as cautionary. The riders guiding the horses could obviously have included the killers—like the man who'd retrieved Frank at the inn. Considering that she'd viewed him close enough to detect his facial scars, he too could have taken note of her face.

An unsettling thought.

For all she knew, he could be the leader Frank feared. Or the man who'd wielded the axe.

On Portland's city streets, she found herself looking over her shoulder from worries of being followed. Men who merely stopped and angled her way were making her jumpy, particularly as she carted around Pearl. Roving leers had never been more discomfiting.

Concerns over safety did ease with the passage of weeks. Reasoning helped. Taking all factors into account, really, how was she a threat to anyone? As the officer had made abundantly clear: lacking actual evidence of the crimes, she was but a lowly maid, relating a secondhand tale from a drunken stranger.

She told herself she'd tried—by going to the police, confronting Frank. It would be only prudent for her to move on. And so she resisted doing anything more.

Until April.

———

Running work errands during Pearl's nap on a temperate Monday afternoon, Celia slowed her steps to cast a glance across the street. Beyond the passing horse-drawn carts stood Hal's Feedstore. It had become a habit of hers to survey the entrance whenever she frequented the vicinity. In her wishful visions, Frank Vaughan would happen to be there and catch her gaze, and the sight of her would compel him to finally do the right—

The entry door opened. A man of lean build emerged, his face obscured by the wide brim of his hat and the burlap sack over his shoulder.

Celia halted, swiftly irritated by her own reflexive hopes.

Chaps covered his trousers. Spurs adorned the heels of his boots. He tossed the sack onto a wagon, adding to a pile of other goods. Then he made his way up to the driver's seat. Finally lifting his face, he revealed...unfamiliar features.

Disappointment stung. Once again.

What more should Celia have expected? For her path to cross

Frank's would have required the sheer coincidence of them being there on the very same day, at the very same time…

The thought stalled all others, an idea grabbing hold. One of, say, a premeditated fluke.

Before sensibility could overrule it, she wove across the bustling street and entered the store.

Inside, through air thick with the scent of grains, she scanned the room filled with bins, barrels, and pyramids of varied sacks. Frank wasn't among the customers sprinkled about, but indeed the clerk was present. Again in an apron that bound his wide middle, the balding fellow was pouring a large sack of oats into a trough-like bin. Straggling bits littered the surrounding planked floor.

"Good afternoon, sir," Celia said upon reaching him. "I apologize for troubling you."

He shook the bag until it was empty, then replied, "No trouble, miss. How can I be of service?"

"Somewhat recently, you kindly assisted me in locating a gentleman. A man by the name of Frank Vaughan, working over at Collins Ranch."

"Ah, yeah. One of the hired hands."

"Exactly." She smiled.

"You were looking to…fetch a special book from him, I believe."

She hesitated, impressed he recalled her excuse for seeking Frank's whereabouts. "You have quite the memory."

He shrugged. "A key to survival in my house. Got a wife with the memory of an elephant." He sneered, but playfully. "So tell me: You manage to get that book of yours back?"

"I did, yes. Thank you." The fibbing was just as much for the clerk's sake as her own.

"Well, that's just fine."

She nodded, preparing to casually ask if Frank still came around regularly and which days were typical, when he added, "Good thing you handled that in the nick of time."

Mentally stumbling, she said, "I'm sorry?"

The clerk hitched a fist on his hip. "Ah, guess he didn't tell ya. Word has it he and his pal up and moved along."

Moved along. The term implied permanence.

She aimed for a level expression. "You wouldn't know where they went per chance? Or if they'll be back anytime soon?"

The clerk shook his head. "No inkling of either. I'd be obliged to ask the rancher next time he's in if you'd like."

She was about to accept when questions of reason swirled. If given the information, she would do what with it? Go on a hunt and chase Frank down? To what end, at what cost?

She was a mother. Pearl's sole protector as of yet. No matter how disheartening, the choice was clear: she needed to let the issue go.

"I...appreciate the offer," she replied, "but that won't be necessary."

CHAPTER THIRTY-TWO

Just outside the zoo at Portland's City Park, under a sunlit sky brushed with feathery June clouds, a resting area featured a pond that promoted serenity—for those without a toddler.

Celia tensed on the wooden bench as Pearl, roughly a dozen feet away, inched closer to the water. From her pocket, she tossed more pieces of stale bread to a family of swimming ducks. Among the strangers ambling about, a few were nearer to the pond than Celia, yet she trusted herself more than anyone to get to her child in time. Especially today, with energy replenished after a night of decent sleep.

Although her nightmares hadn't vanished along with Frank, in the three months since his departure, they'd at least become more sporadic.

"Pearl darling," she called out, and the girl turned with sweetly glimmering eyes that often made admonishing her difficult. "Remember what Mama said: Not too close to the edge."

With no acknowledgment of the heeding, Pearl resumed pitching crumbs—ironically more interested in the birds than she'd been in Grace and Brownie, the zoo's widely famed bears—though she did obey by ceasing her advance.

Another mishap dodged.

That the crux of a mother's duty lay in simply keeping one's child alive had always been evident; what came as a surprise was the evolution of the perils. Throughout infancy, it was Pearl's own biology that most threatened her survival. By the grace of God, sheer luck, or both, she'd evaded stillbirth, malnourishment, and a fatal illness—only to have her curiosity and impulses emerge as rivaling hazards.

Though Celia no longer feared her crawling toward stairs or putting everything and anything graspable into her mouth, and indeed worries had lessened over her touching hot or sharp objects as well as over stumbling while honing her balance, Celia now fretted most about Pearl's affinity for wading and climbing—into water, onto tables, up bookshelves and trees. And, of course, there were all kinds of running: toward horses easily spooked, into streets treacherous with wagons, and one day toward the wrong sort of fellow. Then toward the right one.

Granted, Celia's concerns over the latter were rooted not only in a mother's common dread of separation but also in the possibility that their secret lineage would surface. For just as troubling as public ridicule were the steadily rising laws oppressive to anyone born at least a quarter Chinese.

Which prompted the question: If Pearl's features and those of her offspring never hinted to their heritage, could Celia withhold the truth forever, even from them? Unless otherwise necessary, sparing them the burden might well be compassionate...

Giggles burst from Pearl. A duck was racing toward crumbs she had tossed. Pearl glanced toward Celia to confirm an audience, beaming with an innocence Celia had no desire to see end.

Still, she acknowledged, there was a balance to be struck. While riding here on the streetcar, a new splendid machine-powered invention, Pearl had been antsy to explore the transport. Yet with several strangers eyeing her, Celia became acutely aware of her daughter's need for a suitable manner, to not draw attention, to remain unsuspecting.

Always, you must be a proper lady, Celia's mother had insisted from early on, whether discussing posture and manners or studies and diction. *It is essential to be dignified and viewed respectably at all times.*

Pondering the memory, Celia's breath caught. Only in this moment did she suspect a deeper reason for all the years of stringency and lectures.

"Miss Celia?"

She turned to trace the caller. Nearby, in a dusty-rose bustled day dress, the woman held a parasol overhead, its shaft angled upon her shoulder. As her features registered, so did the familiar address she had voiced.

"Abigail," Celia realized.

Abigail tendered a smile, brightening the crystal-blue eyes Celia recognized from a past that, in an instant, felt equally close and distant.

"My, how you've grown. Heavens. How old are you now?"

"Seventeen"—a small shrug—"nearly."

At the time of their last encounter, Pearl was still nestled in Celia's belly. All the same, how did little Abby—with whom Celia used to share hugs, games, and giggles—mature this quickly? "Well, you've certainly become a very lovely woman."

Abigail's cheeks, now defined like her mother's, pinkened with warmth. "Thank you," she said. Her posture too emitted a statuesque quality reflective of Mrs. Bettencourt—a thought that spurred a question of who had accompanied Abigail here.

As ever, Celia dreaded an encounter with Georgia Bettencourt, but perhaps even more with the mayor. She glanced around, wondering if he'd come to the park to deliver a speech, as he was now a candidate in a tight senate race, according to local papers. "You're here today with…others, I presume?"

"I am. Some school friends," Abigail said, and Celia relaxed slightly. "We've heard the German park keeper is crafting a new garden, fashioned after those in Europe. Anyway, I told the girls to go on without me, that I would catch up." She nodded toward the footpath.

There, a couple of young ladies, dressed just as primly and shaded by parasols, were strolling past a cluster of trees and out of view.

"Miss Celia…" Abigail's tone turned hesitant, regaining Celia's focus. "I've intended to come see you. I just wasn't… I didn't think…"

Celia's residence was evidently not a mystery.

"I understand," she offered, even as she recalled that Abigail's parents had been the ones to relegate her to that very home, deeming it fit for even her child, a granddaughter they still refused to claim.

Abigail nodded, though stiffly. "For some time now, in spite of my mother's wishes, I've wanted to speak with you. To share details," she said, "of my brother."

Celia blinked at this, surprised—if less so by the fact that she herself hadn't immediately thought to ask. Preoccupied with motherhood and what had evolved into her normal routine, she'd become mostly resigned to a wait that would last just another year.

Just, she mused before prodding in earnest, "Yes? Go on."

Abigail adjusted her grip on her parasol, suggesting further uncertainty over her phrasing. "Miss Celia, for your own sake, if you haven't yet done so…I implore you to move on with your life, and most especially your heart."

Another unexpected remark. But in this case, the concept was so ludicrous that a laugh escaped Celia's mouth. "Move on?"

Abigail's expression affirmed her sincerity. She believed it was that easy. Clearly her emotional maturity hadn't kept up with that of her physical. Or perhaps her parents had just convinced her that Celia's claims about Stephen were outright false or exaggerated—delusional, at best.

To what was likely meant as a merciful gesture, Celia replied with a simple truth: "Abigail, I'm afraid you cannot possibly relate to my situation."

"Actually, I can," she replied, quick to counter. "At least...to an extent." She angled her face away, though not before revealing in her eyes a somber sheen. Celia had no chance to dissect this, however, for a splashing sound tugged at her ear. Reminded of her surroundings, she jolted at a thought.

Pearl.

Her attention swung toward the pond, to the spot where Pearl had been yet no longer stood. Celia came to her feet and scanned the water. A scattering of ripples sent her pulse into a sprint.

Then she found it. Her daughter's small, precious form.

Squatting by a hedge off to the side, Pearl was tossing bread to a squirrel that was nibbling a morsel in its tiny claws.

Celia released but a short sigh. "Angel, be careful," she called out. "Not too close."

Pearl remained in place, entranced by the bushy-tailed critter.

"Is that—rather, is she..." Abigail stammered in a near whisper. Her gaze too had lit on Pearl.

"My daughter—yes."

Together, they watched Pearl in silence, and it dawned on Celia that she herself wasn't the only one here with a relationship to the child. Abigail was her aunt. In fact, beyond the commonality of their big blue eyes and light-blond curls, Pearl looked uncannily like Abigail as a young girl. Particularly at this age, based on portrait photographs in the Bettencourt home.

Celia was tempted to acknowledge this aloud when Abigail spoke in a low tone, still staring off.

"He's coming home."

The statement eased in slowly at first, then hit with jarring impact. Who else would she be referencing other than Stephen?

But did she mean sooner than planned?

Celia attempted to restrain her hopes. "When?"

Abigail faced her then and visibly swallowed. "July, midway."

"July—as in the coming month?"

After a pause, Abigail gave a nod. "Figuring you might hear the news elsewhere, I was worried that you'd..." She trailed off with reluctance.

Celia sensed where this was going, spiking her indignance as Abigail pushed on.

"I just think it would be best, Miss Celia, if you didn't come around during his stay."

Obviously, the advice was meant to prevent discomfort for her parents. But their embarrassment was inevitable, this time from a confrontation with the undeniable truth.

"Oh, and why is that?" Celia demanded, curious whether Abigail possessed the audacity to verbalize it.

"Because my mother, she... She recently informed me of my brother's engagement."

So Abigail had been kept unaware of his proposal in the barn. Given that she'd uncovered Celia's secret heritage, the girl's prolonged ignorance on the matter struck as unexpected.

Then Abigail added, "She's the daughter of my father's

friend, the American professor who's been teaching at King's College."

Celia failed to follow the comment, thrown off by details of a person seemingly irrelevant to the discussion.

Who is "she"? The query readied to leap off her tongue, until Abigail's news gained clarity. Rendering Celia motionless, it stole the breath clean from her lungs.

"My brother is returning," Abigail finished with a note of sympathy, "to wed."

1888

—

JULY

CHAPTER THIRTY-THREE

Enclosed on a ship—docked on the Willamette presumably—Celia strove for calm despite her daze and confusion. Only slits of natural light aided her visibility.

On the damp planked floor, she pushed herself up to a sitting position. A burlap sack fell away from her body, a blanketlike covering. Where her head had lain was a matching sack but stuffed. Situated like a pillow, it smelled of wool.

Her gaze moved around the dim space too quickly, and her head again began to throb. Its rhythm nearly coincided with the creaking of the room. A cargo hold, it seemed. Loaded with crates. A range of sizes. Stacked like children's building blocks.

There were piles too of the stuffed burlap sacks. Coiled ropes dangled from hooks. They swayed from the rocking of the ship, which would soon be headed for only God knew where. Away from Portland, away from—

Oh mercy. Her beloved Pearl!

From sudden panic, Celia clambered to rise in her bulky boots and scanned for an exit. The crates spanned every wall. There was a hatch on the planked ceiling but much too high to reach.

A rumbling seized her awareness: the sound of an engine. It sent vibrations through the floor.

She needed to disembark, specifically before making it past Astoria and over the bar, before the currents of the Columbia swept her out to the Pacific.

Using a wall for balance, she rounded the nearest crates and spotted two more hatches high above. The smaller of them bore a ladder, bolted in place, near vertical for access.

She worked her way over, staggering against the motion of the floor. At the ladder, she grabbed hold of its rails. She steadied herself only briefly before endeavoring to climb. Dizziness chased her as she ascended, one rung after the other.

Men's voices drifted from outside, muffled, indicating a buffer of distance. An ample one, she hoped.

Once at the top of the ladder, cautiously she pushed the hatch up a mere inch, then another, to test its resistance. Unlocked— thank heavens. She opened it a tad more, daring a peek, yearning for an unobstructed route straight to freedom.

Spread over the length of the ship, which looked to be at least a hundred feet, were ten or so crewmen. All in grubby seamen's attire, they were scrubbing decks, toting lines, managing sails. The enormous sheets of ivory canvas billowed from masts that appeared tall enough to poke holes in the pale-blue sky.

Then came the sight of birds. Below smudges of summer clouds, they flapped their wings and rode the air. Their calls, resembling laughter, suddenly registered as the ones she'd heard but couldn't place. Seagulls, after all, were far more common on the Columbia than locally on the Willamette.

The thought jostled her just as a breeze delivered a touch of salt, both its taste and smell. Her skin prickled more from dread than the wind as she searched frantically for the docks.

Finding none, she feared how far she'd traveled westward on the river. She strained her vision to assess the area surrounding the ship—to her left, her right.

Her stomach plunged.

There was no land to be seen. Just cresting and foaming waves stretched out in every direction.

Walloped by fear, she retreated into the hold and realized she had awoken too late.

She was a hostage already at sea.

1888

—

JUNE

CHAPTER
THIRTY-FOUR

Since the encounter with Abigail a week earlier, Celia had gone through the motions of her daily routine absently, disconnected, as if floating outside herself. Snippets of the news continued to file in and out of her thoughts the way childhood memories drifted back in pieces.

It was to be a short visit, Abigail had said of Stephen's return. To gather his belongings. A stop en route to California. Some city in the southern area, a name Celia didn't know, didn't catch. The origin of the woman's family, a natural location for the wedding. Then back to England he would go, to finish school and to live. Permanently. He with his wife.

His wife.

A cherished title Celia had believed would be hers.

The thought trailed every glimpse she caught of the string still binding her finger. Removing the token would feel like acceptance, even as she imagined Stephen presenting an elegant gemmed band to his newly betrothed, surely a woman of stellar pedigree and worthy heritage.

The added vision of Georgia Bettencourt greeting her with open arms would have ensured reality speared Celia clear through if not for the numbness of her shock. Her mind, after all, was still struggling to reconcile how the sustaining promise she'd clung to for nearly three years, the dream of a future awaiting her and her child—Stephen's child—was but an illusion.

True, she couldn't deny that concerns had clawed at her before he left: that their courtship wouldn't survive the separation, that his acquired worldliness would eventually demand his leaving her behind. But she had dismissed all such notions. Foolish and naive, she'd chosen to believe he loved her enough to wait. Whether he ever loved her at all was suddenly a question with no certainty of an answer. Namely from him.

If she defied Abigail's heeding by descending upon the family home, would Stephen bother to even come to the door? Would his fiancée—another stolen title—be right there with him?

All this time, Celia had pictured her letters tossed in a bin of some London mail room, their lack of specifics labeling them undeliverable. The more likely scenario—that he'd received yet discarded her messages after growing smitten with a new girl—was cause for even greater humiliation than she was prepared to register.

Oh, how she wished the theory was outlandishly dramatic. But his apparent ability to travel back now, a year before completing his degree, not for Celia but for the benefit of another woman, spoke volumes.

And what about Pearl? Where would this leave their young, innocent daughter?

Seated beside her on their bed, Celia stroked Pearl's back in a mindless, habitual rhythm. The child was drifting off for her afternoon nap, breathing in and out peacefully, oblivious yet to the ways her mother had doomed her life.

From the hardships of Celia's childhood and those endured by her parents, Celia should have known better than to believe in a fairy tale and to act on selfish whims. And now Pearl, more than anyone, would be the one to pay. For even if Stephen were to accept her as his own, how would she be treated by all others, including his bride, as anything but a mistake? A bastard child branded as "different."

Lettie barged into the room, ceasing the spiraling of dark thoughts. "Ah, Celia. You just won't believe it."

Celia managed a reflexive shush to prevent waking Pearl.

Obliging, Lettie lowered to a whisper but with a grin widening her lips. "You did it, girl. Whatever you said to him, it worked."

Celia struggled to understand. Fortunately, she needn't explain her jumbled state; days ago, Lettie's questioning from a sense that something was off produced Celia's meager reply: *Stephen's marrying someone else.* Lettie had sat beside her, supportive in silence, empathetic due to her jilted past.

"Who..." Celia began to ask.

"Frank. The fella who confessed to you. He went to the authorities, he did." Lettie padded over with a newspaper and displayed an inner page. "See the proof for yourself."

Celia accepted the offering, careful to minimize any rustling. Her eyes roamed over the print until a headline stopped her.

TRIAL SET FOR MURDERS OF CHINESE MINERS

Mustering her focus, Celia waded through the brief article. Frank Vaughan of Wallowa County had turned state's evidence, it said. His testimony to the grand jury resulted in indictments of the other six gang members for murdering ten Chinese gold miners. As independent laborers under the Sam Yup Company, the victims were allegedly ambushed in their cove encampment, where they had been mining for eight months in the remote canyons of Deep

Creek, locally known as Dead Line Creek. The trial was slated to begin on June 12 in Enterprise, Oregon.

As Celia digested the announcement that just over a week ago would have granted her cathartic relief, she attempted to calculate just how soon the legalities would begin. She could recall only that the current month was June.

"The date—" She regarded Lettie. "What's today's date?"

"Well, it's...the eleventh."

Which meant the trial would start tomorrow.

"And Enterprise, where is that located? Do you know?"

Lettie shrugged. "Nearly as far as Joseph, I think."

Joseph was a town in the far northeastern portion of the state. It made sense for the trial to be held there, given the proximity of the crimes.

"I need to be there," Celia realized.

"There? At the trial, you mean?" Lettie's face pinched with confusion. "But, Celia, that's miles from here."

More than a few, she meant. Indeed, travel would take the better part of a day, requiring round-trip train vouchers in addition to lodging after arrival. With Celia's future so greatly in flux, conserving her accrued savings would be more crucial than ever. Her compulsion to attend, however, to see *this* particular of all missions through, was overwhelming.

And yes, almost as strong was the need for a distraction from her worsened plight, too devastating to yet fully absorb, and the impossible decisions that lay ahead.

First, though, came an imminent, daunting task.

Unless she wished to squander her job as well as her home— the only foreseeable one for her and Pearl—her leave of absence would require permission.

CHAPTER
THIRTY-FIVE

The instant Marie answered her bedroom door, the flushing of her face served as an alert. Wordless in her fastened robe, she stepped away from Celia and settled on her vanity seat. Her slightly drowsy eyes, reflected in her oval mirror, only confirmed Celia's suspicion: She was in the descent of an opium high.

How far down, Celia couldn't yet gauge. Even if at the tail end, it wasn't ideal for a discussion; Marie could be dazed and rambling or nonsensical and combative.

But Celia's window of time was fast shrinking. Marie would soon be preoccupied with a stream of evening customers—no matter her state, somehow she always played the charming hostess—and Celia still needed to prepare for a morning departure, starting with schedules of eastbound trains.

Presuming Marie said yes.

Bolstered by purpose, Celia ventured into the room through wisps of lingering smoke. Although the newspaper remained in her hand, she didn't pause to fan the air. "Marie, if I could trouble you for a favor..."

"Mmm..." It seemed an invitation to continue. A sign of listening at any rate.

Thus, as Marie dabbed on rouge from a tin, Celia delved in by setting the scene for an appeal. Mindful of Marie's attention span, perhaps even more limited than her norm, Celia relayed only the essentials of the case, followed by a mere mention of its personal relevance, being the loss of a dear one in Rock Springs.

A subtle arching of Marie's eyebrow indicated interest, possibly making her receptive.

Celia cut to the conclusion. "I'd therefore be terribly grateful for the opportunity to attend the trial."

Silence reigned as Marie set her cosmetic tin aside. Then she gingerly powdered her neck, presumably mulling over the decision.

Celia needed something to tip the scale. Recalling the article, she moved to stand beside Marie. "There's more information here if you'd care to read—"

Marie waved the paper away. "Go. Finish work," she said and resumed her powdering.

Although the woman possessed a softer side—at least for Pearl, revealed during the child's high fever and since then in affectionate, if furtive, glances—Marie was still Marie. As pressuring her was always a risk, Celia continued gently and with reason.

"Marie, I assure you, you'll scarcely notice I'm gone. As it is, I'd be traveling the first day of the trial. And with one of the guilty men having confessed, I can't imagine it lasting beyond a few days." Her lodging expenses would dictate the same, though she refrained from saying so, not wishing to be accused of wasteful spending. "Should you like, I could even double up on my chores when I'm—"

"*No*," Marie hissed, instantly agitated. "Read verdict in paper."

Her stance couldn't be clearer.

And yet given the case's importance to both society and Celia—including a direct tie in fact—she refused to concede so easily, despite all she could lose.

"One of the murderers confessed to me."

This narrowed Marie's eyes. When she raised them to meet Celia's in the mirror, Celia proceeded to quickly summarize her encounter with Frank behind the inn, how the horror of his tale spurred her to seek him out and press him to come forward.

After taking this in, Marie gradually swiveled in Celia's direction. "Mmm," she said with a nod that seemed promising, until she added, "Of course he do this for *you*." The remark was as bemusing as it was maddening. Did she not believe the claims?

"I'm telling you the truth."

Marie came back firmly, "I not say you lie."

"Well, then…I don't understand." Celia would blame the opium, but Marie was speaking well enough to convey otherwise.

"You think he tell this to *me*? No." She sneered and shifted back to her mirror. "And look, now you are hero."

Celia struggled to determine whether Marie's issue was with credit—if so, absurdly—or with race. But should it be the latter, how could she treat news of the trial and Celia's desire to attend as trifling?

"The miners were Chinese," Celia reminded her, offended—on their behalf or maybe just her own. "I would think you'd be happy, that you'd see this as a good thing."

"Oh, yes. Very happy!" Marie's brightness dripped with sarcasm, reiterated by pats to her chest. "I so grateful to a white woman for helping my people."

Stricken, Celia scraped for a reply. "That's…not fair."

"Not fair—for you?" Marie scoffed, then flicked a nod toward the newspaper Celia still clutched. "This killing not special. Many Chinese killed every day. No reason *you* go to trial." Bitterness filtered into her voice as a flush returned to her skin. Then she touched her temple as if fending off a sudden ache. "Now, go work."

Celia's legs were rooted. Overcome by the frustration of it all—the mistaken assumptions, the endless violence, her own simmering fears and inability to share, the perpetual denial of closure—she felt she might burst from holding in so much for so long. "My father was Chinese," she blurted out. "He was one of the miners murdered in Rock Springs. And *that* is the reason I need to be at this trial—for him. To witness the kind of justice he will never have."

Marie stared at her through the mirror. In the strident quiet, she twisted back to face Celia, and intrigue settled in her eyes, as if assessing not just Celia's features but also pieces of her life. Then something shifted in Marie's gaze, whether favorably or not was yet unclear.

Feeling bare, Celia wanted to run but couldn't. She had just gifted the woman with another layer of control, a secret to wield.

"What of Pearl?" Marie intoned.

Celia wasn't sure why she needed to explain. Naturally, her child too was part Chinese.

But then Marie clarified, "While on trip, what you do with Pearl?"

With the question reframed, Celia strove to collect her thoughts and noted Marie's phrasing: *while*, she'd said, not *if*.

Celia responded with regained composure, "She would come with me, of course."

Marie's expression soured. "On many trains and long hours at trial? You want her hearing talk of killing Chinese?" She *tsked*, blending disapproval and disgust in a single sound. "No," she spat, a nonnegotiable.

Celia went to dispute her—as Pearl's mother, she herself would know best—but Marie's points were valid. Irrefutably so. It had been challenging enough to deliver the mildly worded summary to Officer Glenn in Pearl's presence; the testimonies at trial would be even more gruesome. Furthermore, if any protests broke out like the one in Chinatown, it wouldn't be safe for a child, which meant...

There would be no trip, no witnessing of justice. No closure. Celia's stomach sank, a sharp plunge.

"Pearl stay here," Marie declared. "You will go."

Celia balked at the very idea. Stints of a few hours were the longest they'd been apart, and certainly never overnight. "I...I don't know..."

Marie huffed with impatience, though only lightly. "We care for baby," she said.

Pearl wasn't really a baby anymore—admittedly, another reason to consider the option. Besides, in addition to Marie's skills from other jobs, at an orphanage and as a nanny—albeit both surprisingly yet—she'd proven herself more than capable with Pearl.

"Go to trial," Marie stated. Then, after a pause: "For others."

That word—*others*—had long been shelved in Celia's mind as a label to be feared and avoided. A classification for outsiders, minorities of society, those who didn't belong. But in this moment, combining context with Marie's subdued yet halting tone, it seemed to transform into one of inclusion. *Others* felt like another word for *us*.

While reluctant to leave Pearl, even in the most trusted hands beyond her own, Celia couldn't deny the singular decision to be made.

She agreed.

CHAPTER
THIRTY-SIX

The trial marked the first ever held for a murder case in Wallowa County. In a brick building at the center of town, a bank encompassed the main floor, and above it, adjacent to the offices of the sheriff and other county officials, awaited the teeming courtroom. Though Celia's knowledge of trials was limited to stories and articles, the apprehension she discovered there aligned with the expected. Murmurs pervaded the morning air, thick with pipe smoke, as she strove to find a seat.

Her previous day of travel—trains and transfers, tedious waits in between, and at last a wagon ride from the final depot—had wearied her to the bone, only to end with a tiny, rented room bearing walls thin as thread and a raucous saloon just below. Not that she would have otherwise enjoyed a restful night of sleep. Nerves and impatience, from both the case and missing Pearl, had been coursing through her ever since departing. And news from her curmudgeonly driver had further magnified her trepidation.

Once charged with murder, three of the gang members had turned tail and run, he'd said. Following Celia's initial pang of disappointment, she assured herself that the fugitives would eventually be found, and anyway all the others involved—except for Frank, due to his confession—were already standing trial. For now, that was enough.

It had to be.

"Need a seat, honey?" A plump, older lady in a plaid bonnet offered a gentle smile. On a bench just off the center aisle, she scooted over and patted the widened vacancy. Freckles dotted her fair skin.

"Thank you, ma'am." Celia smiled back. Only then did she note a voluntary division of seating in the room. The majority of white attendees, including those surrounding her, dominated at least the front half of the room; Chinese faces spanned the back.

In light of the gathering's purpose, for the first time to her memory, she yearned for a spot that straddled the border.

"Another long day ahead, I reckon," the woman said with a sigh.

Celia absorbed the remark, having just settled beside her. "You attended yesterday?" As the wagon driver had no updates from the trial, she asked in earnest, "Was there much that I missed?"

"Oh, jury selection took up most the morning. Ran into a pool shortage to start, with all the witnesses not being able to serve. Once that got sorted, there was opening statements. A few testimonies about family histories and character. So far, no surprises."

"Well," Celia said, aware of the brutal depictions to come, wanting to prepare her, "I imagine that could change..."

A bump to the shoulder turned Celia toward the middle aisle. Weaving past was a young man in a suit—notable, given his age of no more fifteen. Two other fellows—one appearing in his latter teens, the other in his thirties and with dense facial hair—followed in his wake, both also in suits befitting the country more than the city. The brisk way people were stepping aside to clear a path made the trio's roles unmistakable.

These were the accused.

Celia must have reacted with a sound, because the neighboring woman gave her arm a tender pat.

"Don't you fret now. In the end, the law—like the Lord—is good."

Celia nodded gratefully before wondering with dread: Was the woman rooting against the killers or for them?

———

The trial procedures for the day promptly commenced. Any attendee lacking a seat remained standing, lining the gallery. A scattering of ladies fluttered fans due to the warmth of the crammed space. Parked at the defendants' table, the youngest of them—Robert, Celia deduced—gazed out the window at the lush pastures and farmland that stretched southward to the Wallowa Mountains, surely lamenting his freedoms soon to end.

Likewise on display in their designated seats were the judge, a jury of twelve, and the opposing counsels—the district attorney, acting as prosecutor, and a whole team of defense attorneys, one each for the three accused in the room. All were white men boasting a mustache, if not also a beard, as well as stern looks apt for the occasion.

When cued by Judge Isom, a middle-aged man with a sturdy build, the prosecutor came to his feet. "Good day, Your Honor. If it pleases the court, the state hereby calls Frank Vaughan to the stand."

Whispers rolled through the room like tumbleweeds common to the surrounding high-desert region. The judge banged his gavel twice to restore order. From one of the foremost benches, Frank emerged with hat gripped at his side.

This was the first Celia had seen of him since the barn. Now on the stand and guided by a clerk, he took an oath on the Bible to speak the truth, and Celia found herself conflicted.

It couldn't have been easy for him to testify before the grand jury, specifically resulting in charges against his friends. Given his own part in the crimes, however, his apparent immunity left her ill at ease—ironically so, as she herself had baited him with the possibility of leniency.

As he lowered himself onto the witness chair, she consciously tapered her thoughts: *All else aside, ultimately, he was doing what it took to make things right.* In a world darkened by inequality and wrongs, one had to bask in the small rays of justice when they came, despite their rarity.

Rather for precisely that reason.

The prosecutor adjusted the spectacles on the bridge of his broad nose and glanced at the page of notes in his hand. "To begin, Mr. Vaughn, please tell the court all you know about the killing of some Chinamen on Snake River in Wallowa County, Oregon, approximately one year ago."

Frank's gaze ricocheted between the prosecutor and the jury as if uncertain where to direct his reply, no doubt also avoiding the wrath of his friends' eyes. "As nearly as I can recollect"—opting to address the attorney, he projected with a formal quality—"it occurred the last of May. The seven of us was staying at a cattle camp, about a day's ride from Imnaha."

"By the party of seven, you are referring to Bruce Evans, J. Titus Canfield, and Omar LaRue as well as the defendants present today"—he gestured to their table—"Robert McMillan, Hiram Maynard, and Hezekiah 'Carl' Hughes. Is that accurate?"

"It is, yes."

"And Imnaha is where you attended school with two of the defendants?"

"That'd be Robert and JT—yes, sir."

"Thank you. Please go on."

Frank opened his mouth to continue just as his gaze caught on Celia, and his words stalled. Her presence was unexpected.

On sheer reflex, she raised her chin toward him in acknowledgment, if only fractional.

"Mr. Vaughan, you were saying?" The prosecutor stepped closer to the stand.

Refocusing, Frank steered clear of Celia's eyes. "Bright 'n' early," he said, dropping his volume a notch, "the bunch of us loaded up and proceeded to ride for Snake River Canyon. We were taking some of Blue's horses to sell to the army."

"'Blue' being a familiar name for Bruce Evans, correct?"

"Yes, that's right—sorry."

"And those horses were, in fact, among the very ones for which he and JT Canfield have been charged with rustling, I presume."

Mutters arose from the jurors, their head shakes further expressing disapproval. The crime of stealing livestock by altering the animal's brand was a severe one, in rural areas even more.

"I—I don't know if those were them *specifically*," Frank insisted.

The prosecutor pinned on a knowing smile. Should Frank say he had been aware at the time, he'd become an admitted accomplice—for a separate offense.

"A matter for another trial," the attorney replied, and Frank nodded with a dash of relief. "What happened then?"

"Then, well..." He straightened as if resuming proper decorum. "We encountered some trouble crossing the river. This resulted in a loss of several of the horses. A band of Chinamen were camped nearby, over in a cove at Dead Line Creek. They were mining on the gravel bar and had a boat in their possession. Then Blue—Bruce, I mean—trekked over and requested to borrow it to help get the horses across. When the Chinamen refused, Bruce became very agitated."

Celia was puzzling over the accrual of unfamiliar details when the prosecutor responded, "I daresay that's understandable, on account of what seems a reasonable request."

So absurd was the comment that Celia half expected him to cap it with an eye roll. How was it *understandable* for a stranger to commandeer a vessel essential to a mining group's livelihood? In a reversal of roles, no chance would the same view hold.

But then, from the prosecutor's conversational style, it occurred to her: he could be aiming to gain Frank's trust. Maybe that of the jury too.

"And what did all of you gentlemen do next?"

"We returned to the cabin. To hunker down for the night."

"Were there any plans made at that time regarding the Chinamen?"

Frank paused, the line of questioning gaining greater weight. "I...do not recollect exactly—that is, not to my recollection. I recall only that there was a discussion—by Bruce Evans, JT Canfield, and Omar LaRue—about returning to Dead Line Creek. I did not figure there was any killing to be done, just that we would again attempt to get the boat."

From his choice of language to his use of their names, the answer bore a stilted quality; it struck Celia as memorized and rehearsed. For a murder trial, perhaps that wasn't uncommon, as every word could be vital. But much more worrisome was his reiteration of the boat being the goal. Not a single mention of the gold and a desire to play so-called Robin Hoods.

"So then you all went back there?" the prosecutor asked.

"In the morning—yes, sir. But not with the whole party. Hiram Maynard and Carl Hughes"—Frank tipped his head toward the older defendants, appearing to make eye contact—"stayed in the cabin. To cook us up some breakfast."

"What happened when you approached the Chinese camp again?"

"JT and Omar, they went up on the hillside. Bruce stayed below. I remained down there as well but a ways off and close to Robert, who was watching the horses."

"That's when the shooting of the Chinamen happened?"

"Yes, sir."

"How far away were the two of you from the place of the killing?"

"Around three hundred yards, I would say."

"Did Mr. McMillan do any shooting?"

"No, sir, none at all," Frank said pointedly, sliding the kid a look.

"Did you and Robert go to the actual campsite?"

"We did. Yes."

"What was done by the gang after you got there?"

From the grisly scene Frank had painted in Celia's mind, she could still see the slain miners, stripped of not just their clothing but every shred of their dignity, even after death.

"I did not go to the camp till *after* the shooting," Frank clarified, not yet answering. "Same as Robert."

"*After* the shooting then, what did you see at the camp?"

"We saw four or five dead Chinamen."

"Were there ten dead in total?"

"There might have been. I couldn't be sure."

Celia's hands balled up on her lap. He hadn't sounded unsure in the least when he confessed to her.

In contrast, the prosecutor started to pace quite casually. "What occurred next?"

"We all returned to the cabin again. Then the next morning, it was just Bruce, JT, and Omar who rode off for the day."

"What reason did they give for leaving?"

"They said they was planning to go back and burn all the clothes and other belongings. And to throw the...the rest of, well, the evidence in the river."

"The corpses, you mean?"

Celia cringed. They were people, innocent victims. *Corpses* made them inhuman—the way Frank claimed to have viewed them until it was too late. In fact, hadn't he told her that he'd assisted with the acts of disposal that were nearly as horrifying? Yet now it was only a story he'd heard?

"Yes," Frank replied more quietly.

"But they were interrupted—is that right? By a boat of other Chinese miners who were happening by?"

The whirring of Celia's thoughts halted, diverted by a new reference that seemed already established in the trial.

"To my knowledge, yes."

"How many did you hear were in the boat?"

"Eight, I believe."

"And Mr. Evans, Mr. Canfield, and Mr. Hughes then killed them too?"

Celia gawked at Frank in anticipation of the response.

"Just according to what I heard," he stressed, "that is correct."

Celia covered her mouth in shock, but not before her lungs pulled in a sharp breath.

A few heads twisted her way, only then to turn back—except for one. Several rows ahead, a fellow with pockmarked cheeks continued to stare. He was the man Celia had suspected to be one of the murderers—evidently not so, but when his recognition of her face plainly set in, his gaze turned piercing.

A sudden touch to Celia's lap gave her a start. It was a pat for comfort from the neighboring woman, accompanied by a solemn look. Celia glanced back at the scarred man, but he'd returned his attention to the prosecutor, who pressed on with his questioning.

"Mr. Vaughan, what were you told happened next?"

"I was told they got rid of the bodies, then rode the boat to another Chinese camp about four miles away."

"And they did the same to the Chinamen there?"

A weighty pause. "Yes."

Celia felt a numbness coming on, as it was all too much to take in.

"How many did they say there were mining at this spot?"

Frank mumbled his answer.

"Could you please repeat that?"

"'Bout fifteen."

Ten…eight…fifteen…

Celia couldn't think well enough to calculate but sensed a sum of around thirty. Behind her, she vaguely detected the sounds of shallow breaths. A sideways glimpse traced the source to several Chinese women battling their emotions, restraining their sobs.

Meanwhile, the prosecutor referred again to his notes in a level manner. Obviously, the information wasn't new to him and murders fell within his usual scope; still, his show of acceptance only made the moment more wrenching.

"After your return to the cabin," he said, "did you discuss the killings with anyone in the party?"

"No," Frank declared, "I did not." Then, again in a practiced tone: "To the best of my knowledge, both Hiram Maynard and Carl Hughes knew nothing of the circumstances before or after the killings. Likewise, they—the same as Robert McMillan—had no means of preventing the affair."

The prosecutor nodded as if expecting the response. At last, Celia realized the attorney himself could have shaped Frank's retelling to fit their immunity agreement.

"Permit me then to ask you this…" As if readying for a culminating query, the prosecutor planted himself before the stand. "Were you a witness before the grand jury that indicted the men for this very trial? The men accused of the killings that took place at Dead Line Creek?"

"I was—yes."

"Why, therefore, did you implicate the defendants in this courtroom back then but not now?"

"Well, I didn't," Frank argued. "That is, I didn't implicate them any more than I have today."

A preposterous claim. If he hadn't accused all six of participating, how would the grand jury have ever charged them? The blatant contradiction was ripe for the prosecutor to pounce upon and force out the truth—finally.

"Mr. Vaughan, one last question."

No. No, wait—*that was it?* He was moving on?

Celia wanted to scream in protest. But to whom?

"Is there a reason you waited so long to make the entirety of this matter known?"

"Indeed, there is," Frank asserted. "Because of the parties who did the killin'—Bruce, JT, and Omar—being real desperate men."

With the spotlight of blame directed solely, conveniently, at the three on the run, Celia came to understand why the remaining defendants hadn't fled along with them: they'd well known they had nothing to fear.

Again, the youngest was peering out the window.

Celia was wrong, as it turned out, about his reason for gazing at the serene pastures and mountains that lay beyond the glass. Smugly comforted, he was admiring the freedom he stood no chance of losing.

"Thank you, Mr. Vaughan," the prosecutor said as Celia's heart dropped to an immeasurable depth. "I have nothing further."

CHAPTER
THIRTY-SEVEN

Long before the final witness spoke, far prior to the lawyers' closing arguments, the verdict became a foregone conclusion.

If Frank's testimony—requiring no cross-examination—hadn't made that excruciatingly clear, those of the defendants in the courtroom provided ample confirmation. Each took the stand separately, but outside of highlighting their families' communal roots—as original pioneers and homesteaders, a devoted teacher, and even a doctor turned judge—they could have testified in unison, for their answers involving the massacre weren't merely aligned; some of their verbiage was an identical match.

That they would deliberately bear false witness after swearing on the Good Book was an astonishing thing. There appeared to be no limit to the despicable nature of some.

As for the additional witnesses called upon to speak, none proved impactful to the case—for either side. Not even the rancher who owned the cabin. Having neither observed nor overheard the gang's activities at the hideout, he instead described finding, with his son, bodies washed up on gravel bars and lodged in rocks deep in the canyon, much of the flesh picked clean by coyotes or buzzards. Similar testimonies from the stand only solidified the irrefutable: that dozens of Chinese miners had been slaughtered by perpetrators who'd attempted yet failed to hide all the evidence.

Nevertheless, out of respect for the victims and their families, for the countless others akin to them, and yes, out of a vexing hope for the minuscule chance that the jurors would see through the coordinated lies of the accused, Celia remained in town a second night to hear the outcome firsthand.

—

In the silence of the courtroom, muted rays of morning light dimmed the judge's pallor as he turned in his seat toward the jury. "Mr. Green, what say you?"

All went still. No fluttering of fans. No puffing on pipes.

The lean foreman, with his mild slouch, appeared to push against the weight of anticipation as he rose. From the note in his hands, he read: "In the Circuit Court of the State of Oregon for the County of Wallowa, in the case of the State of Oregon versus Hiram Maynard and Robert McMillan and Hezekiah 'Carl' Hughes—implicated with defendants J. Titus Canfield, Bruce Evans, and Omar LaRue—we the jury in the above-entitled action hereby find the defendants Mr. Maynard, Mr. McMillan, and Mr. Hughes...*not* guilty."

Cries of devastation collided with exclamations of joy. The judge banged his gavel and demanded order as the more subdued in the gallery, including the plain-bonneted woman, murmured prayers of thanks to the Almighty and pleas that the "true killers" would soon receive their due.

Celia's stomach roiled so fiercely she feared she might retch. The feeling did anything but dwindle on the wagon ride back to the depot. While the bumps and sways of the road were no help, the greater cause was the driver's insight about predicting the verdict from the start.

Apparently, in the lead-up to the trial, the three now-acquitted defendants had been released on bail due to a petition signed by a score of local men. Strangely—astoundingly—at least one of them had been on the very grand jury that had issued the charges.

The flagrant conflict jarred Celia, though nothing should have at this point. Not after the prosecutor's paltry cross-examinations. Repeatedly, he'd failed to challenge inconsistencies nor home in on any ambiguous or odd answers. And what about the gold?

Frank had explicitly told her the miners' windfall was a chief motivator for the attack, yet the prosecutor barely grazed the topic.

Throughout Celia's return train rides and transfers, this peculiarity among others swelled in her mind, an unreachable itch. Sure, the fugitives might have spirited away the gold, but the rest of the gang would have had access to it before then, likely keeping a share for themselves.

The longer she considered the combination of elements, the more probable it seemed that the precious metals had somehow contributed to how the trial played out—from the apparent reversal of Frank's testimony to the grand juror's incongruence to the prosecuting attorney's dubious approach.

Once she'd boarded the last of her trains, logic and intuition firmly supported the theory that bribery was involved. Paired with threats perhaps. Some form of corruption anyhow.

By the time the locomotive delivered Celia to Portland, she was certain. And fuming.

She disembarked at the depot, the handle of her valise tight in her gloved grip. Evening light was fast dissolving into darkness. Amplified by the quiet, the despairing sobs from the courtroom still reverberated in her ears.

As much as she wished to retreat to the comfort of her bed and curl up with Pearl, rest would be impossible until she made even the smallest effort to stop the perpetual cycle of madness. Of brutality. Of evil.

Once more recalling her dismissal by Officer Glenn, she had no illusions of initiating remedial actions on her own. But there was someone who could. And this time around, when standing before him, she'd refuse to let him ignore her and turn away.

CHAPTER
THIRTY-EIGHT

The cool night air crept into Celia's overcoat, although for her mood, she barely felt the chill. Through the moonlit shadows before the Bettencourt home, she veered from her habitual path to the servants' entrance, clutching her travel bag, and marched straight to the front door.

Two rounds of interspersed poundings with the knocker summoned a greeter. Miss Waterstone. The lit kerosene lamp she carried accentuated her familiar glower but with added creases of bewilderment.

"Miss Hart," she said. "Paying an unsolicited call at such an hour is highly inappropriate."

It was late. Past nine, if Celia had to guess.

A trivial concern.

"I've come to speak with the mayor."

Miss Waterstone huffed, exasperated. "I believe the Bettencourts have made it quite plain to you—"

"This is of an urgent legal matter. And I will not leave until he sees me."

The woman flinched, surprised by Celia's resolve. She was no longer the meek girl who'd been forced to slink away, even willing to return with hands cupped, begging for a crumb of help.

After a pensive moment, Miss Waterstone's expression eased, but just a smidge. "Wait here." Her commanding tone made clear she was agreeing strictly to try. Then she shut the door.

With the passing of seconds, then minutes, stoked by pride and the bitter notion of relying again on the Bettencourts' whims, Celia's festering anger grew. Not just toward the mayor and his wife but at Stephen. For his betrayal. For not having the decency to at least write and rescind his offer.

In truth, she was just as angry at herself for trusting him enough to believe in the fairy tale. How foolish she had been to refuse Timothy's proposal, which, at minimum, promised a decent life for Pearl.

The door reopened. Miss Waterstone stood alone. "He'll see you in the den."

Celia gave a nod, too agitated to be thankful, and proceeded into the house.

"Follow me," the woman said after closing the door.

As if Celia could have somehow forgotten her way.

She sealed her lips, preventing a quip to that effect, and allowed Miss Waterstone to take the lead. In the lamplit foyer, eyes stared from framed images on the surrounding walls. Celia slowed only enough to set aside her valise.

As she continued on, a reminiscent wave rushed in. Two years ago, Miss Waterstone had similarly led her to the mayor, but to learn of her father's death. Another savagery unpunished. Why she now needed to fight.

At the doorway of the den, Miss Waterstone paused for Celia to enter alone.

Orange flames crackled in the mantled hearth as she stepped

inside. The cozy room, with its ceiling-high shelves of leather-bound texts suffused with history and knowledge, had been Celia's favorite, even before it drew her and Stephen together. The ivory chess pieces still glinted on the table flanked by a pair of chairs, on which they'd spent countless nights laughing, playing, talking. And soon he would be back in this room, though with another.

The door shut, halting the thought—gratefully.

She turned to find the mayor seated at his imposing desk, where a candle illuminated piles of paperwork. Coatless, he wore his sleeves rolled to his elbows. Ink blackened his fingers from the pen he now placed at an angle in its holder.

"Please." He gestured to one of the matching tufted chairs a few feet from the desk, but Celia was far too edgy to sit.

"I would prefer to stand, thank you."

He leaned back with a look of intrigue, also seeming to detect a change in her. Not long ago, that recognition would have been satisfying.

She dove straight in. "I've just returned from the town of Enterprise. I attended a murder trial there—rather, a sham of one. Which is the reason I am here."

"Ah... Yes." He nodded. "The Chinese gold-dust miners."

She balked over how fast the news had spread. "You know, then, that the three were found innocent?"

He sighed and shook his head regretfully. "I hadn't yet heard. Though I confess I would have speculated as much." While his disappointment was welcome, genuine as it appeared, it would mean nothing without action.

"There needs to be an investigation."

He cocked his head, perplexed. "Into the murders?" he said. "But this must have occurred already for there to have been charges—"

"Into the trial," she corrected. "The grand jurors, the witnesses—Frank Vaughan in particular—and the prosecutor most of all. They need to be questioned. Once the corruption is rooted out, I presume the defendants could be retried fairly."

After a beat, the mayor leaned forward, elbows on his desk. "Celia, it's understandable for you to be distraught, given the most unfortunate business with your father."

Unfortunate business? She almost laughed. One might think her father had run a lumber mill or a shipping company that failed.

"He was *murdered*." The mayor apparently needed a reminder. "Same as the miners at Dead Line Creek. And unless something is done, just as before, the killers will continue roaming free." A mockery of a trial, as it turned out, was worse than no trial at all. "I was there, in that courtroom, and witnessed it myself. The whole process reeked of impropriety." Compelled, she added, "I'd wager my life on it."

The vow wasn't meant lightly, which his eyes confirmed that he grasped. When he glanced away, the fire's glow highlighted a look of unease. "Celia," he said before dragging his gaze back to hers, "even if your suspicions are entirely valid, what would you have me do? I'm not a judge or a lawyer and certainly not an investigator."

She strode forward, unwittingly heartened. "But you know men who are. Or ones who have the connections to effectively examine the matter. Politicians. Reporters. If enough of a ruckus is made, those in power will have no choice but to address it." Even Sylvester Pennoyer, now as the governor, could be forced to act contrarily to his racist rhetoric.

The mayor sat back again, vacillating. At last, he nodded, a ruling made. "It's all a tremendous tragedy, and I very much want to help." Sincerity carried his tone, but not without a hedge; a caveat was coming. "With the election approaching—a rather tight one at present—I'm afraid my abilities are highly limited until it's over. However," he added warmly, "if everything goes as hoped, I will soon be in a position to better pursue the issue."

His senatorial election was only a few months away, yet measured by the attention span of modern society, that translated to a lifetime. By then—notwithstanding the loved ones of the victims—people would have moved on. There would be new murders and crimes and outrages, all guaranteed to likewise pass without consequence.

"No," Celia snapped. Her tone was unplanned though unregretted. "This cannot wait. It must be handled *now*."

Based on the abrupt thinning of the mayor's lips, he wasn't in agreement nor intrigued any longer by her fortitude. His response turned curt. "Clearly the trial has clouded your judgment and made you irrational."

Irrational? More aptly cast-off and patronized. The combination scorched her restraint.

"In other words, I need to be obedient and quiet and not cause trouble—for your family above all, heaven forbid."

She had long believed silence was the best way to protect herself and, more recently and crucially, her daughter. But what if, in the larger scheme of things, the opposite was true? Even if Pearl never learned of her Oriental lineage, the fact remained that this trial, these injustices, pertained to her.

And so Celia charged on.

"You know in your heart this is the right thing to do, and yet you're too cowardly to offend those you call *friends*. Like the governor and Gordon Humphrey. Despicable thugs full of hate and deficient of morality."

The mayor's posture stiffened in his chair, his skin flushing.

"The *gentlemen* you've named are supporters. Significant ones. And I need to remain in the favor of each if I am to win this race."

The race. His primary worry. In the role of mayor, he used to be driven by a desire to serve—a key word he'd often cited—and improve the lives of others, those of Chinese heritage included. But he'd since become consumed with climbing the political ladder, not caring who was stepped on during the ascent. How many injustices, how many slain immigrants, would it take?

How much hypocrisy?

"I do wonder," Celia mused, "how strong of supporters they'd be if aware of the truth. Namely that your own grandchild is *tainted* with Chinese blood?"

He stared, and his nostrils flared. "You...you have no proof of that."

Aside from Pearl's existence, he wasn't wrong.

Or was he? The family portraits she'd passed on her way in supplied a reminder.

"Only if you blatantly disregard the physical resemblance. No doubt Abigail's photographs at Pearl's age make quite the case." Boosted by his continued fluster, she added, "If not you, surely your opposing candidate would take keen interest in such a thing."

The mayor shot to his feet, and for a second, it appeared he might lunge. Celia tensed just as he bellowed toward the door. "Miss Waterstone!"

Almost immediately, the door opened. She'd waited nearby. "Sir?"

Seething, the mayor pinned Celia with a glare. "See our guest out."

This wasn't at all what she had come to do—blast it! Whether salvaging the situation was possible or even if she wished to, she couldn't say. She therefore seized the most rational option:

she turned with chin raised and reversed her path in Miss Waterstone's wake.

They were passing through the foyer when Celia slowed to retrieve her valise. As she grabbed the handle, the sense of an onlooker drew her focus upward. On the stairwell landing, in a long silken French robe, stood Georgia Bettencourt.

How greatly Celia had longed at one time for her acceptance. For even a semblance of care, to someday be treated as family.

Now Mrs. Bettencourt simply peered down at Celia—the woman's forte—saying nothing and everything all at once.

Good riddance, Celia said in her mind and left the Bettencourt house, decidedly for the very last time.

CHAPTER
THIRTY-NINE

"Ah, Celia. There you are." Lettie's usually welcomed voice came from behind. "There's somethin' I need to share with you."

At the kitchen counter, with flour specks lingering in the late-afternoon light, Celia stilled her hands on the dough. She grumbled to herself despite her friend's good intentions. For the past four days, in futile attempts to lighten Celia's mood—over the trial and mayor, much less Stephen—Lettie had been relaying amusing tales about her regulars. Like all Marie's girls, she'd assigned secret nicknames: "Jabbering Justin," who incredibly spoke through *every* waking act; "Rowdy Ricardo," the rambunctious Spaniard; and several others with adjectives worthy of a blush.

But for now, with Pearl off drawing with some of the ladies in the parlor, Celia yearned for a moment of meditative kneading to block out all the thoughts and feelings that could otherwise overwhelm her.

"I'm sure it's quite the story," she replied without turning, "but really, if you wouldn't mind waiting..."

Either not hearing or flat out ignoring her, Lettie continued at a rambling pace.

"I know you've been awful distressed about the courtroom

shenanigans and all. So I...I took the liberty of asking round, starting with the local old-timers, the real gossipmongers. And then there was my usual customers, placing special attention on the miners and ranchers, even a lawyer—for any possible connections, you see. After all, once fellas get the drink in 'em, some'll even confess where their penny jars are buried."

Or they could confess far worse.

Celia withheld the dark, useless comment and proceeded to knead the dough.

"My point is," Lettie went on, "I didn't uncover anything more about the trial in and of itself, but, well, I did manage to gather some stunning news nonetheless."

As the words sank in, Celia's hands slowed but didn't stop. Braced by cynicism, she offered only a blithe "Oh?"

Lettie's steps brought her closer. "There's a fella—Owen's his name—says he knows where the missing killers are hiding out. After we got to chattin' about it, he decided he's going to ride out there and try to snatch the gold for himself."

Celia faced her finally—out of incredulity, not interest. "He told you all of that? And you believe him?" She didn't intend to be demeaning, but Lettie well knew how deceitful men and their stories could be.

"He swears it's the truth. Been a customer awhile, paying me visits more and more. Says he wants the funds so he can make me his bride." She added in haste, "Sure, you must think me daft after being hoodwinked before. But I believe him, Celia. When he says he loves me, he means it. Trust me, I know the difference."

Celia had to admit, precisely because of the past, Lettie wasn't one to be gullible; she was skeptical and shrewd, which made it difficult now to discount her claims.

"You're not daft in the slightest." She reached out and squeezed

Lettie's hand. Noting her own coated in flour, she almost reflexively let go but then remembered the way it had added a layer of comfort to her mother's hands, roughened from cooking and washing and scrubbing. From a reality that had also failed to be a fairy tale.

Not that Lettie's outcome was destined to be the same.

Celia prayed it wasn't.

"You'll make a lovely bride," she insisted. "And you deserve to be happy."

Lettie hesitated before edging out a nod, and emotion moistened her eyes. She angled her face aside, leaving Celia's mind to linger. On news of the hideout in particular.

It was a foolish thing to consider. Raising her hopes over just about anything anymore verged on pitiable, but...what if...

What if this fellow really knew where the killers lurked? Would Celia be the one this time to let them get away?

She crossed her arms tightly, feeling torn. While her faith in the legal system was meager, she couldn't deny that the trial had built a strong case against the fugitives. Their rustling charges alone threatened prison time that would likely, if appallingly, be longer than those for the massacre. If the three men were captured, their testimonies, perhaps with new evidence, might even land the whole gang behind bars.

"Lettie..." she said. "This fellow of yours—Owen—could you get him to tell you the specific location of the hideout?"

Drawn back to the original topic, Lettie turned toward her and appeared to reset. "I tried to, of course. All he'd share is that it's in Idaho Territory. But then an idea came to me—one that'd be safer for him and with a higher chance of success for all. I told him what you said, about the mayor seeming sympathetic yet the election taking priority. So I suggested Owen offer a trade."

"A trade? How do you mean?"

"I figured the mayor might be willing to pay for details of the like. If he was able to nab the fugitives with a group of lawmen, the publicity might gain him a nice number of votes."

Celia cringed at the thought of him touting credit—worst of all, capitalizing on the murders—though both, she supposed, would be secondary if they led to rightful punishments.

"And? What did Owen say?"

"He was reluctant, I'm afraid, thinking the gold might be well worth the risk. Which is why," Lettie stressed, "you need to convince him yourself."

Celia strained to understand. "Why would he listen to *me*?"

"Because I told him all about you. How you're likely the reason there was ever a trial, only to have it end so wrongly. Also that you know the mayor personally, so that maybe, if needed, you could ensure the mayor agreed."

As if Celia would ever be allowed to approach the mayor again or that she possessed any real swaying power over him. Based on his recent silence and inaction, he'd recognized her threats for what they were: empty. For her to even suggest creating a scandal centered on her own daughter had been lowly and selfish, a fact she loathed to dwell upon.

"I'll think it over—later." She sighed. At present, she wanted to merely finish the dough in peace. She was rotating toward the counter when a hand on her elbow halted her.

"But he'll be ridin' out at dawn, he said."

The implication was jolting. "You're telling me I'm too late?"

"Not if you talk with him tonight." Lettie's tone, its near-desperate level of hope, even more than the timeline, eliminated the opportunity to debate. As if the choice was ever actually in question.

Besides, what harm could come of simply speaking to the man?

"You know where he is?"

Lettie nodded but then shrugged. "Where he'll be anyway. A place over in Chinatown."

"But...I have Pearl. And you're working tonight."

"You can just go after she's drifted off. Although she sleeps like a log, I'll gladly keep checkin' on her. Marie won't mind. Got a soft spot for that little one, she does."

All were true points, giving Celia no reason not to concede, save for one.

"Except it's Chinatown. Venturing there at night..." Out of caution and lack of need, it was something she'd yet to do.

"Sounds a bit daunting, I know. But I've done it myself. You'd be surrounded by loads of people. After a quick chat with the fellow, you'd be back in a wink. Ah—also, I've got something sure to protect you."

The immediate thought of an object most used for protection, possibly left by a customer, caused Celia to tense. "If it's a gun, I have positively no interest." Weapons of the like already caused too much death and despair.

"Oh, no, 'tis nothing like that," Lettie said. "Just a special outfit to wear."

At the peculiar reply, Celia recalled the fancy dress and wig Lettie had lent her eons ago for their prance through the boutiques in town. "A disguise, you mean?"

Lettie's lips curved partly up. "Come to my room," she said, "and I'll explain."

CHAPTER FORTY

Dusky light draped the city like a cloak. At least Celia preferred to believe it did, for as she entered Chinatown with chin tucked and shoulders hunched, she felt rather bare despite the layers of her facade.

Lettie was right about the number of people on the streets at even this late hour. Celia could only hope her friend's assurances were as accurate regarding the theatrical glue she'd helped apply—specifically to secure a short, brown wig and a matching beard and mustache. Lettie had claimed the paste was harmless and removable yet impressively strong. There had been no warning, however, of its itching effect from drying.

Then again, the issue might lie more in the tickling nature of hair. Real hair, in this case.

A regular patron of the inn, a barber in an apparent struggle with his attraction to men, had crafted the accessories for Lettie to wear during his visits. He'd also provided her with a brimmed hat, chambray shirt, vest, and trousers—all smelling of tobacco yet fitting Celia relatively well—whereas the boots and overcoat were from a drunken customer who'd departed free of outerwear.

When Lettie first pulled out the disguise, Celia had laughed.

She'd figured her friend was teasing until Lettie specified that Owen would be found in a gambling den. Then Celia understood, as only men were allowed in such places. While the illegality of the vice was of little concern, with the related laws rarely enforced thanks to payoffs, she found the idea of passing for a man—even a relatively young one, given her build—utterly ludicrous. But Lettie was insistent. Thus, with doubts—and while retaining her own knee-length bloomers, of course—Celia had allowed the attempted transformation.

The result was startling.

So altered was her appearance in the vanity mirror, she'd shifted her arms and legs instinctively to confirm the movements were hers. In fact, caught up in the amusement of preparing for a role—a nightly specialty of Lettie's—Celia had briefly forgotten about the task ahead. The weight of it, the challenge. As an absolute stranger to this man, she was to persuade him into abandoning his quest for a jackpot or at least to disclose the hideout details first. For while she wouldn't voice this to Lettie, logic told her that once he'd left for his trip, odds were high he would never return.

—

With her gait at shoulder width to feign masculinity—in sheer opposition to her upbringing—the farther Celia treaded, the more aware she became of an unusual response from gentlemen in passing. No whistles, no leers. No vulgar remarks. The refreshing invisibility bolstered her confidence, giving her a sense of how men navigated through the world, and she found herself walking a bit taller.

Above a series of storefronts, decorative lanterns swayed from a light breeze that again tickled the hairs on her face. Striving to leave them be, she went to pocket her hands but stopped. Best not to risk rubbing away their dirt, transferred from a potato to veil their feminine nature. If one could even say that of her roughened fingers and calloused palms.

At the next corner, a wooden awning featured the sign she sought:

LEE TAO, MERCHANT TAILOR

Following Lettie's instructions—based on details from her fellow—Celia snaked through the stream of people to reach the shop. Unlike the nondescript door that led to the opium parlor, there was no daunting peep-through to gain admission, just flickering lamps illuminating the windows. Even so, to bar any second thoughts, she entered without pause.

A variety of fabrics spanned the walls of shelves. Seated behind the counter with a measuring ribbon draping his shoulders, a lone Chinese man in bifocals read a book propped low. He raised only his eyes.

Celia prepared to speak as rehearsed. Guttural tone, clipped words. "Shop open?"

He surveyed her for just a moment. "It is running," he murmured. Then he tipped his head toward the back of the store and returned to his book, an apparent signal to proceed. Easy as that. Almost oddly so.

She had passed her first test as a man—evidently one who looked primed to lose money.

It occurred to her only then that she should have brought a handful of coins in case wagers were required for entry.

Too late for that now.

She plodded through the room and down an adjacent stairwell. In the dim basement at the bottom, she continued to a far brick wall to reach what appeared to be a closet door made of steel, as described.

She took a breath, reminding herself that being turned away was the worst that could happen.

Applying a fist, she pounded twice. As she waited, the sight of her left ring finger haunted her with its bareness. Her costume had demanded the removal of the string, an overdue need. Still, perhaps pathetically, she'd stored it in her trouser pocket. Grief occurred in stages after all. Even in a fantasy.

Just then, the door opened partway, and a young Chinese man peered out. As he looked Celia over, she resisted lowering her head enough to shield her face with the hat. He must have arrived at the same assessment as the pseudo tailor, for he widened the gap and waved her into a lively room before shutting the door behind them.

In an illuminated haze of tobacco smoke, assorted tables were sprinkled about, numbering at least a dozen. Behatted gamblers were seated at some, standing at others, dictated by the game. Coins lay strewn across tables of men engaged in fan-tan, placing wagers on estimated tallies of divided beans from a cup. A burst of cheers came from a table running dice—craps, perhaps, or Sweat. Fittingly, the air smelled of perspiration.

From another direction came a barrage of clacking. Dominoes marked with Chinese characters and designs were being mixed for a game of mah-jongg. Elsewhere, cards were being dealt, shuffled, and played. Celia narrowed her focus to these. Faro, Lettie had said, was her fellow's game of choice, typically at a table near a gilded *Qilin*.

Celia craned her neck and spotted, on a pedestal across the

room, the statue—half dragon, half horse—said to symbolize good fortune and prosperity. She used to roll her eyes at the superstition that she now hoped, for her sake, held an element of truth.

Granted, the issue would be moot unless she located Owen, at which point she'd reveal herself as Lettie's friend. But only once away from others.

Projecting a casual stroll, she worked her way through the brick-lined room. Furtively, she scanned the sea of faces, seeking a white man in his midtwenties with a slender nose, downturned eyes, and, most distinctly, a hairless line on his bearded chin, the result of a scar.

Table after table, there was no sign of him, even among the faro players by the statue. Perhaps he'd simply yet to arrive— though how long could she wait without raising suspicions, particularly without money to bet?

She was rounding the statue for another walk through the room, hope fading, when a man seated alone in a nearby corner caught her eye. A smoldering cigar rested between his lips as he regarded a piece of paper. On a small wooden table, he'd set his weathered hat, exposing russet hair that matched his neatly groomed mustache and beard. A bare segment in the latter suggested a scar. His other features too aligned with Lettie's description, including the sturdy build accentuated by his coat.

Indeed, this had to be him.

Celia's pulse accelerated, though not in earnest. Rather, everything about the plot that had seemed rational before arriving suddenly felt as ridiculous as her male getup. She was tempted to dash back up the stairs and out the door but fought the inclination. Having ventured this far, the only thing more ridiculous would be to leave without making contact.

She strode over and stopped at the man's table. With his eyes intent on a list of names and numbers—some sort of betting, it appeared—she couldn't help but note his handsomeness. A perk Lettie deserved, obviously.

She affected a husky tone. "Owen?"

The room's noise had surely smothered the word. She geared up for a louder attempt, but then he looked up and replied, "Yeah?"

She touched the back of the empty chair across from him and ground out, "May I?"

In lieu of answering, he studied her face. Should he see through the disguise, detect her as a woman, he could demand her removal with little more than a holler.

He withdrew his cigar, its plume smelling of cinnamon and cedar. Thankfully, he nodded. "Be my guest." His timbre surprised her with its raspy deepness.

Ready to transition to her natural register, she settled on the wooden seat and more acutely felt the binding around her chest. Though the long linen strip flattened her breasts effectively, it confined her lungs as if by a corset.

"Glad you made it," he said, then finished while holding her gaze: "Miss Hart."

Alarmed, she retracted slightly. "You know me?"

"From a distance."

The inn. He must have seen her there. But for him to detect her now with such ease, her disguise couldn't have been as strong as she'd thought. That concern, of course, slipped away as his full greeting sank in. "You knew I was coming?"

He gave an aloof shrug, consistent with his overall manner. "I had hoped." As he puffed on his cigar, the most apparent explanation formed.

"So Lettie mentioned I might approach you." She thought to tack on, "About the deal that would be mutually beneficial."

"Those are definitely the sort I favor," he said. A positive indicator. "Except the only deal we'll be discussing is the one I have for *you*."

Her optimism dissolved into confusion as she waited for him to elaborate. From an unseen gambling table, collective groans indicated an unlucky dice roll.

"You see, ma'am, a quite powerful gentleman feels your presence could complicate his, shall we say, grand ambitions. Fortunately, he's willing to extend an offer."

The mayor, he meant. Plainly—but how?

She struggled to track how the men were already associated until she realized: Owen had indeed followed the suggestion of meeting with the mayor. From her own links to the situation, however, she seemed to have become part of the trade. A deplorable thought.

"Likewise," Owen added, "it's a solution beneficial to all involved."

"What exactly is he proposing?"

"Relocate."

"As in from the Dewdrop?" The instant the words were out, she knew he'd meant beyond there.

"The state," he said. "You do that, and I guarantee you'll be well rewarded."

"A bribe then."

"I'd think of it as…incentive."

Her threats to the mayor weren't viewed as empty after all. Although with good intentions, Lettie had sent her fellow, an apparent hustler seeking a nest egg, into the clutches of an affluent, corrupted man.

"And what would that *incentive* entail?"

Owen drew again from his cigar slowly, as if to mount suspense. "A grand, new life, Miss Hart. Enough money to buy train tickets to just about any city across the country. Enough to afford a nice, cozy home. To buy your daughter the finest clothes and bonnets, shiny leather shoes. And all in a place"—his volume lowered—"where no one knows of your secrets. Or Pearl's."

Highly unnerved that he knew her child's name and even more by the mayor's disclosure of their bloodline, Celia worked to maintain her composure.

She replied through a clenched jaw, "What if I refuse?"

As he seemed to be the mayor's henchman now, she half expected him to unleash a litany of prescribed threats: that she and Pearl would be kicked out of their home, that the mayor would utilize his power and connections to arrest her for blackmail or sue for defamation, that he would pillage every cent she had saved.

But Owen said none of these things.

He merely leaned forward with chestnut-brown eyes reflective of his pensive tone. "From what I've gathered, ma'am, I just don't see what's left for you here. How is sticking around truly in your best interest? And above all that of your daughter? A brothel is no place for a little girl. I'm confident you see that. How long before a big, ugly drunk wanders in and...causes her harm?"

Celia cringed inside, mainly from his last point—but from each of them really. None of which she could rebuke. It made her all the more eager to return to Pearl. Yet before she could do so or even consider the offer, she needed to understand one thing. Why had he waited for her to—

Voices burst out, overriding the thought. Her agitation over the interruption fell away at the sight of a table being flipped. Playing cards fluttered through a crisscrossing of shouts. Gamblers were throwing tantrums over a hefty loss or the discovery of a rigged game. At least that was her assumption until the toss of another table launched a spray of mah-jongg tiles. The blocks pelted fellows who were stooping with hands covering their heads. Even dealers were scattering every which way.

Celia jumped to her feet. Angry bellows competed with a rise of panicked yelling. Chairs toppled in the chaos.

"We have to go." It was Owen, suddenly at her side with hat donned, cigar abandoned. "A tong raid. Let's go. *Now.*"

Her gaze shot toward the entry door. There, the doorman was brawling with a Chinese man in all black, evidently one from a gang disgruntled over the competition of this particular den. Several other invaders were scooping money from the floor into sacks. Among the men were at least two with queues bound atop their heads. Highbinders—known to be killers.

"This way," Owen said over the pandemonium, gesturing in the opposite direction.

She nodded, or perhaps she just meant to, and he rapidly led her to the perimeter of the room. As they followed along the wall, her free hand brushed the rough bricks, aiding her balance.

A cracking noise caused her to stop and duck. Her mind flew to a vision of bullets.

She dared a glance backward, heart thrashing against her ribs. Above gamblers' heads, wielded by a tong member, arose a hatchet. At its downward swing, Celia gasped in anticipation of a skull being split. Instead, it struck a chair, which shattered as if built of twigs.

"Move!" Owen's order. Reinforced by his tug on her wrist, she continued behind him. She flinched from every strike of the axe. Then Owen pulled her sideways, through an opening in the bricks. The toe of her boot nicked an edge, and she barely caught herself from tumbling to the ground.

A tunnel stretched to the left and right, disappearing into the cool darkness. Her vision strained to adjust as she surveyed the options, same as Owen. Gamblers and dealers were fleeing in both directions. A couple of men behind Celia bumped past her shoulder and scurried off.

"Now this way." Owen maintained his hold while towing her to the right in a rush. She scrambled to keep up, coughing on air that tasted of dust and smelled of dirt. They were like mice outrunning a flood. In an underground maze. A labyrinth with no clear exit.

A chill rode her spine even as sweat dampened her back.

On a near-constant verge of tripping, she couldn't tell if Owen's grip was a help or hinderance, but either way, vaguely recalling the dynamic of their meeting, she gradually wriggled her arm free. Her regained sense of control would have brought greater relief if not for the tunnel darkening with each stride.

Owen halted abruptly and checked a door, rattled it. Locked. He gave it a knock. Then pounded.

A few more men fled past.

Owen squinted, looking ahead. "There's another door." He hustled forward, focused. Here was Celia's a chance to decide: stay with him or break away.

This time, he cut straight to pounding.

She was a good fifteen feet from him when shouts erupted distantly from behind. Hostile voices in Chinese suggested tong members had entered the tunnels. She recalled the hatchet men at the protest and wondered if, based on her features, she'd be viewed as an enemy.

A whistle shrilled—from the other direction, causing Owen to turn. The note held like that of a train, a warning. The type of whistle standard for police. Whether cops were in pursuit of the assailing tong members or the gamblers or both, there was no way to know. Not until a confrontation that could land Celia behind bars.

Fear squeezed her chest just as Owen used his elbow to ram the door, and it gave way. He twisted back with lips parted as if to urge her to follow, but already she'd nearly closed the gap between them.

She glanced through the doorway—simply access for transferring goods, it appeared. For there were no gambling tables or cots cushioned with opium pillows, only stacks of barrels outlined by a soft beam of light. The all too familiar scents of liquor further hinted at the storage room of a saloon.

The Chinese shouts were growing. Another whistle pierced the air.

She hurried over the threshold, followed directly by Owen. He closed the door, shutting them in the basement, alone.

Her impulse to escape swung her attention to a light at the top of the stairwell. There, a din of voices and the clinking of glassware affirmed the nature of the establishment, one that would have an exit to the street.

She headed for the stairs.

"Wait."

Her defenses flew up.

"I'll go first."

She was ready to defy him until he added, "Don't want them thinking we're thieves. We could wind up shot before even questioned."

Sage advice.

And a fine motive, actually, to allow him the lead.

CHAPTER
FORTY-ONE

With quiet steps, Owen climbed the basement stairs. After reaching the top, he scouted the area with equal caution, then waved Celia up.

On ascent, throat dry and dusty, she was stifling a cough when she again caught herself from stumbling, the toe of her boot having snagged on the ground.

Not *her* boot, rather—a man's. She'd forgotten the whole of her attire. No wonder her steps had been challenging. She needed to adjust.

Aware of reentering a public place, she regathered her masculine deportment and trailed Owen through a short corridor, which emptied them into the saloon's main hall. At least half the tables were filled, most of the customers as grimy as the place's furnishings. Among the drinkers standing, one was urinating in the spittoon trough at the base of the bar, an appalling act that accentuated the room's undesirable odors.

More pressing reasons to leave.

With lengthened strides, Celia maneuvered past Owen. She was almost at the door when his deep voice piped up.

"I wouldn't do that."

Wary of a threat, unsure if it was, she looked back to gauge him.

"Best to wait. Let things settle out there."

She traced his gaze toward the window. Police were combing the area. A few were loading figures onto a paddy wagon stationed across the road.

Owen's warning was maddening, though valid.

Even if the officers had no interest in anyone but members of the raiding tong, her attempting to sneak past in disguise could be hazardous. If she were caught and identified as a woman, how would she explain?

Strictly to sustain a natural act, she joined Owen at a corner table set away from the others. It couldn't have been more than a minute before a woman sidled up, swaying her feather boa and wafting cheap floral perfume. Her face was as worn and aged as her dress, which, despite its fraying seams, pushed up her generous bosoms to the brink of overflowing.

"Evenin', fellas. New to the place?"

It didn't take living in a brothel to recognize her occupation. Whereas Celia once viewed ladies of her like as inferior—shamefully at that—she now felt only compassion.

"Just briefly in port," Celia murmured, voice and eyes low.

"That's all right, sailor." The woman leaned on the table. "Don't need to be in town long to enjoy yourself. If you're wanting, maybe, some trousers mended, I'm quite the skilled seamstress, they say."

At the feel of her hand, brazen on the knee, Celia jolted in her seat. The woman pulled back, but with a seductive giggle.

"Well, ain't you a ticklish one."

Celia was about to decline politely, but Owen cut her off with an icy tone.

"The answer's no. For us both."

The woman extended a tepid smile. "Then how's about a drink?" As if expecting a refusal, she pointed toward a wall by the bar, where a wooden sign featured an engraving.

SALOONS ARE NOT DOCKS
DRINK OR SHOVE OFF

"We'll have two ales," Owen stated, once more rather gruff and on Celia's behalf.

The woman smiled a bit brighter, though Celia well knew the honesty it lacked. "Two ales it is." Straightaway, she retrieved the tawny pints. She exchanged them for a couple nickels from Owen, who readily partook of his drink.

Celia waited until the woman was out of earshot to address him quietly with a scowl. "Just because you're devoted to Lettie doesn't mean you had to be rude. I'll also have you know I was entirely capable of handling that myself."

"Oh, I have full faith you're capable of handling just about any situation." He conveyed this not as mockery but a statement of fact, a pleasant surprise as he downed more of his ale. "Which is why," he added pointedly, "I trust you'll see how taking the deal you've been offered makes all the sense in the world."

How naive of her to think him sincere for even a second. On account of whatever agreement he'd reached with the mayor, he too was putting on an act.

Celia scoffed to express her stance. With the dust lingering in her throat, it provoked another cough.

Owen slid the second pint toward her. "This will help."

She hated to accept anything from him. Only for practicality did she proceed to take a sip.

Unlike the few ales she'd sampled before, this one didn't make her wince. She had long been averse to such drinks due to their bitterness, but this was smoother than the others. A second, longer sip subdued the tickle in her throat and went down even easier. Of course, it wasn't as pleasant as the cordials she and Stephen had shared on occasion, alone by firelight...

Criminy, Celia—stop.

She longed desperately to purge the memory, along with all her others involving Stephen and spoiled by him. Aiming to drown them out, she swallowed a series of gulps as Owen resumed his coaxing. She followed his words far less than the rise and fall of his voice, the inflections applied for emphasis, the increasing staunchness, much like the mayor's orations.

The fellow was tenacious, she'd grant him that much.

She interrupted without courtesy. "What is it you stand to gain, I wonder, by persuading me to clear out? Money? Gold?"

Owen glanced away before replying, "Just doing a job to help someone in trouble."

The answer, while vague, wasn't as abysmal as anticipated. Still, the resulting conflict remained: Celia's principals versus her maternal duty.

For her to accept the mayor's funds seemed filthy to even consider. And yet for her daughter's well-being, how in good conscience could she refuse?

Requiring time to wrangle with the decision and yearning to reunite with Pearl, she went to stand, set on revisiting the window to assess the street. But a dizzying wave of exhaustion pulled her back down. A consequence, surely, of fright and adrenaline from the raid. Compelled to rest for a minute, she circled back to a mystery that remained.

It was obvious why the mayor would assign a middleman to present a bribe—and to communicate with her at all, for that matter—but not this: "Explain, if you will: As a messenger, why did you wait for *me* to come to *you*?"

Owen finished off his drink and set down the glass. "Rest assured, Miss Hart, I had every intention of seeking you out."

But when? His story gained an issue. "I thought you were leaving at dawn to reach Idaho Territory."

From his coat, he drew a cigar, then searched his pockets. He was hunting for a match, it appeared, though she greater sensed he was stalling, at a loss for a response.

In that instant, the rest of the tale that had lured Celia to find him tonight returned in a rush. With it came Officer Glenn's words about Frank's late-night confession.

You feel confident this young fella wasn't just spinning a tale, trying to impress you?

She submitted to Owen warily, "Lettie said you know where the fugitives are hiding out, and so she sent you to the mayor. Please tell me you didn't make a trade based on lies."

His eyes turned guarded as he replied evenly, "Ma'am, the only dealings you ought to concern yourself with are your own."

His evasiveness all but outright confirmed her initial doubts, his supposed knowledge of the fugitives much too convenient. She should have known better, and yet disappointment flooded her, adding weight to her heart, her head. Even if all done for the sake of courtship, he'd been dishonest. How was she...ever to...tell Lettie...

Celia struggled to connect the words going adrift, like snowflakes she was reaching for, unable to capture. The harder she tried and farther she stretched, the more distant they became. They were disappearing at the lightless fringes of her mind. Strangely, from there, a blackness swelled. It encircled her vision like a hollowed fist telescoping her view, closing in on the saloon and Owen, shrinking all to a pinpoint until, in a blink, her last speck of the world vanished.

CHAPTER
FORTY-TWO

Chinatown, the gambling den. The tunnels, saloon, the underground cell. Despite Celia's haze, her memories at last were falling into place.

At the base of the ladder in the cargo hold, she held tight to a rung while trembling from her peek through the hatch overhead, one that revealed her baffling location—on a ship at sea.

Creak…creak…

The incessant sway of her dim, musty surroundings increased her wooziness as she attempted to decipher how she'd arrived onboard. Perhaps by way of the tunnels. Though just as easily, she could have been lugged openly down the streets, like any number of drunken sailors due at their ships.

Not that the logistics mattered, only figuring out how to escape and return to Pearl. Her single consolation was knowing her daughter was safe with Lettie and even Marie.

A sudden light shone from above.

The hatch was opened, and a man was climbing in. Presuming he was her captor, Celia scrambled backward until bumping into a stack of crates. A blockade. There was no place to go nor hide.

The hatch fell shut as he descended in his black boots. Facing away, he was dressed as a crewman: dark knit cap, loose shirt, trousers. No weapon—at least not that she could see.

If only she had one for herself.

"What do you want?" she demanded, ready to employ her fists, her nails.

He dropped early from the ladder with a thud and whipped toward her. "*Keep it down,*" he whispered, his urgency mirrored in his downturned eyes.

It was Owen.

Her body sagged with relief.

"You can't be using your usual voice," he said. "Not when any of them can hear." He sent an upward glance to indicate those on deck as *them.* "Here, put this on." He handed her a knit cap resembling his.

Reminded of her altered appearance, her role, she touched her face. The beard and mustache were still adhered—though not as fully secured—and the wig too remained. The disguise, she recalled, had managed to work well at the gambling den as well as the saloon—where her ale must have been drugged.

She realized with a start: "You did this. The cell, the ship… You brought me here." Her mind scrambled to identify the steps required to have made it possible.

"Just calm down," he urged.

"But how did you—with the raid?" she said, incredulous. "Did you know it was coming?"

The mayor. He might have known somehow and passed it along, orchestrating her tunnel run, the "seamstress," the drinks. A means to dispense of Celia…if rather complex.

"Of course not," Owen said. "Don't be foolish." His brow knotted, emphasizing the absurdity of her whole theory—justifiably.

"Fine. Then how did I get here?"

"Dumb, rotten luck. You got shanghaied, same as I did."

"Shanghaied?" she repeated, not for lack of understanding. From living in Portland—said to be the nationwide capital of the scheme—she obviously knew the term that involved the doping of unsuspecting sailors. As the story went, they'd be sold off by so-called crimpers to fill spots in shorthanded crews, hence would awaken on ships headed as far as Shanghai and be forced to work, lest they be tossed overboard.

Given the nature of seamen and their tall tales, Celia had long chalked up the scenario as fabled—yet here she was.

Creak…creak…

She noticed the bruise then on Owen's cheekbone, the healing cut on his temple. The wounds, combined with his raspy voice, supplied her with another revelation. "You were in the next cell. The inmate who was killed—I'd thought."

"Just got a little roughed up." He shrugged, a movement that caused him a small wince. "At any rate," he said, diverting, "when you poked your head out just now, it was a relief. Seemed you'd been overdosed. The crew didn't want you in the berths in the event that…" He didn't finish, didn't need to.

She nodded, wondering if she'd been drugged beyond the two times she surmised.

"I did though come down to check on you whenever I could."

She glanced over at the burlap sacks—her makeshift pillow and blanket—and sensed he had provided both. She went to offer her gratitude but squelched it, her feelings about him mixed. Besides, she had greater concerns.

"How many days has it been?"

"About two at sea. Before that, a day or two down the river, best I can figure. I was in and out of it so am pretty foggy on those."

"Do you know where we're going?" She prayed the actual answer wasn't Shanghai.

He hitched his hands low on hips. "Crew's been awful tight-lipped. Sounds like there's a long voyage ahead, across the Pacific. But we're southbound for now. I've heard a mention of swapping goods somewhere in California. No doubt that's our best shot. Maybe our only one."

Even California was staggeringly far—from Pearl, from home. To stay calm, Celia refused to consider what would happen if they failed. One issue at a time. Such as, until reaching the next port, what was she to do? Hiding out in the hold for days longer would naturally draw investigation. But as forced labor, she hadn't the first clue about working a ship, and she hardly possessed the level of strength men typically provided.

Then it dawned on her.

"Why don't I just tell them?"

He waited for her to clarify.

"That I'm a woman. Surely they'll let me off—on another ship or at the closest port. What use would they possibly have of me if they knew? Then I could alert someone and send help."

Owen stepped closer, his expression grave. "Miss Hart, you listen up. Aside from being docked here and there, some in the crew have been months at sea. Trust me when I say that informing them you're a woman is the last thing you want to do."

The implied usefulness they *would* find for a woman entrapped on their ship—another form of forced labor—sent rolling nausea through Celia. The sway of the room became abruptly more prominent. Feeling herself blanch, she strove for soothing breaths.

"C'mon," he said. "You'll feel better above deck."

Though wary of approaching the crew, it was an inevitability and the sole way to reach fresh air.

She put on her cap, checking for loose strands of her own hair, then returned to the ladder. She was gearing up when he interjected, "Don't forget: Keep your head down and voice low. Speak only when you have to."

A speedily assembled costume and a few practiced phrases had been the sum of her preparations for passing as a man, just enough to enter a gambling den at night. Not for this. Not in daylight with an all-male crew in close quarters.

"Do you think they'll get suspicious?" she asked and thought to raise her coat collar, shielding half her face.

"There are a couple talkative ones but also plenty who keep to themselves and scarcely say a thing. You ought to be fine."

Ought to.

Not the strongest reassurance.

CHAPTER
FORTY-THREE

On the weathered main deck, Celia barely had a chance to recover when the time arrived to eat. Having gone days without a meal, she might have been eager if not for feeling ill—from both the ship's motion and the shock of her predicament. Still, since it was the last breakfast shift and a means of keeping in Owen's company, she joined him and a portion of the crew in descending the narrow steps into the galley.

The menu of watery porridge, hardtack, and bitter coffee did nothing to aid her appetite. And yet the worst of her queasiness derived from boasts subjected upon the table by an oaf named Leonard—Lecherous Leo, she labeled him silently, as the ladies at the Dewdrop would appreciate. With a mouth outsized only by his head, he rattled on about the poor women in various ports with whom he'd had his way.

"If they don't put up a fight, lads, it's just too easy. It'd be like a bear handing her cub right over. No challenge at all."

A couple of the men snickered.

Celia strained to block them all out, Leo especially, not just to complete the already challenging task of forcing down her food but also to prevent herself from tossing her metal bowl at his face—an easy target.

The sailor seated across from her was proving no quieter with his German-sounding accent. Befitting his elfin features and lean frame, strong though it appeared, his nature was sprightly at least—though it did seem overly so to the scowling crewman at his side whom he was prodding for conversation.

"Jonathan Smith, I hear you are sailor—from England. *Ja?* Like the famous captain. Captain John Smith."

Jonathan, with a stocky build and crooked nose suggestive of rough-and-tumble encounters, kept his attention on eating.

"Except you are bigger. Much stronger. *Ja?* Maybe we call you Big Jon. What you think?" The chipper man grinned over the clever dub.

But Jonathan was neither amused nor impressed. His irritation was palpable. Celia only hoped the chatty one sensed this before pushing too far.

"*Hallo.* You—new fellow."

With sprouting dread, Celia met his gaze. She was the fresh target.

"I am Calum. From Zurich. What is your name?"

The room plummeted into silence, or it just seemed that way. She didn't dare glance around for fear all eyes were on her, aimed like spears and just as pointed.

"What do you call yourself?" he pressed.

A name. She needed just that, any name, anything male.

"Stephen," she mumbled.

"Ah, Stephen. A fine, strong name."

She fought a grimace—at herself. Now, for however long her time on the ship, she would have to answer to those cursed two syllables. Even more reason to find a way off.

"Where you from? You are from America, Stephen?"

She debated which was safer: a muttered reply or silence. Which would gain less attention?

He continued to wait, expectant.

Then footfalls came, heavy down the stairs, detouring Calum's interest.

Wearing a captain's hat askew, a hefty man entered the room in a greatcoat, threadbare and missing several brass buttons. Above deck, Owen had described Captain Sterling as a bulldog. Celia had wrongly assumed this referred only to the man's demeanor, not his face and build.

"Back to work, all of you!" His voice, suitably, was gruff as a bark.

Celia followed Owen and the others in hurrying to wash and store their dishware. As the crew began to disperse, a command shot toward her.

"You. Stay."

Her heart set to thumping.

Head down, voice low. Owen's reminder. She raised her eyes toward the captain just enough to show acknowledgment.

"Finally awake, I see." He spat this while eyeing her dismally—as if she were at fault. As if she'd actually drugged herself. "Well, I certainly didn't pay for your bleeding size. For the love of God, tell me you've at least worked a ship before."

Though reluctant to agitate him further, she shook her head.

"Bastard crimpers. Liars, the lot of 'em." He cursed unintelligibly under his breath.

The reaction provided her with a dose of hope: that he just might view the safety risks of unskilled labor as strong enough cause to drop her at the closest port.

Then he addressed her with more of a snarl. "I imagine you've at least shoveled coal before?"

She pushed down her disappointment and nodded that she had—comparatively, one of her lesser deceits.

"Calum!"

The chatty sailor paused from leaving and scurried over. "*Ja,* Captain?"

Sterling jerked his chin toward Celia. "This one's working the fireroom with you. Teach him what's needed."

Celia bristled at the pairing. The odds of Calum simply teaching her the process, then leaving her quietly to her work, was horrendously unlikely. The more she had to reply, the higher her chance of being discovered.

A request for an alternative rushed to her tongue, but the captain—far from accommodating—snapped around and plodded away.

Owen had lagged subtly behind. "Calum, wait," he said, tone hushed, almost conspiratorial.

Lured in, the sailor whispered back, "What is it?"

"Could I possibly interest you in a trade of duties?"

No answer came as Calum's eyes turned dubious.

"Just untangling nets today. Yours for the taking if you'd like."

At that, Calum's mouth stretched into a grin. "Yes. *Gut.*"

A disaster averted—though with many more waiting, Celia feared.

CHAPTER
FORTY-FOUR

The fireroom had been aptly named. With its contraptions resembling large potbelly stoves that housed burning coal, the confined space was hot and sooty. Celia chose to remove only her coat, cautious of shielding her physique.

Shovel coal into the stove. Per Owen, this was her one essential task.

Her capped wig and facial disguise hardly made things cooler, but removing them wasn't an option—not voluntarily. Sweating increased her worries that the adhesive wouldn't last, thus amid her shoveling, she regularly pressed the pieces to her skin and dabbed away any drips.

The lone saving grace of her duty, aside from it allowing her and Owen privacy, was the rhythmic monotony of the action, decluttering her head enough to think.

She whispered to him as they scooped the coal into a stove: "Perhaps silly to ask, but you *have* attempted to speak with the captain, demanding he let us go, haven't you?"

"*Of course.*" Though quiet, Owen's tone alone said it had failed. "He claims he was given documents we supposedly signed ourselves, so our showing up a little drunk didn't make a difference."

A *little* drunk? A laughable characterization.

"How can he honestly believe that?"

"He doesn't. But he paid for us. Told me I'm welcome to take it up with port authorities when we circle back to Astoria."

"Astoria?" By that, he meant after completing the entire loop of their shipping route, which thereby confirmed to Celia: escape was the solitary goal.

Continuing to shovel, she mentally sought features on a ship that could be useful. "I assume there are dinghies stored somewhere…"

"There is—one."

She brightened. "Then why not use that? We could sneak off at night."

"Because there's always a lookout. And the dinghy looks to be heavy and on a pulley system. It would take at least two men to heft the ropes and lower it to the water."

Fine. He'd already thought that through.

"Well…is there anyone who might be willing to help?"

"The money I had on me was stolen, at the saloon or in the cell. So unless you've got some funds here…" He raised a brow at her knowingly, then returned to shoveling.

But money wasn't the only motivator.

"What about out of compassion? Or just because it's right?" While perhaps foolishly idealistic, particularly given what she knew of the crew so far, the idea had to at least be considered. "There must be someone."

"The sailor at breakfast." Owen stated this as if he'd pondered this too. "The angry one."

"Jonathan," she recalled.

"He's made plain he has no desire to be here."

She halted her shoveling. "Shanghaied too?"

"Seems so."

It hadn't occurred to her that there could be others. "You think he'd work with us?"

"Can't say yet. I haven't been able to talk to him. Not in private."

At the room's entry, a figure appeared.

Lecherous Leo, his face stern.

Celia hastened to resume shoveling the coal and worried how much he'd heard, if anything.

"Cap'n don't want you two together. You"—he glared at Celia—"come with me."

Relief mixed with dread as her thoughts raced. Knowing better than to question him, she surrendered her shovel to Owen, whose eyes hinted at concern, and pulled on her coat despite the heat. With reluctance, she followed Leo out.

Once up the ladder, she trailed him down the main deck. From his purposeful barefoot steps, she remembered hearing of shanghaied victims, specifically those ruled useless and tossed overboard.

Would pleading make any difference, or yelling for help? How long would she last afloat in the ocean?

Abruptly, he stopped near a rail, and her breath held.

As he turned to face her, she kept her gaze low while seeking glimpses of any land or other ships—all of which she found none.

Then Leo reached down into a pail of water by his large, hairy feet. He produced two rocks, each rough like pumice and about the size of a hand.

"See these?" he grunted. "Holystones. The small one's called a prayer book. The bigger one, a Bible. 'Cause you'll be spending a whole lotta time on your knees." A sneer curled his lips, reminding Celia of his disgusting talk of women.

Or did he suspect her secret?

"Every morning, use the seawater and sand from the bucket, and scrub with a stone till the deck's good and clean. If these boards get mold and moss or go dry, they'll shrink and leak. That happens, I'll hold *you* responsible. You hear me?"

Celia was still processing the details but nodded.

He cocked his head and stared. "You mute?"

She hazarded a gravelly reply. "No, sir."

He held in place, and she envisioned him scrutinizing her as the captain had. After an interminable beat, he muttered, "Damn half-wit." Then he turned and continued down the deck, peppering sailors with orders as he went. Among the crew, a few were scrubbing the deck. Others were tending to lines and sails.

The breeze was crisp but pleasant. For a moment, she could breathe.

She grabbed a stone and knelt. Glad for an unsuspecting reason to keep her head down, she scrubbed as directed. All the while, surreptitiously she scanned for anything that could be of help.

Done with a section of the deck, she found relief in standing and moved her bucket to another area to scrub. But first, she nabbed an opportunity to stretch. The sight of a man at the bow of the ship, seated with trousers down, gave her a start. He was relieving himself on an open seat that extended over the water.

She'd been half listening to Owen while venturing down to the galley. He had said something about the facility called "the head" not being ideal for Celia—but good gracious, that couldn't possibly be the ship's version of an outhouse. If so, how she'd navigate that, she couldn't yet fathom. She knew only that she yearned to avert her eyes.

In doing so now, she at least located the crew's stored dinghy. Unfortunately, Owen was right about the ropes and pulley being unwieldy—though not, perhaps, with help.

A mere dozen feet away, Jonathan was heaving different lines, adjusting a sail.

Under the guise of scrubbing, she could work her way over and perhaps sneak in a discussion. Owen would have her wait, no doubt. But every available minute not spent plotting and combining forces was time lost that they could ultimately regret.

And so she resumed her task, gradually moving closer. Her palms felt increasingly tender from the sandy water and stone. She paused to gauge the damage just as a shout burst out, an unrefined English accent.

"I don't need your orders, mate! Not any more than I need to work on this bloody ship!" It was Jonathan, who promptly threw a large bundle of rope, knocking Leo backward.

Leo's initial surprise quickly turned to fury as he flung the pile back at Jonathan's feet. "You'll pick that up—now!"

"I'd be obliged to. For proper wages. Otherwise, you'll do it yourself."

Tension hung in the air as the crew on the deck froze. It felt like hours though was likely just seconds before Jonathan—or maybe it was Leo—took the first swing. Whoever it was, the hit launched a brawl of punches and grunts and smacks. From grips on each other's shirts, together they tumbled onto the deck, toward Celia.

She sprang to her feet, prepared to move out of the way, unsure where they'd land. They were still punching, now rolling. Blood splattered from their mouths. A ticking noise sounded as something hit the deck—a tooth.

Some crewmen hurried over. Celia expected a few to intervene, to stop this insanity. But as if betting on a prizefight at a saloon, they only gathered around to whoop and cheer for their favored competitor.

Jonathan, on top then, pounded away at Leo's face before shifting to his ribs. Leo's hand was lying at his side, no longer a fist—a sign of weakening, even giving up. The fight would be over soon, the victor evident.

But then something glinted in the sunlight. A blade.

Celia resisted the impulse to cover her mouth, a feminine response, and realized Leo hadn't yielded. Rather, he'd reached for his ankle to draw a stowed knife. Enwrapping Jonathan's back with his free hand, Leo now shoved the blade into the middle of the man's torso, a move punctuated with a jerk toward the heart.

Jonathan bent from the impact, ceasing his efforts. He traced the sensation to Leo's grip, to the clutched handle protruding from his own shirt, where blood was spreading.

Celia's lungs pulled in a gasp, yet she managed to cut it short. She applied every ounce of her will not to turn away with eyes squeezed shut. She couldn't afford to act like anything but a man accustomed to witnessing brutality at various points in his life. To survive this moment, she couldn't be a proper lady.

More than that, she couldn't be human.

The spectators went silent as Jonathan spat red. His gurgled breaths were the only sound, save the flapping of sails.

When Leo yanked the knife out, Jonathan rolled off and landed on his side. He clutched his middle as if trying to patch the opening with his hands, as if he could somehow keep the blood from pouring out of his body. Over the deck seeped a red stream. It encircled Celia's pail, staining the holystones.

"What in damnation is going on here?" The captain's bark of a voice turned heads as Leo scrambled to rise, the tainted knife still in his grasp.

Celia watched in shock as the small mob receded enough for the captain to step into the arena.

"What the devil have you done?" he said to Leo, then went to Jonathan's side and lowered onto a knee.

Jonathan was writhing. His eyes beseeched the captain, who raised Jonathan's shirt. After a brief assessment, he released the garment and stood, fuming, chest heaving beneath his greatcoat. He walked over to stand before Leo, their faces mere inches apart.

Celia braced for the captain to snatch the knife and stab Leo in turn. Instead, he said through gritted teeth, "Deal with this. And I'll deal with you later." With that, he stormed off, leaving Leo surely to attend to the wound.

If not him, there had to be someone on board with even basic medical skills, given all the mishaps and illnesses that could occur during months at sea.

"Pick him up," Leo growled. It was a near echo of his earlier order, but now for a body, not rope.

Three crewmen obeyed, two lifting Jonathan by the shoulders, one by the feet. He groaned from the pain, still challenged to breathe. They'd be carrying him to an infirmary-type area, it seemed.

But then Leo said, "Toss him."

Horror shot through Celia as the men swung twice and, over the rail, let go.

CHAPTER
FORTY-FIVE

The strained and muffled screams that followed the splash of a half-living man flung into the sea was, incredibly, only a bit more alarming than the sight of the crew snapping back to their duties. The episode seemed but a brief detour from their day, the man's life not worth a whit.

Except to the captain, of course. In passing, he continued to seethe and mutter about having wasted perfectly good money on feeding the sharks.

The vision of Jonathan being torn to shreds in a circling frenzy haunted Celia as she aimed to scrub the deck clean of his blood. The sandy seawater, turned pink, stained her nails and stung her hands, her palms rubbed raw from the "prayer book" she proceeded to shove back and forth over the planks with wordless aggression.

Even three nights later, the shanghaied man tormented her sleep. In her dreams, both of them underwater, he floated before her, lifeless with an unseeing stare. But then, miraculously revived, he reached for her. He was seeking her aid, she thought, to return to the surface. Instead, he covered her mouth. He was trying to drown her, to take her with him.

"Quiet," he said, an urgent undertone—heard under the ocean somehow.

She clutched his wrist, combating his grip, wriggling to get free. "*Celia, wake up.*"

She noted the use of her real name—not Stephen—then the directive, and her eyes shot open. A face hovered. Owen's. His hand was indeed over her mouth.

"Couldn't risk your screaming," he whispered.

Her gaze darted past his shoulder. By the light of a swinging lantern, she hastened to assemble clues to explain her coffin-like surroundings. An upper berth. On a ship. Swaying at sea.

Remembering it all, she nodded, and Owen released her mouth. He stood with cap on and coat fully buttoned. "All hands have been ordered on deck."

This explained his rare presence. As it was, the captain had gone to marked lengths to keep them separate, from daily duties to meal and sleep shifts, surely to prevent any scheming until the ship would be so distantly west that there was little chance to flee.

Owen was about to say more but glanced over his shoulder, confirming the crewmen in the room were distracted. Those not scurrying out of their berths or throwing on coats and boots were already headed for the ladder, navigating the dramatic tilting from side to side. Celia noticed then the exceptionally loud creaking and the sound of waves pounding the walls.

A storm.

Fear rushed through her, powered by a notion: that the ship would never reach a port at all.

Owen resumed a quiet voice. "Once above deck, I'll find a way to sneak you into the cargo hold to wait out the weather."

The suggestion of the storm passing, indicating it wasn't wholly severe, was at least cause for hope.

She agreed with a nod, mind racing. Swiftly, by feel—an automatic habit by now—she assessed and adjusted her capped wig along with the rest of the adhered yet loosening parts of her disguise. Scrapings of pitch, from crates in the cargo hold, had helped to an extent. How much longer the pieces would stick was distressing to even consider, though less a priority in this moment.

With coat and boots on, always, she dropped from her berth, ready to follow Owen. But then thoughts of his plan spurred memories of Jonathan—specifically, where the shirking of his duties had led.

"Owen, stop." She gripped a bunk rail for balance as he faced her, the room otherwise vacant. "If someone finds me below deck, I could end up overboard. Harshly punished at best." Blending in had long been her key to survival—quite literally, in this case. "Besides," she realized, perhaps most vitally, "the only way to get back to my daughter is if this ship makes it through." And that would require as much help as possible.

Owen looked to be dithering, so she gave him no chance to argue.

"Let's go." She clambered past him, a split second before a roll of the ship sent her sideways. Hand braced against a wall, she raised her collar high around her face, then stumbled toward the ladder.

"Just…take care up there," Owen insisted as he trailed behind.

Grappling with the rungs, she lumbered her way up. She'd barely reached the deck when a swath of cold water slapped her face, sobering her to the ominous scene.

Since the end of her duties at dusk, aside from her stew sloshing during supper, there had been no portending signs—or perhaps she'd been too tired to notice, as much physically as mentally: constantly on guard, avoiding the likes of Chatty Calum and Lecherous Leo, and anxiously impatient for a port that could enable escape.

But now, under the dark blanket of clouds yielding only strips of moonlight, the wind, sea, and sky appeared to be colluding in a quest to smother the ship.

Through the sideways falling rain, Celia grabbed on to the closest rigging. She was collecting her bearings when the bow of the ship crested a swell and plunged. The gusts whipped at her eyes, pelting her with salt crystals that stung her skin.

The captain stood at the helm, tying a rope to the wheel to stabilize control, and bellowed at Owen, "Where've you been? Man the bleeding sails!" The sheets of canvas rippled and snapped like laundry on a line.

Owen hustled off and assisted a cluster of crewmen who were lowering a sail by feeding out line. The masts creaked and swayed, as if threatening to break.

From off to the side, Leo's voice came for Celia: "Ya half-wit! Don't stand there lollygagging! Help batten down the hatches!"

Though daunted, she obeyed by setting off for the hatch she knew best—the laddered entry for the cargo hold—by wading through water already a couple of inches deep. It seeped into her boots, sending a chill through her socks. Owen's plan became more tempting with every step.

She was nearly there when a crewman beat her to it. He shut the hatch and slid its bolt into place.

The sea blasted a frothy arc her way. She turned her head and hunched, but still icy runnels bypassed her collar, slipping down her neck and back.

The captain ordered another sail lowered as the ship rode a

larger swell. The bow went up, up, and higher still. Celia scanned for a structure to grasp on to. But too soon, the ship slammed down. Losing her footing, she went rolling and sliding across the deck, straight toward an opening in the rail, a gap that would send her into the sea. She fought for purchase with her legs, clawing with her hands, until all at once, she stopped.

A railing post had caught her. Heart pumping, she braced hard against it and breathed.

"*Hilfe!*"

The word drifted through the rain, the wind.

"*Hilf mir!*"

The cry had come from behind her, past the rail.

She twisted just enough to peer over the edge. Several feet down, dangling from a narrow ledge with arms fully stretched, was Calum. He strained to pull himself up, but the ship pitched and dropped him back down. Celia clutched the post as he looked up. Upon finding her gaze, his eyes sparked with hope.

"*Hilf mir!*"

Her instinct was to help; of course it was. But to do so required a level of risk that could easily make Pearl an orphan. And yet, should she do nothing, what kind of person would she be? What sort of mother?

Defying her screaming nerves, she knelt on the slickened and shifting deck. She maintained a grip on the post with one hand and, leaning over, reached for Calum with the other. He was too far down. Even when she lay flat, a foot-long gap remained.

But then his face flashed with determination. Relinquishing one of his holds, he lurched for her hand. Missing by a few inches, he swung downward. Celia gasped, fearing he would plummet. Somehow his other grip held, and he dangled by his fingers. Salvaging enough might, he returned his second hand to the ledge. Still below him, the waves swarmed, insatiably hungry, nipping at his feet.

For her to extend her body farther over the edge seemed an act of suicide. This wasn't going to work—not without help.

She turned toward the crew and shouted in the lowest voice she could fast summon. The word died, however, in the cacophony of the wind and sails and water. Various crewmen, including Owen, traded muffled yells, endeavoring to keep the ship upright and afloat.

Desperate, Celia scanned the deck for anything of use. No more than eight feet away, a coil of thick rope was fastened to an anvil-shaped fixture.

"*Hilfe!*" His plea was now a shriek.

Through the standing water, she sped in a crawl to the rope. It was rough and heavy. Determined, she lugged it back with her to the edge and, in Calum's direction, shoved it over. From a sudden drop of the ship, she grabbed a rail, barely, and kept herself from flying into the ocean.

Striving to settle, she glimpsed Calum working his way up the rope. All the while, the ship bobbed and shook like an unbroken horse intent on bucking him off and Celia along with him.

When Calum was close enough, she reached down and guided one of his hands to quicken his ascent. He was about to crawl onto the deck when again the ship pitched, launching a spray. Seawater doused her eyes and filled her mouth. She blinked and coughed and spat, only to discover Calum missing.

She snapped around and confirmed his body had been tossed—thankfully onto the ship.

The captain was shouting commands about lowering another sail.

Calum offered Celia a quivering smile. "*Danke,*" he said. "*Danke!*"

Before she could respond, Leo appeared and hollered orders at Calum, who scrambled back into action. Another crewman just as soon shoved a bucket into Celia's hands, rattling off instructions for the areas where water needed bailing.

The night stretched on this way, the assignments endless and taxing, until the wind, sea, and sky gradually abandoned their mission, perhaps having ruled the crew formidable.

Through the relative calm of the morning, while all resumed their usual duties, exhaustion lingered. This was no less the case for Celia—nor for Owen, judging by the look of him.

But Celia was also fretful. Her beard, now battered and dampened by the storm, was scarcely hanging on. She could keep her head only so low and for so long before one of the crewmen noticed. Although adhered separately, the mustache was sure to follow.

Thus, come midday, the captain's alert—delivered in the form of two gloriously barked words—couldn't have been more welcome.

"Land ho!"

CHAPTER
FORTY-SIX

The crew's anticipation rose with every passing mile. Many, though none more than Lecherous Leo, boasted of the delights they would relish while docked in San Francisco—specifically its infamous district dubbed the "Barbary Coast." Aside from general lawlessness, the area comprised of several blocks was known for its concert saloons, variety shows, and dance halls and naturally brimmed with brothels.

Celia's focus, of course—hampered though it was from compounded lack of sleep—centered on escape.

According to snippets she'd amassed, having become near invisible to more than a few crewmen, the ship was to anchor in the harbor upon its evening arrival; then, after docking at first light, the crew would exchange one load of cargo for another, including an additional haul of provisions that suggested a lengthy trip.

In sum, tonight would be her sole and final chance.

She saw no other opportunity to flee before otherwise sailing to a country as far away, perhaps, as her father's homeland—not by choice and in a withering disguise that, to the entire crew, could soon make her the opposite of invisible. To some, a glaring target in the most lascivious of ways.

She did her best to shun these thoughts while continuing to blend in. After hours of holystoning the deck, she forced her body, aching and bruised from the storm, through a full scrubbing of the galley, as ordered.

The second she finished, she defied the impulse to rest and went on a hunt for Owen. They needed to devise a plan. More than one, for an array of scenarios. For though he and Celia had helped brave the storm, as much as any others in the crew, she couldn't fathom the captain trusting them with shore leave.

But would he actually think it safe to leave them alone on the ship?

She emerged above deck, pondering, and a shout jolted her.

"There you are, dammit!" Leo scowled, as if she was petulant for not predicting his oft-changing needs—despite the fact that she'd been precisely where he had sent her. "Ya got another chore. Cargo hold."

The detour was irksome, even without the idea of shifting and hefting more supplies. But as she followed Leo, she at least recalled a benefit of the actual crates. Their drippings of pitch were rather scant, and many were too dry for adhering, yet even small dabs would be helpful—especially now, with the moderate breeze fluttering a loose portion of her beard.

She dropped her head even lower behind the barricade of her collar as Leo opened the hatch for her to enter first. Hustling past his close view, she descended the ladder to receive instructions. She'd barely reached the bottom when he sneered, "Get cozy."

Before she could comprehend the meaning, the hatch slammed shut.

Her gut retracted, hard, as if hit.

Her immediate instinct was to climb back up, but a metallic

scraping, from the sliding of the bolt, proclaimed it pointless. And she well knew the other hatches were kept locked. She was trapped again in the lantern-lit cage. Struck by the repercussion of being kept from Pearl, she wanted to scream. Why hadn't she paid closer mind? How could she have gone so willingly?

A noise came from behind, swinging her around. Something was being punched, repeatedly. On the floor, a man's legs were peeking from around a crate. Recognizing Owen's boots, she rushed to help.

There, indeed, she found him, but seated and alone. He was punching the stuffed burlap sack behind him, shaping it as one would a pillow. "Gotta confess," he remarked as if to himself, though clearly for her, "I always said I wanted to go and explore the world. Just never pictured it like this."

Her relief was fleeting, pushed out by aggravation. She had to remind herself to whisper. "You must have known I was climbing down. Why didn't you warn me?"

He answered without looking up. "And if I had, what would you have done?"

She scoured for any reply other than *nothing*. "I could've taken a stance."

"Ah. Sure. A declaration in your most authoritative masculine voice. That definitely would've done the trick."

She narrowed her eyes at him. "I don't hear any of your ideas."

He reclined and laid his head on the makeshift pillow. "That, Miss Hart, is because there aren't any—none that'll work. Not unless you want to brawl your way out of here. Frankly, I don't see you faring all that well. And in the process, they'd be sure to discover you're not exactly the strapping sailor they thought."

His argument wasn't wrong. Which made it all the more infuriating. Still, there was too much at stake to simply, what—take a nap? "So you're just giving up."

"I'm accepting my losses for the time being. It's what people do who aren't gamblers—or," he added with distaste, "fanciful dreamers. I'll figure out a plan once we're not stuck in this hold."

The hold. Full of cargo.

That reminded her: "They're scheduled to unload and reload in the morning, over at the port. I presume they'll be moving crates in and out of here, maybe for hours." Growing encouraged, she pointed out, "All with hatches open."

Owen threaded his fingers over his middle. "And...you thought we could sneak right out?" The arch of his brow gave her pause.

"Well—no..."

All right, possibly. But she was tired, to put it mildly.

She strove to block out the room's creaking and rumbling to better think. "We could yell toward the dock, call out for help."

"Let me guess," he said, closing his eyes. "Your first time to the Bay." He left it at that, making clear that cries of the like, perhaps commonplace, would go unheeded. The notion was almost as disquieting as his conversational tone, a thinly veiled dismissal.

She could—and would—find a solution on her own.

All around were crates and ropes. Nothing else visible. Packed in the containers, however, could be objects capable of knocking a man out, creating a chance to run.

At the closest crate, she attempted to pry free the lid. She combated gouging splinters and firmly secured nails. Unsuccessful, she tried a second crate and a third. Nothing budged.

Darn it all!

The sliding of a bolt sounded from above. She looked up as the main hatch reopened. A crewman descended the ladder, facing away while balancing a tray with his free hand. All the while, Owen stayed reclined and Leo peered down from the main deck, standing guard as if at a prison—which, in essence, this was.

Once at the bottom, the sailor turned and revealed himself as Calum. He set a tray of two dinners on the floor, and resentment rolled through Celia. After all they had gone through, all she had done to save his life, here he was, aiding her captivity.

He stood fully and gestured with a smile. "For this night, it is usual meal. There is beef stew and bread. Plenty of food. *Ja?*"

His chattiness had never been more maddening, now accentuated by his volume. He was speaking as if she were across the room, not a few feet away. The only thing preventing her from storming off, aside from the confinement of the space, was her compulsion to peg him with a close, bitter stare.

He rattled on regardless. "Also, you have ale. So if you need, you have pissing pot, over…" His gaze bounced around, found it. "There!"

She wasn't about to explain her heightened aversion to the drink. She'd sipped it on board only when necessary—which, incidentally, helped keep her use of the ship's head minimal and mostly to nights.

She did, though, consider declaring she wasn't foolish enough to consume anything she was currently served, but then Calum's voice dropped to a whisper.

"They will tie you up, both of you, at dawn. Before unloading goods." Barely moving his head, he threw a look up and to the far left, toward the deck above. A message.

"That's enough!" Leo hollered down. "They got what they need."

Calum resumed addressing Celia at his prior volume. "I go now. But you both have fine sleep. *Ja?*" His projection had been for Leo. Calum further clarified this by sliding Celia a tender smile, reflective of the gratitude in his eyes. Then he scurried back to the ladder and up the rungs.

As soon as the hatch was resecured, Celia studied the planked ceiling by lamplight and tracked the aim of Calum's gaze. "Owen," she urged quietly.

"Yeah, I heard," he muttered. "Could've told you they'd keep us bound."

"No—not that. I think he was trying to help. The smaller hatch over there." She pointed. "The way he looked at it makes me think it's unlocked."

Owen climbed to his feet and walked over to survey the spot.

She tempered her hopes due to the height of the hatch until noting the resources all around. "If we stacked some crates, we have to be able to reach it."

He glanced about, then back upward, mentally measuring. "I'd say so. But we'll need to wait until the crew leaves." As if to preclude any challenge to the idea, he cut his gaze to hers and said, "Anyone looks in on us and sees what we're up to? They won't be waiting till dawn with that rope."

She highly doubted there would be another check-in tonight, not with their chamber pot and meal provided to last through morning. But for the off chance she was wrong—or that a crewman was sent down for supplies—she agreed it wasn't worth the risk.

So now, the eternal wait.

CHAPTER
FORTY-SEVEN

Loud as a tornado bearing down on a house, a merciless mix of rattling and clunking reverberated through the cargo hold. It was the anchor dropping, the chain unwinding.

Once it ended, the captain launched into a litany of orders.

Celia hurried to the top of the ladder and strained to catch any developments. Enough of his words leaked through the cracks and seams of the deck for her to deduce that a watchman would be posted on the ship. To that man's great dismay, as much as Celia's, the task was assigned to Leo.

While Celia figured the captain would reduce Leo's pay—and he might well do that too—the duty was received like a sentencing. Whereas a denial of shore leave for murdering a man struck her as impossibly trifling, Leo felt the opposite. His grousing didn't stop until the rest of the crew rowed away in the dinghy, turning the ship eerily quiet and—as Celia accepted with dread while pacing amid the crates—leaving her and Owen only one way to reach the shore.

To swim. Through a bay of dark, icy currents. With her moderate skills and, far from trivial, the potential of sharks.

"Don't worry," Owen insisted as they outlined the plan. "We won't find them this far into the bay."

Was he saying that only to assure her? How did he know for certain? She couldn't imagine sharks just collectively agreeing on an invisible line in the water not to cross. And anyway, how could he know how distantly the ship was anchored and therefore the length of the swim?

Granted, all this would prove moot if they couldn't even make it above deck.

From a thorough search, they found what they needed: two accessible medium crates that felt liftable between them while also being sturdy enough to withstand each of their body weights. Using a larger crate as a base, the vertical column needed be only tall enough for Celia and Owen to stand upon and reach the targeted exit.

Further heartened by Leo's murmured shanties near the main hatch, a sign of liquid indulgence that could benefit the escape, Celia was eager to begin stacking.

Owen stopped her. "To be safe, crates should stay where they are till we're fully ready to go."

"Why? What else do we need to do?" Their clothes, she recalled, answering her own question. They needed to strip down to a minimum to enable their swim. A practical idea from Owen, if slightly daunting.

"Let's give Leo some time," he said, "to get more booze in him." Then Owen sat to rest against a crate.

"But...how much? You can hear him. He's had a decent amount. And the crew could return at any time."

"They'll be gone a good while yet." She went to protest, when he stressed, "Trust me."

Taking this in, she couldn't help but laugh. "Trust you? I'm in this mess because of you."

He gave her an exhausted look. "I think we've established

we're in the same boat—literally, in fact." A hint of levity entered his eyes, but Celia restrained any show of amusement.

"Really though," she challenged. "How am I supposed to trust someone I know almost nothing about? Especially when you seem to have extensive knowledge about me."

He simply glanced away, not the type to volunteer his personal matters. But what of those that pertained to her and Pearl?

She sat directly before him. In part, she merely craved a distraction, to curb her mind from the mission ahead. "You can at least tell me the deal that landed you here." What little he'd shared had left her curious. "In acting as a go-between, you said you were helping someone in trouble. So what did that mean? How is the mayor supposed to help?" She pressed him with her gaze, intensified by the quiet, not letting up.

At last, he looked back at her. His lips parted, the words seeming primed to flow out. Yet before they could, a sense of guardedness returned, as cool and solid as armor. "Let's just concentrate on getting us home."

It seemed he needed to be told that she wasn't the one holding things up.

But he closed his eyes and rested the back of his head against the crate, their discussion over.

She withheld a scoff, not wanting to satisfy him with her agitation. Rather, she moved to sit against a crate set away from him, where she impatiently endured Leo's off-key singing. His lyrics about women were predictably lewd, a reminder of yet another reason the escape couldn't fail.

As each shanty rolled into another—the extent of his catalog almost impressive—an escalation of slurring and pauses midverse illustrated the alcohol taking effect.

Celia was on the brink of prodding Owen when Leo's voice faded away.

Owen straightened at the silence, as did she.

Hopeful, she whispered, "Surely he's had enough to be knocked out. Don't you think?"

Of the crewmen known to snore, Leo surprisingly wasn't among them. For the current situation, she wished he were.

Regardless, Owen replied, "Let's find out."

By that, he meant it was time.

CHAPTER
FORTY-EIGHT

Working together, still cautious, Celia and Owen stacked the crates gently to minimize any questionable noise from the cargo hold.

Then came the next step: undress.

They faced away from each other, of course. Perhaps a silly thing, since they'd be in proximity for the entirety of the escape. But there was Lettie to consider—presuming Owen's dishonesty about the hideout wouldn't be enough to end their courtship. Also, not all the habits ingrained by Celia's mother—modesty, in this case—could be simply wiped away. Nor, she realized, should they be.

Once down to her bloomers and chambray shirt, beneath which the linen strip remained, she stepped toward Owen with eyes averted and passed along her boots, cap, and clothing. At the edge of her vision, he stood in only his drawers, bare from the waist up and knees down. Feeling a sudden flush of her face, she was grateful for the room's dimness as well as the busyness of his actions.

He stuffed her garments and shoes along with his own into the empty burlap sack that at one point had served as her blanket. Then he used the shortest rope he could find to tie the bag closed. As he bound it to his back, she couldn't avoid glimpses of his chest, his shoulders. The lamplight flickered softly over the lines and angles of his muscles, which shifted and flexed with his movements.

In an instant, she was back in the barn. At the memory of Stephen's arms around her, her heartbeat picked up pace, reviving feelings she had forced into dormancy.

"I'll go first," he said.

Owen's voice. Not Stephen's.

Jarred, she nodded before even digesting the words.

As he endeavored to climb, she shook off her ridiculous, unbefitting thoughts. Clearly a consequence of being tired beyond measure.

Focus, Celia.

The sway of the room added to the challenge of Owen's ascent. She tensed at his series of unavoidable creaks but far more so from the raising of his hands when he reached the top crate, specifically from the discovery. Even on the balls of his feet, a solid meter separated him from the hatch.

Celia's impulse to try for herself shattered under a burden of logic, her height being several inches lower than his. Instead, she searched for another suitable accessible crate—despite already knowing there was none. She refused to believe a couple of lousy feet would keep them from freedom and, above all, her from her daughter.

If only it were possible to combine Owen's reach and her own...

As he stepped down onto the lowest crate, a solution seized her. "Wait—stop there." She managed to heft herself up, arms shaking a tad from exertion, and stood to join him. "If you lift me from the top box, I could make it through the hatch."

For Owen to then follow her out, she thought of Calum in the storm. "Once I'm above deck, I can sneak over to a rope to toss down."

He glanced up at the hatch with reservations but didn't dispute her; honestly, what were their choices?

In earnest, she climbed onto the second crate, staving off images of a disastrous fall, not only for its injuries but also a ruckus that could summon Leo.

Owen followed as she mounted the third box, where she worked to maintain her balance. The rocking felt expansive at the summit, particularly when allowing Owen sufficient space.

Would it hold their combined weight? Too late to worry.

"Are you ready?" he rasped.

At her nod, he lowered himself so she could use his thigh as a step, then guided her to climb up and sit on his shoulders. He gripped her knees to hold her in place as she looked up at her goal. Stretching her arms high, she could sufficiently reach.

"Careful," he said. "Open it just enough for a peek."

Heedful of his warning, she pushed gently on the hatch. Too gently, for it neglected to budge even the slightest. She tried again with more strength. Still, it wouldn't move. Alarm swept through her.

Had she misread Calum's signal? Had there been no signal at all?

Owen's shoulders began to quiver from holding her up—he too was worn from laboring on the ship. And so hurrying, she pushed even harder, the resistance feeling like a lock, until suddenly the door gave and lifted an inch.

Her relief arose, only to retract at the squeak of a hinge. Gradually, she pressed upward a few inches. Hatch held atop her head, she peered down the moonlit deck toward the glow of a lantern at the helm. Structures and equipment partially obstructed the view of the area around the main hatch, where Leo would be seen if standing.

Which he wasn't.

Listening for movement, Celia scanned every direction possible. "I can't find him," she whispered to Owen.

"Are you sure?"

"He must have passed out at his post. It looks clear."

"All right," he said. "Be cautious yet." He guided her up to kneel on his shoulders. Her pulse hastened as she lifted the hatch fully, the hinge luckily quieting. Soon she was out and crawling barefoot onto the cool deck.

A near-full moon illuminated the neighboring vessels in the harbor, all generously spaced and casting shadows from their masts, forging a bay of ghost ships. Those at the docks resembled toy models built in large bottles, appearing smaller from a distance that still seemed manageable for a swim.

She glanced around once more, for fear of Leo roaming but also the dinghy returning. Seeing neither, she shuffled on her knees to reach the closest rope, the very one she'd tossed to Calum. This time, though, the loose end wasn't there. The rope was pulled taut across the deck. She tugged, but it held firm, secured to something over the side.

There were other ropes, she recalled, coiled and hung in the cargo hold. Though figuring she could secure one to a rail, she wondered if she was strong enough to help pull Owen up and through the opening. But before reversing her path, needing to confirm Leo wasn't an imminent threat, she dared raise her head just enough for a clearer view of the main hatch.

Spotting no hint of him, she stretched higher and higher until discovering he wasn't there at all. Anxiously, she scanned the deck again until the obvious came to her: he'd gone down to his berth to sleep.

This left the main hatch unguarded. A fast, reliable exit. The thought sent her straight back to Owen.

"Leo's not there. Go over to the ladder. I'll release the bolt." She didn't wait for him to respond, just rose and rushed off to meet him in a vigilant stoop.

Up ahead on the deck, a liquor bottle lay abandoned. She pictured Leo, chugging away between songs.

Suddenly, as if willed from the vision, the silhouette of a blocky figure arose on the bow. At the ship's head, it was Leo, pulling up his trousers. Before she could think to react, he saw her and halted, causing her breathing to do the same. "Oy!" he bellowed.

If she dove into the bay now and swam away, his odds of catching up would be slim. But that would leave Owen trapped.

"Stay *tharr*!" Leo shouted with a slur. "Damn ta hell!" He was heading for the deck, fastening his trousers. Given his state and inclinations, who knew what he'd do to Owen, the sole remaining captive, with no one here to stop him?

Oh, blast it!

Celia raced through the final strides to reach the main hatch and knelt at its bolt. She went to slide it, but stubborn and rusted, it barely moved. She gave it a yank, realizing she'd never unlocked it herself.

She threw a glance over her shoulder. Leo was staggering but closing in.

Using both hands, she grabbed the bolt again and gave a sharp pull. As it scraped with movement, she didn't ease up until sliding it free. With no time for relief, she swung open the hatch and found Owen starting up the ladder.

"Hurry!" she yelled down. "He's—"

She got no further before feeling herself grabbed and slung through the air. Her body slammed onto the deck, face down, knocking the air from her lungs. Dazed while rising, she made it onto all fours, but a booted foot pushed into her side and sent her onto her back.

Towering over her, Leo reached down and clutched her hair with his hand, which reflexively she grasped with both of hers. A glimpse of his other arm, cranking back, fingers curled into a fist, caused her to wince. She braced for a punch straight to the face, for the implosive, jaw-breaking pain of it. But then, in his effort to raise her head, her wig slipped free. He startled at the accessory in his grip. From a quick survey of her real hair, her bloomers, his comprehension set in—that he'd been deceived, that she was a woman—twisting his face into something both vengeful and crude.

He was a man beyond reason.

She scrambled backward. He was reaching for her again when he was yanked from behind. It was Owen, who managed to throw him sideways. Amid the fall, however, Leo grabbed hold of the bag on Owen's back and used it to heave him at the deck. As Owen flew into a railing post, the sack broke away and knocked into the liquor bottle. Gathering his bearings, Owen clutched a rail while climbing to his feet, but already Leo had stormed over.

Panic hurtled through Celia as Leo clamped a hand around Owen's throat. Immediately, Owen fought to pry it off.

Nearby on the deck, the bottle was rolling. An object to strike Leo.

Celia crawled after it in a rush. It was approaching the open hatch in a drive toward the edge. She lunged with hands out and brushed the bottle as it fell. The glass clunked down the ladder and shattered at the base.

She snapped her attention to Owen, now arched backward over the rail, held there by a strangling hand. Raised in Leo's other grip and poised to strike was a knife that Owen was simultaneously struggling to ward off.

Celia sprinted over and lurched for the weapon. But Leo deflected her with an elbow to the cheek, a slug that sent her hard on to the deck.

Moonlight glinted off the blade as Leo strove to bring it downward, aimed for Owen's chest. A repeat of Jonathan's grisly end. In a flash, Celia saw the blood on the planks, her nails stained pink, hands raw from scrubbing...

The holystones.

From a moment of clarity, she hastened to a nearby pail where some of the stones were kept. She snatched the top one, a Bible, then dashed back and, driven by primal instinct, swung at Leo's skull. The contact stunned him enough for Owen to knock the knife free. It plummeted toward the water and disappeared with a splash.

When Leo turned to her, she struck again without thought— his temple now—and he collapsed into a heap. On his side, he lay unmoving.

Celia's fingers trembled around the stone.

There was no blood, and his eyes were closed, not blankly staring. Still, she regarded Owen. "Did I... Is he..."

Panting while recovering upright, Owen peered down at Leo in silence.

Did he not want to answer? Or was he assessing, looking for signs of life?

Then, with his foot, he nudged the man's leg. Leo moved, and Celia jumped back. But his body stopped there, his breathing heavy.

"He'll be fine," Owen said. She exhaled a mix of emotions as he stated, "We need to go."

The stone slipped from her hand.

He scooped up his bag and, retying it onto his back, led her to an opening in the rail. "You ready?"

She looked at the water, dark as tar. The ripples reminded her of the captain's words, about people being feed for sharks. Her knees too were trembling now. What if she couldn't do this?

"Celia…" A wide, warm hand encased hers, drawing her gaze to Owen's. "We can do this. Together. You can trust me."

Trust him.

This time, she didn't laugh. Instead, noting the sincerity in his voice, mirrored in his eyes, she nodded. And on the count of three, they jumped.

CHAPTER
FORTY-NINE

The bites came all at once. They spread over every inch of Celia's body—or maybe the sensation was more like a thousand pricking needles. She could think of no better way to process her plunge into the icy bay.

The instant her head resurfaced, she gasped. Her lungs fought to suck in air that the cold was determined to drive out. She was surrounded by the blackened sea.

And she was alone.

She kicked and paddled her arms to rotate, searching for Owen. Her nightmares of Jonathan slung back at her. She pictured him underwater with his lifeless stare, readying to reach up and pull her down. Her legs had never felt so vulnerable, an easy target. Bait. She strove not to panic.

A splash sounded from behind.

Her already fast pulse raced as she spun sharply for a view, her freed hair swaying around her like kelp. She expected to find a protruding fin. But it was just Owen—thank heavens—his head above the surface.

"The bag," he said, catching his breath. "The weight took me down a ways."

"Will you…be all right?" Her voice rode shallow breaths. "Do you need to…take it off?"

"Nah. I have it. So long as we go now."

She gave a nod—at least tried to as her jaw clenched from shivering—then turned with him away from the ship and began to swim. Seeking calm in a rhythmic tempo, she focused on her breathing and arm sweeps, her stiff but steady kicks.

A ribbon of moonlight created a path lain practically to shore. As numbness set in, her shaking waned. But then came a tightening, a cramp invading her calf.

She slowed and flexed her foot, desperate to prevent a knot. It teetered on the verge, threatening a crippling pain that could end in her drowning.

Owen was several strokes ahead. Weighted already by the bag on his back, could he really help in time if she suddenly went under? Could he even find her in the depths and darkness?

She breathed hard, coaxing the muscle to relax.

"Celia?" He'd stopped to face her, treading water.

Needing to concentrate, she couldn't answer. She visualized a knotted rope within her leg, her fingers untying it. She continued her breaths, and gradually the binding eased, melting away.

"It's fine now," she replied. "I'm fine."

"Float on your back…if you're tired."

If she was tired. Heavens, was she ever tired. But she pushed out the thought and resumed her strokes. Intermittently applying his advice, she floated on her back while kicking, always kicking, as the destination neared.

At last, safely away from the docks, they emerged on a dark beach. She felt relief though briefly, sliced through by the night wind. The revived quaking in her limbs heightened the already difficult task of redonning her outfit, which came out drenched from the bag.

Owen's lips similarly quivered with his voice. "Let's find some…place to get warm."

The idea was logical, a necessity, but also, as they soon learned, an inordinate challenge.

They hadn't a penny between them, and entering any of the local establishments open at this hour—saloons, inns, especially brothels—meant risking a run-in with Sterling or those loyal in his crew. Even if she and Owen managed to find a port authority to hear their case, their claims of identity would fail to supersede the captain's forged documents. And a ruling of desertion could land them right back in a cell.

To at least shelter from the wind, they ventured into a vacant alley. There, they sat huddled together for warmth as the chill clung to Celia. Straggling from her cap, a lock of her wet hair brushed stiffly against her cheek. The chattering of her teeth echoed so loudly in her ears that when a hatted fellow approached and traded words with Owen, she wasn't sure why Owen then guided her to join him in trailing the stranger.

"Just another block," the man said over the shoulder of his coat.

Fixated on temperature, Celia's brain puzzled over his clean-shaven face as a nonsensical choice, astounded that he wasn't suffering from pneumonia. A concern for herself, in fact, with her cap and hair sending cold rivulets down her neck. Her boots squished with every step, her toes still numb and shriveled.

She was relaxing her jaw enough to ask Owen about their destination when they rounded a corner, and the stranger again glanced back and said, "Home sweet home."

Celia's awareness expanded past his common stature, where campfires glowed in an area speckled with lean-tos, tents, and clusters of men.

Like moths, neither she nor Owen needed persuading to head for the flames.

At the closest fire, they sank onto the ground. Celia's exposed skin voraciously soaked up every degree of heat from even the sparks of the crackling logs. Her bones, in contrast, were stubborn. The cold that had settled in the marrow refused to leave.

As if predicting this, their guide, Matthew—his name one of the few details she'd caught—produced a woolen blanket from a nearby tent and laid it over her and Owen's shoulders. Then he circled around the fire and squatted to speak to a silver-bearded man who sat with the hunch of a retired miner. The old-timer looked over and eyed Celia, scrunching his wrinkled face in consternation, likely for her sopping wetness. But then, in a begrudging motion, he ceded his ceramic liquor jug to Matthew, who returned with the offering.

"I highly recommend y'all take a nip. Be cozy in no time." His soft smile revealed dimples, conveying a charm equally inherent in his drawl.

"We're much obliged." Owen accepted and, after a few swigs, exhaled a breath suggestive of moonshine. Then he passed Celia the jug with a look that said she'd be foolish to decline.

Indeed, she agreed.

As expected, the first sip went down like liquid fire. She had to stifle a cough as the booze burned a path down her throat. In her frozen state, she couldn't say she entirely minded. After indulging in a longer, smoother swallow that spread heat through her chest, she passed the jug back to Owen. They both took a couple more turns before she surrendered the bottle to Matthew, now seated at her side.

But rather than drink, he said, "You folks passing through, I reckon?"

Owen was polite but to the point. "We need to hop a north-bound train the soonest we can. Know where we could do that?"

It was among the possibilities he and Celia had discussed in the cargo hold, though she'd given little thought to anything past making it to shore. Now safely on land, she relished being one enormous step closer to home—which was to say, Pearl.

"Sure do," Matthew said. "That's my favorite way to travel. First train headed north passes through at about…half of nine, if I recall. I'd be glad to take ya to a good spot to catch it. Got an odd job lined up tomorrow but not till midmornin'."

"We'd appreciate that." Owen then turned his attention to holding his palms to the fire, never one for chitchat.

As prickles again needled Celia's body, this time from thawing, Matthew addressed her tentatively. "Hope you don't mind my asking, ma'am, but are you in some sort of variety show?"

She recalled her tattered disguise with a start. She knew even before touching her face that her beard was gone, lost in the bay or in her tussle on the ship, and her mustache was barely adhered. No wonder the old-timer was dismayed. She must have seemed a sideshow oddity, like Siamese twins or a bearded lady. Mustached, in this case.

"No, actually. Nothing like that." She didn't so much pull off the accessory now than allow it to fall into her hand. "This was all just a costume for…" Even if not for her mental fatigue, where would she begin? "It's quite a long story."

"Is there any better kind?" Matthew smiled with a joviality that reached his eyes. "Truth be told, in cities like this, I reckon it's a whole lot safer to look like us fellas."

The reputation of the Barbary Coast certainly supported the theory. "Well, even so, that's clearly no longer an option." Thanks to her cap, she could do without her abandoned wig, but the same couldn't be said of her mustache. Gesturing to it, she submitted lightheartedly, "Not unless you have some glue or pitch lying around."

"Afraid you got me there." His eyes gleamed. "Anything else that might do?" He understood she was joshing him, though the question did make her think: in baking, there was a delicious yet sticky substance, often a hassle to wash off.

"You wouldn't have any molasses, would you?" She knew it was a stretch, so she wasn't surprised when he shook his head. But then he sat up and wagged a finger.

"I do happen to have something else." With that, he hustled back to this tent.

By the time he returned, Celia was a smidge woozy, but still she listened as he sat and untied a little ball of checkered fabric on his lap.

"Nice couple gave me a ride on their wagon, so I whittled toy soldiers for their youngins. The missus insisted I take a loaf of rye and this here as a thank-you. It was real kind of her. I just never been fond much of sweets." Out of the swatch came a square of honeycomb. "Could be worth a try."

The moonshine was definitely taking effect, because not only did Celia agree, she also found the experiment increasingly funny—to the point that when her honeyed fingers ripped patches of hair from the mustache, she became teary with giggles. "It looks like a sad, molting caterpillar."

Matthew chuckled along. Then he picked up his kettle. "Just might have an alternative if you're game."

The next thing Celia knew, he was applying a mix of coffee grounds and honey to her face as faux stubble. Once done, she twisted around to show Owen, exaggerating a deep, husky voice: "Whaddya think, partner? I look like a train hopper to you?"

He raised a brow, his eyes lightly glazed. "You sure look like...something."

She rotated back to Matthew, and they burst into laughter. She'd almost forgotten the feeling of such pure, innocent merriment, the nostalgia of someone she used to be—particularly when in the company of the man she'd loved. It was a joy no sooner fueled now by Owen's rare smile.

Contrarily, the old-timer shook his head, his silvered bushy eyebrows drawn. He muttered about their silliness and drank his moonshine. What he didn't do was leave, giving Celia a sense that, in spite of himself, he enjoyed the company.

Since food seemed wise at that point, Matthew shared pieces of dried salted beef. The old-timer reciprocated, though cantankerously, by passing around half-stale bread along with his jug. Through the group's conversations under a starry sky, Matthew made clear he was raised in Kentucky but his family was Yankee through and through. And when he finally circled back to ask about the "long story" of Celia's disguise and their drenched attire—her recalling only then the cold she now barely felt, even out of the blanket—she delved into the highlights of their nautical adventures...granted, a bit out of order and with occasional slurring.

Seeming ponderous, Matthew released a long whistle. "Two survivors in a storm at sea, you say? I reckon I've heard that one before." He squinted, focusing, and switched to a dramatic stage voice. "'We are plunging madly within the grasp of the whirlpool—amid a roaring, and bellowing, and shrieking...of ocean and of tempest—'"

Owen assertively chimed in, "'The ship is quivering—oh God! And going down.'"

Celia gawked at him despite her slightly blurring vision. And she wasn't the only one impressed.

"You know Poe…" Matthew smiled as if speaking of an old mutual friend.

"Never had much of a choice." Owen shrugged with nonchalance, yet a corner of his mouth curved up and warmth entered his eyes. "In our house, my father quoted his works more than a preacher does the testaments."

Matthew nodded. "So your pa was a devout man of literature."

"Of my mother," Owen corrected. Matthew was as confused as Celia, based on the tilt of his head, until Owen explained, "Her name's Annabel."

"Ah, sure." Matthew sighed. "As in the beloved 'Annabel Lee.'"

Celia recognized the reference, having studied the poem by Edgar Allan Poe in school. Believed to have been written for his late wife, it expressed love that transcended their insurmountable separation.

"Your pa must quote that one often," Matthew said.

"He used to, but…then she got sick…" Owen's expression gradually fell, and he finished simply: "It's been a while since I've heard it."

Absorbing this, Matthew nodded with a look of compassion.

Celia expected Owen to reapply his armor, even go for a walk to distance himself in every way. But perhaps due to the alcohol or just from Matthew's demeanor—so personable and disarming he could tame a rattlesnake—Owen proceeded, in turn, to ask Matthew about his family and fondness for literature.

This softer, vulnerable side of Owen was a lovely thing—of which Lettie was no doubt aware. An enticing reason to marry the fellow. It seemed Lettie's fortune was changing for the better. Not unlike Celia's, in fact. For soon, she'd be back home with Pearl.

From the comfort of the thought and crackling fire, Celia's eyelids grew heavy, along with her head. She lowered to rest it on the wadded blanket, fully overcome by the booze and exhaustion of a tremendously surreal day. Further soothed by the men's alternating voices, she let her eyes close. When next she opened them, it seemed only seconds had passed, but the fire had diminished to smoldering embers.

Once again, she was alone.

Owen was gone.

CHAPTER FIFTY

The old-timer's moonshine, which had so effectively helped warm Celia, now became her greatest hindrance. Still woozy, she rose to her feet with an altered sense of balance. The darkness shrouding the sky was lifting ever so slightly, revealing the sparsity of the camp, with most people surely asleep.

Perhaps Owen was simply dozing elsewhere. Though why stray from the fire—and from her? Unless seeking more food or water or...

Matthew would know.

Straining to focus, she ventured toward his tent. The bay air filtered through her clothes, still damp, spreading a shiver over her skin. When she reached his home, she found it vacant. A possibility unsettled her: Owen, having grown antsy, could be using Matthew's guidance to hop an earlier train.

But would they really leave her behind?

Fear gnawed at her as she proceeded to comb through the area, attempting not to stagger while avoiding bumps and divots in the dirt. Toward the edge of camp, at the base of a tree, sat two male figures, side by side in silhouette.

Hopeful, she moved closer.

She was seeking familiarity in their faces when Owen's voice, layered with Matthew's soft laugh, confirmed neither had left.

Relief flowed through her, tinged with surprise. It was remarkable that they'd managed to keep talking so long. Owen especially.

Then Matthew looked at him, and they both fell quiet. Their gazes held, their bodies just inches apart.

Maybe the liquor was clouding Celia's perception, but something about the exchange felt...intimate.

From her sudden grasp of the situation, instinct shifted her back a step. The scuffing noise caused Owen to twist toward her. His eyes expanded in alarm, only affirming her suspicions.

"Celia, wait." He scrambled to his feet.

This wasn't her business. She turned to leave, awkward, embarrassed.

But then came thoughts of Lettie, specifically how much she'd already endured, how undeserving she was of another man's betrayal. And Celia stopped.

She spun around to face Owen, doubting all she'd heard and believed of him to be true. "Was everything you told her a lie?"

He halted just a few feet away, looking out of sorts.

Did he actually not recognize the reference?

"Lettie," she spat. "Did you lie about being in love with her? About your plans to marry her?"

Comprehension appeared to settle over him. But then his mouth formed a straight line, and he replied in a murmur, "I don't know what you're talking about."

She shook her head, appalled at his convenient loss of memory. "Well, at least she'll understand you're not worth the trouble. For you best believe I'll be telling her the truth. She and any other woman who'll listen will learn all about you and...and about *this.*" She waved a hand toward where Matthew had been seated before striding away in the direction of his tent.

Owen stepped closer, turning steely. "You won't say a word. Because you don't know a thing."

Anymore, this wasn't enough to intimidate her.

"I know Lettie's my dearest friend in the world. And she deserves far better than the hurtful liar you are."

He huffed a laugh, irking her further.

"You find that funny?"

"I find it amusing you think this woman—this Lettie—is your friend when she's anything but that. Can't you see that by now?"

"Don't be absurd. Of course she is. Why would you say such a vile thing?"

"You think I'm the liar? Nothing I've told you has been untrue. Your *friend*, on the other hand, reeled you in with a whole string of lies. The story of some hideout and fugitives? Me going to the mayor with it? Evidently, even an imaginary courtship for some reason—to get you to trust me, I suppose."

His words were so unexpected that part of Celia couldn't help but question their veracity. Seeking to discount them, she challenged, "Oh really? And what on earth would she have gained from all that?"

He shrugged but with a lack of casualness. "Honestly, I couldn't tell you. For her role in the deal, she obviously had a price. The truth of it is"—he paused before finishing—"I've never met the lady."

Celia blinked, taken aback. Of all his claims, the last one struck as the most outlandish. She wanted to accuse him of spewing more falsehoods, yet the sudden gravity in his bearing, pronounced in his eyes, told her otherwise.

Though still wary, striving to make sense of things, she dared ask, "What are you saying? That Lettie took part in your deal with the mayor, trying to drive me out?"

He looked away, as if second-guessing how much to share. The authenticity she sensed in his hesitation was more distressing than anything he'd said yet. She refused, however, to let him shut down this time.

"Owen, tell me. No more secrets." She was exhausted enough by the burden of her own.

After a reluctant beat, he dragged his attention back to her. "The deal wasn't the mayor's. It was Humphrey's."

"Humphrey...as in Gordon Humphrey?"

Owen nodded, baffling her. That couldn't be right; she distinctly recalled, at the gambling hall, his saying how her presence could complicate the ambitions of a powerful man...

The memory trailed off, and she balked at her initial presumption—natural, if mistaken.

"I don't understand. What does Humphrey have to do with *me*?"

Owen cocked his head slightly. "Aside from the Dewdrop?"

She stared at him, even more perplexed.

"You don't know?"

She shook her head, inviting an explanation.

He raised a shoulder. "From what I've gathered, when you were with child, the mayor went to him for help. Wanted to move you into one of the man's hotels—to live and work. Humphrey opted for a brothel, since he owns that too. Same as the gambling hall where I was sent to make you the offer."

The discovery that the Dewdrop was owned by Gordon Humphrey sent Celia's mind into a whirl—as much from the connection as the hypocrisy. No wonder the "big boss," as Marie called the owner, never showed his face: to maintain his public persona. A repugnant charade.

Just to think...the man was grandstanding for the betterment of the nation, all while running illegal businesses that catered to vices—employing even a Chinese madam. Despite his racist diatribes, so long as the immigrants made him money, clearly they were fine by him.

"Our meeting was supposed to be on the docks," Owen continued. "But Lettie would only agree to lure you out, apparently, to a place with plenty of people—the one good thing she did for you. So Humphrey switched it to his gambling hall. You'd have to be in disguise that way, and no one would remember seeing you if...if you suddenly..."

"What?" Celia said. "Suddenly what?"

"Disappeared."

Stunned by the implication, the extreme measure, she breathed, "Why?"

"He's invested too much into the mayor's career. Presuming any of the bits I've caught about you are true—and even if not—he can't risk your sabotaging Bettencourt with a scandal."

Political influence, he meant. Guaranteed to increase with an elected senator.

But this scheme couldn't have all come from Humphrey. The mayor too was obviously involved, given the timing Celia had been deemed a threat—to a level worthy of murder, a task assigned to more than a messenger.

"You're a killer," she realized with a start. She stepped backward, away from Owen.

"No. Never." He held up his palms, a display of innocence. "Look, I've done things I'm not proud of. After my mother passed, my father went down a real dark hole, with gambling and... Anyway, I did what I had to do to chip away at his debt to Humphrey."

His father. So that was the person in trouble he'd meant to help. Yet at what cost to others?

"I'd never hurt a woman though. I swear it."

"But you agreed to!"

At her raised volume, he glanced around. Though no one appeared in the proximity, he responded in a hushed voice, "If not me, you think he wouldn't have found someone else to do it?"

"And what if I'd refused the deal? Then what?"

"I wouldn't have given up until you said yes." His tone was insistent—the same as when he'd first tried to persuade her, right before they happened to be drugged. Or was that also Humphrey's doing?

"What about the raid? And being shanghaied? The truth this time."

He shook his head. "It was never part of the plan. Like I said, just dumb, rotten luck. Believe me."

Now she was the one who laughed, darkly. "Sure. Why would I not?"

"Celia, just listen."

But she couldn't listen to more of his reasoning, because a thought suddenly shook her to the core. She wasn't the only one potentially viewed as a detriment to the mayor's career. "What was to happen to Pearl if I'd so-called disappeared? Were you supposed to…"

She couldn't complete the question, the mere idea too ghastly for words.

"No," he asserted, "the child was never to be hurt."

She released a breath. "Thank heavens."

But Owen's expression didn't share her assurance.

"There's more. What is it?" She tensed further, for again he appeared reluctant.

"She was to be given to some family, off in another state. Far enough away that her ties would unlikely become a threat."

Just then, a notion dawned on Celia and washed her in terror: "I did disappear though. What if they already gave her away?"

"We'll start back tomorrow," he quickly supplied. "First thing. And if needed, we'll find her, wherever she is." He reached for Celia's arm as if for comfort, but she jerked back from him and gaped.

"You've known all this time and never said a word..." How dim of her, how reckless to have trusted this man, particularly after Stephen's duplicity. And once more, Pearl stood to suffer the consequences. Celia's throat turned impossibly dry, though she managed to bite out a final order. "Stay away. You hear me? I want nothing from you—ever."

Head pounding, she didn't wait for a response, just turned and strode off, directionless. She yearned to distance herself yet had no clue where to go.

Except home. She needed to head home—tonight if she could.

The old-timer was walking nearby, stooped with a slight limp. "Sir. Sir, please!"

"Huh?" A sharp groan.

She nearly tripped while approaching him, struggling to think, to not panic. "The trains. Bound for north...to Portland. Do you know where...where I can jump on one?"

"In your condition?" He scoffed. "I wouldn't bet on it."

"But I have to. For my daughter."

His lips curled as he studied her, deciding. Then he shook his head. "Won't be anything passing through this early. You want a chance of hopping one at all, you'll want to soak up that moonshine." With that, he continued to lumber away, leaving her at a loss until he looked back. "Well? You comin'?"

Befuddlement prevented her response.

"You need to eat, don't ya?"

Between the lingering booze and her fears over Pearl, nothing about food sounded appealing. Of course, by improving her hampered state, she could better plan what to do.

And so she accompanied him, away from the camp, toward an unknown destination.

Unfortunately, too late she sensed the decision was a mistake.

CHAPTER FIFTY-ONE

"Wait here." The old-timer didn't explain his reason for stopping Celia just before the end of the city block, but his manner made clear he had one.

"Sir...what are we—"

"*Sh.*" He flapped his hand behind him and advanced without her.

Through the muddling of her thoughts, she sought to understand his skittery glances at their surroundings, suggestive of paranoia. A sign of senility, maybe. Whatever the cause, his ambiguity added to her unease.

As he deepened his stoop and stretched his neck for a peek around the corner, apprehension drew her in close enough to trace his attention.

SCIULLI'S ITALIAN BAKERY

Across the street and midway down the block, the name emblazoned the side of a bread-delivery wagon with a hitched horse waiting idly. At the rear of the vehicle, outside its rolled-up canvas, stood a man with a mop of black hair. He was passing a variety of hard loaves from a rolling cart to a boy aged around eight who, inside the wagon, hustled to keep up. They were the only two in sight.

Though Celia couldn't pinpoint the current hour, the predawn light and her familiarity with bakeries told her the shop was still closed. Perhaps before opening, the baker gave away bread too old to sell or at least discounted it for a negligible price.

She dearly hoped that was the old-timer's purpose, even as he turned to her with an undertone that indicated otherwise.

"All right, missy. When I say so, we'll hurry over to that there wagon to snatch two loaves, one for the each of us."

Dread gripped her, increasing the challenge to voice a clear thought. "But...I can't," she whispered back. "That wouldn't be... It's stealing."

His bushy eyebrows dipped in slants. "Well, ain't that a humdinger. Look who's suddenly high 'n' mighty. How exactly did ya think we was gonna get you fed?"

In all honesty, she hadn't bothered to think that far. If she had, though, she'd have figured on a charitable home or a church that doled out offerings.

Not this.

"I guess I just didn't plan on—"

"What? Taking something you didn't pay for?" A succinct description.

"*Yes.*"

His mouth quirked into a sneer. "You sure didn't take any issue with drinking my moonshine, now did ya? Eatin' food that could've filled my own belly? Where you think that bread came from—that I'd baked it myself?"

She had no response. She felt foolish and, deservedly or not, ungrateful.

He set his fists on the hips of his ratty trousers. "Missy, I obeyed plenty of rules in my time. Heck, I put on a uniform and helped drive out the Mexicans, battlin' men I had no personal gripe with. All it got me was a bum leg and an even harder life." He paused then, blew out a breath, as if trying to rein in the topic or maybe his impatience. "Now, you listen here—no bakery is going under on account of a couple measly loaves. You wanna starve, so be it. But least you could do is help me get in and out of the wagon so I can replace the loaf I was good enough to share."

His points were difficult to counter, due as much to her haziness as a resonance of injustice. Moreover, she suspected he'd proceed even without her but slower and hindered. She therefore found herself nodding.

"Good," he said. "Now, when they go back into the shop, we'll have five minutes. Got that? Just five." Again, he peeked around the corner, and before she could reconsider, he urged over his shoulder, "They're gone already—let's get to it."

Pulse instantly doubling, she followed him in charging toward the wagon. He was brisker than expected, given his age and limp. Ironically, she had to concentrate on her own strides to keep them straight and maintain her balance.

There was no one else on the street, not in front or behind them. The door of the brick bakery was shut. Wafts from heated dough thickened with their approach, the first time to Celia's memory the scent wasn't a comfort.

At the rear of the wagon, the old-timer lifted the canvas, which had been dropped back into place. It made sense why he had to climb inside rather than just reach in: there were loaves aplenty, stacked high and sorted by varieties, but filling only the front half of the transport. She imagined the baker now in the kitchen, restocking his cart to fill the rest of the wagon in preparation for his route.

"Hold this up," the old-timer whispered and transferred the duty of propping the flap. Then he quickly placed a hand on her shoulder and a foot up on the wagon. Aided by her grasp on his arm, he heaved himself skyward, but midrise, his foot slipped off onto the ground, sending his shoe tumbling into the street. The horse snorted from the movement.

Right away, the old-timer gripped Celia's shoulder to try again. He raised his socked foot, big toe exposed.

Her head throbbed harder as she looked back at the bakery, saw nobody, but that could change any moment. This was taking too long.

"Here, let me do it." A single loaf—that was all they needed. She could snag one in a few meager seconds.

He scooted aside, allowing her entry. She began the climb but struggled—a surprise, though it shouldn't have been. Exhaustion from the swim, the ship, from everything, had weakened her muscles to those of a newborn's. She felt the booze swish in her stomach.

Summoning her will, she pushed herself up, the wagon tilting a bit under her weight. The shifting of hooves sounded as she rose into a stoop, limited by the ceiling. Behind her, the canvas dropped—the old-timer needed to fetch and don his missing shoe.

She moved toward the bread just as he said something from outside. She strained to process it, her brain murky, before reminding herself to hurry. From atop the closest stack, she snatched a hard loaf, causing a few others to fall. They thumped upon landing, loud as an alarm. The wagon jerked backward, the horse apparently startled, knocking Celia into the flanking columns. A storm of bread rained down, and the loaf slipped from her hand.

Heart hammering, she abandoned her mission and rushed to get out. She stumbled over loaves that collapsed under her steps. When she gripped the edge of the canvas, the old-timer's hand was fortunately there to help. He grabbed her wrist and guided her down. She was ready to run, but he didn't let go.

It was then that she looked up and discovered the old-timer was gone. The man clutching her with paw-like hands—strengthened from working dough, toughened from the ovens—was the Italian baker.

"You are thief!" The rolling *r* in his accent did nothing to soften his tone; it exuded as much anger as his huge brown eyes, which snapped toward his shop. "Antonio!" he roared. "Antonio, *vieni qui! Sbrigati!*"

The young boy reemerged. He gaped as the baker rattled off more words that Celia was unable to interpret, save for one. That single word stole her breath just as the boy sped off down the street.

Polizia.

CHAPTER
FIFTY-TWO

"Lieutenant, please." Celia worked to control her anxiety as the tall officer, hair close cropped and eyes set a little too close, opened the cell door for her to enter. "If I could explain—"

He raised a splayed hand. "Just get in."

The younger policeman who'd arrested her had assured her the lieutenant was the one to speak with. Had that simply been a way to quiet her?

Wishing again not to seem defiant, she proceeded into the cell already occupied by two women, both on thin, striped mattresses—of which a couple more were vacant. One gal lay curled up on her side, coughing. The other, reclined against the wall with a tousled updo and dinner gown, sat up.

"*Heyyy*," she slurred. "This cell's for ladies. Put him in with the fellas."

"Calm yourself, Bitsy," the lieutenant said. "It's a she."

The woman's face twisted, but she sank back against the wall.

Celia swiped away the remnants of her coffee-ground stubble and addressed the officer as he shut the barred door. "Sir, I need to get back to Oregon as soon as possible. If you'd just hear me out. It would take only a moment."

"Save the effort. You'll be telling it all to the judge."

A trial. *For a solitary loaf?*

She suppressed panic that would do her no good. "How long before that happens?"

The officer's ring of keys rattled as he inserted one into the lock. "When it's your turn on the list. According to the schedule, about a week."

A week? She'd been away from Pearl for at least that. And now she knew that every passing day was crucial.

"But no—no, that's too long."

His gaze finally lowered to hers. "I guess you'll have plenty of time then to mull over the choices that got you here."

As if she could possibly think of anything else!

"Please, Lieutenant, I have a young daughter—"

Absent of interest, he walked back to the office area, deaf to her words.

—

The minutes stretched on endlessly.

As the liquor wore off, Celia reminded herself that already she'd been a prisoner and achieved escape. She could do it again.

Somehow.

Lying on her musty mattress, a pad that barely separated her from the concrete floor, she mentally cataloged all the goings-on around her: the duties of the few other policemen who passed through the cell room, the snippets of their conversations, how and when they carried a ring of keys.

During the lulls, she was actually grateful for Bitsy's snoring and the other woman's periodic coughing. Even for a drunken man's grousing from a nearby cell. The diversions helped limit her thoughts of Lettie, the friend she would have called upon at a time like this.

While she wanted desperately to dismiss Owen's claims, Lettie had indeed set her up with the disguise, the meeting, the false tales about Owen. Celia hadn't believed her own heart capable of aching again from betrayal, not after Stephen's, but she was wrong.

She could only hope she wasn't as wrong about Marie, specifically that the woman cared enough about Pearl to protect her.

Then again, for that very reason, Marie—and even the midwife—might still think the child best belonged with a proper married couple, a threat Celia had feared on more than one occasion. Perhaps for both women, there remained a profit to be made. Even if not, under Humphrey's employ, how could Marie refuse his order?

Distressed by the scenarios, Celia was attempting to shut them out when the lieutenant reappeared. Now a couple of hours after her arrival, he stopped at her cell and again inserted a key.

"Time to go."

His announcement was astounding—only slightly less so after the one feasible reason occurred to her.

Owen.

The old-timer must have reported back at the camp. After everything she and Owen had survived together, despite her commanding him to keep away, he'd tracked her down and come to fetch her.

Though eager to leave, she sat up without rushing, figuring she'd lessen the sway of the room if she rose in stages.

"Come on, hurry it up." The officer waited at the open door. "Your brother's here to take you home."

Brother?

Celia paused, then recognized the reason for the false title. Prisoners, particularly women, were unlikely released to a person not of relation.

The lieutenant sighed with impatience as she climbed to her feet. "I said shake a leg, Bitsy."

At the name, Celia froze. Reality shattered her hopes, including those regarding Owen. With her conveniently out of the way, essentially completing his side of the bargain, odds were high he was already on a train bound for Portland.

She sank back onto her mattress as the woman in the gown stood and sauntered past.

"You know, Lieutenant," Bitsy remarked, brushing off the skirt of her dress, "you really ought to wash these mattresses sometime. You wouldn't want this place gaining a poor reputation." Posed before him with hand on her waist, she winked, eliciting what seemed a rare smile from the man.

"I'll see what I can do before your next stay."

"Well, don't dawdle. Might be soon," she said, exiting the cell.

"I have no doubt," he murmured and resecured the door.

Celia brimmed with envy, wishing she could stroll out as easily. Of course, she wasn't here to just sleep off some booze; she'd been arrested for theft. Though well intentioned, she was guilty—and not only, she realized, for the crime at hand.

Threatening the mayor, in and of itself, had been rash. But pointing out Pearl's likeness to Abigail as evidence for a scandal had been infinitely worse, an irresponsible mistake that could mean losing her child forever.

Already Pearl might have been placed in another home. At night, would the child cry herself to sleep, thinking her mother had abandoned her? Would she come to believe she hadn't been loved?

In time, would she forget Celia completely?

CHAPTER
FIFTY-THREE

The coughing was no longer a helpful diversion; it became quite the opposite.

As the morning hours passed, not only did the woman's intensified hacking prevent Celia from drifting off, it enveloped her thoughts, linked to memories from her past. Her mother's coughs had sounded much the same, her breathing similarly labored, until they just stopped.

Celia's cellmate, likewise, remained curled on her mattress, her face largely veiled by her straggly, brown hair. Whereas Celia at least ate a portion of her own served oatmeal—no easy task, feeling the way she did—the other bowl remained untouched.

Concern growing, Celia crawled over from her own mattress. "Ma'am, are you all right?"

Another round of deep, hearty coughs came in response. They convulsed the woman's body before she fell limp. A shaken rag doll.

Celia hazarded to slide the hair from the woman's face, dampened from sweat. Her skin was pale yet hot, her lips shivering from chills. On the mattress were spots near her mouth. Fresh red stains.

Alarmed, Celia looked up just as the lieutenant was passing the doorway. "Sir! Please, this woman is ill."

He glanced from a distance. "Yeah, I've heard her. The lady's got a cold."

"She's coughing up blood," Celia argued. "She needs a doctor."

He appeared skeptical. Surely tricks of the like were often attempted as a means of escape, but he sighed and stepped closer. His eyes, from their subtle flash of apprehension, marked the instant he found the stains.

"All right," he said, tone even, though he wasted no time in recruiting help.

Celia remained in place until he returned with two cops carrying a stretcher. As the three entered the cell, she gave them needed space by returning to her mattress.

Though a bit less gentle than Celia preferred, the woman was transferred onto the canvas.

"Do we know who she is?" one of the officers asked the lieutenant.

"Just a vagrant," he replied. "As far as I can tell, no one of consequence."

The phrase poked at Celia, stinging her from familiarity. It took her a moment, but she recognized the echo of Georgia Bettencourt's voice. Several years ago, the gal had described Celia in near-identical words, dismissing her to a prim friend on the street, as if Celia's entire existence held no value. As if she could vanish and not a soul would notice.

She dreaded to think the same applied to this stranger.

"Lieutenant," she called out, delaying him from following the officers carting the woman out. "Do you know where she's going?"

"Any place that'll take her, I'd say." He went to leave again, but the answer was too vague for Celia's comfort.

"You mean a hospital, yes?"

Grudgingly, he turned back. His brow furrowed, for valid reason. It wasn't as if the women were truly acquainted.

"I'd just like to know she'll be getting the care she needs."

He considered this, and his expression softened. "There's a hospital not far away. They're fairly good about taking in patients like her."

Celia nodded, appreciative. "I'm pleased to hear that."

He lifted his chin in return. When he caught her gaze, it held, a moment of unspoken understanding. Together, their combined efforts might well have saved the woman's life.

Once the lieutenant exited and inserted the key, he paused and exhaled, contemplating for several seconds. Then, instead of locking the door, he swung it back open. "Stand up. Follow me."

She hesitated, confused. Would she be going along to the hospital?

"You want to see the judge, don't you?"

The offer was a surprise. "Well, yes. Of course." But her spark of delight was immediately extinguished by the rush of it all. She needed time to prepare as well as to recover. Her mind was still fuzzy, her mouth both dry and sticky.

"It's nothing formal," he explained. "Judge doesn't start his trials till midmorning. I can't promise you more than a few minutes. But it might be enough to appeal to him, get yourself in his favor before your hearing next week."

Encouraged if somewhat daunted yet, she realized she hadn't responded when the lieutenant muttered, "You don't want to? Fine by me." As he started to close the door, she clambered to her feet.

"No, wait—I do."

"Well then," he said. "Follow me, this way."

She trailed him out and, with his grip light on her arm, continued into the neighboring building, aware she would need more than an understanding judge. She'd need a merciful one for any chance of walking free.

CHAPTER
FIFTY-FOUR

He had exceptionally kind eyes. It was the first thing Celia noticed about the judge, who looked to be in his fifties. His other features had an equally soft quality about them, traits she focused on when, cued for her turn, she entered his chambers.

Needing to appear respectful and amenable, she stood with proper posture before his expansive maple-wood desk, where files lay neatly near a framed photograph—of family, she presumed. Behind him, flanked by bookcases crammed with fancy legal books, a framed diploma featured the name Alexander James Earnest in Old English script.

"Miss Celia Hart, is that correct?" he asked from his burgundy wingback chair.

"Yes, Judge—Your Honor."

He nodded while perusing a page. "This report is rather interesting. It says you've attempted to present yourself fraudulently as male, even going so far as to wear coffee grounds to portray facial hair. Is that accurate?" His gaze remained down, still reviewing.

"Yes—I mean, no." Her head regained a throbbing at the realization she was still in men's clothes. More importantly, she'd expected to have an informal conversation, not to make her case yet. And even then, only pertaining to the bread. "That is, I wasn't trying to be *fraudulent*, Your Honor. The coffee grounds were only needed because my mustache and beard had fallen off."

Goodness, how could she better explain? How far would she need to back up?

"I was on a ship, you see, where I'd worn the disguise. But to protect myself."

He looked up at her now. "You're saying you presented yourself as a man to work fraudulently as a sailor?"

That word again.

"No, sir. I never actually signed the captain's documents. Someone did that on my behalf." That hadn't come out right. "You must understand, it started only because I went to meet a gentleman in a gambling den, regarding a massacre of miners and his plan to get their gold—from the killers, that is, not the miners. Rather, I thought that's what the meeting was to be about."

A line of intrigue split the Judge Earnest's brow, and his speech slowed. "So if I understand this correctly, you were in an illegal gambling den, once again impersonating a man?"

She wasn't helping her cause, not a whit. His inclusion of the word "illegal" made that plain. How was she to answer his question without incriminating herself further? Unsure, she jumped forward in her story.

"I was drugged, sir, in a saloon, after a woman—a lady of the night—approached me, offering to mend my trousers. Of course, that's not what she intended, of which I am sure Your Honor is aware."

"Certainly," he interjected with a soft smile that just as soon leveled. Before she could continue, he asked, "And what of your theft at the bakery? Would you care to speak to that?"

The switch of topics jarred her. "I...yes, I would." The bread. Finally. "I was simply trying to assist an elderly man. Originally, I believed he was guiding me there for food to help soak up my moonshine...not mine, actually. It was his. But I'd only drank too much—or any of it, really—to warm up after swimming in the bay..."

Celia, what are you saying? Her nerves and lack of sleep, the growing pounding of her head, the booze—all of it had left her thoughts meandering and explanation rambling. Yearning to start over though doubting at this moment she could do much better, she veered back to the relevant points.

"And that is why...I climbed onto the delivery wagon for him, not for myself. He has a limp, from serving in the army. And then he slipped and lost a shoe—"

"Miss Hart, it's all right." The judge's voice was reassuring, as was his tender smile. "I am confident I've heard a sufficient amount. I've also read the arresting officer's report in detail." As he sat back in his chair and rubbed his chin, Celia's breath held. "You've clearly been through some harrowing experiences— much like a lively aunt of mine who often had similar tales of adventures, even creative attire as well. So I do understand."

Celia offered a grateful smile. Bridling her hopes, she refrained from speaking, worrying she'd only do more damage.

"For this reason," he said, his tone declarative, "while there are crimes you have clearly committed—about which you are at least forthcoming—I cannot say that I believe you belong in jail."

At the definitive judgment, relief burst through her and stretched her lips into a grin. "Oh, thank you," she blurted out. "Your Honor, thank you very much."

"I do, however, believe you require appropriate help to become a much more productive, healthy, and functioning *woman* in society. Therefore, you shall be relocated," he said, "to Brentwood Asylum."

The words had just sunk in when he yelled toward the door, ordering the lieutenant to take her back and arrange for transport.

CHAPTER
FIFTY-FIVE

Daylong ice baths and perpetual sedations. Bed restraints and solitary confinement. Forced sterilization and experimental surgeries.

Celia had heard many a rumor regarding asylums over the years. In markets or at dinner parties, she'd caught whispers about women sent away after being labeled "hysterical" by doctors— sometimes for merely being outspoken or because their husbands wished to move on with a mistress.

It had all seemed too preposterous to be true. And yet having presumed the same about shanghaiing and underground cells, she now feared the horrors that could well greet her come morning, when she'd be transferred in a secured wagon to an institution.

Perhaps forever.

Though she'd succeeded in fleeing captivity on a ship, the opportunities to escape a place that specialized in confining its patients for the supposed safety of the public would be close to nonexistent. And even if she managed it, which treatments would she have endured? Would she be remotely the same person?

Her pleas to the lieutenant as he escorted her back to jail once again fell on deaf ears. The more she protested, the more the judge's ruling appeared suitable. She detected the same perception on the other policemen's faces as she attempted, though briefly, to explain from her cell.

Their skewed view of her wasn't real. She knew this. For she knew who she was and that she wasn't mad.

But who among them would believe her?

———

The daylight hours ticked their way toward evening.

Alone, resigned to her mattress, Celia ate only nibbles from her served meals, her stomach in knots. In the adjacent room, the lieutenant was bidding his colleagues good night, sounding tired and glad to have completed his day.

Celia wondered if she'd be gone by the start of his next shift.

But instead of leaving, he began conversing with another man. Back and forth they went, their voices vague, before the lieutenant entered the cell room, trailed by a fellow in a brimmed hat. Not an officer's uniform.

"Sir, is this your wife?" The lieutenant gestured to Celia.

Her thoughts leaped to Stephen, despite her having no inkling how that could possibly be, but then the man hastened into full view with a rucksack in his grip.

"Oh, darling," Owen said, his tone refined. With beard neatly trimmed, he wore a smart coat and trousers that evidenced just a few mended holes. "Thank heavens I found you. Come, let me see you."

She smiled, nearly overwhelmed with relief, and didn't hesitate in rising to meet him at her cell door. Against her sensibilities, given all he had shared, she couldn't deny the comfort of his hand on hers through the bars.

"Lieutenant," he said and snapped his gaze toward the officer. "I demand you release my wife at once. It is a travesty to find her in such a state after less than a day in your care."

The lieutenant moved closer, and for a second, Celia expected a rattling from the lifting of keys. Rather, he replied with a hardened voice.

"Mr. Hart, I assure you, the state your wife finds herself in is not of our doing."

"Yes, well, all the same. Now that I'm here, there remains no good reason for her detention."

"I'm afraid that is not accurate, sir."

"Oh, but it is," Owen replied. "A gentleman I know personally happened to witness the alleged crime, and he would readily vouch that she emerged from the delivery wagon empty handed. As such, I see no thievery that was committed."

Celia pictured the old-timer peering from around the corner, watching the scene unfold after shuffling off.

"Mr. Hart, a ruling for theft is no longer being pursued."

Owen's eyes brightened. "Why, that's splendid. But then… why haven't you released her?"

Celia was about to fill him in but recalled how her earlier efforts had worsened her situation, and so she stayed quiet.

"Your wife has been found to suffer from identity issues—as I'm sure you can see and perhaps were already aware." The officer indicated her appearance with a quick up-and-down look.

Owen sighed casually as if amused. "This is obviously just a mix-up. In fact"—he raised the rucksack, seeming to suddenly remember it—"having heard she was dressed in costume, I brought her a favorite outfit from home."

Wherever the attire actually came from, it was a nice touch to support the claim of marriage.

"Sir, it seems you're unaware of the extent of the problem. The judge has reviewed her case and decided she would benefit from proper medical care at Brentwood Asylum."

Owen fell silent, thrown off by the development, worrying Celia.

She couldn't dispute that she'd long struggled with identity issues. But not of this sort and certainly not solvable by extreme therapies in an institution.

Letting go of her hand, Owen turned to the officer with renewed indignance. "Lieutenant Gregory," he ground out, "regardless of some judge's assessment, I assure you, I am fully capable of caring for my wife in the comforts of our own home."

Only then did Celia learn the officer's name.

"Well, *sir*," he shot back, his patience running equally thin. "Judge Earnest feels differently."

"Indeed, I heard you the first time."

Oh, enough. Celia groaned. If they kept up like this, they could well go to blows. Then Owen too could wind up behind bars, perhaps even quickening her trip to Brentwood.

She jumped in, "The judge was correct."

Both men startled, though for different reasons. With their stares upon her, she raced to gather her words while slowly facing the officer.

"Lieutenant," she said in a sheepish tone, "sadly, I was too embarrassed to tell the judge the true story—which even my husband doesn't know. You see, yesterday evening, when he claimed a need to depart on business, I got the silly notion in my head that he was sneaking off to… Oh, I hate to even say it…" She lowered her eyes, dangling the bait, hoping the officer would latch on.

But a quiet beat passed.

"Go on," he prodded at last, thankfully, and folded his arms. He was listening, but a small huff reminded her that he was antsy to end his shift.

"Of course," she said, picking up her pace as if eager to put the experience behind her. "Sir, I feared my husband was committing a romantic indiscretion with a woman who lives locally. To know for certain, I dressed as a man to follow him, only to witness him going straight to the depot. On my way home, however, I found myself a bit turned around and was lured into a camp by an older fellow who was much more cunning than I—naturally so, my being a woman. When he asked me to help him reach a loaf on a bread wagon, I presumed he was planning to purchase it. I learned shockingly too late that this was not the case. And due to my costume, I was without my coin purse to pay for it myself."

The officer's fingers were quietly thrumming his sleeve. Since it seemed a sign of wavering, she ventured to continue.

"I'm confident you can understand why, when the judge asked about my odd appearance and actions, I was so ashamed to have doubted my husband's devotion that I became utterly discombobulated, creating a ridiculous tale to explain. If only I were better at lying," she stressed with a shrug, "I suppose I wouldn't be here, asking for my dear husband's forgiveness—and for your mercy now."

She angled back to Owen with an apologetic look, cueing him to chime in.

"Darling...I had no idea." He took her hand again, a look of sincere awe in his eyes. "Though I'm the one who need apologize. You deserve never to feel inclined to question my devotion to you."

She nodded and forced her lower lip to tremble as if to hold back tears.

The lieutenant's lack of objection was promising.

But then he narrowed his eyes at her. "Ma'am, what about that daughter of yours, whom you supposedly need so urgently to return to? Up in Oregon, I believe you said?"

Doggone it. She was surprised he'd paid enough mind to recall that. Now he was using it to test her.

She shook her head regretfully. "Once again, just a poor excuse, which you shrewdly saw right through. I was simply trying to return home before my husband could discover how foolish I'd been."

Owen addressed the lieutenant with a calm demeanor. "Now that the situation is entirely clear, I respectfully give you my word that, as her husband, I will assume full responsibility for her actions."

The officer looked at her, then Owen, then her again and exhaled an audible breath. Whether he believed their alibis or was merely too tired to tussle with them anymore, he replied to Owen, "Get her dressed, and take her home."

CHAPTER
FIFTY-SIX

Under the evening sky, clear and peach hued, Matthew was waiting anxiously a block from the train depot. Based on the gleam of his eyes beneath his brimmed hat, his relief over Celia's liberation was nearly as great as her own.

After an exchange of hugs, he expelled a whistle. "Well, miss lady, don't you look spiffy."

"All with thanks to you." She trailed his glance over the outfit he'd resourcefully supplied. Procured through a trade, the powder-blue day dress fit rather well, and the heeled boots were just a little snug. The ribbon tied beneath her chin now brushed her neck, a reminder of the dainty hat that topped her updo— hastily pinned, so suffering a few stragglers. Still, even if Captain Sterling's crew remained in town, which was highly doubtful, they'd be hard-pressed to recognize her.

"I'd wager you've got another long story I'll want to hear sometime." Matthew smiled.

She nodded wearily, as there was plenty to tell.

"For now though..." He sighed, and regarded Owen. "We'd best get y'all to your chariot."

—

Tucked behind one of the many lines of freight cars parked at the station, the three waited for the 7:25 p.m. train to depart. Distant mumbling wafted from passengers climbing on board, preparing to travel north, the same as Owen and Celia, but in the comfort of seats.

Today, she cared nothing about such luxuries, only that if all went as planned, she'd be back in Portland in roughly two days, where she prayed her daughter safely remained. And if not, without question, this much she knew: no matter how long or far the search might take her, she would never give up until Pearl was in her arms.

Owen peeked around a boxcar, back toward the depot, to gauge the status of the idling locomotive. Already Matthew had snuck over to collect helpful details while avoiding the lone patroller—what freighthoppers called a "bull," he'd said, warning that some could be ruthless.

"Still got a little time yet," Matthew said in assurance now, checking his pocket watch again while seated on the graveled tracks.

Owen, back in his own clothes—having borrowed the others from Matthew—settled near him with elbows on his propped knees. One of his legs bounced from the wait, from the anticipation Celia too felt.

She didn't join them in sitting. Rather, she stood before the neighboring open boxcar, its floor at chest height, mentally rehearsing her boarding. She and Owen had already practiced a few rounds of his yanking her up and inside. Their actual hop would naturally be more challenging, with the train pulling out of the station.

"How 'bout that?" Matthew said.

Concerned, Celia turned to him, but he only motioned his chin toward the sky.

"The sun and moon both out. Take a gander."

It seemed a pesky distraction, until she recognized that relaxing might help—which surely he intended.

And so she looked up. A fading sun and a three-quarter moon hung distantly yet indeed were sharing the stage. She'd seen this many a time, of course, but in this instant, something about it felt different. In the best of ways. As if witnessing a secretive meeting.

"That's lovely," she said.

Owen too gazed upward, and his knee stilled. After a moment, clearly stirred by a memory, he murmured, "'For the moon never beams without bringing me dreams...of the beautiful Annabel Lee.'"

This time, Matthew was the one who provided the ending: "'And the stars never rise, but I feel the bright eyes...of the beautiful Annabel Lee.'"

The two exchanged not a glance, just let the words float between them, along with a palpable sense of connection. Celia recalled a similar feeling deep inside from what seemed a previous life.

Then two short whistles sounded. The train was about to depart.

When the men rose, Celia hugged Matthew again. "Thank you, dear friend. For everything."

"Pleasure was mine," he insisted. Then he angled toward Owen, and with warmth in his eyes, he extended his hand for a shake. Their hold lingered as he said, "Take care of yourself, Owen."

"You do the same." Owen seemed on the verge of saying more but offered a gentle smile, and their hands parted.

"All right then," Matthew said and looked at Celia. "Ya ready to run?"

Fortunately, he didn't wait for an answer, because after these past endless days—nine, by Owen's calculations—she definitely was not. But that didn't change the fact that she needed to and therefore would.

Matthew hustled in leading them to the next line of parked freight cars, which neighbored the track of the coming train. The sounds of slow chugging grew, and soon the engine passed by, towing a series of passenger coaches.

Celia took a bolstering breath, waiting for the freight cars to appear. Amid their total of around fifty, the fourteenth—a safe distance from the crew up in front and those in the caboose and with a door sufficiently ajar—was the one they'd be jumping. Hence, by the eleventh, they would start to run. Ready to count, she regarded Owen, his eyes intent on the train.

Finally, the first of the freight cars rolled past. Her nerves ratcheted with every rotation of the wheels.

Two...three...four...

As the count rose, Celia's legs grew restless despite their fatigue. In preparation, she gathered the hem of her dress and held it to her side, then Owen clutched her free hand. He would run closest to the train.

Five...six...seven...

Huffs from steam blended with rattling from the tracks. Even Matthew was counting under his breath.

Eight...nine...ten...

"Now!" Owen said. Together, they set off, leaving Matthew behind.

In a few strides, they reached the eleventh freight car. The locomotive was picking up speed. They jogged alongside it with hands still joined, letting the eleventh car pass. The ground was patchy and graveled. Celia kept her heels up by staying on the balls of her feet, causing her boots to pinch her toes. The skirts of her dress brushed heavily against her legs.

As the twelfth car passed, she glanced back at the thirteenth.

One more, just one more. Her breaths were thinning, her legs burning. She concentrated on maintaining her balance as number fourteen arrived.

"This is it," Owen said and released her hand. They sustained their pace. Once close to the partially open door—just as Matthew had described—Owen grabbed on to the floor of the boxcar and, while in motion, heaved himself through. Then he scrambled onto his knees and turned to face Celia. Gripping the doorframe, he prepared to help her board.

But the fabric in her hand—it was slipping from her grasp. The skirts were hampering her strides. *Keep going, keep going.*

He held out his free hand for her to grab. She reached for it, still running. Their fingers were but an inch apart when her boot tangled in the hem of her dress. She stepped hard on the fabric, and her body flew forward. She barely caught herself from sprawling over the ground but stumbled onto one knee. Their boxcar was charging away.

"Celia, hurry!" Owen shouted.

She couldn't run without regathering her skirts. She rushed like the devil to do so, pulling them higher with one hand. The front of the next car began to pass her by. Her body was begging to collapse.

"Run!" he yelled.

Somehow, she mustered enough strength to launch into a sprint. Heart thundering, feet throbbing, she strained to catch up. The train clacked faster.

At last, closing in on Owen's outstretched hand, she reached for it. The gap between them persisted, so he extended his arm farther. Upon the brushing of their fingertips, she dared to lurch toward him, risking a tumble onto the ground that would end their efforts. But just in time, he managed to grasp her wrist, and in a single jerking motion, he pulled her up and on board. As she slid on her belly, he fell back and landed with a grunt.

Panting, she connected with his gaze. They traded looks of relief before she discovered they weren't alone. Between stacks of crates sat a pair of adolescent boys and a lone older man, all staring wide-eyed. She presumed it was strictly from the excitement until remembering her attire—more suitable to the rider of a passenger car than to a train hopper, for certain. What an oddity she must have seemed, but at least an amusing one.

She joined Owen in standing and brushing off their clothes. Then, against a wall, she sat beside him—slumped there, actually—and fully caught her breath. On the closest crate, *SEATTLE* was stenciled in black. Same as the next crate and the next. The stated destination suggested that this particular boxcar would be passing through Portland and not unloaded until well after that. A welcomed assurance.

As the train rocked and rattled onward, Owen set his hat on his lap and reclined. "I'll keep watch. Get some rest."

The idea of resting, the fact that she could—for the moment anyhow—was undeniably inviting. Shifting onto her side, she used her elbow for a pillow and wriggled to get comfortable. As it was a slight challenge given her outfit, to help doze off, she set her thoughts adrift. Soon, they were wandering through her stories. Not just of the jailhouse but those of her daughter, her parents, her journey.

She recognized more than ever: the stories people tell, to themselves above all, were often what kept them going.

When looking back on life, really, who was anyone without them?

CHAPTER
FIFTY-SEVEN

Jostled by the train's motion, Celia groggily opened her eyes and found the space beside her vacant. While weaving in and out of half sleep, through various stops, she'd glimpsed figures hopping on and off the boxcar. It occurred to her now that one of them might have been Owen.

She sat up and discovered the lone stranger and adolescents gone. In their place sat a Chinese couple who looked to be in their thirties—thus were likely a good decade older. Dressed in quilted travel clothes, they conversed softly in their dialect.

And against a wall near the door sat Owen.

Face aglow from the pink-orange sunset, he was watching the passing scenery. From the absence of his coat, she noticed her head had been cushioned by the balled-up garment. She smiled with gratitude and caught a whiff of snacks from one of the coat pockets. Matthew had packed cheese and dried salted beef in a handkerchief for the trip.

Her stomach consequently growled just as the Chinese couple unpacked a meal from their scarf, including food familiar at a glance. It was bao. The favorite treat she used to share with her father.

She could still see him rolling the dough, then folding it around the filling. Steaming the buns perfectly, each round and smooth and pillowy. Laughing with her over the mess they had made...

"You want?" The man raised a bao toward Celia, alerting her that she'd been staring.

"Oh...sorry. I'm fine. But thank you." She tendered a meek smile. How embarrassing to come across as silently begging.

The woman replied, "Come." She waved Celia over, then patted the floor. "You eat."

Out of courtesy, Celia stayed reluctant, and the man smirked a bit, as if to say challenging his companion was a fruitless endeavor.

The woman patted the floor again, less an invitation than an order.

As it seemed more of an offense to decline, Celia complied by joining them but with an offering of her own. She presented a portion of her meat and cheese, which they accepted before courteously bowing their heads. Then the man placed the bun in Celia's hand, and a word she'd long forgotten floated back, the name of the dessert.

She lifted it. "Nai wong bao?"

The couple looked pleased that she knew the term, though the man shook his head. "Pork bao."

The woman flicked her hand toward the bun, a command for Celia to eat, and so she did. The bread was soft in the way only bao could be, in her hand and even more in her mouth. Although its filling, being a tangy-sweet pork, differed from the custard held fondly in her memory, it still tasted—in the best way she could describe it—like home.

"Good?" From the man's question and the couple's chuckling, she realized she had closed her eyes and must have looked foolishly lost in bliss.

She smiled, wanting to at least explain. "As a child, I used to make bao with my father."

The couple's amusement faded, replaced by expressions of intrigue, understandably. The activity was a rarity for someone who looked like her.

The added explanation formed on Celia's tongue, yet in contrast to countless times before, she felt no desire to swallow it down. "My father was Chinese." The words flowed out so easily that in their wake emerged two more: "Like me."

A sense of pride filled her, a deep connection to her father, her heritage. Herself. Never again, she decided, would she feel ashamed of her lineage, most especially when it came to Pearl.

Appearing confused, the couple conferred in their dialect. Then, as if comprehending, they turned back to Celia and smiled. Perhaps they were simply being polite, but it seemed a message of acceptance.

The man held up another bao. "Take more."

They were being far too generous. Celia was about to resist, but he gestured with it toward the door. "For your friend."

"Oh my. That's so kind of you." After accepting and bowing her head in gratitude, Celia ventured over to Owen. "Delivery," she said, settling before him and passing along the gift.

"Thanks." He gave a tender smile, then enjoyed the bun in just a few bites. But as they sat there, gazing at the sunset, she sensed the rebuilding of a wall that seemed to have briefly dropped away—one much like the kind she'd unknowingly built within herself.

Unaware of what would become of their friendship once they faced all that lay ahead, she felt compelled to voice a thought for any impact it might make while the opportunity remained.

"Owen, at the risk of overstepping, I wanted to tell you…"

He waited, warily curious.

"I know the feeling of needing to hide who I am." She was tempted to end there but dared to add, "I also know what it's like to love someone you can't be with."

A muscle in his jaw tightened. His attention cut to the scenery, clearly wanting her to stop. So she would, but with a final point.

"Just know that I understand and you're not alone."

Owen didn't reply. But after a quiet stretch, he gave an almost imperceptible nod.

There was no need to say more.

Leaving him be, she returned to her spot by the other wall. There, she reflected on her own heart's path, one that ended with regret and resentment. In her darker moments, she had wished she'd never met Stephen. But then she wouldn't have experienced the most joyous love imaginable—first with him and then with Pearl. So although he was gone from her life, if given the choice, she'd do it all precisely the same.

Comfort from the thought helped fend off her worries through the remainder of the night and through the next day as the train rattled on. She and Owen took turns napping while the other kept tabs on their progress and an eye out for patrollers.

After nearly two full days on the train, she'd grown so accustomed to the sounds of the door sliding opened and closed from a rotation of travelers that when she jolted awake, it took her a moment to decipher the noise that had roused her.

The blast of a gun.

CHAPTER
FIFTY-EIGHT

"Celia, get up," Owen urged after a glance from the partially open door.

Somewhere outside, in the dim evening light, a man was bellowing orders to halt. Regaining her bearings, Celia realized a patroller was clearing out hoppers—a "bull" using force, as Matthew had warned.

She hastened to rise as several fellows scrambled from the boxcar. This left only her and Owen. To lead them out, he jumped from the car just as another shot fired. At his vanishing, her heart contracted.

She hustled toward the door despite fears for herself and braced for the sight of him sprawled on the ground. Instead, having merely crouched upon landing, he sprang to stand and turned to reach for her. "Come on."

Relieved, if briefly, she rushed to sit at the edge and, given her cursed heels and dress, accepted help without hesitation. He gripped her sides, and with her hands on his shoulders, she landed on gravel lining the tracks.

In the train yard, freight hoppers—dozens of them—were scattering every which way. Many were jumping out of cars, some descending ladders from the roofs. Others climbed out from the undercarriages.

"*Stop there!*"

"*You—halt!*"

The patrollers' voices varied, soaring from indiscernible directions.

"Let's go." Owen tugged her arm, and they launched into a sprint alongside the boxcars.

A slew of hoppers zipped past, headed the opposite direction. The most likely reason arose from the sight up ahead, slowing Celia's feet. A uniformed patroller with a club was beating a man huddled on the ground, arms shielding his skull.

Owen too must have seen this, because he paused and scanned the area, then said, "Follow me, this way." He veered toward a freight car parked on the next track, expecting her to trail him.

And yet the directive stalled her. Although common enough, it was the lieutenant's very phrase that had led her inadvertently into what could have been a lifelong trap.

Owen dropped down and crawled to pass under the boxcar. As soon as he cleared it, he rose and turned. "Celia, hurry."

Mere days ago, she'd viewed this man as not just a betrayer but also a henchman assigned to take her life. Although he'd come to her aid at the jailhouse, was she indeed mad to place her faith in him now?

Allowing her gut to guide her, she made a choice.

She followed his path under the freight car. She was about to stand and join him when yet another shot fired, close enough to ring in her ears. Instinct pulled her into a crouch, and she shut her eyes. Opening them, she found Owen on his back, gripping his thigh.

She gasped. "Owen, no…"

He looked at her, pain tightening his face. "Go," he ordered, then shifted his attention to the stocky man holding a revolver just thirty feet away. Whether or not the bull had been aiming at another target, he was now focused on Owen, and a click suggested his cocking of the barrel.

Before Celia could act, even deter him with a scream, a scuffling sound intervened. The bull swung toward it and faced the other way. Not far from him, a lanky fellow had jumped from a boxcar and stumbled on gravel, toppling to the ground.

"Halt!"

The train hopper, perhaps from seeing Owen wounded, refrained from running. He raised his hands in surrender, and the bull moved toward him.

Celia's spinning thoughts narrowed. The patroller clearly considered Owen subdued, enough to apprehend the other man first. A brief window of distraction. Celia raced quietly to help Owen to his feet and supported him to round a boxcar on the neighboring tracks. The other hoppers had grown sparse.

Cautiously, she assisted in weaving Owen through the lines until reaching a ditch. She guided him to sit with her, low and out of sight. He stifled a groan, still holding his leg. Blood tainted his trousers, his fingers.

"I'll get you help," she told him, having no clue how or where, only that it was vital.

Seeking a frame of reference, she dared a glimpse out of the ditch. A sign in the distance declared the area Oregon City. Just two stops from Portland.

"You need to go," he argued, a shake in his voice. "Leave while you can and get to your daughter."

Staying meant the possibility of remaining in harm's way, but no chance would she leave him to fend for himself—not like this.

She recalled from Stephen, from his shared highlights of caring for wounded animals, that stemming blood flow was crucial.

For a bandage, fabric would do.

She snatched the hem of her dress where her boot had ripped a hole, tore off a strip, and folded it into layers. "Here, press this to the wound."

As he accepted the fabric, the ribbon dangling from her hat spurred an idea.

She pulled the satiny tie free and tossed the hat aside. Her fingers trembled from adrenaline and worry. "You're going to be fine," she insisted, wrapping the ribbon around his leg to help secure the bandage. "Everything will be. We'll get your father's debt all sorted, and you'll set out and see the world. Understand?" She tied the knot, causing him to grimace. "You'll even swing through San Francisco, see a friend who wants to explore the world too." She wasn't just assuring him; she was rambling, yes, but also commanding him, not giving him any alternative.

"We'll see," he rasped. As she finished adjusting the bandage, he murmured as if having given it more thought, "Yeah. Yeah, maybe..."

She sat back to take a breath and noted the quiet. No footsteps, no voices.

Twisting back over the ditch, she again assessed their surroundings. Not a hint of anyone remaining, neither travelers nor patrollers.

They could make it to the road. But what then?

Two whistles blared. The train was about to resume its journey.

To reach Portland by foot would take a full day, half that by wagon—if they even found a driver willing to pick them up. By locomotive, they could be there in less than an hour.

Struck by a notion, she faced Owen. "With my help, could you climb back into a boxcar?"

His brow dipped. "After all that, you want to jump the same train?"

"It's a blatantly foolish thought, I know. Which is why I figure we ought to be in the clear."

He pondered this, no doubt hindered by his pain. As they didn't have time to mull further, she repeated his demand that had served them well.

"Trust me," she said.

He met her eyes, and he nodded.

"Good. Now let's go." She helped him to stand, and again with caution, they retraced their path to the very freight car that had delivered them here. She looked on with relief at the door that remained open enough to permit them to board.

She had just given Owen's booted foot a lift, hefting him into the car, when the train started to roll. With both hands and every ounce of her strength, she heaved herself up and inside.

Two more stops, that was all they needed.

She still didn't know how they would treat his wound from there. She knew only where they would go for help—the same place she prayed she would find her daughter.

CHAPTER
FIFTY-NINE

Even from the street, it was clear the inn was bustling. Though standard in the evenings, the sight was both welcome and daunting.

Once through the front door, Celia remained at Owen's side, a defense against any distracted patrons apt to bump into his wound. One such customer was swaggering from the base of the stairs, where Harriet had just seen him off.

Her gaze caught on Celia's, and she beamed. "Celia, you're back," she said before shifting toward Owen. "Well...my oh my..." Her assumption evident, she thought romance had drawn Celia away.

Since correcting her would waste time, Celia just stated, "He's hurt and needs help."

Harriet's look of intrigue morphed into concern as she noticed his bloodied grip pressed to his makeshift bandage. "Let's bring him to the kitchen," she said.

Guiding Owen in limping behind Harriet, Celia considered sending for the midwife. While bullet wounds doubtfully ranked among her specialties, Mrs. Downey was well adept in emergencies and, during Pearl's birth in this very home, had likely saved Celia and her child.

The instant Celia helped Owen into a chair at the table, however, Harriet perked up at a thought. "There's a fella in the parlor. Served as a medic in the cavalry, I think. I'll go fetch him."

"Wait—before you go," Celia said, stopping her midturn. "Is Pearl here?"

Harriet balked. "I...I thought she was with you."

The vault within Celia, where she'd managed to contain the worst of scenarios, suddenly flew open. Fear engulfed every fiber of her being and appeared to spill over to Owen, whose eyes shone with worry.

Despite this, he spoke with confidence. "You'll find her. Like you said, everything's gonna be fine."

Celia focused on his words, determined to believe them. Besides, she realized: someone knew where Pearl was, and that person was darn well going to share.

Swinging back to Harriet, Celia demanded, "Where's Lettie? And Marie?"

"Marie's been out since morning." Even without Harriet's tone, Celia knew this was peculiar. "Last I saw though, Lettie was upstairs."

About to charge straight there, Celia glimpsed Owen's leg. She hesitated over leaving him in such a state.

"Go on," he said, understanding. "The medic will get me all fixed up."

She nodded and, desperately hopeful, flew past Harriet and up to the second floor, dodging customers and several of the inn's ladies—a few of whom zealously commented on her return—and burst into Lettie's room.

Though the lamplit space looked vacant at first, on the bed lay a blanketed object, shaped like a small body. Like Celia's precious girl, all cozy and curled up.

Deciding Harriet had been mistaken, she treaded over with breath held and slid back the cover, only to find a bundle of sheets and clothing.

Panic tightened her throat as she rotated in place. Visually scouring the room, seeking even the slightest clues of Pearl's whereabouts, she inadvertently kicked something.

A leather-bound sketchbook protruded from under the bed. Lettie had never shared its contents. The one time Celia had inquired over them, Lettie declared them "personal," which Celia had respected easily. But that was back when Lettie's secrets seemed harmless. Now Celia envisioned notes for schemes covering the loose papers inside, maybe even details key to locating Pearl.

She moved the sketchbook to the bed and flung open the cover. Yet she found no words, only drawings of a female child at various stages—as a baby, a toddler, a young girl.

Was it Pearl in all the sketches?

Celia inhaled a shaky breath.

For the past two years, she'd viewed Lettie as family and thought the feeling mutual. Instead, had Lettie been acting on her own hidden purpose? When the opportunity arose, had she struck a deal to steal Pearl? Perhaps she'd even pursued the trade herself.

"Celia! Oh, thank the heavens." Lettie stood just inside the doorway, her hand over the bust of her corset. "Been frettin' to death that something horrible happened to you."

Celia held up a page, her whole arm trembling now. "What is this? All this time, you've been obsessing over Pearl? Biding your time to take her as your own?"

Lettie's eyes went wide. "What? Of course not. That's ludicrous. I would never!"

"Then explain this to me." She snatched up more papers. "And this one. And this."

"They're..." Lettie's pale skin flushed as she struggled to answer. "They're my daughter."

Lies. All she told were lies. "You said you gave her up when she was a baby. So how could you possibly know the way she looks?" Celia relinquished the pages, letting them fall onto the coverlet.

Lettie strained to reply, her eyes welling. "By imagining it." She lifted a shoulder. "Whenever I see Pearl or any wee one on the street. A girl in a park or a shop. Try as I might, I can't help but wonder: Is that how my sweet Clementine looks now? Her face, her hair? Does she have my hands? Any trace of me at all?" Lettie's chin quivered, yet she pressed on.

"So when Humphrey came to me, saying he'd take me to her—not to keep, mind you, but to at least see how she's fared—I could barely think. He said all I need do was get you to meet a feller in private about a special offer. The best I could figure was that in some way, it might involve the mayor's son. Given how Stephen left things with you, I was doubtful you'd agree to go, and I couldn't take that chance. Even though deep inside I knew Humphrey was lying about me ever seeing my babe, how could I not have tried? Not hoped?" A tear broke free as she stepped closer, an appeal in her eyes.

"I'd insisted on your meeting in public, of course, to make sure you were safe. I thought you'd be even more so, what with your being dressed as a man. But then you didn't come back, and I've been just sick over it. Even went to Humphrey, I did—the mayor too—demanding to know what came of you. But they both swore they hadn't an inkling, that they were as stumped as I was."

On that account, Celia acknowledged, the men were telling the truth. But then she abruptly reminded herself that none of it mattered. Only this: "Where is Pearl?"

Lettie paused and swiped the moisture from her cheeks, her feelings being secondary; same for questioning where Celia had been these many days. She replied simply, "Marie placed her elsewhere."

Celia stared, terrified over what that meant. "Placed her where?"

"I was still so worried about you that I told her all I knew, about you and your daughter, and she shared the same with me. Wary of the boss man, days ago she took Pearl somewhere safe, at least till we could know for certain the child was out of danger."

"Do you know where that is?"

"I do," Lettie said, then hedged. "About."

The ambiguity was unnerving. "What does that mean?"

"Marie's kept it a secret from even me. As a precaution, I thought it wise to find out what I could. So yesterday morning, when she left to call on friends, taking them food as she does, I followed her…to as far as I was able."

Celia almost probed further, but she was done with questions. She'd heard enough to act.

"Take me there."

CHAPTER SIXTY

A dim alley in Chinatown wasn't the last place Celia would have imagined Lettie guiding her, but it was close.

At the door with the peep-through—a place Celia hadn't visited since before Pearl's birth, while on an errand for Marie—Lettie applied several knocks. Apparently, this was where Marie had entered with her usual basket of dumplings the prior day.

Summoned, the doorman slid open the lookout. "Yeah?" He had the same youthful Chinese face that Celia recalled, same casual English.

Lettie replied, "We're here to see Marie." She stood staunchly in the day dress she'd donned in haste.

"Haven't seen her."

"But are you sure?" Lettie's immediate challenge barely prevented him from shutting the peep-through. "She's been gone most the day, and I know she comes here regularly—for more than the opium."

Celia's skin prickled from a thought. If Marie had just come for a periodic check-in on Pearl—presuming the child was indeed here, as Lettie figured—why hadn't Marie returned yet to the inn?

"Listen," he said, "I let them in, but that was several hours ago. She probably left while my cousin was manning the door."

A word—*them*—snagged in Celia's ear. Thinking of Pearl, she cut in, "Who do you mean?"

He turned to Celia. "How's that?"

"You said you let *them* in. Who was with Marie?"

He shrugged his brows. "I don't know the name."

"But was it a little girl?"

"Nah. A white man in a suit and hat. He didn't say much, seemed intense."

Gordon Humphrey.

Celia bristled. She looked at Lettie, whose eyes said she dreaded the same. He'd either pressed Marie for information—her safety as much as her livelihood at risk—or he'd followed her here, same as Lettie had.

Celia charged to the point with growing certainty. "I know Marie has been hiding my daughter to keep her safe. And while grateful, I will *not* leave before searching for my child." The primal instinct she'd discovered within herself hadn't been left on the ship. She felt it now buzzing through her, which the doorman appeared to sense.

Not arguing, he at last granted them entry.

By lantern, with Lettie in the rear, he led them down the steps. From the bottom, he continued away from the opium parlor and through a squatty opening in the rock wall under the staircase. At the threshold, the familiar air of the underground, cool and dank, smelling of stale dirt, swarmed Celia with a feeling of entrapment.

She was back at the tunnels.

Memories descended—the panic of the raid, the blurry terror of the cell—constricting her lungs and slowing her feet.

Her distance from the doorman was growing.

"Celia?" Lettie's voice, concerned.

Celia took a breath, recalling her purpose. Her daughter. Hopefully within reach, potentially in danger.

She pushed herself onward and into the tunnel. Their guide soon led them to a propped wooden slat, the very one she'd stumbled upon years prior, lured by the cries of a baby.

The doorman slid the board aside. In the lamplit residence, murmurings ceased as a slew of Chinese faces angled toward the entry. Among them, totaling around ten and ranging widely in ages, Marie sat a few feet from the doorway. She paused from helping a woman tear leaves from vegetables into a bowl, and her expression tightened. Celia's arrival was surely as surprising as her unexplained disappearance.

Just as Marie's features softened with relief, a giggle drifted through the air. As light and sweet as a confection, the sound was so familiar, so beloved, it caused Celia's breath to catch.

"Pearl," she managed, stepping forward, scanning the room. "Pearl!"

On a grass mat halfway across the space, the child rose from the lap of a man seated in a suit and hat, his back to Celia. "Mama!" She squealed and dashed forward, threading through the strangers. Celia knelt just in time for her daughter to literally leap into her arms. Pearl clung on, like a baby chimp to its mother in the wild, and Celia embraced her no less fervently. The girl's natural scent soothed Celia as never before.

But then she recalled Humphrey. His audacity to interact with her child, let alone to hold her, heated Celia's blood. Readying for battle, she stood while clutching Pearl and aimed a glare at the man. As he rose to face her, his jaw slackened.

As did Celia's.

For he wasn't Gordon Humphrey; he was Stephen.

"Celia," he breathed, causing her chest to squeeze.

The soft flickering over his face from the kerosene flame magnified the moment's surrealness.

He moved toward her with a stride she recalled as distinctly as the feel of his sandy-blond hair. When he stopped before her, he studied her face as if to verify it was real. "Marie said you vanished... Love, are you all right?"

It was difficult for Celia to think, much less to answer. "I am... now."

Clearly he detected her puzzlement, reading her as he so insightfully used to do.

"I returned home only last night," he explained. "With my parents out for the morning, I was just settling in when Abigail told me everything—about you and Pearl..." He glanced at the child, and a smile touched his lips, but then they leveled as he continued. "She told me about your father too. Darling, if I'd known about any of it, I would've returned right away. You must know that."

Pearl squirmed restlessly and climbed down from Celia's arms. As she scuttled off and retrieved a marble from the floor, Celia felt compelled to pull her daughter back, to never let her go.

But then, from her side, Lettie chimed in, "Don't you fret. The lass won't be going anywhere far." Given Celia's thoughts of Lettie over the past few days, her offer now to keep watch over Pearl shouldn't have brought comfort, yet still it did.

All around, the murmurs resumed. With the doorman gone, the board was set in place, sealing them in. Any sense of confinement, however, was offset by the distraction of Stephen's claims. For as wondrous as they sounded, Celia recalled the most likely reason he hadn't come back all these years, along with her consequent hurt and shame. The utter humiliation.

She forced a swallow, then pointed out, "What does it matter now? You're engaged."

He shook his head. "I'm not though."

She stared at him, recalling what she knew to be true. "Your sister... She told me at the park, about a professor's daughter—"

"On our sail together from London," he interjected gently, "the closer I got to home, the more I realized it wasn't fair to her. Maybe even selfishly, I couldn't marry someone I didn't love, a woman who..." He finished simply, "She wasn't you."

The sentiment was moving, undeniably so. Nonetheless, Celia upheld her guard, remembering he'd once used words just as tender in a promise he failed to keep.

"In the barn, Stephen, you'd already proposed—to me."

He conceded with a nod, though she'd nearly expected him to deny it.

She glanced away, as much to subdue the longing she felt as her need to check on Pearl. On the floor, the girl was playing marbles with two other children. Her willingness to already stray from Celia displayed an independence that spurred parental pride, if not without a slight sting.

"My mother wrote to me," Stephen went on, "shortly after I left for school. She told me you'd moved away to be with your father. That you'd married a Chinese man arranged by the matchmaker."

Celia snapped back to face him, dumbfounded. How would his mother have known of—

The thought broke off at the recollection of her father's last letter, which, in her sudden departure from the house, she'd evidently left behind.

"But none of that is true," she insisted.

"I know that—now. Because of Abigail, I learned it was all

lies," he said firmly. "It was outright cruel of my mother. Rest assured, I'll be having quite the discussion with her." The muscles in his jaw deemed this an understatement.

Celia wanted to be just as bitter—and, on the flip side, to revel in the promising news—but there was too much to digest, including his very presence. "How did you know where to find Pearl?"

"I went over to the Dewdrop Inn, looking for you both, and found *this* tenacious woman." He glanced toward Marie, who was still helping with the vegetables nearby but now eyeing him and listening. "It took some convincing—and by that, I do mean a lot—but she agreed to bring me."

The jumbled pieces, one by one, were falling into place. "The doorman, he said you've been here for hours."

Stephen smiled a little. "Not exactly by choice."

Marie inserted a *tsk*. "He demand to take Pearl. I say no. Maybe not safe. So we stay."

It was a standoff. Between Marie and Stephen. Celia could almost laugh.

"Honestly," he said to Celia, "I haven't minded a bit." He directed his attention back to Pearl with a look of awe that matched his voice. "It's given me hours to gaze at this beautiful creature of yours."

Ours, Celia amended to herself.

She only realized she'd said it aloud when he turned back to her with a warmth in his slate-blue eyes that threatened to melt the entirety of her defenses. She clung to what remnants she could, as there were other considerations, practical ones.

"How soon are you going back? To school in London, I mean."

He contemplated this as if it hadn't occurred to him yet. Then he replied, with the tone of a revelation, "I'm not."

"But…you have a year left."

"And there happen to be some fine universities right here in the States."

Taken aback, she peered at him. "Are you sure?"

"I'm not leaving you, Celia. Not ever again. That is, not if you—and Pearl—will have me." With that, he cradled Celia's face with his hand, and she allowed herself to sink into it. "I love you," he said, "more than I can ever describe. I missed you in ways I didn't even know I could." His sincerity was unmistakable, paving the way for her decision.

Though she'd spent years yearning for their reunion, fearing she couldn't survive or parent sufficiently on her own, she had since discovered otherwise. Whether to proceed together or apart was no longer a need but a choice.

"I love you too," she told him, her voice soft yet certain. "Just as dearly."

His eyes glimmered before he pressed his lips to hers. It was a tender kiss that, while different from before—as it couldn't help but to be, as surely he too had changed in some ways—already she knew she would cherish this memory until her final breath.

CHAPTER SIXTY-ONE

In the underground haven, Stephen had just returned to his seat on the floor, joining Pearl and the other children in a game of marbles, when Celia took note of Lettie. Off to the side, leaning against a wall, she continued to watch over Pearl, just as she always had when needed. Beginning even before the child was born.

If roles had been reversed, with Celia in Lettie's situation, baited by even the slimmest chance of seeing Pearl again, in all likelihood she would have done precisely as Lettie did.

At that moment, Celia realized Owen was mistaken. Humphrey, in his scheming, hadn't found Lettie's price. Just as he did with Owen, he had found her weakness.

Celia approached Lettie to convey her understanding, yet got only as far as "Lettie…"

"Let me say to you first," Lettie interrupted, as if about to burst from withholding the words, "just how very sorry I am. About the lies I told, the pain I caused. Celia, I do pray you can forgive me one day."

Celia shook her head, though only as an assurance. "I already have."

Lettie looked at her with relief, with gratitude, and released a breath. Then together they stood, enjoying the infectious laughter from Stephen and Pearl.

Still gazing upon them, Lettie remarked to Celia in a warm tone, "Well, it seems you'll be enjoyin' a lovely new life, as you rightly deserve."

Celia considered only then what lay ahead for the three of them—from a simple, intimate wedding to a real home befitting a family. It seemed Pearl would indeed be blessed, as Celia's father would say, with a path of good fortune.

Yet what awaited Lettie? As she had long paid off her debt to the inn, surely more than money was keeping her there.

Celia recalled the drawings of Lettie's child, each line etched from pain. From grief. Perhaps most of all, from shame. She decided right then: if allowed, she'd do everything she could to help Lettie with a fresh start of her own. As she too rightly deserved.

But for now, she merely reached over and squeezed her friend's hand. Lettie hesitated before turning to Celia, and with emotion brimming in her eyes, she smiled.

———

Once Celia settled on the floor beside Stephen, he at last raised a question initially lost to the bedlam of other topics and thoughts. It was the very one Lettie would undoubtedly soon ask and Marie would demand Celia answer.

Where on earth had she been?

So she told him, in broad strokes anyway, beginning with highlights about his father and Humphrey. Much of her subsequent adventures would wait for another day, due not only to the energy she would need but also to Stephen's demeanor, his frustration mounting with every detail. By the time she paused, he was fuming.

Suddenly, he stood and offered his hand. "Ready to go?"

She wasn't sure of the destination; neither the brothel nor his parents' house seemed appropriate at this point.

"Where to?"

"A dinner party."

Thrown off, Celia glanced down at her dress—ripped, dusty, and spotted with blood. "Stephen, I'm hardly suited for a fancy affair."

"We're not going for the festivities," he said. "Aside from my father, there's just one guest I'd very much like a word with."

It took little effort to envision which guest that would be.

Celia rose on tired legs and replied, "As would I."

CHAPTER
SIXTY-TWO

Upon answering the front door of the Bettencourt home, Miss Waterstone recognized that the group hadn't come for a casual visit. She surveyed Stephen and Celia briefly. But it was her glance at Pearl in Celia's arms, head resting sleepily on Celia's shoulder—just as it had throughout the paid carriage ride—that eased a hint of gentleness into the woman's face.

By Stephen's clipped request, Miss Waterstone guided the three of them to the den, then set off to retrieve Stephen's father and Humphrey from the drawing room, where the guests were enjoying after-dinner brandies.

Celia stood waiting by the fireplace, rocking and holding Pearl close, not wanting to let go anytime soon. At the center of the room, Stephen silently paced, though not for long. The summoned men arrived shortly. They appeared unsettled by the surprise arrivals, but Stephen dove straight in, beginning with his father, who planted himself before his desk.

"Is it true? Were you part of trying to bribe Celia, to get her to leave town?"

The mayor straightened, and his mouth firmed. "It was a generous offer, a chance for her to start over."

"You mean to get her out of the way for your damn campaign? Is there anything else that matters anymore?"

"It was just as much for your sake," the mayor argued, right as his wife entered the den. She wore a proper evening gown and an appalled expression.

"What in heaven's name is this about? We have guests."

The mayor called out past her, "Abigail, shut the door."

Abigail, also in an evening gown, trailed her mother into the room. She sealed the door behind them as Mrs. Bettencourt addressed Stephen. "Where have you been all day?"

"With me," Celia stated. "And our daughter."

Mrs. Bettencourt looked just as disconcerted by the discovery of Celia and Pearl. In contrast, Abigail sent a kind smile from where she stood nearby.

"As I was saying," the mayor continued, "the offer was made for your benefit, Stephen. For pity's sake, you were marrying another woman."

"Because I was lied to," Stephen charged back, then addressed his mother. "In a letter, you told me Celia ran off to marry another man. Even when you knew she was with child. My child."

Immediately, Mrs. Bettencourt countered but with her voice slightly faltering. "How were we to know if she was telling the truth about your being the father?"

Again, Celia took the liberty of responding. "You could have written to him and asked, as I'd suggested."

"Well..." The woman appeared flustered by this. "That would've been highly inappropriate."

"Inappropriate?" Stephen laughed under his breath. "Yes, let's discuss that, shall we? How appropriate would you say it was of Mr. Humphrey to order his henchman to make Celia *disappear* if she refused Father's offer? And for my daughter to be secretly given away?" He shifted to his father directly. "Or were both of these ideas yours?"

"What? No, that's preposterous," the mayor insisted, flabbergasted. "I would never do such a thing."

"Edwin," Mrs. Bettencourt said. "What is he talking about?"

As her husband appeared at a loss—genuinely so, based on Celia's years spent with him—Celia at last confronted Humphrey, who stood off to the side, casually observing. "Mr. Humphrey, you've been awfully quiet. Have you anything to say about these charges?"

He eyed her smugly. "I didn't realize I was in court."

Stephen broke in, "No, you're not. *Yet*. Though I imagine a jury would be very interested in hearing all about this." Perhaps from Humphrey's nonchalance or from the fact that the situation could have ended tragically with a henchman other than Owen, Stephen's volume and gruffness escalated. "Of course, between running a brothel and a gambling den—both illegal businesses, last I heard—the newspapers, at the very least, ought to find your story rather fascinating."

"*Stephen*," his mother urged, "keep your voice down. There are guests."

He continued his assault on Humphrey regardless. "You know, maybe we should start right here—tonight. Find out what our guests think of who you really are. About your claims of building a better society, all while polluting it with your racist filth and hypocritical corruption."

Humphrey glared at him, no longer smug. "You will do no such thing."

"Oh, yes? Let's just see about that." Stephen wheeled and headed for the door. While he crossed the room, Celia trained her focus on him, stunned by what he was about to do.

"Stephen!" Abigail yelled.

As his face snapped toward her, Celia realized it had been a warning. For that was when she glimpsed what Humphrey had pulled from his dinner jacket: a gun from a holster.

"Don't you dare touch that door."

His menacing words swung Stephen around to find the revolver pointed his way. When he raised his hands, Celia's pulse spiked from panic, and the den plunged into silence. She heard only the thumping of her own heart and the distant murmurs of conversations from unseen guests, people entirely ignorant of the scene in this room.

"You come back and listen," Humphrey said through clenched teeth.

Gripping Pearl protectively in her arms, Celia raced to think of what to do as Stephen complied with slow steps.

"That's right, keep comin'." Humphrey was reveling in the show of obedience. Stephen was no more than six feet from the man when the mayor interjected, overly calm.

"Gordon," he said, stepping in front of the gun, blocking Stephen. "That's enough now. Your point is made."

"I'll say when it's enough. And my points are only beginning. Now, move." Humphrey jerked the revolver to the side to illustrate, but the mayor persisted with his appeal.

"We can figure this out. Together. No one here is going to incriminate you."

Humphrey sneered, his temper rising. "Oh, I know they're not. Because if that happens, you'll go down with me. Understand? You and your whole righteous family! You think you have troubles now—all because of this dirty half-breed and her Chinese kid—"

As he spoke, he flailed the barrel in Celia's direction. With a gasp, she turned Pearl away, a split second before Stephen lunged for the weapon.

All at once, he and Humphrey were wrestling over the gun. Men's shouts clashed with Mrs. Bettencourt's screams as Abigail rushed to Celia's side. She layered an arm over Celia to shield Pearl, who wriggled, rousing from the commotion.

Then a shot blared out.

Celia's heart stopped, along with all motion in the room.

Humphrey and Stephen just stood there, the moment stretching out endlessly, the silence deafening. Then Humphrey crumpled and landed face-up on the floor. Red pooled at the gaping hole in his chest, and any sense of time blurred. At the dimming of his widened eyes, all life seemed to leave his body.

Stephen looked on in shock, still gripping the gun, yet relief swooped through Celia. He glanced over at her and Pearl, confirming they were safe.

The mayor lowered himself onto a knee and checked Humphrey for signs of a pulse, a heartbeat. Appearing not to find one, he slowly came to his feet. His eyes were darting; he was thinking. Then, gently, he removed the gun from Stephen's hand. "Now, you listen, son. It's going to be all right. I'll hire the best lawyers in the city, the whole state. You hear me? You will not be going to jail."

"No. He will not." Mrs. Bettencourt's statement drew the room's full attention. "Because our son didn't pull the trigger."

The mayor scrunched his brow. "What are you saying?"

"I am saying…" She fed the words out gradually, as if formulating the answer as she went. "When you—the upstanding Mayor Bettencourt—confronted Gordon Humphrey about his illegal and unsavory dealings, he threatened your loved ones with a gun. Naturally, you defended your family, as any respectable man would do." She looked straight at Celia, making clear how this applied to Stephen; then she turned back to her husband. "It was self-defense, plain and simple."

"Yes, but...Georgia..."

"It's over, Edwin. It's all over."

Whether she meant his senatorial campaign, his political career in general, or only the current discussion about how to proceed—her statement seemed to address them all.

Though with reluctance, the mayor nodded.

A pounding came at the door. "Everything all right in there?" a man yelled. "We thought we heard a gunshot!"

Guests were gathering outside the room.

Celia gave Abigail's arm a grateful squeeze, then rushed over to Stephen. He embraced Celia and Pearl, his arms quavering.

With deliberate strides, Mrs. Bettencourt walked over to the door and paused. She glanced at Celia again, then Pearl and Stephen, the three of them standing as a family. Finally, straightening her posture, Georgia Bettencourt unlocked and opened the door, not a mere crack but wide, in plain view of the world.

1995

—

AUGUST

EPILOGUE

The cemetery is vacant, almost eerily so.

But this allows my darling collegiate granddaughter to park us in a nice, shady spot a short walk from our destination, which the paper in my coat pocket has made me immeasurably eager to reach. Granted, that's not the only reason I'm quick to open my door and unfold from my seat on the passenger side—*quick* being a relative term at my age of eighty-four. I'm strong-willed inherently, even proudly, so I can't say I've ever been very good at being a passenger. My patient late husband could have vouched for as much.

"Nana," my granddaughter says to me, exasperated but caring, having just circled around to my door. "You should have waited. I would've helped you get out."

"Oh, shush, I'm not dead yet. Of course, if I were…I've come to the right place."

She groans, though the frame of her charming pixie cut softens her frown. "Don't joke about that."

The thing is I'm only partially joking. The last survivor among my siblings, I'm quite at ease with the thought of death, and not just because I've lived a full, gratifying life but because more than ever, I feel connected to the lineage of my ancestors. I suppose you could say, a lot like a bead on my good-fortune bracelet—bought on my last trip to Shanghai, an ongoing effort to explore my heritage—I've become a small but integral part of a beautifully infinite loop.

As we pass the first row of headstones, my granddaughter surveys our tree-lined surroundings. "Wow, looks like we're the only ones here today. Not another soul around."

"Mmm, I think there's more than a few."

She takes this in and giggles, more than the remark deserves, transforming her eyes into thin little arcs. They pair perfectly with her sweet bao-like nose. The traits that make her "different" have become all the rage, specifically those from mixed ethnicities, like mine. A mutt, I call myself, though with a pride instilled by my late, dearly missed mother.

Given that she was a quarter Chinese and my father a quarter Korean, they would quip sometimes that together they made half an Oriental—pardon me, *Asian*. That's the term I'm supposed to use. My son, particularly as a professor of Asian history, likes to tease me warmly: *Repeat after me, Mom: Orientals are rugs, Asians are people*.

So I do, and we laugh.

Frankly, it's hard to keep up anymore, to know which descriptors are appropriate or not. Sometimes they even swing from PC to taboo and back again. By nature, I'm a consistent person—a gentler word for stubborn—so I've mused, for instance, why the word *Chinaman* is offensive (though admittedly, something about it rubs me wrong too), whereas Irishman and Dutchman are considered just fine.

I've found myself wondering about the root of the difference. What I've come up with, plain and simple, is this: intent.

If you ask me, it's the only factor that truly matters. But I also concede that I see life through the limits of my singular lens and so will have to rely on others, like my children and, these days, also my grandchildren, to widen that view when possible and called for.

The graves I'm here to visit, today for more than sentimental reasons, await a few yards away. My steps can't help but hasten a little at the sight of the stone-etched names of my grandparents: Celia and Stephen Bettencourt.

While most of my memories of them have dissipated into a kaleidoscope of faded images, what remains bolder than the words on a marquee are the stories that have riveted me since childhood, highlights of their remarkable lives.

Grandma Celia was a woman who didn't wait for good fortune to fall her way; she fought for it. Earned it. More importantly, she paved a road of it for others. Aside from the daunting task of mothering four children—the eldest being my ever-loving and feisty mother, Pearl—she spent many of her years actively protesting anti-Chinese laws and fighting for women's rights. In fact, her status as a "convict" from her arrests as a suffragist leader are still cited in our family as a point of pride. Similarly inspiring, Grandpa Stephen was a devoted doctor who helped countless women by treating them properly rather than allowing them to be easily labeled "hysterical" and sent away.

Often, relatedly, I've claimed that my daughter's resolve to battle injustice as a civil rights attorney is the product of the couple's genes, but there's more to it than that. Though she was only in grade school when Pearl Harbor was bombed, she still remembers when her Japanese American friends too were sent away, perhaps as clearly as I recall seeing a classmate of hers wearing a button that read "I AM CHINESE."

How tragically ironic that at one time, the hierarchy was reversed. Same for the targets whose rights were likewise stripped due to fear sparked by ignorance, enflamed in a maddening game of politics. The cycle reminds me of a Chinese proverb that my mother—as a teacher, like me—used to quote: "Knowledge changes destiny."

It's especially fitting for this moment, as I stand before my grandma's grave and pull from my pocket a folded page from the *New York Times*, a portion of its contents a hundred years overdue.

FILES FOUND IN OREGON DETAIL MASSACRE OF CHINESE

The article, in which a historian ranks the atrocity as the worst massacre of Chinese by whites in America, reports that even an uncle of Frank Vaughan, one of the gang members responsible for the killings, told others that his nephew was downright guilty. My hands trembled, more than usual, when I first continued to read about the Wallowa County clerk uncovering related case files from 1887. From a curiously sparse court journal to contradictory depositions that strongly suggest a sham of a trial, they appear to have been tucked away in a safe with the goal of being forgotten.

The premeditated slaughter of more than thirty Chinese gold-dust miners in a remote area of northeastern Oregon—later dubbed Hells Canyon—was a topic Grandma Celia spoke of rarely but with vehemence. This is precisely why I felt compelled to bring her the article today, hoping to provide a small sense of closure for at least this case, even if not for that of her father.

"Nana, could I do it?" The earnestness in my granddaughter's voice assures me she's asking to place the paper for her own reasons, not just to prevent me from leaning down that far—though in all honesty, it's not the wisest idea for me anyhow.

"Of course, dear."

She smiles, and from my grip, she delivers the article to the in-ground vase at her great-great-grandma's headstone. An offering to her ancestor, like bouquets from Westerners and food from the Chinese, this is our means to connect. As I watch her, I touch the heirloom dangling from my neck, a family locket, for much the same purpose.

If Grandma Celia is looking down from above, I imagine she too is smiling, awed by the continuation of her lineage and pleased by the validation from the article's news. For though it's far too late to reward the victims or their loved ones with justice, at least the truth finally surfaced, enabling others to learn from the past.

After retirement, I became a docent at the Oregon Historical Society for that very reason. Although I've long considered Portland a warm and welcoming place for Asians and their families, it wasn't always that way. So it's vital, in my opinion, to speak of the darker events that never make it into textbooks, especially ones that folks have striven to erase from history, like chalk from a blackboard.

At the museum, I've related details of the Hells Canyon Massacre more times than I can count, and not yet have I stumbled upon a visitor already familiar with the occurrence. So I keep telling the story, heart-wrenching as it is, again and again.

Some evenings, with the encouragement of family or friends and a few sips of wine, I even share a tale about Grandma Celia, a jaw-dropping adventure involving Portland's seedy saloons, brothels, and Shanghai Tunnels—legends of the latter naturally viewed as exaggerated and kitschy by strict historians yet intriguingly authentic by its tour guides. The story charges on to her harrowing escape as a hostage on a ship and her brief stint in a San Francisco jail, soon followed with a ruthless chase by patrollers on a hunt for train hoppers. Then, at last, comes the happy ending, derived in part by a woman who saved my mother as a child and hence became my namesake, known in our family as Marie Ah-Yi, or Auntie Marie.

Tales of the kind have been circulating in my family for generations, perhaps gaining sprinkles of lore on the way—or b'gosh and b'golly, as my mother called it in baking, a passion of mine, also passed down. Just as with dough, I'm always one for adding a pinch of spice. And whose life—and thus stories— couldn't use more of that?

AUTHOR'S NOTE

Despite being raised in Oregon practically since birth, I learned a mere dozen years ago about the existence of Portland's Shanghai Tunnels. Legends surrounding the underground labyrinth were making the rounds—propelled, I daresay, by an episode of *Ghost Hunters*. Admittedly fascinated, I soon embarked on a city walking tour that included venturing into the basement of a pizza parlor, where a jagged opening in a brick wall allowed for a peek at a portion of the abandoned tunnels.

Since then, the Shanghai Tunnels often tugged at my mind as a setting ripe for a novel. Only a few years ago, however, after a marathon plotting session with an author friend (thank you, Therese Walsh!), did the premise begin to take shape. Gradually, it expanded with a spark of inspiration from *hapa.me*, a photography book gifted to me by teacher-librarian extraordinaire Nancy Sullivan at McDaniel High School. The book of portraits by Kip Fulbeck spotlights people of Asian or Pacific Rim mixed-race heritage, referred to as *hapas* (meaning "half" in Hawaiian, long used as a term of endearment by my father), and their experiences with identity, ranging as widely as their appearances.

Still, a key story element was missing—that is until Shelley McFarland, a dear friend and impressive history buff, asked if I was familiar with the Hells Canyon Massacre.

"The *what*?" I believe was my reply.

In no time, I was deep down the online rabbit holes, uncovering yet another piece of Oregon history I had somehow missed. In this case, the ghastly details I found left me stunned, including the fact that even with a confession that prompted the grand jury's indictments, all three of the accused who appeared in court walked free after a markedly brief trial. The sparse court documents—seeming hidden until stumbled upon by Wallowa County clerk Charlotte McIver in 1995, when a safe was being donated to the county museum—further confirmed the questionable nature of the trial and collective efforts to have brushed away the incident.

Estimates of the victims slain in Hells Canyon in an atrocity also known as the Snake River Massacre typically range between thirty-one and thirty-four Chinese gold-dust miners. In 2005, though not without a measure of conflict and controversy, the U.S. Board of Geographic Names granted the five-acre Deep Creek (or Dead Line Creek) murder site the designation "Chinese Massacre Cove." There, a granite memorial now stands to honor the victims while reminding visitors:

No one was held accountable.

In a *New York Times* article, even Frank Vaughan's great-grandnephew Vern Russell stated, "Father told me old Frank was guilty as sin." Yet far more damning, in a published deathbed confession, Robert McMillan, before reportedly succumbing to rheumatic fever just two years after the trial, claimed that the murders were indeed premeditated by the gang and that $55,500 worth of gold (valued today at nearly $2 million) was stolen from the miners' camps. What became of the gold is a mystery with many theories but no firm conclusion.

Due to the trial's limited documentation, Vaughan's testimony in this novel is based largely on various historians' accounts and a deposition he gave, in which he appeared to suddenly shift blame to the three gang members who had fled the county. Creative additions, of course, helped fill the gaps. Similarly, Frank's encounters with Celia are obviously fictional, providing imagined reasons for his official confession that resulted in six gang members being charged. Also adjusted for story purposes, aside from some liberties taken with transportation to reach Enterprise, the real trial lasted one day longer and took place in August (not June) 1888.

Unfortunately, save for the inclusion of Celia's father—and the unlikely publication of the victims' names in the newspaper, particularly given their ethnicity—the details surrounding the Rock Springs Massacre are factual (though the precise number of victims differs slightly among reports). When my research of the Hells Canyon murders led me to this equally heartbreaking assault, I once again found myself shocked and horrified. That, likewise, not a single punishment was handed down fueled my compulsion to spread word of both heinous occurrences, along with the mass expulsions and other shameful anti-Chinese acts of the time.

While all these elements contributed to crafting Celia's journey, her struggle with identity was informed in part by my own experiences. As the daughter of a Japanese immigrant whose inherent customs and culture haven't always blended with his ardent desire for his children to be proud Americans, I recall early in life not knowing exactly where I fit in. Only as an adult did I come to fully appreciate being "different" and recognize the beauty derived from my two interwoven cultures.

On that note, throughout the novel, I enjoyed borrowing name variants from my family lineage, most notably for Celia's father, Chung Jun. Her father's writing style too is reflective of my own father's, the latter expressed not through letters but texts, made even more endearing by a consistent plethora of repetitive emojis. Just as personal, Marie's speaking style and other mannerisms, with her gruff exterior yet soft heart, were fashioned after a combination of two of my favorite aunties. As for bao, it's been a beloved treat since my childhood and hence a reminder of my family's regular Saturday outings to a small Asian market in downtown Portland, a city with no shortage of history, stories, and secrets—for even longtime locals like me.

Recommendations for further reading include *Massacred for Gold* by R. Gregory Nokes and *The Oregon Shanghaiers* by Barney Blalock. For other features related to *The Girls of Good Fortune*, including a book club guide and tour information for the Shanghai Tunnels, visit KristinaMcMorris.com.

THEMED RECIPES

Lemon Snaps

Specifically during childhood, Celia loved these popular cookies. Crisp, tasty, and notably simple to make, they're perfect to enjoy with a cup of hot tea.

- ½ teaspoon baking soda
- 2 teaspoons hot water
- ⅔ cup unsalted butter, room temperature
- 1⅛ cups sugar
- 1⅛ cups all-purpose flour
- 1 teaspoon lemon extract
- Zest of one lemon (optional)

Preheat the oven to 420°F. In a small bowl, dissolve the baking soda in the hot water. Set aside. In the bowl of a stand mixer, beat together the butter and sugar until light and creamy. Add the baking soda mixture. Gradually add the flour at low speed, occasionally scraping the bowl, until well blended. Add the lemon extract and, if desired, lemon zest. Lightly flour the counter and a rolling pin, then roll out the dough to the thinness of a piecrust, approximately ⅛ inch. Use a cookie cutter (or similar) to cut into circles slightly larger than silver dollars. Place them on an ungreased cookie sheet, allowing space for the cookies to spread. Bake until the edges turn golden brown, roughly 5 to 6 minutes.

Silver Cake

The precursor to white cake, this delicious specialty of Celia's, baked for Pearl's first birthday, includes a great number of egg whites (whereas gold cake, today's yellow cake, features egg yolks), resulting in a fluffy texture akin to angel food cake.

For the cake:
- 1 cup unsalted butter, room temperature
- 2 cups sugar
- 8 egg whites
- 3 cups cake flour
- 2 teaspoons baking powder
- ⅓ cup sour cream plus milk to make ½ cup
- 1 teaspoon vanilla extract
- 1 teaspoon peach, orange, or coconut extract (or any other flavored extract desired)

Preheat the oven to 350°F. In the bowl of a stand mixer with a paddle attachment, beat the butter and the sugar together until creamy. With the mixer going, add the egg whites in about four additions. Sift together the flour and the baking powder, then with the mixer on low speed, gradually add to the butter mixture, stopping occasionally to scrape the bowl. Combine the sour cream, milk, and extracts, then add to the batter, mixing until smoothly blended. Line the bottoms of two 9-inch round cake pans with greased parchment (or simply grease the bottoms). Pour in batter, and bake for 20 to 25 minutes. Once cool, turn out and stack the cakes with buttercream frosting in between, then frost the rest of the cake.

For the frosting:
- 1½ cups unsalted butter, room temperature
- 6 cups confectioners' sugar, sifted
- ½ teaspoon salt
- 1 tablespoon vanilla extract
- ½–¾ cup heavy cream
- Food coloring (optional)

Again using a stand mixer, beat the butter until soft and fluffy. Gradually add the confectioners' sugar, occasionally pausing to scrape the bowl. Add the salt, vanilla, and a small amount of the cream. Blend on high speed until light and creamy, periodically scraping the bowl. Add the remaining cream as needed for desired consistency, as well as any drops of coloring (gel recommended for vibrancy) if preferred. Recipe makes a generous amount of frosting.

For the more ambitious dessert enthusiasts, perhaps even as a book club activity, visit KristinaMcMorris.com for details of how to make Celia's and her father's cherished custard bao.

READING GROUP GUIDE

1. Several Chinese proverbs are woven through the novel, including "Fortune rests in misfortune" and "Knowledge changes destiny." How do these apply to the story? Do you believe they also apply in real life? If so, how?

2. By the end of the book, which characters would you consider "girls of good fortune" and in which ways?

3. Were you already familiar with the Shanghai Tunnels and the practice of being crimped or "shanghaied"? What is the most interesting thing you learned about the topic?

4. Similarly, had you ever heard of either massacre featured in the story? What was your impression of the outcomes? Do you believe the results would differ if the incidents occurred today?

5. Of all the characters in the novel, who are your favorites? Did your impression of anyone significantly change?

6. Motherhood is a central element of the story, with a range of emotions including love, joy, pride, self-doubt, shame, and guilt. By the end, Celia comes to view her mother's behavior differently upon reflection. Can you relate to a similar shift of perspective involving family or other loved ones?

7. During a run-in with Celia at Portland's City Park, Abigail solemnly claims she can relate to Celia's romantic plight, "at least...to an extent." But interrupted, she fails to expound. What do you imagine her experience might have been, and how does her sense of commonality with Celia ultimately affect their relationship?

8. Celia's journey entails numerous twists and turns. Were there any you found especially surprising?

9. Through much of the story, Celia wrestles with identity. At their core, how are Owen's struggles with the issue similar? How are they different?

10. In the epilogue, the narrator ponders the evolution and usages of racial terminology over time. Do you agree or disagree with those views?

A CONVERSATION
WITH THE AUTHOR

While researching to write *The Girls of Good Fortune*, were there discoveries that surprised you? Relatedly, what was the most interesting thing you learned?

Several of my previous novels have been set during WWII, so I've grown well accustomed to researching heart-wrenching atrocities, many of them stemming from hatred and ignorance. And yet the details of the Wyoming and Oregon massacres still managed to shock me, even more so when I learned about the trial and cover-up.

As for the most interesting info I gathered, the origins of the tongs as well as the existence of highbinders and how they got their name fascinated me. But most of all, especially being a virtual native of Oregon, I was continually intrigued by tidbits involving the darker side of the state's history.

What would you say was the greatest challenge of crafting this particular book?

Initially, I'd planned for Celia's story to take place

around 1910. Since my novels are typically set between the 1920s and '40s, I'd joked with friends that I was proudly spreading my wings by backing up an entire decade. It was only after being assigned a deadline (naturally!) when I discovered that the evolution of steamships made shanghaiing a rarity by the 1900s.

I had little choice then but to switch to the 1800s, which meant the daunting task of researching the history of countless words, inventions, garments, transports, cities, and so much more I wasn't familiar with! In the end, of course, I'm thrilled by how much I've had the opportunity to learn and that, best of all, I was able to help highlight some incidents that too often verge on being lost to history.

Were there specific characters you enjoyed writing most?

The first who comes to mind, surely not a surprise, is Marie. Inspired by my relatives, she's like a teacher who rarely gives out A's so that when you succeed in earning her approval, it's that much more rewarding.

Some less obvious choices would be a few of my secondary characters. Matthew was one I instantly adored, as was Calum, whose dialogue I often found impossible to read aloud without laughing. And then there was the sweet Chinese "bao couple" on the train. Since one of my dearest friends since childhood is Filipina, almost every time I visited her house, Angerene's adorable grandparents, Lolo and Lola, would be eating a Filipino snack at the kitchen table, beaming and insisting I sit down and join them. All to say the fictional bao couple is my ode to this beloved pair.

Speaking of characters, in the Author's Note, you explained how at least one of their names carries personal familial significance. Did you use another method for choosing the rest?

As usual, I began by reviewing an online list of names popular in the years my characters were born, seeking out options that reflect the characters—not just in personality but ideally also their heritage and even station in life. And of course, I borrowed names from people outside of family whom I care about (as you'll likely note from those mentioned in my Acknowledgments). I do, after all, own a T-shirt that reads: *Be careful or I'll put you in my next novel... and it won't be pretty.*

Pearl's name, on the other hand, does bear more unique importance. Aside from finding it a lovely name popular among girls at the time, for Caucasians in particular, I liked that it also offered a subtle Asian element, given the typical correlation to pearls. Even more than that, however, I loved the name's pertinence when I considered that pearls are formed initially from an "irritant," and only through patience, time, and multiple layers of protective coatings do they become gems viewed widely as beautiful and cherished.

On a similar note, throughout the novel, are there any other subtle nuggets you included that only you know the significance of?

There is one, actually. Upon first meeting Marie in her bedroom, Celia notices in the background a cabinet-like shrine, a reminder of her father's. I mentioned how when she happened across it as a child, she was especially intrigued since both parents were Christians, but her mother "shut and removed the cabinet, which was never seen again."

My original plan was to circle back to this later in the story and explain the significance. But besides not seeing a natural spot for its placement, I ultimately preferred to leave it as a scrap of a forgotten mystery—for the reader as much as Celia. In my mind, I viewed it as a glimpse into her father's own struggle with identity and connections to his heritage and ancestors. So even though his physical traits had made no secret of his ethnicity, the reality was that he too had resorted to hiding parts of himself while riding a line between two worlds—a point I like to think Celia would one day contemplate and recognize in her father.

ACKNOWLEDGMENTS

As with each of my stories, though for this book in particular, I managed to type *The End* only with the support of many tremendously generous people.

Therese Walsh—my (poor) friend, without you and our countless, hours-long brainstorming and plotting calls, this story literally would not exist. I owe just as many hugs, once again, to my dear friend, research savior, and editing queen Aimee Long—how you resisted dodging all but a few of my twenty-plus calls a day was no small feat. *(On that note, chat in five minutes?)*

Elisabeth Weed, though I regularly refer to you as a "dream agent," even that descriptor fails to encapsulate how much I value your guidance, cheering, trust, and friendship; in short, I'm immeasurably grateful to be on this journey with you. Sending heaps of appreciation as well to the rest of the savvy, stellar team at The Book Group.

Likewise, I'm equally in awe of the shrewd vision, infinite patience, and unwavering belief and support of my editor, Shana Drehs—to say I'm thankful for all that and more would be a massive understatement. The same goes for my publisher, Dominique Raccah, an undeniable force of nature and a shining inspiration. Dom, your fervent refrain that "Books. Change. Lives." is a truth that would mean far less without proponents, like you, who ensure that books actually reach readers' hands—and a great number of them at that.

As ever, sharing that mission with no less passion and my utmost admiration is the rest of my Sourcebooks team—especially Molly Waxman, Cristina Arreola, Valerie Pierce, and Margaret Coffee; your clear devotion to both storytellers and storytelling is not only treasured but infectious. Also, Lucy Kim, I couldn't have asked for a more stunning cover!

I'm enormously thankful to Janie Chang for reviewing a draft and providing invaluable feedback and insights into Chinese traditions and various related elements; Sarah Chung and Kapiolani Lee from the Portland Chinatown Museum for their language and research assistance respectively; the Oregon Historical Society for their fascinating archived materials; American West historian/scholar Laura Ferguson, PhD, for her insights and guidance for accuracy; Matt Wilson for his historical sailing knowhow; Claire Organ for yet again being my go-to for all things Irish; David Macleod for confirming my British-sailor speak; Steven Burke for his ever-reliable legal input; and Traci Wheeler, once more, for her horse expertise and eagle-eye reading, let alone her ceaseless enthusiasm since book one.

With heartfelt appreciation, I'm raising a toast to event masters and visionaries Susan McBeth, Liz Hamilton, Pamela Klinger-Horn, Robin Hoklotubbe, and Christie Hinrichs; the extraordinary impact you all continue to make on the literary world is indelible.

Sending so much love, always, to the rest of my beloved TASK group: Tracy Callan and Shelley McFarland. Together with Aimee, our sisterhood reminds me of the good fortune bracelet described in the story: a beautiful, infinite loop. I can't imagine my life without our friendships, nor would I ever want to.

For their unfailing kindness and support through an impossibly eventful year, I'm eternally grateful to Matthew Pitts (not least of all for the "delucious" brioche cinnamon rolls and, unwittingly, some of my favorite bits of dialogue); incredible lifelong besties Stephanie Stricklen, Brandon Anderson, Sarena Talbert, Ben Rodriguez, and Kellie Jewett; my "one brain" sister, Erika Robuck; and my wonderful "breakout" Zoom gang: Kate Quinn, Fiona Davis, Pam Jenoff, Marie Benedict, and Kristin "Mystica" Harmel. Also to easily the best neighbor possible, Cynthia Miner, whose last-minute editing swoop-ins were undoubtedly tush saving.

Additionally, I'm thankful to the "clubhouse boys"—Nicholas Leonard Sciulli, Greg "Zesty" Zhdanov, Sam Glenn, Tyler Smith, Johnny Vorobets, and Calum Fischer—for helping fill our house near-daily with much welcomed laughter, warmth, and, indeed, stray Ping-Pong balls. I'm truly excited to see where your amazing paths take each of you!

I'm also indebted to my parents, Linda and Junki Yoshida, for so very much—including the resilience and strength they instilled, along with the importance and joys of storytelling, and for the special blending of our cultures.

Above all, I'm grateful to my sons, Tristan and Kiernan, my two favorite people in the world and biggest cheerleaders always *(Ma, lock in! More cowbell!)*. There are no words to fully express the love and pride I feel for you both. Being your mom will always be the greatest and most rewarding honor of my life.

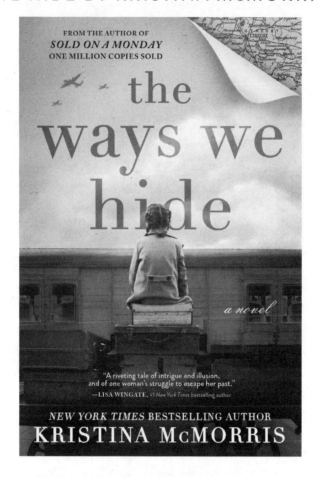

CHAPTER 1

September 1942
Brooklyn, New York

Deep within me, a sense of dread buzzes and crackles, an electrical wire threatening to short. I'm trapped by the stage lights, the performance well in motion. I assure myself that Charles's behavior, subtle oddities throughout tonight's tricks, falls within reason. It was at his prodding, after all, that a top New York critic agreed to attend. As a faceless judge in the shadows, the lone man can render a verdict that could pack future shows—or trigger a decline.

Even so, what I detect from Charles differs from nerves.

Only with disciplined effort do I resist rushing through the grand finale. I distribute a padlock to each of the volunteers: two airmen, a banker type, and a trio of sprightly ladies. With all the poise and undulating cadence of a showman's assistant, I encourage their inspection. My narration flows out, as programmed as a song on a player piano. On this stage alone, it's my fourth performance in two days.

Stewing in a haze of cigarette smoke, aftershave, and floral perfume, the medium-sized theater could be any one of a hundred. The attendance is respectable at two-thirds full. Largely from the "cheap seats" of the balcony, periodic catcalls remain standard fare, with no help from my galling if customary outfit. Astoundingly, the sequined halter and midthigh skirt are rather modest for my role.

Displayed on the prop table are two pairs of handcuffs and a set of minuscule keys. I'm retrieving them all when Charles reappears in the right wing of the stage to await my cue. He's traded his top hat and tails for a black bathing costume that hugs his lean build from shoulders to thighs. All in line with our usual act, save for the object in his grip.

An ax.

I bristle, less from startle than confusion. A stagehand was supposed to brandish the tool, not Charles. And certainly not yet.

For a show that blends illusion and danger—from the magical mending and vanishing of items to mind reading and death-defying feats—there's purpose to every step, glance, and gesture. To timing above all. At the climax of the act, as fears arise over the escape artist's ability to elude his bonds, a harried display of the ax implies need for its imminent use, amplifying suspense.

It's hardly to be used as—what? A parading of bravado?

Still, we've performed together with such frequency over three years of touring that my speech hitches only slightly. "Now… that our 'committee' of volunteers from the audience has keenly inspected the padlocks for authenticity"—I pause, prompting nods from the lock-bearing group—"death-defying escapologist Charles Bouchard shall be sealed into the galvanized-iron milk can, airtight and filled with water to its very brim." Grandly I gesture toward the barrel-size container, just as Charles interjects.

"Een fact!" He reemerges prematurely with his faux French

accent, turning the sea of heads. "So superior are my abilities to those of Harry Houdini himself, I balk at even zee most basic safeguards."

The affront to my late idol, a legend for this very trick, irks me but briefly. More pressingly, I struggle to decipher Charles's intentions as he strides past the volunteers to reach center stage, his slicked ebony hair tousled from his costume change. "Observe, for instance, zis emergency tool, which I have primed with a hacksaw. For what, you ask? Why, to do...*zis*." Against an edge of the milk can, he slams the ax handle—once, twice—and breaks the handle in two.

My chest tightens, despite murmurs of surprise and delight. Charles slings the pieces aside with a hearty "voilà," barely missing my T-strap heels. Even the four-piece band, routinely dispassionate in the pit, gawks with interest.

"What is more," he proclaims, swooping toward me barefoot, "one with supernatural gifts has no need for caution. Is it not so, Mademoiselle Vos?" I'm still eyeing the can—finding no damage, gratefully—when he snatches from me the tiny ring of keys. He jangles them high, pinkie in the air, as if ringing a bell for tea service, before tossing them into his mouth and swallowing them whole.

A ripple of gasps. A mix of groans.

Another maddening, bewildering detour.

Unless vitally called for, never stray from the act. Of the many rules I've taught him, this was the first. The most crucial.

I dredge up a smile nonetheless, bright with Victory Red lips, ever accustomed to wearing a mask as much onstage as off. And besides, I'm well aware the keys are unnecessary, the padlocks a ruse. The neck of the can is, after all, rigged with an outer and inner wall. Telescoped upward, the lid detaches with secured locks intact. It's a deceit based on presumption, a twist on a story viewers convince themselves to be true. Just as experience tells them a book holds full-sheeted pages and a shoe heel is built solidly through, to their minds, a milk can opens only one way.

Mind you, Charles's ingesting of the keys is real. For escapologists, a trained resistance to gagging is required to handily swallow an item, then reproduce it on cue. Compliments of a sword swallower, I learned the rather unsavory skill while on breaks from my old sleight-of-hand acts. It was at the very dime museum where I first met Charles, back when his unruly black hair wasn't yet slicked with tonic, his average if pleasing face still free of smugness; when labeled a "curiosity," he drew the upper crust of society to point and cringe.

Who could have guessed he'd become my greatest illusion?

"*Alors*, zee final touches!" Charles holds out his wrists and regards me with a jerk of his chin, a sign to administer the handcuffs and resume my patter. His granting of permission.

Annoyance curls my fingers, interrupted by a heckling sailor.

"Hey, honey, I could think of some better ways to use those handcuffs!"

"Yeah, Kazlowski, like to lock up your ugly ass," calls another.

"Pipe down, all you! We got ladies here!"

The exchange is typical nowadays, with an abundance of enlisted boys high on hormones and sips from their flasks, antsy for glory half a world away. For people like me, the war could as easily be set in another universe.

Ordinarily I'd toss out a clever comeback, but distracted, I simply reassume control with a clearing of my throat. Somewhere in the room, a critic looks on.

"As you will see," I declare in a voice that, based on a rare press mention, *outsizes my graceful ladylike frame*, "both pairs of handcuffs, also diligently inspected by our committee, will be fastened to Monsieur Bouchard's wrists."

More nods from the group.

Back on script.

I apply the cuffs, tempted to attach them overly tight. Evading my glare, Charles makes a display of being firmly bound. After I remove the milk-can lid, he wriggles into the container with more sloshing than usual. The theater's stagehands—one burly, one bearded—join us with prefilled buckets and quickly remedy the water displacement.

I discovered long ago, for help with shows and rehearsals in any theater, advance gratuity ensures a job done right. Or done at all.

"Once sealed," I continue, "the milk can will be enclosed by a three-walled cabinet. Its triangular shape allows no room for trickery and, most notably, can be unlatched only from the inside." The stagehands are now fetching the roofless structure from just offstage. "Upon a countdown of five, I challenge each of you fine ladies and gentlemen to hold your breath along with Monsieur Bouchard, who shall be submerged in five...four..."

The audience joins in. Charles inhales and exhales in exaggerated preparation. On the collective utterance of "one," he plunges below the surface. My internal timer begins as I affix the cover, catching a whiff of his breath. Under the faint sweetness from his usual cherry Luden's drops comes a citric-juniper scent, one I know well from my past.

Gin.

God in heaven...

CHAPTER 1

August 1931
Laurel Township, Pennsylvania

It was their eyes that first drew Ellis in.

Seated on the front porch of a weathered gray farmhouse, among the few homes lining the road surrounded by hayfields, two boys were pitching pebbles at a tin can. Ages six and eight at most, they wore no shoes or shirts. Only patched overalls exposing much of their fair skin tinted by grime and summer sun. The two had to be brothers. With their lean frames and scraggly copper hair, they looked like the same kid at different stages of life.

And then there were their eyes. From as far as twenty feet away, they grabbed hold of Ellis Reed. They were blue, like his own, but a shade so light they could have been cut from crystal. A striking find against the blandest of settings, as if they didn't quite belong.

Another drop of sweat slid from Ellis's fedora, down his neck, and into his starched collar. Even without his suit jacket, his whole shirt clung from the damn humidity. He moved closer to the house and raised his camera. Natural scenic shots were his usual hobby, but he adjusted the lens to bring the kids into focus. With them came a sign. A raw, wooden slat with jagged edges, it bowed slightly against the porch, as if reclining under the weight of the afternoon heat. The offer it bore, scrawled in chalk, didn't fully register until Ellis snapped the photo.

A breath caught in his throat.

He lowered the camera and reread the words.

Really, they shouldn't have shocked him. Not with so many folks still reeling since the market crashed in '29. Every day, children were being farmed out to relatives or dropped off at churches, orphanages, and the like, hoping to keep them warm and fed. But selling them—this added an even darker layer to dire times.

Were there other siblings being spared? Would the brothers be separated? Could they even read the sign? Ellis's mind whirled with questions, all lacking presumptions he would have once made.

Even, say, six years ago—at barely twenty and living in Allentown under his parents' roof—he might have been quicker to judge. But the streets of Philly had since taught him that few things make a person more desperate than the need to eat. Want proof? Sit back and watch the punches fly at just about any breadline when the last of the day's soup is ladled out.

"Whatcha got there, mister?" The older of the boys was pointing toward the small contraption in Ellis's hand.

"This? Just my camera."

Actually, that wasn't altogether true. It belonged to the *Philadelphia Examiner*. But given the situation, clarifying seemed unimportant.

The small kid whispered to the older one, who addressed Ellis again as if translating for his brother. "That your job? Makin' pictures?"

Fact was, Ellis's job of covering fluff for the Society page didn't amount to much else. Not exactly the hard-nosed reporting he'd envisioned for his career. A gopher could do the same work.

"For now."

The older boy nodded and tossed another pebble at the can. His kid brother chewed on his dry bottom lip with an air of innocence that matched his eyes. They showed no hint of knowing what life held in store. Probably a good thing.

While children who were adopted as babies were often raised as real family, it was no secret how kids acquired at older ages were valued. The girls as nannies, seamstresses, maids. The boys as farm and field hands, future workers at the factories and mines. Maybe, though, it wasn't too late for these two. At least, not with some help.

Ellis peered at the front windows of the house, searching for movement beyond the smudges. He strained to catch the clinking of pots or a whiff of boiling stew, any indication of a mother being home. But only the distant groan of a tractor and the earthy smell of farmland drifted in the air. And through it all came thoughts of reason.

What could he possibly do for these two? Convince their folks there had to be a better way? Contribute a whole dollar when he could scarcely afford his own rent?

Both brothers were staring at him, as if waiting for him to speak.

Ellis averted his attention from the sign. He scoured his brain for words with real meaning. In the end, he came up empty.

"You boys take care of yourselves."

At their silence, he reluctantly turned away. The plinking of rocks on the rusted can resumed and then faded as he retreated down the country road.

Fifty yards ahead, the Model T he'd originally salvaged from a junkyard waited with windows open. Its radiator was no longer hissing and steaming. Somehow its surroundings, too, had changed. The sprawling acres, the crooked fencing—only minutes ago Ellis had found them interesting enough to photograph for his personal collection. A decent way to pass time while his engine cooled from the August heat. Now they were mere backdrops to another tragedy beyond his control.

As soon as he reached his old clunker, he tossed the camera inside, a little harder than he should have, and retrieved his jug of water. He refilled the radiator and prepared the motor by adjusting the levers and turning the key. Back at the hood, he gripped the fender for leverage and gave the crank a hearty jerk. Thankfully, a second attempt revived the sedan.

Once behind the steering wheel, he chucked off his hat and started on his way, more anxious than ever to return to the city. In less than an hour, he'd be in a whole different world. Laurel Township would be a speck of a memory.

Spread over his heaped jacket beside him, his map flapped against air breezing through the car. Just this morning, that wrinkled page, penciled with notes and circled destinations, had guided him to his latest rousing assignment: a quilting exhibition by a ladies' auxiliary of the American Legion, headed by the sister of Philly's mayor. No doubt much of the needlework was impressive, but Ellis had grumbled with every click of the shutter.

The fact that it was Sunday had further soured his mood, as he still needed to develop the photos and draft the article for his deadline tomorrow morning. So much for a day off. Yet now, humbled by that pair of boys, he felt ashamed of grousing over a job many would envy.

Though Ellis tried to push the kids from his mind, they circled back again and again as he rattled down the highway and out of Chester County. Still, not until he approached the *Examiner*'s building did he note the real reason they'd resonated so deeply.

If Ellis's brother had survived, he wondered, would they have looked just as similar? Would they both have been wanted?

ABOUT THE AUTHOR

Kristina McMorris is a *New York Times* bestselling author of two novellas and eight novels, including the million-copy bestseller *Sold on a Monday*. Initially inspired by her grandparents' World War II courtship letters, her works of fiction have garnered more than twenty national literary awards. Prior to her writing career, she owned a wedding-and-event planning company until she had far surpassed her limit of "Y.M.C.A." and chicken dances. She also worked as a weekly TV show host for Warner Bros. and an ABC affiliate, beginning at age nine with an Emmy Award–winning program. A graduate of Pepperdine University, she lives near Portland, Oregon, where she somehow manages to be fully deficient of a green thumb and not own a single umbrella.

THE WAYS WE HIDE

The wars we fight—between nations and inside ourselves

As a little girl raised amid the hardships of Michigan's Copper Country, Fenna Vos learned to focus on her own survival. That ability sustains her even now as the Second World War rages in faraway countries. Though she performs onstage as the assistant to an unruly escape artist, behind the curtain she's the mastermind of their act. Ultimately, controlling her surroundings and eluding traps of every kind helps her keep a lingering trauma at bay.

Yet for all her planning, Fenna doesn't foresee being called upon by British military intelligence. Tasked with designing escape aids to thwart the Germans, MI9 seeks those with specialized skills for a war nearing its breaking point. Fenna reluctantly joins the unconventional team as an inventor. But when a test of her loyalty draws her deep into the fray, she discovers no mission is more treacherous than escaping one's past.

Inspired by stunning true accounts, *The Ways We Hide* is a gripping story of love and loss, the wars we fight—on the battlefields and within ourselves—and the courage found in unexpected places.

"I love this book!"

—Kate Quinn, *New York Times* bestselling author of *The Rose Code*

FOR MORE KRISTINA McMORRIS, VISIT: **SOURCEBOOKS.COM**